D0404139

SEARCHING FOR A KILLER

It was 10:20 in Chicago, but Stephanie knew Ryan Farrell was still awake. She grabbed the phone and dialed his number. It rang once and then he picked up.

"Is that your brother-in-law in the picture?" he asked.

"Yes."

"Do you know who the fourth guy is?"

"No. But you realize—"

"That means three of the four guys in that picture are dead," he cut in.

"That's exactly what I was thinking. All three knew each other. They were all widowers. And shortly after they got remarried, all of them were killed—along with their families. You said in your email that you didn't see anyone in your father's yearbook who looked like the fourth young man in the photo. We need to find out who he is. If he isn't already dead, he could be next. Plans could already be in motion to murder him and his family. Or who knows? He could be the person behind everything that's happening . . ."

Books by Kevin O'Brien

ONLY SON

THE NEXT TO DIE

MAKE THEM CRY

WATCH THEM DIE

LEFT FOR DEAD

THE LAST VICTIM

KILLING SPREE

ONE LAST SCREAM

FINAL BREATH

VICIOUS

DISTURBED

TERRIFIED

UNSPEAKABLE

TELL ME YOU'RE SORRY

Published by Kensington Publishing Corporation

TELL ME YOU'RE SORRY

KEVIN O'BRIEN

PINNACLE BOOKS
Kensington Publishing Corp.
www.kensingtonbooks.com

PINNACLE BOOKS are published by

Kensington Publishing Corp.
119 West 40th Street
New York, NY 10018

Copyright © 2014 Kevin O'Brien

All rights reserved. No part of this book may be reproduced in any form or by any means without the prior written consent of the publisher, excepting brief quotes used in reviews.

If you purchased this book without a cover, you should be aware that this book is stolen property. It was reported as "unsold and destroyed" to the publisher, and neither the author nor the publisher has received any payment for this "stripped book."

All Kensington titles, imprints, and distributed lines are available at special quantity discounts for bulk purchases for sales promotions, premiums, fund-raising, educational, or institutional use. Special book excerpts or customized printings can also be created to fit specific needs. For details, write or phone the office of the Kensington special sales manager: Kensington Publishing Corp., 119 West 40th Street, New York, NY 10018, attn: Special Sales Department; phone 1-800-221-2647.

This book is a work of fiction. Names, characters, businesses, organizations, places, events, and incidents either are the product of the author's imagination or are used fictitiously. Any resemblance to actual persons, living or dead, events, or locales is entirely coincidental.

ISBN-13: 978-0-7860-3160-3
ISBN-10: 0-7860-3160-3

First printing: May 2014

10 9 8 7 6 5 4 3 2

Printed in the United States of America

First electronic edition: May 2014

ISBN-13: 978-0-7860-3161-0
ISBN-10: 0-7860-3161-1

*This book is for my friends and coworkers
at Broadway Video,*

*Paul Dwoskin, Tony Myers,
Sheila Rosen & Chad Schlund*

With Love from the Part-timer.

ACKNOWLEDGMENTS

Many thanks to my terrific friend and ever-patient editor, John Scognamiglio. I love working with you, John. I'm grateful to everyone at Kensington Books, and feel incredibly lucky to be one of their authors. And a very special thank-you goes to the fantastic Doug Mendini.

Thanks to my dear agents, Meg Ruley and Christina Hogrebe, and the wonderful people at Jane Rotrosen Agency. This Honey Badger would be nothing without you!

A huge thank-you also goes to my Writers Group for their help and friendship. John Flick, Cate Goethals, Soyon Im, David Massengill, and Garth Stein, you guys are the best.

I also get so much support and encouragement from my Seattle 7 Writers pals. Check them out at www.seattle7writers.org.

My thanks also to the wonderful folks at Levy Home Entertainment.

Thanks to the following friends who inspired and supported me—whether they were helping me with ideas, pushing my books to their friends, or just listening to me whine: Nancy Abbe, Dan Annear and Chuck Rank, Pam Binder and the gang at PNWA, Marlys Bourm, Amanda Brooks, Terry and Judine Brooks, Kyle Bryan and Dan Monda, George Camper and Shane White, Carol Cassella, Barbara and John Cegielski,

Barbara and Jim Church, Pennie Clark Ianniciello, Anna Cottle and Mary Alice Kier, Dennis Delk, Debi Donahue, Tommy Dreiling, the gang at Elliott Bay Books, Laurie Frankel, Tom Goodwin, Dennis and Debbie Gottlieb, Cathy Johnson, Ed and Susan Kelly, Elizabeth Kinsella, David Korabik, Lori Lyn, Cara Lockwood, Stafford Lombard, Roberta Miner, Jim Munchel, the gang at The News Group, Meghan O'Neill, my pals at Open Road Media (especially Jane, Jeff, Luke, and Danny), Midge Ortiz, Eva Marie Saint, John Saul and Mike Sack, the kids at Seattle Mystery Bookshop, Jennie Shortridge and Matt Gani, John Simmons, Roseann Stella, Dan, Doug and Ann Stutesman, George and Sheila Stydahar, Marc Von Borstel, and Michael Wells.

And thank you to my family.

PROLOGUE

Saturday, August 8, 2009—12:32 A.M.
Lake Geneva, Wisconsin

The blond woman beside him in bed was a stranger. The sheets covered her to the waist, and she had on Vanessa's nightgown—the pink, lacy number that got him hot whenever she wore it. But from the moonlight coming through the bedroom window he could see she wasn't Vanessa.

And he could see she was dead.

With her head turned on the pillow, she faced him. Dick Ingalls stared at the bruises around her throat and her pale, gray-tinged skin. It looked like she'd been strangled. Her open eyes held a vacant stare and her tongue protruded from one side of her mouth.

Horrified, Dick told himself it was all a nightmare. He tried to move, but couldn't. He felt helpless, paralyzed, in some awful limbo state between sleep and consciousness.

Yet he knew exactly where he was, in the master bedroom at their summerhouse. He told himself that his wife of two months, Vanessa, was asleep beside him in bed—not this dead stranger, this hideous apparition from some nightmare. This wasn't real.

The last thing Dick remembered was watching *WALL-E* with Vanessa and the kids, and trying to keep his eyes open. For their first night here, he'd planned to barbecue. Vanessa had suggested they eat at the picnic table in the backyard, overlooking the lake. He'd bought nearly two hundred dollars' worth of groceries at the Piggly Wiggly. But it had rained, so they wound up ordering pizza from Gino's East, which was just fine with the kids. Dick wasn't sure if it was all the pizza he'd eaten, or the two martinis he'd had before dinner. Or maybe it was the three hours of stop-and-go traffic from their home in Glencoe to the lake house this morning. Whatever, not long after Vanessa had passed around her special caramel-covered brownies for dessert, Dick had started to nod off—and so had the kids.

He remembered his youngest, 8-year-old Griffin, curled up and snoring on the braided oval rug. Yet just an hour before, Griffin had been so excited about the whole family watching his DVD of *WALL-E*. He'd been shushing everyone and telling them where to sit. Dick's two older children, Kip, 16, and Allie, 14, had simply rolled their eyes and let their little brother take charge.

The two of them had bellyached for the entire drive up to Lake Geneva. It was bad enough that they were being torn away from their friends for *three whole days*. But worse, the summerhouse didn't even have cable or Internet access. Dick may as well have been sending Kip and Allie to Outer Siberia. He tried to impress upon them that this would be their first family trip since Vanessa and he were married. It was an important bonding experience for everyone. He wasn't sure if he'd used the word "bonding," but that had been the message he'd tried to put across.

He and Vanessa had already spent a pretty wild weekend here by themselves *before* the wedding. They'd had a whirlwind courtship. He'd met her in late April, a year after his first wife, Sandy, had died—from a stroke of all things—at age 38. Dick remembered talking to Sandy on the phone that morning, and she'd complained of having "a colossal headache." Yet she'd still planned to meet her girlfriend, Judy, for their eleven o'clock Zumba class at the Community House in Winnetka. The three Advil she'd downed hadn't done the trick, and she'd hoped to sweat it out.

Less than an hour later, the tearful call came from Judy saying Sandy had collapsed in the parking lot outside the Community House. The paramedics hadn't been able to revive her.

It had been so surreal and preposterous, a woman in her thirties in terrific shape suddenly dying of a massive stroke. No warning signs, nothing.

Dick hadn't imagined ever emerging from his grief—until he met this gorgeous, red-haired, blue-eyed creature at the Glencoe Metra station while waiting for his morning commuter train into the city. She seemed so vulnerable and sweet. They boarded the train together and sat next to each other. Seven weeks later, he and Vanessa were engaged. Two months after that, they were married.

The kids liked her all right. But Dick was impatient. He wanted them to feel she was part of the family now. And what better way to make that happen than a family trip to the Lake Geneva summerhouse?

Once they'd arrived, he'd told Allie and Kip: "Okay, I know you hate every minute of this. But you're here now. So you might as well make the best of it—instead of acting so pissy and put-upon . . ."

The talk must have done some good, because his two older children stopped bitching about the trip. Allie even helped Vanessa wash the dinner dishes in the kitchen while Griffin put *WALL-E* on pause. Vanessa had shooed Allie back into the family room. Though she insisted they go back to watching the movie, Griffin kept it on pause for her while she heated up the caramel sauce for the brownies.

Not long after Vanessa collected the sticky, messy dessert plates, Dick felt himself nodding off in front of the movie. He woke up to the sound of her yawning. "Help me get Griff up to bed, will you?" she muttered.

The TV was off. The family room windows were shut and the ceiling fan was still. Dick didn't see any sign of the two older children—just Griffin, conked out on the rug. Vanessa, in shorts and a tee, stood over him with her shoulders slumped. "C'mon hon," she moaned. "Help me out. He's too heavy for me to carry, and I'm exhausted . . ."

Griffin was seventy-three pounds of dead weight in Dick's arms as he hauled him up to his tiny bedroom on the second floor. It had a set of bunk beds—with his older brother's faded *Pirates of the Caribbean* sheets. There was also a small closet and one window with a box fan in it. Dick and Vanessa managed to get Griffin into his pajamas, and then into the upper bunk. It was all Dick could do to keep from flopping onto the lower berth and surrendering to sleep.

He wasn't aware of the time—or where Kip and Allie were. He assumed they were in their rooms. He remembered the rain had stopped.

"I can hardly keep my eyes open," Vanessa groaned as the two of them made their way to the master bedroom. She turned on the ceiling fan to high speed.

Without brushing his teeth, he stripped down to his briefs and crawled under the cool sheets of their squeaky old brass bed. "I'm not setting the alarm," he heard Vanessa say. "No need to."

Dick was already half asleep.

At some point in his slumber, he felt her weight shifting on the mattress. He heard the bedsprings squeaking. Then he heard her whispering to someone in the hallway, outside the bedroom door.

He'd wondered if he was dreaming.

Dick wondered the same thing now. His eyes were closed, but he could still see the empty stare of the corpse beside him in bed.

All at once he sensed someone hovering over him. He tried to scream and wake himself up, but he couldn't. Something started crushing his chest. He couldn't breathe.

He opened his eyes with a start, and saw a woman standing over him. She had one knee pressed against his sternum. In the dark, it took him a moment to see her face. Was it Vanessa? She looked so ugly with her mouth twisted into a scowl, and she wore a strange

kind of uniform jumpsuit. It was gray with a zipper up
the front. She held one end of a thick piece of rope in
her hand.

"What—" was all he could say past the pressure
against his chest.

She yanked at the rope, and suddenly his hands shot
up. He felt something pinching around his wrists as his
arms swung over his head. His knuckles banged
against the brass-rail headboard, and it hurt like hell.

"I've been practicing this," she murmured—almost
to herself. Leaning over him, she tied the rope around
one of the brass rails. "If I pull this just the right way,
it'll unravel—and the rope will fall off your wrists in
one quick motion. Your hands will be free again. But
by then, it'll be too late for you. . . ."

It felt as if his arms were being pulled from their
sockets. The skin at his armpits was stretched thin.
Wincing, Dick arched his back to stop the pain. He
tried to kick, but couldn't move his legs. He couldn't
even feel them.

She let out a long sigh. "The pills I ground up and
put in the caramel sauce are pretty strong, aren't they?
I'm sure you're still kind of groggy. You barely
flinched when I rolled you over in bed and gave you a
spinal block. Your breathing didn't even change. That
paralysis in your legs—it's from the spinal."

In a panic, Dick again tried to move his legs. But
nothing happened.

"The paralysis is temporary," she continued. "It
doesn't last more than a couple of hours. In your case,
Dick, that means you won't be able to move your legs

for the rest of your life." She leaned down closer to him. "Do you understand what I'm telling you?"

He just shook his head. He heard someone's footsteps in the hallway—heavy and hard. As he glanced toward the corridor, Dick once again saw the dead woman at his side—staring back at him. Behind her, beyond the open bedroom door, a shadow moved along the hallway wall.

"That's a friend of mine," she said. She must have seen that he'd noticed the movement in the corridor. "And this is a friend of his—beside you."

Dick glanced up at this woman he thought was his wife. He felt the weight lifting off his chest slightly. He tried to move, but from the waist down he was dead. He felt so helpless and confused. None of this made any sense. "W-what's happening?" he finally managed to ask. "Why are you doing this? The kids, where—where are they?"

"In their beds," she replied. "They're asleep. They probably won't even wake up. They got a helping of the same stuff I gave you earlier. I gave them spinals, too. They won't be able to move, either—when the fire starts."

"God, please, no . . ." he cried.

"Yes, that's gas you smell."

"C'mon, let's get cracking!" called the man in the corridor. "Wrap it up in there . . ."

Dick felt her knee pressing harder on his chest again. He still couldn't comprehend what was going on. He remembered one of the last things Vanessa had said to him before he'd fallen asleep, something about no need to set the alarm clock. He now realized that he and his children would never see the morning.

"You know, I really don't need this ugly flame-retardant suit," she said. "I'll be long gone when the fire spreads from room to room. But I wish I could be here. I wonder how you're going to feel, lying there, getting hotter and hotter, and listening to your children scream."

Staring up at her, he could barely breathe or get any words out. "Who—who are you?"

Her knee crushed his chest again, and she leaned forward. Her red hair fell down, forming a tent around his head. In the darkness, he couldn't quite see her face. But he felt her warm breath on his face.

She whispered to him, "Tell me you're sorry."

CHAPTER ONE

Friday, June 15, 2012—1:43 P.M.
New York City

It was the only handwritten envelope among the letters on his desk. There was no return address.

Scott Hamner, a 43-year-old ad executive with the Whetsell-Lombard Agency, had just returned from a long business lunch. He was chewing Orbit gum to combat the aftereffects of two vodka gimlets and linguine with clam sauce. Dressed in a black suit and a white shirt with no tie (it was casual Friday), he looked dapper. Though not necessarily handsome, Scott did the best with what he had. He kept his receding brown hair trimmed to a quarter of an inch to give it that balding-is-sexy look, and he visited a tanning bed weekly. He had a slight potbelly, but was in better shape than a lot of guys his age.

Whetsell-Lombard occupied the thirty-third floor of a building in Midtown, across from Bryant Park and the Public Library. From his office window, Scott had a covetable view of the skyline—with the Chrysler Building as the star.

His assistant had set the mail by his computer keyboard while he'd been out.

Scott left the other letters on his desk, and tore open the hand-addressed envelope. He stopped chewing his gum for a moment as he took out a card. On the cover was an illustration of a man's shirt with a loud, jazzy tie. Over the shirt pocket it said in script: *For a Very Special Dad . . . Fashions come and go . . .*

Scott opened the card, and read the inside:

But our family ties last forever!
Happy Father's Day!

The card wasn't signed.

Scott frowned. With Father's Day coming up, he should have known what to expect when he'd seen the anonymous, handwritten envelope. Every year for the last three years, he'd received an unsigned Father's Day card at work. The first one had been postmarked from New York City. He'd figured one of his kids must have sent the card and forgotten to sign it. The children had been seven and ten at the time. But when he'd asked them, neither his son, Ernie, nor his daughter, CC, had known a thing about it. He'd asked his wife, Rebecca, if maybe she'd sent it on behalf of the kids.

"Somebody sent you a Father's Day card and didn't sign it?" she'd countered. "Are you trying to tell me that you might have a kid out there I don't know about?"

They'd almost had a huge fight about it. He'd insisted he'd never been unfaithful to her, which was a lie. Still, Scott was 99 percent certain he hadn't gotten any of those women pregnant. And as far as he knew, he hadn't knocked up any of the girls he'd dated before Rebecca. Scott had quickly dismissed it, telling his wife that the anonymous Father's Day card must have been a prank or some mistake. He'd hoped the sooner he stopped talking about it, the sooner Rebecca might forget about it.

Scott had decided to forget about it, too. But another unsigned card had come to his office just before Father's Day the next year. The postmark had been Phoenix. He didn't know anyone in Phoenix. And last year, the card—a syrupy Hallmark card with a father and his kid in silhouette walking along a beach at sunset—had been from St. Louis.

For a while, he'd figured Rebecca's younger sister, Stephanie, might have been sending the cards. She was an airline pilot, and always traveling. Maybe that explained the cards coming from different cities. Stephanie had moved in with him and Rebecca back in their Portland days when they'd practically been newlyweds. Considering the circumstances that necessitated her living with them, Scott couldn't really object to the arrangement. But it hadn't been easy putting up with Rebecca's kid sister and all her late-teen traumas. They'd moved to New York while Stephanie had been attending the University of Oregon in Eugene. That had been twelve years ago. Stephanie was still single, and she visited them frequently—too frequently as far as Scott was concerned. The kids adored her. She and Rebecca were still extremely close. Scott couldn't help feeling like a third wheel whenever Stephanie was staying with them. He'd managed to tolerate his sister-in-law's visits for the sake of Becky and the kids. And he always sensed the feeling was mutual from Stephanie.

He would have asked her if she was the one sending the unsigned Father's Day cards, but good God, what if she wasn't? She was so fiercely protective of her older sister. Scott could just imagine her reaction—so much worse than Rebecca's, all the questions and accusations and bitch bites. No, thank you.

He'd decided long ago not to say anything about it to his sister-in-law. And he hadn't told Rebecca about the follow-up cards. It had become something unsettling and irritating that happened every Father's Day, a secret between him and the anonymous creep sending the cards.

Scowling at the envelope for this latest one, Scott saw the postmark was Croton-on-Hudson, New York, where he lived.

"Damn it to hell, what's going on here?" he muttered.

He liked it better when the cards had been mailed from hundreds of miles away. Sure, the first one had been postmarked from New York City, but that had been before the sender had started making the cards a yearly ritual. And besides, the city was a whole hour away from Croton-on-Hudson.

This new card had been sent by someone just minutes from his house.

He remembered Rebecca mentioning to him last night that someone had called the house three times. "I could tell they were listening to me when I answered," she'd said. "And each time, they didn't say a thing. They just hung up. It was strange, creepy . . ."

Scott couldn't help wondering if it was the person who had been sending the Father's Day cards. Maybe they'd called Rebecca again today—only they hadn't hung up this time. They could have even stopped by the house. They could be talking to Rebecca right now.

Scott didn't want to find out from his wife who this person was.

Reaching for the phone on his desk, he speed-dialed the landline at home. After two rings, it went to voice mail. "Hey, hon, it's me," he said. "Just checking in. I—um, I was wondering if you want to go to Tino's tonight. Let me know as soon as you can, okay? Give me a call. I'll try you on your cell."

But when he called her cell, it went to voice mail, too. Scott left another message about going to Tino's, an old-style Italian steak house in Hawthorne they both liked. He'd had no such plan for dinner until he'd desperately blurted it out while leaving the first message. He just needed an excuse to have her call him back. And he needed to make sure everything was okay. All these alarms were going off inside his head because of this goddamn card. His stomach was in knots.

An hour later, Scott left another message on her cell as he finished up at the office. Then on the crowded, hot, noisy Metro train to Croton-on-Hudson, he tried texting her.

Still no response.

He started to imagine Rebecca sitting at a table in Black Cow Coffee, getting an earful from some woman he'd unknowingly impregnated five or six years ago. He tried to think of who it might be. He remembered the brunette from Buffalo with the rocking ass, Marcia. He'd met her on the plane to Miami for a business trip. They'd spent three nights together at the Marriott Marquis. He remembered her saying he didn't need a condom, because she was on the pill. She'd been dynamite in the sack, but kind of clingy-crazy, too. He'd been somewhat relieved when it had ended. But he'd faked a sad good-bye to her the morning he'd caught his plane home. He'd never heard from her again.

Was Marcia the one sending him the cards? Or was it someone else? There had been a few one-nighters around that same time, women he'd met in hotel bars while out of town. But he'd always been pretty careful and discreet. He'd kept track of his wallet, too—after taking off his pants. Sometimes, he hadn't even used his real name. Could one of those women have somehow gotten pregnant with his child? It seemed impossible.

But our family ties last forever. Happy Father's Day.

He tried to remember the women's faces and wondered which one might be talking to Rebecca right now.

From the train station, Scott practically sped home. Their house was a brick, mid-century split-level on a woodsy, winding road. His wife's SUV was in the driveway. As he hurried toward the front door, he noticed through one of the lower level windows that the family room's big-screen TV was on. Scott let himself in, and paused on the landing. "Honey?" he called, over the blaring TV. "Honey, are you home? Becky?"

He took a few steps down toward the lower level. He

found Ernie ensconced in the recliner chair and CC sitting on the sofa. On TV, two women with bad perms, a lot of makeup, and gobs of jewelry were screaming at each other. It must have been one of those *Real Housewives* shows. His two teenagers were barely watching it. They seemed deeply focused on their respective iPads. They didn't even look up at him as he came down the stairs.

"Well, don't both of you greet me at once," he groused. "I couldn't stand all the attention."

"Hey," said CC, eyes glued to her iPad.

"Hi," Ernie muttered, glancing up for a moment.

Scott felt a little disappointed in how CC and Ernie were turning out. At least CC's complexion was starting to clear up, and thanks to six thousand dollars' worth of orthodontia, her teeth were finally straight. But she still hadn't lost her baby fat, and the tight, black tee and black shorts were hardly flattering. She was going through a punk-goth phase and had recently dyed her brown hair jet black. CC probably thought she looked cool, but Scott was almost embarrassed to be seen with her. "Next time Steffi comes to stay with us," Rebecca had promised, "we'll both sit CC down and talk to her about her fashion choices. She'll listen to Steffi."

Skinny and pale, Ernie was a sweet kid, but a hopeless nerd. Scott had been a jock in high school. But his son had absolutely no interest in sports—or girls, for that matter. He liked antique cars, and decorated his bedroom with model cars and framed illustrations of every kind of automobile from the Tin Lizzie to the DeLorean. He had a pet cockatiel named Edsel. The stupid bird couldn't talk—and it smelled up Ernie's bedroom, even though Ernie cleaned out the big cage pretty regularly.

Scott heard the parrot squawk down the hallway. "Where's Mom?" he asked, taking off his suit jacket.

"I dunno," Ernie shrugged, eyes still on his iPad. He was probably in some antique-car-lovers' chat room.

"Haven't seen her," muttered CC.

"Well, the car's out there," Scott said, exasperated. "Was she here when you guys got home or what?"

CC looked up at him long enough to roll her eyes. "I said I haven't seen her. God!"

Ernie shook his head. "Neither have I, Dad. Sorry."

They both went back to their iPads.

With a sigh, Scott threw his suit coat over his shoulder and treaded up the stairs to the main level. He poked his head in the kitchen, which Rebecca hated. It was small and outdated. The tiny built-in breakfast booth couldn't even accommodate the four of them—which would have been pretty inconvenient if they'd been one of those families who ate breakfast together.

Scott noticed the Mr. Coffee machine on the counter was still on. Beside it sat Rebecca's favorite mug with an old Rosie the Riveter illustration of a factory woman flexing her muscle, and the slogan: *We Can Do It!* Switching off the coffeemaker, he noticed the pot was still half full—exactly how he'd left it this morning. Her mug had some cream in the bottom of it—as if she'd dispensed the cream first, but hadn't gotten around to pouring the coffee.

Frowning, Scott set the mug in the sink. It wasn't like Rebecca to leave an appliance on. She always double-checked that the stove was off and the coffeemaker was unplugged whenever she left the house in the morning. She had a bit of OCD that way.

Scott stepped out of the kitchen and glanced down the hallway toward the bedrooms and the bathroom. Ernie's domicile and antique car shrine was downstairs off the family room. Scott's eyes scanned the open doors to the bathroom, the guest room, and CC's bedroom. Then he squinted at the closed master bedroom door at the end of the narrow hallway.

"Becky? Honey?" he called, heading down the corridor.

He opened the door, and saw she'd made the bed. On top of it she'd laid out a pair of jeans and a black sweater.

Scott looked toward the master bathroom. The door was closed.

"Becky?" He tapped on the door and opened it.

The light was on. The first thing he noticed was one of the blue Ralph Lauren bath towels in a heap on the tiled floor. Then he saw the words scrawled in lipstick on the medicine chest mirror:

HATE YOU

The blue and white striped shower curtain was closed. Along one white stripe near the edge, Scott noticed a red smudge. It didn't look like lipstick.

He heard the faucet dripping steadily behind the curtain. The sound echoed off the bathroom's tiled walls.

Moving toward the tub, Scott pulled the curtain

aside. The shower curtain rings clanked against the rod. "Oh, Jesus, no," he whispered.

Rebecca was lying in the tub with her head tipped back against the tiles. Her eyes were open, and she looked so forlorn. She wore her white terrycloth bathrobe. Blood soaked the front of it.

By Rebecca's hand—in her lap—was an old straight razor that had been her grandfather's. They kept it on a knickknack shelf in the bathroom—along with a shaving brush and cup. It was just a silly, sentimental decoration.

Scott had never thought of the antique razor as functional.

But now he knew the old blade was still sharp.

It was sharp enough to carve a deep crimson slit across his wife's throat.

CHAPTER TWO

Thursday, November 22, 2012—1:55 P.M.
Spokane International Airport

The only other person at Boarding Gate 6 in the A Concourse was a skinny, sixty-something Asian janitor with bad posture. He had a miserable look on his face as he swept around the rows of empty seats. His slumped state had probably come from years and years of working that pint-sized broom and the short-handled standing dustpan. He ignored CNN, playing on the TV bracketed near the top of one wall.

Stephanie Coburn figured this was as good a place as any to eat her Thanksgiving dinner.

She had a Frappuccino and a clear plastic container that held a Starbucks Turkey Rustico Panini. The least they could have done was slip a little dish of cranberry sauce in with the sandwich—for the holiday.

Stephanie had spent the last seven hours in and out of airports, surrounded by people and families making their last-minute treks home for Thanksgiving. They were on their way to see loved ones for reunions, lavish meals, and celebrations. Stephanie was on her way to Pocatello—and then to Salt Lake City, where she'd spend the night alone in a room at the Holiday Inn, before starting a reverse route back to Portland in the morning.

In her blue uniform, the pretty, slender, 33-year-old brunette was often mistaken for a flight attendant. But Stephanie was a pilot. It struck her as weird that some people—men and women—still felt squeamish about a female commanding the plane they were on. But it was something she'd learned to shrug off and not take too personally. Stephanie had been chalking up flight hours as a co-pilot for a small regional carrier, Pacific Cascade Skyways. Usually, pilots had to pay their dues, so to speak, for five to ten years before they would be considered by the major airlines. Stephanie was in her sixth year with Pacific Cascade.

She could think of worse airports in her territory to have Thanksgiving dinner alone. Some of them only had vending machines, where stale peanut butter crackers were haute cuisine. So she was way ahead of the game here with her Starbucks delicacies.

With about forty minutes to eat, she settled down in one of the seats, balanced the container on her lap and the Frappuccino on the armrest. She started eating her sandwich. Past the floor-to-ceiling windows, planes slowly taxied by. A mound of dirty slush and snow bordered the wet runway. The sky was gray, promising white-knuckled turbulence for even the most seasoned pilot. She flew a 74-seater Bombardier Q400, and it could get pretty bouncy even with just a few cloud-

hurdles. Stephanie knew she was in for a choppy flight to Pocatello.

But that wasn't why she felt the awful pang in her stomach right now.

It was because she suddenly missed her sister, Rebecca—more than ever.

Stephanie put the turkey panini back in the container. Even if she forced another bite of the sandwich, she couldn't have swallowed a thing, because her throat was tightening. She did her damnedest to hold back the tears.

She caught the janitor staring, and turned her face away. She took a few deep breaths and tried to look interested in CNN. It didn't help that over the airport loudspeaker they were playing "Silver Bells"—broken up every few moments by a flight announcement.

Some Thanksgiving, Stephanie thought. And Christmas promised to be equally pitiful.

After losing someone, the first holidays without them were the worst. Stephanie had learned that at age sixteen when her parents had been killed. She'd survived those first holidays without her mom and dad, because Becky and Scott had taken her in, and she'd still felt like part of a family. She'd had her older sister sharing her grief.

But now she was alone.

It had been almost six months, and she was still trying to understand why Rebecca had killed herself. Stephanie hadn't seen it coming at all. She'd talked to her sister on the phone the day before Rebecca slit her own throat. They'd been laughing and planning Stephanie's visit at the end of June.

Stephanie wound up going to Croton-on-Hudson two weeks ahead of schedule—to bury her sister.

Scott had been devastated. He'd asked her again and again if Rebecca had given her any indication that she was depressed or discontented. "How could she do something like this—and not leave us a note or any kind of explanation?" he'd asked.

In their mutual grief, she'd never felt so close to her brother-in-law. Scott had insisted she stay with them while she was in town for the funeral—even though it meant his mother had to stay at the neighbor's. He'd said CC and Ernie needed their Aunt Steffi. He'd tried to give her several pieces of jewelry that had been in her family. Rebecca kept them in the safe-deposit box at the bank, taking them out only for special occasions. Stephanie had told Scott to keep them there—for CC when she got older. Scott had cried and given her a fierce hug when he'd dropped her off at the airport. It had been the first time she'd ever stayed with her sister's family that Scott had seemed genuinely sorry to see her leave.

That was why what he'd done just a few months later had come as such a shock. When Stephanie had found out, they'd had a huge blowup over the phone and hadn't talked since. Her sister's funeral had been the last time she'd seen Scott and the kids. She kept in touch with CC through e-mails and texts. She'd spoken to Ernie on the phone and sent him a fifty-dollar iTunes gift card on his birthday the month before. But that was about it.

She used to feel so close to them.

Over the airport's music system "Winter Wonderland" was playing, and it had started to sleet outside.

Stephanie managed a few more bites of her turkey sandwich, washing it down with some Frappuccino. Then she took her cell phone from her overnight bag.

Scott probably didn't want to talk with her right now, but Stephanie clicked on their home phone number anyway. She had every right to wish her late sister's children a happy Thanksgiving. The phone rang twice before the answering machine clicked on. *"You've reached the Hamners,"* Scott announced on the recorded greeting. *"No one can come to the phone right now, but leave a message and we'll get back to you . . ."*

It used to be her sister's voice on that greeting. She ached to hear it again.

Straightening up in the steel-and-vinyl chair, Stephanie waited for the beep. "Hi, you guys," she said. She hated the little quaver in her voice. "I just wanted to say Happy Thanksgiving. I miss you. I—I'm between flights, calling from the Spokane airport . . ." She looked around the empty gate area. The janitor had wandered off. "Ah, not much going on, just thinking of you, that's all. I hope I'm not interrupting your dinner. I'm not sure when you're having it this year. Anyway, I—"

There was a click on the other end. "Aunt Steffi?"

"CC?"

"Did you get our message?" she asked. "Ernie, Dad, and I—we left you a voice mail on your home line about three hours ago. Happy Thanksgiving . . ."

Stephanie smiled wistfully. At least they'd thought

of her. "Happy Thanksgiving, sweetie," she said. "I haven't checked my messages yet today. I've been flying since Monday, lucky me. In fact, I head off to Pocatello in a few minutes. I didn't interrupt your dinner, did I?"

"No, we already ate." Her voice dropped to a whisper: "Halle tried to cook a Turducken—you know, a chicken inside a duck inside a turkey? Talk about disgusting. This was along with soggy Stovetop Stuffing and instant mashed potatoes, which she somehow managed to screw up, too. I guess she didn't read the directions right on the Hungry Jack box."

Stephanie glanced at the remainder of her turkey panini in the container on the seat next to her. Suddenly, she didn't feel so bad.

"I was trying to tell Halle about the stuffing Mom made every Thanksgiving. That was so incredible. What was in it again?"

"Italian sausage and cornbread," Stephanie said. "I can't imagine Halle wanted to hear about it."

"Yeah, at just about that time, she kicked my ass out of the kitchen. Anyway, I'm going vegan after this. I really miss Mom's cooking." Stephanie heard her sigh on the other end of the line. "I miss Mom."

"You and me both, honey," Stephanie murmured. "Her culinary expertise aside, how's it working out with your new stepmom?"

There was a silence on the other end. "Okay, I guess," CC finally replied.

Stephanie had first found out about Halle through CC—in an e-mail, three months after Rebecca's suicide.

Dad started seeing this woman named Halle from
Washington, D.C. And get this, Aunt Steffi, I think it's
serious. Can you f-ing believe it? I mean, she's nice
enough & certainly pretty, but what's Dad doing dating
ANYONE this soon after Mom?

Stephanie had wondered the same thing.

She got the story in bits and pieces. Apparently,
Halle had come to New York for a job offer that fell
through. While out pounding the pavement for work,
she'd ducked into the lobby of Scott's office building to
ditch some creep who had been following her. She
asked Scott if he'd act like they were together. They
stood there and talked for a few minutes. That had been
the start of it. He'd rescued her.

"Really, I was the one who got rescued," Scott had
maintained when Stephanie had talked to him on the
phone about his new girlfriend. "And for the record,
CC's got it all blown out of proportion. There's nothing
going on. Halle and I are just friends. She's a terrific
person—and an incredible help to me right now. . . ."

Scott married her two months later, near the end of
October.

Stephanie wasn't invited to the wedding. In fact, no
one was. Apparently, CC found out about it when her
dad and new stepmother returned from an Atlantic City
weekend, and sprung the news on her. "At first, I was
really PO'd," CC wrote in her e-mail to Stephanie. "But
I guess if he has to marry someone, it might as well be
Halle. She's pretty cool, and lets me do pretty much
whatever I want. I really shouldn't bitch & moan. But
the way Dad did it was just so sneaky. . . ."

CC's e-mail had come with an attachment: a photo of Scott with his bride. Decked out in a wraparound purple dress that clung to her shapely figure, she nuzzled up beside Scott. Arms entwined, they posed on a balcony overlooking the beach, and she gazed up at him with a dreamy smile. But her face—in profile—was partially obscured by her windblown flaxen hair.

Bimbo, Stephanie thought, reviewing the photo and wishing she had a clearer image of her sister's replacement.

She was furious with Scott. Her sister had been dead less than five months, and he'd already gotten married again—to someone she'd never even met. It had to be one of the shortest grieving periods on record. He barely knew this Halle woman, for God's sake.

"Well, of course, you disapprove," Scott had grumbled when she'd once again grilled him on the phone—this time about his fast-track marriage. "You think no woman is good enough to replace Rebecca. But just ask the kids about Halle. They adore her. I'd like you to meet her. But first, you need to be on board with this, Steffi. I mean, if you can't be supportive—well, you're still family and we all love you. But you're so judgmental . . ."

"You know something, Scott? You're a real asshole."

The conversation—their last—had gone downhill from there.

Again, Stephanie had relied on her niece to fill in the blanks. Why had he been in such a hurry to marry her? "Beats me," CC had told her on the phone a few weeks back. "Something to do with Halle getting a job offer in Philadelphia, and Dad didn't want to lose her . . ."

But he didn't seem to mind losing his sister-in-law. Stephanie couldn't help feeling as if she and her sister were no longer part of his life. CC and Ernie were her only family, her last link to her sister. Now those kids had a new stepmother.

Part of Stephanie rejoiced knowing the woman couldn't cook worth shit and they'd all had a lousy Thanksgiving. Another part of her felt sorry for them. She watched the frozen rain slash at the gate area's floor-to-ceiling windows and listened to the misery in CC's voice.

"Does your dad seem happy?" she asked.

"I guess so, I don't know," CC replied. "Why don't you ask him? *HEY, DAD!*"

"Oh, no, listen, don't bother him—"

"He wants to talk to you," CC said. "He told me to call him when we finished. He's right here. I miss you, Aunt Steffi. Happy Turkey Day. Fly safe."

"Thanks, honey," she said. She heard some murmuring on the other end.

"Close the door, will ya, CC?" Scott said, his voice a bit muffled. There was a beat, and then he came in loud and clear: "Steffi?"

"Hi, Scott," she said, trying to sound pleasant. "Happy Thanksgiving."

"From what I heard on the answering machine before CC grabbed the phone, I gather you're in the airport between flights. Can't be much of a holiday for you, huh?"

"No, not much," she admitted. She thought he sounded a bit drunk. Scott always took on a nasally tone whenever he'd had a few drinks.

"Listen, Steffi," he whispered. "I feel crappy about the last time we talked. You had every reason to be pissed off at me. In fact, go ahead with the 'I told you so.' I have it coming. You were right, you know. I shouldn't have married so soon after . . ."

He fell silent for a moment. Maybe he expected her to say something.

"Don't get me wrong," he continued. "Halle's wonderful. But it's been a challenge. I constantly test her patience, because I still miss Rebecca. I miss her something fierce. It's crazy, I know. Anyway, go ahead and say, 'I told you so.' "

"No, I don't think I will," Stephanie murmured. It wouldn't have given her much satisfaction. And it wouldn't have brought her sister back.

"I don't know why I was so hell-bent to marry Halle so quickly," he said. Stephanie thought she heard ice rattling in a glass—and then him slurping. "Guess I just wanted to feel normal again—and I didn't want to lose her. She was the first decent thing to happen to me since Rebecca. But like I say, I'm just not over her. As much as I've tried, I can't wrap my head around what she did. It still gnaws away at me."

Stephanie found herself nodding over the phone. "Not a day goes by that I don't ask myself why . . ."

"Did she ever say anything to you about a Father's Day card?" he asked.

Stephanie frowned. "What Father's Day card?"

"Nothing, it's just Father's Day was that same weekend, and I—well, never mind. If she got some upsetting news that day, she would have called you, right? I mean, you two talked about everything. You two didn't have any secrets from each other."

"Well, that's what I used to think," Stephanie said. She and Scott had been through all this before. It was actually a relief to know she wasn't the only one still haunted by what her sister had done.

"What did you start to say about Father's Day?" she asked, her grip tightening on the cell phone. "If you know or suspect something, tell me. I don't care how far-fetched it seems, any theory you have—any possible explanation—"

"Rebecca scribbled something on the bathroom mirror in lipstick," he said, cutting her off. "I—I wiped it clean before the cops or anyone else could see."

"What?" she whispered. She couldn't believe he hadn't said anything about this before. "Becky wrote something on the mirror—you mean, like a suicide note? You're just telling me this now?"

There was silence on the other end of the line.

"What did she write?"

More silence.

"Scott, for God's sake, what did it say? Why did you erase it?"

"All it said was, 'Hate you,' " he muttered. "I'm assuming it was meant for me, but I'm not sure why—or what it means. I couldn't face anyone asking me about it, especially when I had no idea what the answer was. Whatever, it made me ashamed. So—I—I erased the damn thing."

Stephanie numbly stared at the storm outside. She wondered what Scott had done to push Rebecca toward suicide. What was he hiding? Or did he truly not have a clue?

"Steffi, are you there?"

"Yes," she said, straightening in the chair.

"There was never any problem between Rebecca and me that we couldn't work out," he said, his words slurred. "I just don't get it . . ."

A beep sounded on the line. Stephanie squinted at the screen on her cell:

PAC CASCADE SKYWYS

It was the airline dispatcher. She realized she was late checking in for her next flight. They were probably wondering where she was. It went to her voice mail.

"Scott, I've got to go," she said, gathering up her meager dinner.

"You're mad, you're upset."

"The airline's trying to get ahold of me. And yes, I'm upset, but more confused than anything else. I'll call you tomorrow morning, okay?"

"All right, but listen, I want you to think about something—"

"Scott, I really have to go."

"I get it. But I'm just saying I want you to come stay with us at Christmas—if you can get the time off. Will you think about it? I want you to meet Halle. And besides, if today proved anything, it's that we need you here to help us through the next major holiday."

Stephanie smiled. "I'll think about it. Talk to you tomorrow, okay?"

"Happy Thanksgiving, Steffi."

She stuffed the remnants of her dinner into a trash can. "Happy Thanksgiving, Scott."

Stephanie heard him hang up on the other end of the line as she hurried toward her departing gate. She would have to wait until later to think about Rebecca's cryptic message on the mirror.

Right now, she had to navigate through a storm.

CHAPTER THREE

Salt Lake City

The screen panel in front of Stephanie showed her heart rate was 109. In the last three minutes she'd been going nowhere for 0.22 miles at 66 RPM. After spending most of her day in a cockpit staring at a panel of lights, numbers, and buttons, she unwound on an elliptical machine, staring at a panel of lights, numbers, and buttons. It was one of two elliptical machines in the Holiday Inn's mini-gym.

Stephanie was the only one in the place at 9:20 on that Thanksgiving night.

As one of three female pilots with the airline, Stephanie was sort of a loner. She always felt like she had to set an example. She didn't want to be seen in the hotel bar, not even with a Coke in her hand, because someone might think there was rum in it. The flight attendants didn't associate with her, because she wasn't quite one of them. Whenever they had a layover, and the flight attendants partied in one of the hotel rooms, Stephanie wasn't invited. So she always took to the hotel gym. It beat sitting alone in her room in front of the Food Network.

She hadn't quite worked up a sweat yet. Her brown hair was swept back in a ponytail, and she wore black sweatpants and a Pacific Cascade Skyways T-shirt. With her iPhone headset, she listened to her "workout" compilation of 1980s hits. The same lineup of familiar favorite songs was a comfort while on the road in various hotels. Right now, Corey Hart was singing "Sunglasses at Night." He drowned out the low-volume chatter from the TV on the wall. The E! Channel was having some "Celebrity Train Wreck" countdown, with comments from a bunch of comedians she'd never heard of.

Outside the window to her left, a light snow gently fell. Two big windows in front of her looked at the indoor pool and Jacuzzi—both deserted. The lights were dimmed in there, and the rippling shadows from the illuminated pool made the place look eerie.

As she toiled away on the apparatus, Stephanie tried to focus on the numbers flashing across the panel in front of her. But she couldn't stop thinking about Scott's revelation earlier today. Before slashing her own throat, Rebecca had left a note telling Scott that she hated him. Why? What had he done to her?

Scott had been right: at the first sign of a crisis, Rebecca and she were on the phone with each other. Why hadn't her sister called her that day? Had suicide been Rebecca's only option?

Stephanie wished she could discuss it with someone. But the only person she could talk to wouldn't appreciate her calling right now.

He was having Thanksgiving with his family.

It was an hour earlier in Portland. Still, they should have wrapped things up by now. Certainly he realized her first Thanksgiving since her sister's death would be rough on her. He should have snuck away and called her on his cell. He'd done that last year—or had it been on Christmas?

She'd been seeing Oregon Congressman Jim Dunning for over two years now. But practically no one knew about it.

Rebecca used to say that on some subconscious level, Stephanie had paired up with a man who wasn't really available to her. Maybe after the sudden deaths of their mom and dad, she'd been afraid to depend on anyone again. So it was safer to go after someone who would never fully belong to her.

Perhaps her sister was right. At one time, she'd come to depend on Rebecca and Scott, too. But while she'd been attending college in Eugene, they'd up and moved from Portland to the other side of the country. If she was truly wary of becoming too reliant on someone, her sister and brother-in-law had sure contributed to that hang-up. But she'd never told Rebecca that.

She'd met Jim Dunning during a rare "whitemare" snowstorm that had closed the Portland airport one night two Decembers ago. The airline had sent her home, but she'd missed the last shuttle downtown. Stephanie was shivering and wet from the thick snow that practically came down sideways. Towing her small suitcase on wheels, she'd been trying in vain to hail a taxi when a limousine pulled up to the Arrivals curb. The back window descended with a·hum, and the passenger inside smiled out at her. He reminded her of Tom Hanks. When he asked if she needed a ride, he seemed more friendly than flirty. She liked how he got out and helped her with her suitcase—instead of letting his chauffeur take care of it.

The drive to her house over icy roads was intense and scary. They passed several cars that had spun off the road, their hazard lights flashing in the snowy night. Once she'd told him she was a pilot, Stephanie had to act like the winter storm was no big deal. But after a while, she didn't have to fake it. Something about Jim Dunning made her feel safe.

He was honest with her from the start. On their first date, he told her that his wife had died eight months before, succumbing to a long battle with cancer. He had a ten-year-old daughter, Maura, who still struggled with the loss. He'd just been reelected to his congressional seat, thanks mostly to campaign funds from his deceased wife's rich, influential parents. He had absolutely no business dating anyone at that point in time. Even if he and she ended up hitting it off, they'd have to keep their relationship hush-hush for a while. Stephanie remembered him saying he wouldn't blame her if she refused to go out with him again.

Two years later, she lamented over the phone to her sister that she had only herself to blame. She'd known the score when she'd started seeing Jim. He hadn't deceived her at all.

"Yeah, well, he's deceiving his constituents and his in-laws and his daughter," Rebecca had pointed out. "As far as they're concerned, you don't exist. I don't condone it, but I can understand why he kept you a secret for a few months after the election. His 'handsome widower' image won him the lonely housewife vote. All right, yeah, I get it. But it's been going on way too long, Steffi. You need to tell him, 'Either we go public or I go.' "

Stephanie simply couldn't issue that ultimatum to him. What if he told her to go?

Jim had tried a few times to tell his daughter and in-laws that he wanted to start dating again. But apparently whenever the subject came up, his daughter would get teary and his in-laws turned cold with disapproval. At least, that was what he claimed. So Stephanie never had any dates out with him in public, except at a handful of little restaurants that had become their regular secret spots.

His in-laws were a constant presence and kept him on a tight leash. Jim was always terrified they—or perhaps his political enemies—were having him watched. Whenever Stephanie sensed that paranoia in him, it made everything seem so ugly and sordid. What drove her crazy was that absolutely no one was getting hurt by their relationship—no one except her.

"You're there for him," Rebecca had said. "But he's never really there for you."

In the wake of her suicide, Rebecca's prophecy was fulfilled. Stephanie realized Jim had a tough time fitting her sister's death into his busy schedule. To his credit, he'd managed to drive by Stephanie's house to console her for forty-five minutes before she'd taken off to New York for her sister's funeral. He'd given her a blooming plant with a sympathy card, and arranged for a limo to take her to the airport. During the cross-country flight, she kept thinking, *If only he'd driven me to the airport himself, it might have made a difference.* Instead, he'd just stuck her in the limo and waved a somber good-bye.

Of course, she never voiced her disappointment to him. She didn't make any demands or issue any ultimatums. With Rebecca gone, she couldn't risk losing anyone else who was important to her.

Stephanie remembered the argument she'd had with Scott on the phone after finding out about his hasty marriage to Halle. "Know what I think?" he'd retorted at one point. "I think you're jealous. Makes sense you'd jump all over my ass for not taking a long enough 'grieving period.' Tell me, how long has your congressman-boyfriend been *grieving* for his dead wife? Almost three years, right? Is that how long I'm supposed to wait, Steffi? Am I supposed to string Halle along for another two years—the way Jim's been stringing *you* along? I don't think Halle would stand for it. I'm sorry, but not everyone is as big a chump as you are, Steffi."

As she watched her heart rate go up to 120 on the elliptical machine, Stephanie told herself not to expect a call from Jim tonight. He was with his family. "As far as they're concerned, you don't exist." Here she had this revelation about her sister's suicide, and she couldn't tell the one person closest to her—not until he called her.

Scott was right, damn him. She was a chump.

Looking up, she glimpsed the silhouette of a tall man at the double doors leading to the pool area. He stood in the doorway for a moment.

Stephanie realized she was staring. She glanced up and feigned interest in the E! Channel. Then out of the corner of her eye, she noticed the doors closing. One of them kept swinging back and forth on its own. She didn't see the man. Had he gone? Or had he ducked into the pool area?

Stephanie's heart rate reading on the machine shot up to 141. She stopped walking in place and tried to catch her breath.

The pool area still looked deserted.

She took off her headset. She didn't hear anything past the E! Channel's announcer. She told herself the man had retreated down the hotel corridor. Besides, even if he was somewhere in the shadows where she couldn't see him, he was probably a paying guest of the hotel. He had every right to be there. What was wrong with her tonight? Why was she so on edge?

Stepping off the apparatus, Stephanie moved over to the window to the pool area. She could see her slightly frightened reflection in the darkened glass. No one was in the swimming area. She was alone.

With a sigh, she looked at her iPhone and switched over to call mode. Sometimes, when she was on the road, Jim would leave her a message at home—knowing she wasn't there and wouldn't get it until later. "Hi, honey, I'm scab-calling you," he'd say. He'd scab-call when he didn't have time to talk, but wanted her to know he was thinking of her. Stephanie wondered if he'd scab-called tonight.

She dialed her home phone number and punched in the code for the answering machine. "You have three messages," announced the mechanical voice. She'd checked her landline messages earlier tonight—after touching down in Pocatello. The first two she'd already heard: one from her friends, Ben and Erica Weaver, who had invited her to spend Thanksgiving with them at their cabin in Spokane. She skipped over it. The second message she'd already listened to as well. It was Scott and the kids, wishing her a Happy Thanksgiving. "Halle sends her best," Scott had chimed in. Stephanie had figured she'd been too busy with the Turducken to come to the phone.

She skipped to the third message—the one she hadn't heard yet. "Thursday, eight-ten, p-m," announced the mechanical voice.

The phone to her ear, Stephanie stared out at the pool area and waited for Jim's voice.

"Aunt Steffi?" It was CC, whispering so quietly Stephanie could barely hear her. She sounded terrified. "Oh, God, this can't be happening. Halle, she's . . . Aunt Steffi, she—"

Suddenly, CC let out a startled cry. There was a strange, garbled noise, and then the line went dead.

Stephanie's grip tightened on the phone.

"End of messages," the machine announced.

All at once, she couldn't breathe. Her heart was racing again. She told herself not to panic. Her niece was playing a prank on her. That was what teenage girls did at eleven o'clock at night when they were bored. If it was a real emergency, why call her? She was on the other side of the country, unable to do anything.

Speed-dialing her sister's house, Stephanie glanced up at the clock on the mini-gym's wall. CC had left the message about a half hour ago. Stephanie figured with the time difference, everyone else in the house was probably asleep by now—if they were all okay. She counted the ringtones, hoping to hear CC answer on the other end. Eight rings and nothing. Even the answering machine wasn't picking up.

Stephanie scrolled down the list of numbers on her phone, and tried CC's cell. After two rings, Stephanie heard a click. "CC?" she asked anxiously.

"The cellular customer you're trying to reach is not available at this time," announced a computerized voice. "Please leave a message after the tone or hang up and try your call again later."

Stephanie waited for the beep. "CC, honey, what's going on?" she asked. "I got your message on my home line. What's happening there? You have me really scared, honey. Call me on my cell as soon as you can, okay? I'll try to get ahold of your dad. I don't want to contact the police unless . . ." She sighed. "Well, just call me, all right?"

She tried Scott's cell. After two rings, it went to voice mail—not his personal greeting, but the same automated response she'd gotten when she'd phoned CC.

"Scott, what's going on there?" Stephanie asked after the prompt. "CC left a message. It sounded like someone was attacking her. And now none of you are picking up. I don't know what to do here. Call me—on my cell."

It still didn't make sense that CC would call her home phone. Her niece knew she was on the road. The only explanation was—maybe in her panic CC had dialed the first number that came to mind. It was on the top of a list of numbers by the phone in Rebecca's kitchen.

With a shaky hand, Stephanie dialed directory assistance for area code 914 and asked for Croton-on-Hudson, New York. She was torn between asking for the local police or for the number of Rebecca's friend and next-door neighbor, Kit Boling. She was a divorcee with two daughters. Their house could be seen through the trees from Scott and Rebecca's living room window. It was Kit who had put up Scott's mother for the funeral. Kit also had an extra set of keys to Rebecca's house in case of an emergency—or at least, she used to. Maybe things were different now with Halle in the picture.

"What name, please?" the operator asked.

Stephanie heard herself asking for the number for Boling, Kit, on Woodland Trail. When the automated voice announced it, Stephanie quickly pressed 1 for a direct connection. Kit Boling would probably think she was crazy, asking her to check next door to make sure everyone was alive and well. But at this point she didn't care.

With the phone to her ear, she leaned against the wall in the hotel's mini-gym and prayed someone would pick up.

And someone did.

"Mom?" said the girl's voice on the other end.

Laurie Boling was still cleaning up the blood when she heard the telephone ring.

The digital clock on the microwave in the Bolings' kitchen read 11:43 P.M. At first, the fourteen-year-old couldn't find the cordless amid the mess on the counter. The remnants of their Thanksgiving dinner were every-where—along with the blood. A crimson trail dotted the leftover turkey and the casseroles, as well as several used glasses, plates, and cloth napkins.

Laurie found the phone behind a stray, crusty piece of tinfoil. She didn't even glance at the caller ID. She automatically assumed it was her mother calling from the hospital: "Mom?"

"Ah, is this—the Boling residence?" the woman asked. She sounded a bit confused.

Laurie hesitated. She was confused, too. Had something happened to her mother and Tara? Why else would some stranger be calling at a quarter to midnight? What more could go wrong tonight?

"Who's calling?" she asked.

"This is Stephanie Coburn. I'm Rebecca Hamner's sister. Is this one of the girls?"

Laurie suddenly put it together: CC's Aunt Steffi, the pilot. She'd met her a few times. The last occasion had been at Mrs. Hamner's funeral.

"Oh, hi," she said. "Yeah, this is Laurie."

"Listen, Laurie, I'm sorry if I woke anyone up, but this is kind of an emergency. Is your mother there?"

"No, I'm the only one home right now," she explained. "Mom's at the hospital with Tara."

"Hospital?"

"Yeah, Tara and I were going to wash the dinner dishes while Mom drove our grandma home. Only Tara picked up the carving knife the wrong way and cut her hand really badly—I mean, you should see. There's blood everywhere. Anyway, Mom came home and right away said Tara would need stitches, so they—"

"Did anyone from next door go with them to the hospital?" CC's aunt interrupted.

"No," Laurie replied. If the first Mrs. Hamner were still alive, or if Laurie and CC were still best friends, Laurie would have immediately called them for help. But the new Mrs. Hamner was different, and no one really knew her. And CC had become too cool for Laurie about a year ago. So tonight, when Tara had cut herself, Laurie had wrapped a dishcloth around her sister's bleeding hand and phoned her mother to hurry home. She'd never even thought about the Hamners.

"Have you noticed anything strange next door tonight?" CC's aunt asked. "Has anyone been coming or going in the last hour?"

Laurie balked. Like she'd had time to kill looking out at the neighbors while her sister was bleeding to death? The Hamner house could have burned down an hour ago, and she wouldn't have noticed.

With the phone to her ear, Laurie wandered over to the kitchen window. Through the bare trees, she studied the Hamners' split-level. The house was shrouded in darkness. "I'm looking over at their place right now," Laurie said. "I can't see much. The outside lights are off. I don't see any lights upstairs—"

"Are both cars in the carport?"

"Mr. Hamner's car isn't there." Laurie squinted toward a lower-level window. "Looks like the TV's on in the big room downstairs."

Someone was always watching television down there until eleven or so—later on weekends. It was probably Ernie. Whenever Laurie went to bed, she could almost count on seeing the dim flickering TV light in that lower window across the way. It always sort of comforted her to know someone next door was still up—just in case.

"Listen—Laurie, I hate to bother you, but I have a feeling something's wrong over there. I got this weird message from CC on my voice mail an hour ago, and she was cut off. Now no one's answering the phone. Do you—well, do you see any strange cars parked along the street in front of their house?"

With the cordless in her hand, Laurie hurried to the living room window to peer out at the street. She never would have asked CC for anything. But the notion that her former friend might be in some kind of trouble had her eager to help. Part of her still desperately needed to prove her worth to CC.

"No, there's nothing," she said, staring outside. "Like I said, I'm pretty sure somebody's up watching TV right now. Want me to go over there and ring the doorbell?"

"Oh, I—I wouldn't feel right sending you over there, honey."

"It's really no big deal," Laurie said. "It'll take— like—two minutes. I'll call you right back. Or I'll have CC call you—"

"Do you have a cell phone?" asked CC's aunt.

To Laurie, it all seemed pretty elaborate for a simple trip next door. But Stephanie insisted on calling her back on her cell phone—so they could talk while Laurie walked over to check on the Hamners.

For a minute or two, she wondered if she was on the butt end of some prank. CC still had some creepy friends from her skanky-punk phase a few months back. Laurie was a year behind them in school, and they knew she'd been close to CC at one time. She wouldn't have put it past any of them to set her up for some mean practical joke. But the woman was calling from area code 503. It had to be real.

With her sweater on, and CC's aunt talking to her over the cell phone, Laurie headed out the front door. A cold wind whipped through her as she cut across the leaf-littered lawn toward the street. She listened to the tree branches and bushes rustling.

"If you see anything unusual—anything that doesn't seem right—you'll let me know, won't you?" CC's aunt was saying. "I mean it. I don't want you taking any chances."

"I'm fine," Laurie said edgily. The woman was making her nervous. She glanced on either side of her. The street wound through some woods, where all the homes were tucked back at the end of long driveways. Between her house and the Hamners', the trees and bushes were so thick that at night they created big, black pockets where anyone could have hidden.

"Where are you now?"

"I'm coming up to their driveway," Laurie answered with a little tremor in her voice. She heard a twig snap, and stopped in her tracks. She watched for some kind of movement in the thicket between their houses. She didn't see anyone, not even a raccoon. The trees around her swayed, and Laurie noticed their shadows rippling across the street pavement.

Suddenly, she didn't want to go any farther. She wanted to turn and run back home as fast as she could—then lock the door behind her. She remembered how after CC had started high school she'd dropped her as a friend. Why risk her neck for CC? Still, if something was really wrong at the Hamners' right now, maybe she could help. She imagined how grateful CC would be. CC might even be sorry she'd ever turned her back on her.

"Is everything okay, honey? Do you see anything strange?"

"I really wish you'd stop asking that." Laurie's hand shook as she held the cell phone to her ear. She took a deep breath, and turned down the Hamners' driveway. "I don't see anything out of the ordinary. If anything's stressing me out it's you. I—I'm sorry, I don't mean to be rude."

"No, you're right. I'm probably overreacting. I talked to them earlier today, and everyone was fine. You're incredibly nice to do this for me. Thanks, Laurie. I—I hope your sister will be all right. Sounds like you've already had a pretty nerve-racking night. How old is—uh, Tara again?"

"Thirteen," Laurie said, eyeing the house ahead. She could tell CC's aunt was trying to make light conversation. But it wasn't helping.

The next closest neighbors were about half a block away around a bend in the road. If something terrible had really happened to the Hamners—or if somebody suddenly attacked her—no one could come to her rescue. No one would hear her screaming. And what could this woman on the phone do? She was on the other side of the country someplace.

"I still haven't met the new Mrs. Hamner," she was saying. "Is she nice?"

"She pretty much keeps to herself. I've only seen her coming and going. . . ."

Laurie trailed off as she heard tires squealing in the distance. She stopped halfway down the driveway. Through the trees, she spotted a pair of headlights—pinpoints in the darkness. She prayed it was her mother and Tara coming home—or maybe Mr. Hamner. She couldn't quite see the car yet. It kept darting in and out of the blackness as it wound up the snaky road. She heard a few loose pebbles crunching under the tires.

"Are you still there?" CC's aunt asked.

Laurie stepped back and watched the approaching vehicle. It was a pickup. It zoomed past the end of the driveway, and continued down the road until it disappeared behind some trees. She couldn't hear the squealing tires anymore.

"Laurie?"

"I'm here," she sighed into the phone. "A truck just drove by, that's all."

She swallowed hard and started moving toward the house again. She stared at the TV's flickering light in the lower level window. This close, she should have heard the television—its volume slightly muted by the glass. But all she heard was the wind and that rustling sound. "Okay," she whispered into the phone. "I'm coming up to the front of the house now . . ."

She peeked down into the recreation room. The set was on, but the room was empty. A TV table by the lounge chair was turned over on its side—and there were broken dishes on the floor.

Laurie froze in her tracks. "God, I think you're right," she murmured. "Something's wrong here. . . ."

"What do you see?"

"Hold on." Laurie crept toward the front stoop. She saw the door was open about an inch. Beyond the tiny chasm was darkness.

"Listen, Laurie, maybe you should turn back," CC's aunt said. "If you don't like what you're seeing there—"

Laurie shushed her. "The front door isn't shut all the way," she said under her breath. "I—I'm trying to hear if anyone's moving around or talking . . ." She hovered by the door. Part of her wanted to call inside and ask if anybody was home. Another part of her didn't want to be heard at all. She figured CC's aunt was right. The smart thing to do would be to turn around and tear ass back home.

"Honey, I don't like this. I think there must have been some kind of break-in—"

Laurie shushed her again—this time, because she heard something in the house.

"What?" Mrs. Hamner's sister asked. "What is it?"

"Somebody's crying in there," Laurie whispered. She dared to open the door a bit wider. It creaked, and she wondered if the noise gave her away. Her heart was racing.

Though the sound was slightly muffled, Laurie heard a distinct moaning. It was almost as if someone was in horrible pain. She couldn't turn around now. She couldn't just leave them there. She kept thinking it might be CC. If her onetime friend was in trouble, she had to save her.

"I'm going in," she said into the phone. She pushed the door open wider.

"Oh, God, please, honey, be careful . . ."

Poised at the Hamners' threshold, Laurie studied the layout. She took a couple of steps up the stairs. It was dark on the upper level, except for the hallway closet across from the top of the stairs. The closet door was open and the light was on. Some of the coats had been knocked off their hangers—and it appeared as if someone had rifled through the upper shelf. They'd made a real mess.

Laurie didn't take another step.

The strange groaning sound was coming from downstairs.

"Are you there?" CC's aunt asked quietly. "Laurie?"

"Yes," Laurie replied under her breath. "You're right. I'm almost positive somebody broke in. They went through the closet upstairs . . ."

"All right, that's all we need to know to call the police. Whoever broke in could still be there. Now, get out . . ."

"Okay," Laurie whispered nervously. "I'm leaving . . ." The woman was right. She was crazy to have come this far. Laurie turned and started toward the door.

A loud warbled cry stopped her.

She glanced down toward the TV room—and the flickering shadows on the wall from the television. She'd already seen from outside that no one was down there in the big room. She remembered Ernie's bedroom was on the lower level—down a short hallway from the recreation room. There was also a bathroom and a utility room. The crying seemed to come from one of the rooms off that little hallway. It wasn't the TV.

Her hand clutching the banister, Laurie crept down a few steps. She heard another muffled groan, and then a squeaky, rattling noise.

"What's going on?" CC's aunt asked anxiously. "Aren't you out of there yet?"

"Someone's hurt downstairs," Laurie whispered. "I think it could be CC. I can't just leave."

"Oh, Jesus, I told you to get out of there. Are you downstairs now?"

"Yes," she said, pausing at the bottom of the stairs.

"All right . . . okay then, you should see a phone on the table by the sofa. Pick it up and dial 9-1-1. Give them the address. You know the address? One-fifty-nine Woodland Trail . . ."

Laurie spotted the cordless phone on the end table where CC's aunt said it was. As she crossed the room, she noticed a *Seinfeld* rerun on the muted television. She also noticed the tipped-over TV table by the lounge chair. The toppled plate had held a half-eaten piece of pumpkin pie. Shards of glass sat in a small puddle of milk.

She stepped around the mess and headed for the cordless phone on its stand on the end table. With a shaky hand, she snatched it up and pressed 9-1-1. "Okay, I'm calling them right now," she whispered into the cell.

But the screen on the phone didn't light up. And she didn't hear any tone as she pressed the numbers on the keypad. Laurie glanced down at the baseboard—and her mouth dropped open. "Oh, no, they cut the phone wire . . ."

"Okay, get out of there! Just get out of there!"

Laurie froze at the sharp cry from one of the rooms down the hall. And there was that tinny clanking noise again. For a few moments, she couldn't breathe.

"Laurie?"

Tears in her eyes, she threw the cordless on the sofa and hurried toward the brick fireplace. She grabbed a poker from the antique set by the hearth. Clutching it in her shaky hand, she started toward Ernie's room.

"Laurie?" CC's aunt repeated over the cell.

"Shhhh," she whispered.

The rattling, tinny sound got louder. Laurie switched on the hallway light with her elbow. The doors to the utility room and Ernie's bedroom were closed. The noise came from inside the bedroom. Laurie glanced toward the bathroom—with the door open and the light off, it didn't look like anyone could be in there. Yet she was afraid to turn her back on the dark little room.

"I—I have to put the phone in my pocket for a few seconds," she whispered into the cell.

"Wait! What for? What are you doing?"

Laurie didn't reply. She slipped the cell phone into the pocket of her sweater. She kept the fireplace poker raised and ready to strike. With her other hand, she reached for the knob and turned it. As she opened the door, the hallway light spilled across Ernie's bedroom carpet—where two of the bodies were.

A loud shriek made her jump.

In the corner of the room, a large bird darted about its pen. Feathers flew as it squawked again and clawed at the cage.

Everyone else in the room was utterly still.

Mr. Hamner and Ernie lay facedown on the floor— almost as if they were asleep there and letting the women have the twin beds just beyond them. Thick pieces of rope bound their hands behind them—as well as their feet. On the back of Mr. Hamner's and Ernie's heads, their hair was all mussed and glistening. Blood soaked the backs of their shirts.

The bird let out another piercing cry. Its claws on the cage made a tinny clatter.

Laurie didn't even flinch this time. She still held the poker in her fist. CC's aunt was saying something, but her voice on the cell phone seemed far away. Horror-struck, Laurie stood in Ernie's bedroom doorway gaping at her onetime best friend.

In a tee and panties, CC looked so pitiful, lying on top of one of the beds with her face toward a blood-splattered wall. Her hands were tied behind her, too. On the wall, above all that blood, several framed photos of antique cars had been knocked askew.

Across from her—and past the bodies of Mr. Hamner and Ernie—on the other bed, the new Mrs. Hamner was sitting up with her head tipped against the wall. She wore a white terrycloth robe. The entire front of it was crimson. Unlike the others, Mrs. Hamner's hands weren't tied.

At least, Laurie was pretty sure it was Mrs. Hamner.

She couldn't be certain, because most of the woman's face was gone.

On her cell phone in the Salt Lake City Holiday Inn's mini-gym, Stephanie stood by the window to the pool area. Clutching her stomach, she listened to the screaming on the other end of the line. Then she finally realized it had to be Ernie's pet cockatiel, Edsel, squawking.

Stephanie anxiously waited for Laurie to get back

on the line—and confirm that for her. She still clung to a slim hope that everyone in the house was all right.

"Laurie?" she cried into the phone. "Laurie, answer me! What's happening there? Please, honey, talk to me . . ."

At last, she heard a rustling—and then Laurie sobbing on the other end.

"Are you there?" Stephanie asked. "Honey, what's going on? What is it?"

"They're dead," she whimpered. "They're all dead. They've been shot . . ."

Stephanie gasped. She felt as if someone had punched her in the gut. Her legs gave out from under her. She slumped against the gym's wall and sank to her knees.

The only family she had was dead.

"Get out of there," she managed to say. Her throat was closing up, and she started to cry. "Run home as fast as you can, and call the police. Do you hear me? Get out of there . . ."

CHAPTER FOUR

Stepping inside the Croton Colonial Diner, Stephanie saw the two crisscrossed flags on display behind the cozy restaurant's bar. She immediately thought of Ernie, when he was younger, saluting those flags every time they arrived at and left the diner. She'd eaten here with Rebecca and the kids countless times. All those memories came flooding back to her now.

She found Scott's mother, Marlene, waiting for her in a booth by the window. "I'm sorry," Stephanie told her. "I'll be right back, Marlene." With tears in her eyes, she struggled out of her coat, and tossed it on the seat. Then she hurried to the ladies' room. Stephanie thanked God no one was in there.

She leaned against the sink counter and broke down sobbing.

The last twenty-four hours had caught up with her.

She'd left directly from Salt Lake City yesterday morning and gotten into Westchester County Airport last night. Renting a car, she drove to the DoubleTree in Tarrytown.

She'd talked with Jim, who couldn't make it to New York. He said he wasn't able to get away from his family and his political commitments. Plus, he admitted he couldn't afford to be seen with her there. The Thanksgiving night murders in Croton had become national news, and the funeral would be covered by the press. He kept apologizing to her. Stephanie cut the conversation short. She'd lied and said room service was knocking on her door.

This morning, the police had asked her to accompany them on a walkthrough of 159 Woodland Trail. They wanted her to point out if any items of value were missing. Stephanie did her damnedest to stay focused on their mission—and not dwell on the framed family photos, her favorite comfy spots where she and her sister had talked late into the night, and all the knickknacks that had been in her family for as long as she could remember. It broke her heart to see so many of those pieces—candy-dishes, figurines, and even kitchen utensils—sealed in bags marked EVIDENCE. Those things used to conjure up such sweet memories, but never again. She noticed fingerprint dust everywhere—and some unfamiliar, funky art pieces in the living room and TV room. She figured they'd belonged to Halle.

Sticking to the task at hand, she managed to tell the police about several missing things, including her mother's silver service set, some candlesticks, an art deco clock, and at least a dozen Waterford crystal pieces Rebecca used to display in the dining room breakfront. It was silly, but among all the items that had been stolen, she was most upset about a missing Royal Doulton figure. It was of an old lady selling balloons. It had been her grandmother's, then her mother's, and then Rebecca's. And now some murdering son of a bitch was pawning it someplace. And for what? A little bit of money.

In the kitchen, there was a spot on the counter where everyone recharged their laptops, phones, and iPads. She noticed nothing was there anymore, except the power strip.

The police asked her to check Ernie's room for more missing items, but one glimpse inside, and she had to turn around. Yellow police tape saying CRIME SCENE— DO NOT CROSS cordoned off the entire area just beyond the entrance. The beds had been stripped, but blood had seeped down into the mattresses. Crimson splotches marred the walls and the beige-carpeted floor.

After they finished, Stephanie hurried back to her rental car, where she sat behind the wheel and cried for twenty minutes.

When she'd left for the restaurant to meet Marlene, she'd been stupid enough to think she was all cried out.

Now, at the ladies' room sink, Stephanie splashed cold water on her face and dabbed it dry with a rough paper towel. She glanced in the mirror. Her eyes were still puffy and red. She couldn't do anything about that. So she fussed with her hair, and checked for wrinkles on her standard, no-iron traveling outfit—a black skirt and a dark blue flower-print pullover.

She had a long day ahead. After brunch with Scott's mother, they were due at the funeral home to make the arrangements. She wanted to call Kit Boling to check on how Laurie was doing. Then somewhere along the line, she had to swing by a mall, where amid the mobs of Thanksgiving-weekend shoppers, she had to find herself a halfway decent black dress for the funeral.

Stephanie put on some lipstick. Then she stepped out of the restroom.

The restaurant was busy that Saturday morning— and noisy, thanks to someone who had brought along their screaming twin toddlers.

"Sorry about that," Stephanie told Marlene. She slid into the red-faux-leather seat across from her.

"I ordered us each a Bloody Mary," Marlene said. "I remembered you liked them. Scott served Bloody Marys at that Easter brunch where everyone got so pie-eyed a few years ago." She smiled, but it quickly faded. "Anyway, I figured you could use a drink after what you've been through this morning. We both could. I think I told you, I gave the police the same guided tour early Friday morning."

Scott's mother sipped her water. In her mid-seventies, Marlene Hamner was a handsome woman with carefully coiffured gray hair. She wore a dark paisley print dress with long sleeves. She was holding up well enough, considering the toll the last forty-eight hours had taken on her. Still, she had a slightly brittle look to her—as if one more little knock would shatter her to pieces.

Scott had been an only child, and Mrs. Hamner was a widow. Unlike Stephanie, at least she had two siblings to help her through all this. She also had Ernie's cockatiel—whether she wanted it or not.

A stout, brassy-haired waitress set their Bloody Marys in front of them. "Have you girls decided yet on breakfast this morning?"

Stephanie worked up a smile for her. "We're still waiting for one more."

"Okey-doke," the waitress said. She hurried over to another table, where the screaming twins had finally shut up. Mrs. Hamner took a long swig from her glass.

Stephanie thought about what she and Scott's mother had seen inside that house. How many Bloody Marys would it take until those images were washed away?

According to the newspapers, Scott, CC, and Ernie had all been shot, execution style, in the back of the head. The killers had put two bullets into Halle's face, firing at close range. Stephanie remembered poor Laurie as she'd run home, gasping into the phone: *"Mrs. Hamner—she—oh, God, her face is gone!"*

After her walkthrough at 159 Woodland Trail on Friday morning, Scott's mother had had to go to the morgue and identify the bodies for the police.

Stephanie nervously fingered the celery stalk in her drink. "I'm sorry, Marlene, but I need to ask. Was it—well, wasn't it difficult identifying Halle?"

Scott's mother shook her head and shrugged. "I couldn't. Even if they hadn't done that to the poor girl's face, I still wouldn't have recognized her." She reached for her glass again. "I never got a chance to meet Halle."

"You're kidding," Stephanie whispered. It didn't make sense. Scott had been married to Halle for nearly a month—and he'd been dating her several weeks before that. His mother was a little over an hour away in

Montclair. How could Marlene not have met her? "I don't understand. . . ."

Marlene glanced out the window. Stephanie followed her gaze. They had a view of the parking lot and beyond that, the railroad tracks, the leafless trees, and the Hudson. It was gray and bleak outside.

"I'm pretty sure I was *persona non grata* with Halle and my son for a while," she sighed. "I wasn't exactly thrilled to hear he'd latched on to some woman—a stranger practically—so soon after Rebecca. I told him so."

"Well, that makes two of us," Stephanie said. "So I guess we were both on the outs with them."

Scott's mother nodded. She was still gazing out the window. "A couple of weeks ago, I had a long talk on the phone with Scott, and we patched things up. He invited me over for Thanksgiving. But on Tuesday, he called and canceled. Apparently, Halle was extremely nervous about meeting me and cooking dinner for the family. It was all too much for her. What could I say? I told him it was no problem. My neighbors—Tom and Liz, a very nice young couple—they'd invited me to their Thanksgiving potluck. So at least I had a backup plan."

Stephanie squinted at her. "That's awfully strange. I mean, okay, she was nervous, I get it. But to *disinvite* your new mother-in-law to Thanksgiving dinner when you haven't even met her yet? That's matrimonial suicide. Who does that?"

"Halle, I guess." Marlene looked at her and let out a pitiful laugh. "I decided not to make a federal case out of it. Scott put her on the phone, and she was really very sweet and apologetic. I could tell she was nervous, too. She asked if we could all go out to eat somewhere in Croton on Sunday. 'Nothing fancy,' she kept saying. I told her that would be lovely."

Marlene took a sip of her Bloody Mary. "I spoke with her again, briefly, on Thanksgiving morning. All Halle said was, 'See you on Sunday,' and something about how she was looking forward to it. The sad thing is I never really got to see what my son's wife looked like. The photo of her and Scott that CC e-mailed me wasn't very good. Halle had her face turned to one side." Marlene glanced down at the tabletop and shrugged. "All I'm left with now is what I saw of her in the morgue. I don't know why the police insisted on showing her to me. I didn't know her."

The detectives had told Stephanie this morning that Halle's father had flown in from Manassas, Virginia, on Friday afternoon. He'd identified his daughter from a birthmark on her right shoulder and a scar on her knee. Her dental records had been faxed from Washington, D.C., for a more positive identification. Apparently, there were still enough teeth left in Halle's head for that.

"I must have gotten the same photo you did," Stephanie said. "I'm not sure I . . ." She trailed off as she noticed Scott's lawyer friend, Bradley Reece, stepping inside the restaurant.

Years ago, Scott and Rebecca had tried to fix her up with him, but the chemistry just wasn't there. She'd seen him again—along with his wife—at Rebecca's funeral. They had two kids. Tall and thin, Bradley was 42. With his wavy brown hair and thick, black glasses, he was handsome in an aging-preppie way. He wore a jacket over a crewneck sweater and khakis, and had a laptop case hanging from a strap on his shoulder.

Stephanie waved to him. His face lit up and he smiled at her—but only briefly. As she watched him make his way to their booth, Stephanie had a feeling his somber look went beyond the sad occasion. This meeting had been his idea.

Brad leaned down and kissed Mrs. Hamner on the cheek. "I'm sorry, Marlene," he whispered. "I still can't believe it . . ."

"Thank you, Brad," she murmured, tears in her eyes. She patted him on the shoulder.

He slid in next to Stephanie, and shook her hand. "Steffi, I'm so sorry," he said, his eyes not quite connecting with hers. He set his laptop case on the floor and wriggled out of his jacket. The waitress came by, and he ordered a coffee. All the while, Stephanie wondered what he had to tell them that he couldn't have said over the phone. Officially, Bradley was Scott's attorney. Unofficially, he helped him with his finances and taxes.

Bradley asked how they were both holding up, and admitted that he was still in shock. The waitress brought his coffee, and asked if they were ready to order some food.

"Could you give us a couple more minutes?" Stephanie asked. "Thanks."

Then she turned to Bradley beside her. "There's something you want to tell us, Brad, isn't there? I wish you'd just come out with it."

He gazed down at his coffee cup and frowned. "Scott's money's all gone."

He waited a few moments, perhaps to let the news sink in.

Stephanie looked at Marlene, and then at Bradley again. "How did that happen?" she asked.

"Well, he took a big hit for Rebecca's funeral," Bradley explained. "But that's not what did it. It was the way he spent money on Halle. In the first month alone, he gave her five grand—just to help her out, because she didn't have a job or a decent place to live. I told him he was bat-shit crazy—" Bradley winced at Mrs. Hamner. "Pardon me, Marlene. I just didn't think it was wise. He hadn't known her very long. Anyway, Scott and I didn't talk for a while after that. . . ."

Stephanie stared at him. She could see a pattern here. "Did you ever get a chance to meet Halle?" she asked.

He shook his head. "Actually, no. I ended up calling Scott a couple of weeks after they got married. We talked some more about his finances. He admitted his funds were dwindling, which turned out to be a major understatement. He went on to explain that he hadn't gotten Halle an engagement ring. So he bought her some jewelry to make up for it—several thousand dollars' worth. He converted his savings, checking, and credit cards into joint accounts . . ."

"Oh, Lord," Mrs. Hamner muttered.

"Between the two of them, they drained their savings and maxed out on the credit cards with several cash advances—"

"Are you sure it was the *two* of them?" Stephanie asked.

"Scott did his part," Bradley admitted. "But yes, Halle did most of the spending—on what, I'm not sure. I really don't know where all the money went. Anyway, I'm sorry. There's nothing left."

"What about the house?" Marlene asked.

"There's still a mortgage. It's underwater. Even if you price it way below market value, you'll have a hard time selling—after what happened in there." He sipped his coffee and sighed. "That's why I wanted to meet with you before you made the funeral arrangements. You—well, you should be careful how much you spend. I'm afraid it's going to be out of your own pockets."

"That doesn't matter," Marlene murmured. "It's the least of my worries right now."

"Well, I'm sorry, but it matters to me," Stephanie heard herself say. "Who was this woman? None of us met her or knew her. My sister's body was barely cold, and this stranger came in, swept Scott off his feet, married him, and spent all his money. Where did it go? Was she giving it to someone? Scott was never foolish with money. Not until this woman came along." She turned to Bradley. "Do you know anything about her or her financial situation before she met Scott?"

"Not really," he replied. "But obviously, she wasn't doing too well."

"Do you think it's possible she spent everything on drugs or gambling?"

"Could be," he said, frowning. "Some people can keep their addictions secret while going through money like grease through a tin horn."

"Well, then that's it," Stephanie said. "It might also explain the murders—if Halle owed someone money and couldn't pay. Maybe that's why she was the only one who . . ." Stephanie hesitated. Halle was the only one who wasn't shot in the back of the head. Stephanie kept thinking that perhaps a drug dealer or a mobster Halle owed money to had extracted revenge by executing every member of her new family right in front of her.

Bradley patted her arm. "I'm sure the police are looking into every possible explanation."

Marlene cleared her throat. "This jewelry my son was supposed to have given her, do you know if it was stolen? Or did she have the good sense to store the more expensive pieces in the safe deposit box?"

"Scott didn't give her access to that, too, did he?" Stephanie asked him, a hand over her heart. "My mother's jewelry is in there . . ."

Bradley drained the rest of his coffee cup, and then sat back. "I went to the bank this morning. Halle's listed as an alternate key-holder . . ." He looked across the table at Scott's mother, "So are you, Marlene—in the event of his death. I have Scott's key with me now."

Stephanie and Bradley sat in gray-upholstered chairs kitty-corner to each other in the little waiting area of the Chase Bank branch. Neither of them said a word. In the chair across from them, a thin thirty-something blonde was talking on her cell phone—a bit loudly. Stephanie did her best to ignore her.

She stared past the chatty woman's shoulder at the teller stations behind the tall Plexiglas wall. At the far corner was the gate that led to the stairs and the safe-deposit boxes on the lower level. Mrs. Hamner had been down there for five minutes now—but it seemed longer.

Stephanie felt silly, caring so much about some old jewelry. Maybe it was because those pieces were the only things left of her mother and her sister that hadn't been stolen, police-tagged, or dusted for prints.

But if Halle had had access to the safe-deposit box, then inevitably, those untainted treasures were long gone. *Damn her*, she thought.

Stephanie found herself absolutely loathing this Halle person. She couldn't help wondering if Halle had been manipulating Scott back when Rebecca had still been alive. Was she the reason for Rebecca's suicide?

She remembered what Scott had said about Rebecca having written "Hate You" on the bathroom mirror. Did Halle have anything to do with that?

Shifting restlessly in her chair, Stephanie glanced again toward the gate that led to the bank's basement and the safe-deposit boxes. Still no sign of Scott's mother.

Marlene had given Rebecca a beautiful pearl necklace and a diamond spray pin that had been in her family for generations. They were supposed to be in the safe-deposit box, too—along with some bonds.

Stephanie drummed her fingers on the armrest. She was getting really tired of listening to the woman across from her yapping into her cell phone. Stephanie wanted so much to tell her to shut the hell up.

"What's taking so long?" Bradley sighed. "Is she tunneling her way to the safe-deposit box?"

Stephanie turned toward him and shrugged. He glanced past her—toward the gate area. Then he frowned. "Oh, shit . . ."

She saw he was looking at Scott's mother, who had paused at the gate. With her shoulders slumped, she held her coat and purse. She looked utterly defeated.

Marlene looked back at them and shook her head.

"Thank you so much for coming," Stephanie said, shaking the hand of a middle-aged woman, whose name she'd already forgotten. She was Ernie's history teacher.

Dressed in a black suit she'd never wear again, Stephanie was dutifully meeting and greeting at the wake. She stood alongside Marlene near the entrance to the main viewing room at Sachs-Asher Funeral Home. Mr. Sachs and Mr. Asher had had to clear out a sofa and two potted palms to make room for all four closed caskets at the front of the beautifully appointed room. The funeral home was a big, elegant old white mansion, and all the furnishings inside had the look of sturdy, well-preserved antiques.

Stephanie was exhausted. Her face hurt from maintaining her polite smile. So many of the mourners were people she'd met five months ago at Rebecca's service—and she didn't remember them. She kept blanking out on their names. It was embarrassing. Of course, all of them knew who she was—Rebecca's sister, the airline pilot.

She asked nearly everyone the same question: "Did you get a chance to meet Halle?"

Stephanie heard stories about Halle not returning phone calls or canceling plans to get together at the last minute. What it all added up to was that not one person here had laid eyes on her.

Halle's father, Jay Driscoll, had proved as elusive as his daughter these last three days. He'd flown in alone, because his bereaved wife was in no condition to travel. He was supposed to have met with Stephanie, Marlene, and the funeral parlor people on Saturday, but he hadn't been feeling well. He'd told the funeral directors that after the wake, he wanted his daughter's remains flown to Washington, D.C., where there would be a second memorial service with her family and old friends in attendance. She would be buried there.

Mr. Asher, an impeccably dressed, soft-spoken, fiftyish man who was built like a football player, seemed embarrassed when he explained: "Mr. Driscoll indicated that if either one of you or Scott's estate would care to contribute to the cost of the other service, they would be much obliged."

Stephanie couldn't believe the gall of this guy, who apparently had no intention of chipping in for *this* service, in which his dead, money-sucking daughter was included. She and Marlene agreed that paying for one memorial service was enough. "Maybe Halle's family and old friends can pass the hat around," she'd muttered to Scott's mother.

She heard from Marlene that a cousin of Halle's had come in on Sunday afternoon. As far as Stephanie knew, none of Halle's other family members or friends were showing up for this service—or for the after-brunch she'd spent the last two days planning with

Marlene. Two days to throw together a buffet brunch for a hundred people—it had totally drained her. At least, tending to all the stupid details had been a welcome temporary distraction. There was only time for stolen, little moments of grief—and crying jags as she went to bed at night. She'd ended up securing a small ballroom where she was staying at the DoubleTree. The hotel was catering it, too, at a price neither she nor Marlene could really afford. She barely knew any of the people who would be attending this brunch. It made no sense.

She wondered if Halle's father and her cousin would have the nerve to show up there. So far, they hadn't made their presence known at the wake.

Bradley had let the police know that Scott's funds had evaporated once Halle had come into the picture. So on Monday morning, police detectives had spoken to both Jay Driscoll and his niece about Halle.

"According to the cops," Bradley had told Stephanie on the phone last night, "the dad and the cousin are making out like Halle could do no wrong. To hear them tell it, she was always responsible with money, held a steady job, was good to her folks—a regular Girl Scout.

"But then last July," Bradley went on, "she suddenly quit her job and started pushing her friends and family away. She didn't return calls. In late August, she e-mailed and texted friends that she'd moved to New York and preferred to be left alone 'to start a new life' or some such bullshit. She'd left behind a half-empty apartment with rent that was two months late. She'd maxed out on cash advances from her credit cards— and she had a stack of overdue, unpaid bills."

"So where do you think the money went?" Stephanie had asked, sitting on the hotel bed with her cell phone clutched tightly in her fist.

"It's anyone's guess. Clearly, she must have owed money to somebody, and she was on the run."

"So—are the police following it up?"

"Yes, but they're focusing more on another lead. There's been a rash of robberies in the area. It's the same MO: late at night, families tied up by a couple of guys in ski masks with guns—only none of the victims got shot before."

"I still say it's all connected to this Halle woman—or someone who knew her," Stephanie had insisted.

She wanted to meet Halle's father and her cousin, and talk with them herself. Maybe they were holding something back to protect Halle's memory. Or maybe the police just weren't asking the right questions.

From where she stood by the viewing room entry, Stephanie could peek over toward the main doors to the funeral home. She kept a lookout for an older man and a woman in her thirties, but still no sign of anyone like that.

However, the tall, full-figured redhead stepping into the lobby looked familiar. She had two girls with her—both gangly young teens. One of them had a bandage on her hand. It took Stephanie a minute to recognize Rebecca's neighbor, Kit Boling. She'd just phoned Kit on Saturday—to ask about Laurie.

Marlene already knew them, because the Bolings had put her up for a night during Rebecca's wake and funeral. "Well, here's the brave young lady," Marlene said, giving Laurie a kiss on the cheek. "How are you, dear?"

Skinny and shapeless, with long brown hair and big, sad eyes, Laurie murmured a reply.

Stephanie didn't hear it. She was shaking Kit's hand. "I'm so sorry I put her through all that," she whispered. "I never should have—"

"You and I already went over this on Saturday," Kit said under her breath. "CC was Laurie's friend. She wanted to go see if she was okay. She made it very clear to me that you kept telling her to turn back."

"I know, but if I hadn't called your house, she never would have—"

"It's not your fault," Kit said, squeezing her hand. "Laurie will be okay. Just in case, I'm taking her to see a counselor tomorrow. The police social worker recommended her. Between you and me, I hope this woman offers a family plan. We're all pretty—unnerved. The girls are bunking together and sleeping with the light on. Meanwhile, I'm keeping a rolling pin at my bedside—as if that'll do any good. We'd have been like this anyway—even if Laurie hadn't made the trip over to the Hamners'. Having that happen right next door is just . . ." She trailed off and shook her head.

Tara Boling was showing Marlene her bandaged hand and talking about her stitches. Laurie darted over to Stephanie, and for a second, it seemed as if the young girl was going to hug her. But then Laurie hesitated and stared at her nervously. "Hi—ah, Ms. Coburn . . ."

Stephanie worked up a smile. "After what you went through for me, I think you can call me Steffi." She took Laurie by the hand and pulled her in for a hug.

The girl's forehead rested against her shoulder. "How are you doing, honey?" Stephanie whispered, patting her back.

Laurie gently pulled away and looked over at her mother. "Can I talk with Steffi alone?"

Kit nodded. "Go ahead."

Stephanie let Laurie pull her toward the funeral home's lobby. It had a fireplace and two sofas facing each other. Each sofa end table had a box of Kleenex on it.

"It's weird," Laurie said to her. "I keep seeing all of them dead in that basement room—and I remember the way Ernie's bird kept squawking. Whenever I hear a bird let out a shriek now, it really makes me sick—like in my stomach . . ."

Stephanie stroked her arm. "Oh, sweetie, I'm so sorry."

"I didn't even know Ernie had a bird. He must have gotten it after CC stopped being my friend. I always—well, I always wanted to be friends with her again." She let out a sad, little laugh. "It's kind of funny. All these kids at school, they've been tweeting and texting me, kids who didn't know I was even alive before. There have been a few really creepy people, but most of them have been nice."

"I'm sorry about the creepy ones," Stephanie said.

"I guess this has made me kind of popular," Laurie shrugged. "But the only thing I care about is that—well, on TV and online, as far as everyone's concerned, in the end, CC and I were still really good friends, best friends even." Her big, sad eyes searched Stephanie's. "Do you suppose it's okay I feel like that?"

"I think it's fine," Stephanie whispered. "You were a wonderful friend to her. How many of CC's other friends would have walked into danger for her the way you did?"

Laurie hugged her again.

"C'mon, honey," Kit said, coming up beside them with her other daughter in tow. "Stephanie's on the welcoming committee. There are other people waiting to talk with her. We can chat with her later at the brunch . . ."

Stephanie gave Laurie a kiss on the cheek. Then she watched her, Kit, and Tara head back into the viewing room. Two teenage girls, whose names Stephanie had already forgotten, ran up to Laurie and excitedly whispered to her. One of them was holding a cell phone.

"Stephanie Coburn?"

She turned and saw a petite, attractive, thirty-something woman with an ash-blond pageboy. The woman gave Stephanie a sheepish look.

Stephanie wondered which one of Rebecca's friends this was. "Well, hello, thanks so much for coming." She reached out her hand.

"You don't know me, Stephanie," the woman said, shaking her hand. "I'm Deborah Neff, Halle's cousin."

Stephanie automatically took a step back. She tried to keep a polite smile on her face. Halle's cousin certainly seemed nice enough. She wore a trench coat—open—over a simple black dress.

"I want to thank you and Mrs. Hamner for all of this," Deborah said—with a nod toward the viewing room. "It's very decent of you. My aunt and uncle aren't doing too well financially right now. They feel awful that they can't contribute here."

Stephanie just nodded warily.

"From what the police told us, no one here really got a chance to know Halle. I'm guessing that includes you."

"That's right," Stephanie said.

"You must have a ton of questions for me. The police certainly did. I understand Halle was supposed to have spent a lot of your brother-in-law's money."

"All of it—and then some," Stephanie frowned. "She also raided his safe-deposit box at the bank, taking some bonds and several pieces of jewelry that belonged to my mother. Years ago, Mrs. Hamner gave my sister some pieces, too. They're gone as well."

Wincing, Deborah shook her head. "I just don't understand it. Halle never cared that much about jewelry—unless it was something made by a local artist. She didn't go in for traditional jewels. She'd splurge at street fairs, buying ceramics and handmade knickknacks. Otherwise, she was very down-to-earth and frugal . . ."

Stephanie recalled seeing a few unfamiliar folk art pieces on display in Rebecca's living room and in the TV room. "Well, the money went somewhere," she said. "Do you think it's possible your cousin might have had some kind of addiction she kept secret? Drugs, gambling, or anything like that?"

Deborah shook her head. "Ben and Jerry's, old movies, and tennis tournaments on TV," she said. "Those were her addictions. Halle was a real homebody, very dependable. That's why it came as a shock when she started dumping her friends and then just moved away. It wasn't like her at all."

Stephanie glanced around to make sure no one else in the funeral parlor lobby heard them. "Do you think somebody else could have been behind this sudden shift, some man in her life?"

"No, Halle didn't have any boyfriends. She was very pretty. She kept in shape working out at a gym. But she didn't have much luck meeting any men there—at least, no straight men. She'd signed up for an online dating service about a year ago, but after a slew of bad dates, I think she was ready to give up. Last time we talked, Halle said she was thinking of getting a Jack Russell terrier." Deborah slowly shook her head again. "No, Halle didn't have a man in her life until we heard that she'd met your brother-in-law."

"How did you hear? Did she call you?"

"No, e-mail," Deborah replied. "Some of Halle's friends and I compared notes. She started pulling away from people back in late June, breaking dates and not answering calls. That's when she suddenly quit her job, too. Whenever anyone tried to get ahold of her, she was too busy. She'd send a text or a short e-mail with some excuse. Then she announced she was moving to New York, and the correspondence practically stopped. Her parents got an occasional note card from her. That's how we found out about Scott, and later, that she'd gotten married."

"Well, didn't anyone try to track her down through Scott?"

"She wouldn't tell anyone his last name. And the notes to her parents had no return address on them—just a New York postmark."

"It's almost as if she didn't want to be found," Stephanie said.

"Exactly," Deborah nodded. "It didn't seem like Halle at all. Another thing, the note cards she sent her folks weren't the kind of cards Halle would have picked out. She had a great sense of humor. Even with her folks, she always sent these edgy, funny cards. The cards from New York had flowers or sunsets on them—you know, serious, inspirational Hallmark stuff."

"Were the cards in her handwriting?"

"Yes, I asked her parents the same thing. I kept thinking, *this can't be Halle*. In fact, even after my Uncle Jay identified her body on Friday, I figured he'd made a mistake. I didn't want to believe it. From the moment she started pulling away from people, it didn't make any sense that Halle would do that. I figured they'd killed someone else in your brother-in-law's house on Thanksgiving night. But the police called us this morning, and said the dental records are a match."

Tears welled in her eyes. "I know you're looking for answers about who could have done this horrible thing to your sister's family. I understand why you'd want to hold Halle accountable for some of it—"

"She walked off with all of my brother-in-law's money—and my sister's jewelry," Stephanie interrupted.

"Walked off where? Halle's dead." Deborah plucked a Kleenex from the box on the sofa end table. She wiped her eyes, then looked at Stephanie and shrugged. "Look, I'd like to say for certain my cousin didn't take your brother-in-law's money or your sister's jewelry. I'd like to say she didn't do anything to cause her own death or those—those senseless murders on Thanksgiving night. But the truth is I don't really know what happened to Halle and why she pushed all of us out of her life. You can come down to Manassas and attend her memorial service on Friday. You can ask everyone there about Halle, and they'll tell you what I just told you. I'm sorry. I wish I could be more help to you."

Frustrated, Stephanie frowned at her. "Maybe you can start by introducing me to Halle's father. Why isn't he here?"

"He's here," Deborah replied. She nodded toward the viewing room. "We came in while you were talking to that girl. He's in there now. He'd like to meet you, too. I'll take you to him . . ."

"Fine," Stephanie muttered. She followed her back into the crowded room.

They made their way toward a seating area toward the front—by the closed caskets. "Uncle Jay isn't doing too well," Deborah said. "My aunt's the one he depends on most of the time. She's his brick. But when they got the news about Halle on Friday morning, she completely fell apart. My sister's looking after her . . ."

Stephanie wondered if Halle's parents were elderly. But when Deborah led her to the man sitting alone on one end of the sofa, he looked as if he were around sixty years old. Dressed in a dark blue suit, he was a lean, handsome, older man with silver hair. And he wouldn't stop fidgeting. It took Stephanie a moment to realize his rocking from side to side and the tremors in one leg were all involuntary.

"Uncle Jay, this is Stephanie Coburn," Deborah said.

He struggled to his feet. Stephanie guessed he was suffering from Parkinson's disease. Spasms continued to rack his body, but he managed to stick out a shaky hand. "I'm so sorry for your loss," he said—with some difficulty. "Thank you for—for including my daughter today. I know you never met her."

Stephanie shook his hand. "I—I'm sorry I never got a chance to," she said.

His eyes filled with tears. "No one here knows. My girl, she—she was wonderful."

She felt herself tearing up. She nodded. "I'm sure she was. I'm sorry for your loss, too." She turned toward Deborah and touched her arm. "I was rude to you earlier. I apologize."

"It's all right. We're all a bit—bewildered," Deborah said.

Stephanie retreated toward the lobby again, threading through the clusters of people. They certainly would have understood if she'd cried in front of them. But she couldn't. She hurried out the door—and then around to the side of the funeral home, where a florist delivery truck and a hearse were parked. There, with no one else around, she allowed herself to break down and weep.

She wanted someone to blame for all this. She wanted to scream at somebody, and make them feel as horrible as she did. But obviously, Halle's family was just as confused and devastated.

Tears streamed down her face, and her throat hurt. Suddenly, she realized how cold it was outside. She could see her breath.

"You look like you could use a shoulder."

Stephanie swiveled around. She couldn't believe he'd come all the way from Portland. He'd left his daughter, his in-laws, and his political obligations to be with her. "Jim . . ."

He had a contrite look on his handsome face. Dressed in a black suit and a tan trench coat, he carried a blooming yellow mum plant. "I'm such an ass to make you brave this alone."

She wiped her eyes. "Aren't you—aren't you concerned that someone might recognize you here with me?"

He shook his head. "If they do, big deal. Besides, most of my constituents don't even know me. What made me think anyone in New York would recognize me?" He handed her the plant, which was heavy. While she held onto it, he took off his raincoat and put it over her shoulders. He kissed her, and then relieved her of the mum plant. "I'm so sorry, Steffi," he whispered.

Stephanie wrapped her arms around him and cried on his shoulder.

A few items stolen from 159 Woodland Trail weren't on the list compiled by police detectives with the help of Stephanie Coburn and Marlene Hamner. Ernie's aunt and grandmother hadn't noticed that some of his vintage Matchbox cars were missing.

The man sitting alone at the wheel of a rented Prius had taken a shine to the red Thunderbird in Ernie's collection. Parked across the street from the Croton funeral home, he absently ran his fingers across the tiny car. "I'm watching the sister-in-law right now," he said into his Bluetooth headset phone.

"The pilot?" asked the woman on the other end of the line.

"Right. Her boyfriend brought her a plant. I have a bad feeling about her. I think she's going to be trouble."

"We have her Portland address, don't we?"

"Yeah," he said. "Right now, she's staying at the DoubleTree in Tarrytown."

"Okay, keep an eye on her. But stick to your schedule. We can always deal with her later. I need you here. When are you getting in on Friday?"

"My flight gets into O'Hare at 3:15. How's everything in the Windy City?"

"Cold," she replied. "Buy yourself a warm sweater. We can afford it now."

He looked down at the tiny model car in his hand and chuckled.

"So," said the woman on the other end, "other than that, how's my memorial service going?"

CHAPTER FIVE

"Hey, Billy!" bellowed the stocky seventeen-year-old. His voice boomed over all the chatter and the din of locker doors shutting. In his royal blue and gold letterman jacket, Derek Jesler swaggered down the school's crowded corridor. He was homing in on a tall, slender Asian American named Billy Kim, who stood by his open locker.

A few students in the hallway stopped to see what was about to happen.

"Hey, Billy, how about a little kiss?" Derek called.

Even with his buzz-cut, Billy Kim was so handsome he was almost pretty. Tossing his tormentor an I-Can't-Be-Bothered look, he tucked his books under his arm and quietly closed his locker.

"Don't you want to kiss me, Billy?"

"Not even with a blindfold, two quarts of Stoli, and a gun to my head, Jesler," Billy Kim answered loudly. It got a round of laughs from the other students in the corridor.

"Faggot!" Derek grunted, knocking the books out of Billy's hand. They tumbled to the floor, with notes and papers scattering about. A few people snickered, and someone let out a catcall.

At his locker down the hall, Ryan Farrell was close enough to catch a glimpse of what was happening in the hallway—but still too far away to do anything about it. Handsome with blue eyes and unruly brown hair that the girls liked, he was just as tall as his bullying teammate—but lean and agile. He threaded around the other students, many of them giving him some space, and he zeroed in on the skirmish in front of Billy Kim's locker.

The slender boy was picking up his books and the scattered papers. "You're pathetic, Derek!" Billy yelled angrily. "No other guy on the football team wears his letter jacket in the hallway between classes! What's that all about anyway, huh? How insecure can you get?"

A few people were cackling. Obviously, Derek didn't understand. With a dumb, triumphant smirk, he started to strut away.

"And you're on second string!" Billy continued. "You suck!"

That, Derek understood. He swiveled around and headed toward Billy, who was still bent forward gathering up the last of his strewn notes. It looked like he was about to kick Billy in the ribs.

Ryan stepped between them. He glared at Derek.

"Walk away," he said in a low voice. "You started it, Derek. Now, you walk away."

Staring back at him for a few tense moments, his teammate finally flinched. He let out a defiant laugh, which still had a nervous edge to it. "Huh, I forgot you two were boyfriends . . ."

Hands to his sides, Ryan clenched his fists. "Walk away," he whispered.

Derek turned and started to lumber down the hall. "What a prick," he said—loud enough to be heard over the other students. "Just like his old man . . ."

Billy collected the last of his notes, straightened up, and shoved the papers inside one of his books. He frowned at Ryan. "Y'know, I didn't need your help. I could have handled him myself."

"You're welcome a hell of a lot," Ryan replied. "Want me to call him back so he can beat the crap out of you?"

"You interrupted right before I was about to point out the irony of it all," Billy said, still getting his books in order. "Derek wears his letter jacket to remind everyone that he's on the team. It's the only thing he's proud of, and he sucks at it."

Ryan nodded. "Yeah, I'm sure hearing that would have really devastated him while he was kicking your face in."

Leaning against his locker, Billy cracked a smile. "You know, one of these days you'll get into a lot of trouble standing up to bullies and defending the down-trodden."

"*Downtrodden*?" Ryan repeated. He laughed. "That's why I love hanging out with you. Who else uses a word like 'downtrodden' unless it's in a term paper? Where do you come up with this shit?"

"You know what I'm talking about, and don't try to change the subject."

With a sigh, Ryan turned and ambled down the hall toward his locker. The last period bell was about to ring, and the crowd in the corridor was thinning out.

"And don't try to pretend you didn't hear Derek bad-mouthing your dad," Billy said, walking alongside him. "It's why you're always trying to rescue people who are getting picked on. You even took that loser, Jillie Mari-anna, to the homecoming dance just because everyone hates her guts and ridicules her." Billy chuckled. "You felt sorry for her, and then it turned out people can't stand her for a good reason. Not only is she a drip—she's a racist idiot. What did she say about Martin Luther King again?"

"I don't remember," Ryan muttered. He stopped by his locker and worked the combination. "But I know why certain people—me included—hate your guts some-times. You analyze *everybody*. You took one college-level psych class, and suddenly you're Dr. Phil."

"Tell me I'm wrong," Billy said. "All your life, your dad has bullied you. So you're constantly trying to save people—*the downtrodden*—from bullies. I didn't need to take any psych class to figure that out."

Opening his locker, Ryan pulled out his letter jacket and his books. "No shit," he murmured. "So what's your point?"

"Just quit acting like you're a big hero, doing me this huge favor coming to my rescue when I didn't need your help."

"Fine, Billy," he said, slamming his locker shut. "Screw you."

He headed down the hallway toward the exit.

"*You started this, you walk away*," Billy growled, imitating him. "What the hell does that mean, anyway?"

Ryan stopped in his tracks. Against all his intentions, he started to laugh. "I haven't got a goddamn clue. But it sure sounded threatening, didn't it?"

"Oh, yeah, very *Dirty Harry*," Billy agreed. "It certainly worked on dumbass Derek. And by the way, thank you. So—where are you headed? Don't you have practice in an hour?"

Ryan shrugged. "I thought I'd drive home, see my mom and pick up some more of my stuff. Shouldn't take more than an hour. Want to come with?"

Billy shook his head. "I can't. I'm tutoring that freshman in the library, and I'm already late. Say hi to your mom for me."

"Okay, see ya," Ryan said, throwing on his letter jacket.

"Later," Billy replied with a faint smile.

Ryan headed toward the double door exit that led to the student parking lot. Before he stepped outside, he glanced back over his shoulder.

He saw his friend standing there alone in the hallway, gazing down at the floor. He looked so sad—so . . . downtrodden.

Driving his used 2002 VW bug down Green Bay Road, Ryan spotted a father and his young son throwing around a football in the park. The guy must have been a stay-at-home dad. A yellow Labrador was running alongside the kid, who seemed to be having the time of his life.

Ryan remembered how he used to toss the football with his dad in the park at the end of their block on Spruce Street. They'd started those sessions when Ryan was around five. He wondered if anyone driving by Spruce Street Park back then had thought of the scene as some kind of sweet father-son bonding ritual. If so, they couldn't have heard his old man yelling at him to run faster, jump higher, put some sweat in it, and the oft-screamed, "Want to play for Notre Dame? Then you better make a real effort!"

Yeah, like every five-year-old should give a crap about the college team he'll play for. Ryan never understood his father's obsession over Notre Dame. The old man went to U of I. But from early on, he'd stocked Ryan's bedroom with Notre Dame pennants, posters, souvenirs—and even a Notre Dame bedspread. Growing up, Ryan didn't question it much. He figured playing for Notre Dame was his duty, and an honorable one at that.

Still, Ryan absolutely hated those sessions in the park—and it wasn't just on the weekends, either. Sometimes on weeknights, after he got home from work, his dad would change into his jeans and Notre Dame sweatshirt, then haul him to the park for "a little practice." He was like a drill sergeant. He'd hurl the football at him again and again until Ryan's hands throbbed with pain. He learned early on not to cry or complain.

Handsome, strapping, and sporty-looking, his dad

was a big shot in finance. Usually, he came across as a real fun-loving good old boy. People liked him until they played a game with him—any game, from Monopoly to charades to touch football. Then they realized just how cutthroat competitive he was. He tried to instill that same brand of "sportsmanship" in Ryan, but it didn't quite take.

Ryan's dad never really abused him—except for the occasional slap in the face or smack along the side of his head when he got extremely frustrated with Ryan. He never took it past that. There was never a second hit. Instead, he'd kick over a chair or slam his fist into his open palm. He was more oppressive than abusive.

Still, his dad must have been doing something right, because Ryan was now an honor student and the star quarterback. And yes, a scout from Notre Dame had watched him in a recent game, and apparently, Notre Dame was interested. But as far as Ryan was concerned, it wasn't worth all the bullying he'd endured.

Billy Kim claimed that Ryan had become his friend freshman year just to piss off his dad. Maybe that was partially true. It was obvious Brent Farrell would have wanted his son's best friend to be an All-American good old boy jock—not some Asian American who looked like a ballet dancer and had a smart mouth on him.

It was weird that his dad wasn't nearly as controlling when it came to Ryan's twelve-year-old sister, Ashley, or his nine-year-old brother, Keith. He was more affectionate with them—and so accepting of everything they did. For example, Keith was a sweet, funny kid who happened to hate sports. His favorite movie was *Moulin Rouge*. Ryan loved his little brother, and it didn't matter to him that Keith was probably gay. What amazed him was that his father seemed to have the exact same attitude. Meanwhile, whenever Billy came over, Ryan's dad would get so annoyed. It didn't matter that Billy liked girls (or at least claimed to); he just wasn't Brent Farrell's idea of a man—or of who Ryan's best friend should be.

Ryan couldn't help wondering if his father really had anything at all invested in Ashley and Keith. With them, the old man had no expectations, no charted path for their future. He didn't attend too many of Ashley's dance recitals or Keith's school plays.

Ryan envied them. His dad didn't miss a Lake Forest High School football game.

Six weeks ago, the Lake Forest Scouts were pitted against the Stevenson Patriots. They battled on the Scouts' home turf: Lindenmeyer Field. By fourth quarter, with 49 seconds left in the game, the home team was behind 21 to 24. In his Notre Dame jacket, Ryan's dad had made his way down from the bleachers and was restlessly pacing back and forth on the sidelines. Nothing unusual there, but this time, not only was he screaming at his son, he started picking on Ryan's teammates, too. Ryan whispered apologies to them during the huddles.

"I'm sorry, Farrell," one of his teammates said. "But if he yells at me one more time, I'm going to punch his lights out. I don't know how you live with that."

From the field, Ryan spotted his father at different times arguing with Coach Annear—and with one of his teammates' dads, and then with one of the umps. Ryan almost wished someone would kick him out of Lindenmeyer Field. But then, of course, he would never hear the end of it.

They'd made it to the sixteen-yard line on short passes, and Stevenson probably expected another. So during a time-out, Coach Annear told him to fake a pass, and follow it up with a fake handoff to his buddy Dan Reich. The Patriots' right defense flank had been a bit weak; so Ryan was supposed to tear ass along the right sideline for a touchdown.

After his conference with the coach, Ryan was heading back toward the field when his dad grabbed him by the arm. "Listen," he said, so close to Ryan's faceguard that Ryan almost stepped back. "John Flick has been wide open the last two plays. And I've never seen him drop a pass. He's out there in the end zone with no one on him, just waiting. You pass to him—"

Ryan started to shake his head. "Dad, Coach Annear wants me to—"

"I don't care!" he interrupted. He grabbed Ryan's faceguard. "Do what I say. Pass it to Flick . . ."

"Farrell, get back on the field!" Coach Annear called.

"You heard what I said," his father growled, giving Ryan's helmet a slap. Then he pushed him toward the field.

Ryan hurried back to his teammates. He heard someone on the Patriots' team mutter: "Jesus, what gives with that douche bag on the sidelines?"

As his team went into a huddle, Ryan looked at John Flick. He was about to tell him to go into the end zone for a pass, but he hesitated. "Listen up," he said, his mouth suddenly dry. "I'm faking a handoff to Dan, then I'm making a run for it along the right sideline . . ."

When they got into formation, he tried to block out his dad's voice calling to him over the roar of the crowd. "You heard what I said, Ryan! Want to win this game? Ryan, are you listening to me?"

The ball was snapped into his hands, triggering the sounds of grunts and groans, and bodies slamming into each other. Ryan pulled back and faked a pass. Then his friend Dan darted around toward him. Ryan faked the handoff. All at once, three Patriot defensemen lunged toward Dan. Ryan saw an opening to the right—just as Coach Annear had predicted.

"Pass it! Goddamn it, pass it!" he heard his father bellow over all the noise.

Ryan ran.

He was so angry. All of his humiliation and rage were channeled into a fearless determination to win. He poured on the speed and ran right toward the Patriot tacklers. He just wanted to hurt somebody, most of all himself. But his blockers were looking out for him— and one by one, they cleared a path for him to the end zone.

The home team crowd erupted into a chorus of cheers and howls as Ryan ran past the goalposts. He hurled the football down on the ground, and it ricocheted off the turf. He didn't do the usual victory dance. Instead, he paced around, trying to catch his breath until his teammates closed in around him. They were all high-fiving each other and slapping him on the back. But Ryan was looking over at his father on the sidelines.

The old man stood there with his hands in the pockets of his Notre Dame jacket. He had a strange smile on his face.

After they scored with the extra-point kick, there were three seconds left in the game, not enough time for Stevenson High School to regain its lead. So while the Scouts' fans started gathering at the sidelines to storm the field, the players went through the formalities. The ref's whistle signaled the end of the game, aborting a last-ditch effort by the Patriots to score. The Lake Forest fans and cheerleaders swarmed over the field like locusts.

The throng merged with his teammates, and suddenly Ryan felt all these hands on him. They grabbed hold of his arms, shoulders, and legs. Then they lifted him in the air. Immediately, he started looking for his dad again. But he only caught a fleeting glimpse of him through the crowd. He was still there on the sidelines, waiting.

As he swayed from side to side on a throne made up of his classmates, Ryan imagined shaking his father's hand. He might not have followed the old man's instructions, but he wanted to tell his dad that he couldn't have done it without him.

Eventually, his friends set him down—amid more backslapping, cheers, and whistling. Ryan was making his way toward his dad. He took off his helmet and grinned at him.

His father still had that same strange smile, and he was shaking his head.

Ryan stepped up to him. "Dad, I—"

That was all he got out before his father slapped him hard across the face.

Startled, Ryan dropped his helmet. Several people in the crowd gasped.

"When I tell you to do something, you do it!" his father barked.

Ryan stared at him for a moment. The whole left side of his face throbbed, and tears filled his eyes. All of a sudden, he flew into a rage. "Fuck you!" he shouted, shoving his dad back toward the bleachers. The old man toppled to the ground and almost banged his head against a post. Ryan must have knocked the wind out of him, because for several moments he sat on the ground, stunned.

After that, it was just a blur. Ryan hardly remembered breaking away from the crowd and retreating to the varsity locker room for his clothes. At some point, he phoned his mother and said he wasn't coming home. Part of him was afraid to. Another part of him simply never wanted to see his father again. He spent the night at Billy's. The following night, he stayed at his grandmother's place in Highland Park, the house his dad had grown up in. Ryan chose to sleep in the guest room rather than his father's old bedroom.

His grandmother was a pretty sharp old lady. She was petite with auburn hair and a lot of energy. She didn't dote on him too much. She phoned his parents to tell them he was there. Neither his mom nor dad tried to talk him into coming home. The following afternoon, while his father was at work, Ryan came by the house to pack a couple of suitcases. He'd decided to live with his grandmother.

He wasn't too surprised to hear that his father didn't care. But he felt sort of disillusioned that his mother would go along with it simply to keep peace at home. It made Ryan realize that she'd always been pretty ineffectual when it came to curbing his dad's oppressive ways. She never stood up to him.

The only time Ryan had ever heard his parents argue had been about four years ago. It had something to do with a Father's Day card. He remembered trying to block out the sound of the raised voices and his mother sobbing in their bedroom down the hall. After a few minutes, his dad barged into his room, waving an envelope. "Did you send this to me and not sign it?" he demanded to know.

Baffled, Ryan took the envelope and pulled out a sappy Father's Day card—with a baby's hand clutching a man's finger on the cover—and no signature inside. "No, sorry," he murmured, handing the card and envelope back to his father. "Father's Day isn't until Sunday. I was going to get you something tomorrow. Who do you think—"

"Forget it," his dad grunted. He threw the card and the envelope into Ryan's Notre Dame wastebasket, and stomped out of the bedroom. "Sweetheart!" he called, heading down the hallway. "Sharon, listen, it's just some stupid mistake or someone playing a joke . . ."

He never asked his parents about it. But Ryan couldn't help wondering if that card meant his dad had another kid out there somewhere—a kid who was illegitimate. Maybe that was why his mother had been crying. He tried to imagine his secret half-sibling, disowned by their common father.

The lucky bastard.

If this kid was really out there somewhere, Ryan now had something in common with him—or her. For the last six weeks, their father hadn't wanted anything to do with him, either.

He and his dad hadn't spoken since the game against Stevenson. Ryan had returned to the house several times to visit his mom, Ashley, and Keith—always while his dad was at work. He'd even had dinner with them one night two weeks ago, when his dad had been out of town on business.

His mother had made a lame attempt to reconcile them for Thanksgiving. But neither he nor his dad would budge. So while his grandmother celebrated Thanksgiving with his family over at his house, Ryan went to Billy's and had turkey dinner there. It wasn't so bad.

This morning, he'd talked to his mother. She'd wanted him to come by and pick up his wafflestomper hiking boots, because it was supposed to snow soon. Plus she wanted him to take the two-feet-tall fake Christmas tree she'd been putting in his bedroom every December since he was a kid. It had white lights and multicolored ornaments. She was going to dig it out of the attic so he could have it in his bedroom at his grandmother's. Obviously, she didn't have much hope for a father-and-son Yuletide reunion.

Ryan pulled into the driveway and parked behind his mother's maroon Acura Sport Wagon. The house was a huge Victorian relic—with a big front porch and a turret. Inside, it was bright, graceful, and elegant. But Ryan had to agree with Billy's assessment: "Shit, man,

I'm sorry, but from the street, looking at your house, it's right out of *The Amityville Horror.*" With the neglected front lawn, the place seemed even a little more sinister lately. He wasn't around to rake the leaves anymore. Walking up to the front porch, Ryan pulled out his keys. Though he hadn't seen his father's car, he was still wary when making these clandestine visits. He didn't want to run into the old man.

He took the mail out of the box by the front door. He always used to bring in the mail. He wondered who did it now—probably Keith.

Slipping his key into the door, Ryan found it was unlocked. He opened it and glanced toward the living room in one direction and the dining room in the other. Empty. He closed the door behind him. "Mom?" he called out with uncertainty.

He didn't hear a sound. Wandering into the kitchen and family room, he looked around and then set the mail on the kitchen counter. He'd expected to find the little Christmas tree there. Maybe his mom hadn't taken it down from the attic yet. She knew he was coming over. Where was she?

"Mom?" he called, starting up the stairs to the second floor. "Mom, are you home?"

Still no response.

He stopped by his parents' bedroom. The door was closed. He knocked. "Mom, it's Ryan . . ." The hinges squeaked slightly as he opened the door. He looked across the room toward the master bath. The door was open and it was dark in there.

Frowning, he retreated to his own room, which seemed less and less *his* with every return visit. He'd already moved so many personal things to his grandmother's. But there were still some clothes to collect—and a few old *Playboys* and *Penthouses* he wanted to smuggle out. He figured he might as well take advantage of the fact that no one was home now.

He couldn't help feeling a little ticked off at his mother. He didn't come over that often. He hadn't seen her since before Thanksgiving. What was so important that she couldn't wait around a few minutes for him? The car was still here. She must have walked uptown for something. She could have at least left him a note. *Typical.* She was probably running an errand for his father.

Sitting down at his desk, Ryan opened the bottom double-drawer and started digging past some papers for the adult magazines. He found four envelopes amid all those papers—each one addressed to his dad. Ryan had stashed them in here a while back.

He wondered if his mother would be so compliant toward his dad if she knew about these envelopes. None of them had a return address, but the handwriting was the same on each one.

Four years ago, he'd fished that unsigned Father's Day card out of his wastebasket and saved it. He was curious about this thing that had caused a skirmish between his parents. He couldn't stop thinking about what the card might have meant—that he could have a half brother or half sister somewhere out there.

The following June, when the Father's Day card selections started surfacing in the supermarkets, he remembered that mysterious, unsigned card to his dad. If he hadn't taken it out of his desk and studied it again, he might not have recognized the handwriting on the envelope when another just like it arrived the week of Father's Day. Bringing in the mail that afternoon, Ryan had slipped the envelope under his shirt. Later, he'd steamed open the envelope. Inside, he'd found another unsigned Father's Day card—of a dad and his little boy flying a kite by the lake at sunset.

Ryan had decided to spare his mother any further grief. So he'd stashed the second card in his desk—along with the first. After two more years, he had two more unsigned Father's Day cards hidden in his desk. His father's bastard wasn't giving up.

As far as his parents knew, there had been no other anonymous Father's Day cards after the one his father had thrown into Ryan's wastebasket four years ago. Sometimes, Ryan wondered if he was really trying to save his parents' marriage. Or had collecting and hiding those potentially harmful cards given him a certain, satisfying sense of power over the old man?

He studied the most recent card, with an envelope postmarked from someplace in New York. On the cover was a cartoon of a man's shirt and a gaudy tie. "For a Very Special Dad . . ." it said, over the illustration. "Fashions come and go . . ."

Inside, it read

But our family ties last forever!
Happy Father's Day!

Like the others, the card wasn't signed.

He almost wanted to show his mother these cards

now. He considered just leaving them on the kitchen counter for her. He imagined her finding them when she returned from whatever she was doing that was more important than being here for him.

"Oh, the hell with it," he muttered, shoving the cards back into his desk. "And the hell with them."

He decided to pick up the magazines some other time. He just wanted to get out of there.

Ryan grabbed his boots from the closet. Then he dug into his dresser drawer for some T-shirts. He'd left behind one of his favorites—with Tintin on it. He hadn't worn it in a while, because the shoulder was ripped. He found it along with a couple of others. As he started out of his room, he looked down at the Tintin shirt and noticed the neat threadwork along the shoulder. Without saying anything, his mother had sewn it up for him.

Clutching the T-shirts to his chest, he backed up and plopped down on his bed. He started to cry. The truth was, he missed her—and he missed his family so much that he physically ached sometimes. He missed this room, and what it used to be to him. Hell, there were even times when he missed the old man. But he'd be damned if he apologized to him. It was his father who should apologize. His dad owed him a lifetime of apologies.

Ryan wiped his eyes with the shirt and pulled himself up off the bed. He smoothed out the Notre Dame spread and headed out of his bedroom. He decided he'd go up to the attic and get the little tree. He'd leave his mother a note in the kitchen, saying he was sorry he'd missed her.

He wandered down the hallway and opened the door

to the attic. It was always a bit jarring to go from this clean, carpeted, elegantly appointed hallway to, just beyond one door, a gloomy old staircase to the dusty, unfinished attic. It was a vast space with cobwebs on the beams across its ceilings. The Christmas stuff was stored up there—along with old furniture, suitcases, wardrobe bags, and toys and games no one wanted anymore.

Ryan stood at the bottom of the stairs and gazed up. The light was on.

He set his boots and the T-shirts down on the hallway carpet. Then he started up the old, creaky steps. Halfway up, he saw a shadow swaying across the unfinished attic wall. "Mom? Mom, are you up there?"

There was no answer. He continued up the stairs.

The sun streamed through the one attic window. A shaft of light—with specks of swirling dust—spilled across the top of the staircase. He glimpsed the little fake tree by the top step. His mother must have taken it out of the storage bag and set it there.

"Mom?" he said again. He looked over to his left, where they stored the Christmas junk. Then he turned toward the side with the one window, where the roof came to a point.

There he saw his mother. With a rope tied around her neck, she hung from one of the ceiling beams.

Below her was an old chair turned on its side—and one of his mother's slippers. It must have fallen off as she'd kicked and struggled in the air.

She'd been waiting for him after all.

CHAPTER SIX

The cute blonde smiling in the photo looked like a nice person. But she was surprisingly unsexy. It was hard to imagine her as the vamp who had come into Scott's life, manipulated him into marriage, and then more or less swindled him.

Stephanie sat at her desk in front of her laptop, studying Halle Driscoll's photo on the monitor for the umpteenth time since the private detective had e-mailed it to her last week. She was home for a change—in her study alcove off the living room of her three-bedroom home in the Hawthorne district. The extra bedrooms upstairs had been for Rebecca and the kids when they came to visit.

Dressed in jeans, a sweatshirt, and thick red wool socks, she'd taken a break from decorating the Christmas tree. She had a pine-scented candle burning, because the tree was artificial. But it looked real—and quite pretty with the multicolor lights. She had only about a fourth of the ornaments hung so far. Though she heard nonstop holiday music in the different airports along her routes, she had Chris Isaak's Christmas CD playing.

The private detective had told her that Halle used this photo—taken outside by Washington D.C.'s reflecting pool—for the online dating service she'd joined. He e-mailed Stephanie a dozen other photos of Halle, collected from her family and friends. Halle exuded a kind of bland wholesomeness in those shots, too. The detective hadn't been able to find a decent photo of her after she'd left D.C. In the few pictures that existed of her with Scott or the kids, she always had her head turned to one side or her face was partially obscured. But it certainly looked like the same woman. Even some of her clothes were the same as those in earlier photos.

A friend of Jim's had recommended J. B. Church Detective Agency. Stephanie had met J.B. in his small office in Long Island City. Fortyish, with curly hair and an affable smile, he could have passed for an English professor in his corduroy jacket, oxford shirt, and jeans. His fee seemed reasonable enough: $750 up front, $150 a day plus travel expenses, and $5,000 if he got results. Results in this case meant any information about Halle Driscoll the police would find useful in their investigation into the Thanksgiving night murders.

After a week, it had cost her nearly two thousand dollars for his train fare and lodgings in the Washington, D.C., area, plus his daily fee. J. B. Church told her he didn't feel right taking any more than $2,500 for the results. The police weren't interested in what he'd found out about Halle Driscoll. But Stephanie was.

J.B. reported that Halle's friends and coworkers had echoed what her cousin, Deborah, had told Stephanie at the funeral. Halle was well liked, dependable, and a bit of a homebody. She hadn't had a steady boyfriend in three years. There had been a flurry of dates ("one-date wonders," Halle's best friend, Rachel Porter, called them) when Halle had first signed on with the dating service, but nothing in the last few months before she left.

For six years, she'd worked in the human resources department at Washington Gas. She'd recently been promoted to a management position.

On Sunday, June 17, Halle had visited her parents in Manassas for Father's Day. They'd had an early dinner, and Halle left for her apartment in Arlington around 7:15. She telephoned her mother a little past eight to say she'd arrived home.

Mr. and Mrs. Driscoll said their daughter had seemed in a good mood—and in good health—that night.

But the following morning, Halle e-mailed her boss, saying she was sick. That same day, her friend, Rachel Porter, telephoned her about a dinner date they'd made. Halle replied with a text, saying she was ill, and would get back to her later. Rachel's subsequent calls were all answered with texts or curt e-mails. "It was like she was giving me the royal brush-off," Rachel told J. B. Church. Halle's other friends and her coworkers received the same brisk treatment. In her messages, Halle claimed to be recuperating. But people were still concerned about her. It seemed she suddenly didn't want to talk to anybody or see anybody.

On Thursday, June 28, she e-mailed her boss, explaining that for personal reasons, she wouldn't be returning to work. His calls to her home went unanswered—except for a formal e-mail saying she didn't wish to return to the office. Could they send her any personal items from her desk and any paperwork necessary to terminate her employment there?

J.B. interviewed several of Halle's neighbors in her apartment building. During this time when she'd claimed to be sick, a few neighbors had seen her coming and going—in the parking garage or in the hallway. None of them were ever close enough to talk with her, but they said she looked fairly healthy.

On July 8, Halle e-mailed her building manager, explaining that she would be late with her rent. She would be able to pay it the first week in August—along with that month's rent and any penalty. "It was the first time in six years she was late with the rent," the landlord told J.B. "So I decided to cut her some slack, and told her not to sweat the small stuff. . . ."

On Monday, July 30, a neighbor reported that Halle's smoke detector was beeping incessantly. There was no smoke, so it had to be a battery that needed replacing. The landlord had been in Halle's apartment about two months before to fix the air-conditioning. When he let himself into the unit to tend to the smoke detector, he found that except for a few odds and ends—and the heavy furniture—everything was gone. Moldy food was in the refrigerator.

Down in the lobby, her mailbox was full of bills

with "Second Notice—Open Immediately" printed on the envelope. The landlord notified Mr. and Mrs. Driscoll, whom Halle had listed on her rental agreement as next of kin. He forwarded the unpaid bills to them.

Halle had cleaned out her savings and maxed out her credit cards with cash advances. Her cell phone service was shut off. No one could reach her.

The first week in August, Halle sent her parents a letter from New York, explaining that she'd moved there and would forward an address once she'd settled down. She planned to get herself out of debt soon. If they could cover the minimum balance due on her bills, she would pay them back. The letter was in her handwriting on her stationery, but there was no return address on the envelope.

She notified friends with a group e-mail:

Many of you have been sending me e-mails. Some of you were also leaving me voice mail messages until I dropped my phone service. I appreciate your concern, but I'm fine. I've moved to New York, where an exciting job is waiting for me, along with an exciting new life. I need to break from past ties in order to start fresh. I hope you'll understand and respect that. I wish all of you the very best.

Sincerely,
Halle

"According to both Halle's best friend and her cousin," J.B. told Stephanie on the phone, "this e-mail was—and I'm paraphrasing—complete, utter bullshit.

It pissed off a lot of casual friends, who didn't want to have anything to do with her after that. But the close ones, the through-thick-and-thin friends, were convinced she was in serious trouble. Her friend Rachel even wondered if Halle had been forced to write that e-mail."

Rachel, Deborah, and Halle's parents were about to hire a private detective to track down Halle's exact whereabouts. But then something happened the second week of September. Halle's parents received a birthday card for her father. Inside was a cashier's check for $500. Halle said she would be sending them another check soon, and she'd phone them. She mentioned she was dating a very nice widower with two children.

Stephanie didn't have to guess how Halle had suddenly come into some money.

The five hundred barely put a dent in her debts. But it gave Mr. and Mrs. Driscoll hope that their daughter was getting back on her feet. Moreover, she seemed ready to reach out to them. For the time being, they decided against hiring a detective. They were afraid if Halle found out, she'd cut off communication entirely.

Another cashier's check made out to her parents— for $250—arrived in a Halloween card the first week of November. She wrote in the card:

Sorry this isn't more. It's been crazy & wonderful lately. I married on 10/27. His name is Scott. He has two children. Can't wait for you to meet them. I miss you both!

*Will call you soon about a Thanksgiving
reunion! Let Deb know. Be happy for me.*

*Love,
Halle*

That was the last communiqué.

The Thanksgiving reunion turned out to be Halle's memorial service.

The $750 that Mr. and Mrs. Driscoll received was just a pittance compared to how much money Halle had drained from Scott's bank account, credit cards, and safe-deposit box.

All of J. B. Church's painstaking research didn't really tell Stephanie much that she didn't already know. It just confirmed that Halle had been a sweet, decent person. At least, she'd come across that way. But at some point—obviously, around Father's Day—she'd gotten herself into trouble. Whether related to drugs, gambling, or some man, she'd kept her dilemma a closely guarded secret—a secret she'd taken to her grave.

Was it just a coincidence that Rebecca had killed herself the Friday before Father's Day? She'd written that message to Scott on the bathroom mirror: *Hate You*.

Stephanie had figured that Halle's erratic behavior and the way she'd gone through Scott's money would have warranted a police investigation. Certainly, J. B. Church's findings deserved some kind of official follow-up. In all likelihood, the murders on Thanksgiving had some connection to whatever—or whoever—Halle Driscoll had been running away from.

But the police didn't see it that way.

Chris Isaak sang the last Christmas song on his CD. With a sigh, Stephanie went onto Google, and typed: "Croton, NY Murders, Thanksgiving." The first search result was an article in the *New York Daily News* from the day before. Stephanie clicked on it and stared at the headline:

TWO BRONX YOUTHS ARRESTED FOR CROTON MURDERS
Suspects Tied to String of
Commuter Neighborhood Robberies,
Grisly Execution-Style Thanksgiving Slayings

Mug shot photos of two surly-looking teenagers appeared beneath the headlines. Ronald Mady, eighteen, and Calvin Davis, seventeen, each had police records and gang associations.

Frowning, Stephanie studied their faces. They looked like trouble—especially Mady, with his skinhead look and the Mike-Tyson-style face tattoo. Still, Stephanie didn't think the police had the right guys—at least not for the murder of her sister's family.

"Are you still looking at that?"

Startled, Stephanie swiveled around in her chair. "You scared me," she murmured. "Did you have a good nap?"

Yawning, Jim ran a hand through his mussed hair and nodded. He was wearing a wrinkled long-sleeve T-shirt and jeans. "I thought you were going to give that a rest and decorate the tree."

With one click of the mouse, Stephanie closed the Internet connection and got to her feet. She kissed him on the cheek and then brushed past him and opened up the old Meier & Frank box that held another batch of ornaments. "I was waiting for you," she said. "It's no fun doing it alone."

He flopped down on the sofa. "Can I just sit here and watch for a few minutes? I'm still half asleep. That flight from D.C. always wipes me out."

These evenings at her house with Jim were too few and far between. She liked to cook him a real homey dinner on such occasions, which usually came at the tail end of a business trip. He'd sneak home a day early, spend the night in her bed, and Stephanie could almost fool herself into thinking they were man and wife. Tonight's dinner was pot roast, slow-cooking for the last two hours while Jim had napped.

Stephanie put on Nat King Cole's Christmas CD, and then went back to trimming the tree.

The Meier & Frank box had most of the cherished, fragile old ornaments that used to go on her family's tree. She always put them front, high, and center. Yet it was a bittersweet reminder of her parents—and everything that had been taken away from her. She always got blue around the holidays. This Christmas promised to be downright miserable for her. She might not have even put up a tree this year if Jim hadn't been with her tonight.

"I know you think I'm crazy," she sighed, hanging up a blue ornament with a star pattern on it. "But I'm still convinced the police have the wrong guys."

"Yeah, you can tell by looking at them that they're just a couple of fun-loving, misunderstood, ragtag, innocent kids." He stretched out and clasped his hands behind his head. "Give me a break, honey. The cops found stuff in their apartments they'd stolen during all those house robberies . . ."

"But they didn't find Scott's car or anything from Scott and Rebecca's house," she pointed out.

The two suspects had kept some electronics and high-tech toys from their other break-ins. Police tracked down several jewelry pieces and silverware that had been fenced or sold to local pawnshops.

As for Rebecca's jewelry, Scott's mother had a theory that perhaps Halle had taken it from the safe-deposit box to wear at upcoming functions during the holidays. And perhaps the pieces had been stolen on the night of the murders. But none of it had been recovered yet.

Stephanie put down a bell-shaped ornament and scowled at him. "Scott's car, my mom's jewelry, the silver service, all that Waterford Rebecca collected, the Royal Doulton figurine—where did it all go? Why didn't the police find that along with all the other stuff?"

"That material connected them to four murders," Jim said. "It was red hot. They probably sold it somewhere far from home. Just you wait, it'll turn up."

Stephanie sat down beside him on the sofa. "That's another thing. The police are blaming them for five other robberies in the commuter neighborhoods, but they never killed any of the other people they robbed."

"No, but they tied them up and put them all in one bedroom—same pattern. And they practically beat that man to death in Chappaqua—in front of his wife and kids, no less. That family they robbed in White Plains, they roughed up the teenage boy. These are violent kids, Stephanie. Sooner or later, they were bound to kill someone." Jim shook his head. "I know you're trying to find some connection between the murders and what Halle did with your brother-in-law's money. But the two things probably aren't connected at all. You're trying to make sense out of it. But that's just the thing, it was all senseless." He took hold of her hand. "You need to let go and move on from this. Otherwise, it's going to eat away at you."

His cell phone rang—inside the pocket of his jacket, which was slung over the sofa arm on her end. Stephanie reached for his jacket and handed it to him. Then she got up from the couch and turned down the volume to Nat King Cole. Most of Jim's incoming phone calls were important.

"It's Maura," he said.

"Go ahead, talk to her in here," Stephanie said. "I need to check on dinner anyway."

But she stopped and put another ornament on the tree—one of her mother's favorites, a silly little cherub sitting on a moonbeam.

"Hi, sweetheart," Jim was saying to his daughter on the phone. "I was just about to call you. How are you doing?" He paused. "That's wonderful, honey . . . Oh, I'm just sitting here in my hotel room. It's lonely, but at least I can see the Washington Monument from my window. It's all lit up and beautiful . . . No, I'm going to bed in about an hour . . ." He paused. "Yep, that's right. I'm three hours ahead of you here. I can't wait to see you tomorrow. How are Nana and Grandpa?"

Stephanie quietly retreated to the kitchen.

Jim's daughter, Maura, was a mere twenty minutes

away at his in-laws' Lake Oswego home—an estate, actually. They looked after Maura whenever Jim was out of town—and on some nights, like this one, when they didn't know he was actually in town.

Hearing him on the phone just now made this night of sweet domesticity seem like a total sham. Stephanie felt so stupid, making him this homey dinner—so that for one night, she could pretend to be married to him.

Stephanie opened the oven door and carefully peeled back the aluminum foil over the pot roast. A savory aroma filled her kitchen. It was her mother's recipe. Stephanie had discovered it after her parents were killed. It was scribbled on an index card, one of dozens of recipes in a small filing box that had daisies painted on it.

Her mother had been a wonderful cook. But every Wednesday night—for as long as Stephanie could remember—her family used to go out to dinner. As kids, she and Rebecca would inhale their Cokes and stuff themselves on breadsticks or packaged Saltines with individually wrapped pats of butter—while their parents seemed to take forever with their pre-dinner cocktails. But there had always been something special and fun about it—until they became teenagers. Then the whole thing turned into an insufferable ordeal. Stephanie couldn't understand why her older sister, at age fifteen, had boycotted the Wednesday "cook's night out" excursions—as their dad had called them. But by the time her sister was married and Stephanie was fifteen, she realized why Rebecca had years ago come to loathe those dinners out with their parents. It was just so *uncool,* not to mention a total bore compared to an unsupervised night at home alone—with a microwave dinner and friends on the phone or something on TV. On those Wednesday nights, Stephanie used to sit and snarl at her parents half the time they were eating out at some nice restaurant. And if her mother or father sent something back, chatted too long with the waitperson, or even asked for a doggie bag, Stephanie was utterly humiliated.

She was such an incredible brat. Yet her dad would be so disappointed when she didn't want to go out with them.

"Aren't you getting ready?" he asked, poking his head in her bedroom one Wednesday night in October. He had a jacket on over one of his jazzy sweaters. He always had his coat or jacket on about ten minutes before anyone else was ready. "We're going to your favorite, China Harbor."

From her desk, she turned toward him with a long-suffering look. "Dad, I *used* to like it—like maybe five years ago. Do you know how fattening Chinese food is? God!"

"Well, we can eat someplace else," he offered. "We don't have reservations there. Where do you want to go, sweetheart?"

She sighed and tapped her pen on her pink desk blotter. "Can you guys just go without me? I have this English Lit paper due . . ."

Her dad looked so hurt. "Well, can we bring you something to go?"

Her mother was buttoning up her blouse when she wandered into Stephanie's bedroom. Stephanie's parents always got dressed up for their Wednesday night excursions. "Let her sit this one out, Lloyd. There's a ton of food in the refrigerator. She won't starve." Her mother looked at her with one raised eyebrow. "Eat something! We'll be back around nine." She patted her husband's shoulder. "I'm almost ready. Why don't we just go to Nelo's tonight? They have that veal marsala you like so much . . ."

"Veal is a baby calf!" Stephanie called as they retreated to the hallway. "How can you eat that?"

She heard her parents muttering to each other in their bedroom and then in the hallway. At one point her mother said something about, "Oh, she's just at that age . . ." Then there was the sound of their footsteps on the stairs. "Okay, honey, we're leaving!" her mother called.

"Have fun!" Stephanie yelled, not moving from her desk.

It felt so good to hear the front door shut, and know she was alone.

Stephanie didn't even notice when they weren't home by 9:30.

At about 10:15, she heard a car. Stephanie glanced out the window. It wasn't the family Nissan. Instead, she saw a police car pull in front of their house while a second patrol car turned into the neighbor's driveway. They didn't have their sirens flashing or anything. Stephanie wondered what was happening over at Mr. and Mrs. Gottlieb's house. They were a nice younger couple with two toddlers.

It didn't look like any kind of emergency, and she didn't want to be caught snooping. So after a minute or two, Stephanie went back to watching *Northern Exposure*. The English Lit paper she'd used as an excuse not to go out with her parents wasn't due until Friday.

She was about five minutes back into her show when the doorbell rang. Springing up from the sofa, she ran to the door and looked out the peephole. It was Mr. Gottlieb.

Stephanie didn't notice until she opened the door that a policeman was standing to one side of him. She didn't notice until they were face-to-face that Mr. Gottlieb looked terribly nervous.

"Stephanie," he said. "Honey, something's happened to your mom and dad . . ."

The gunman was a 24-year-old named Roland Shoemaker. Apparently, he'd just been dumped by his girlfriend, Tina Marco, a waitress at Nelo's, a small, family-owned Italian restaurant in Seattle's Wallingford neighborhood. According to one witness, Shoemaker walked into the establishment with a handgun and just started shooting. Tina had been waiting on Stephanie's parents at the time. Stephanie couldn't help thinking that her mom and dad had been keeping her there at the table, chatting with her the way they did with most of the waitstaff at their favorite spots.

The bartender and part owner of the restaurant had a gun concealed behind the bar. He fired back several shots, one of which hit Roland Shoemaker in the chest, killing him instantly. But by then, Shoemaker had shot seven people—including Tina Marco.

Besides the gunman, three people were killed in the restaurant that night: Stephanie's parents and an 18-year-old busboy named Charles Tobin, a senior in high school working to save money for college.

Stephanie couldn't fathom how someone's stupid ex-boyfriend had destroyed so many innocent strangers' lives for nothing—just because he was pissed off and had a gun. But then, she blamed herself, too.

"Dad wanted me to go out with them for Chinese that night," she tearfully confessed to her sister after the funeral. "But I didn't want to. I wanted to stay home. So they went to Nelo's instead. Don't you see? If only I'd gone out to dinner with them . . ."

"No, stop it." She remembered Rebecca hugging her. "You can't say for sure what would have happened that night. They could have changed their minds in the car and the three of you could have wound up at Nelo's. Then maybe you'd be dead, too. And I'd be all alone. You don't know, Steffi . . ."

She moved down to Portland to live with Rebecca and Scott. Starting at a new school, not knowing a soul, and missing her parents terribly—she came to depend on her newlywed sister and brother-in-law. Their once-spartan two-bedroom "starter home" was suddenly full of the furniture and knickknacks they'd inherited from her parents. Stephanie took some comfort in that. Yet she knew she must have been a burden on them, too.

Part of her felt they wanted to get as far away from her as possible—Scott especially—when they moved to New York during her sophomore year at the University of Oregon in Eugene. It put an end to the occasional weekend visits to see her sister. She stayed with them summers and at Christmastime, but always felt in their way.

She learned not to depend on—or expect too much from—anyone.

She'd liked it best when Rebecca and the kids came to stay with her. Now, those rooms upstairs would just sit empty.

Stephanie stood at the stove, listening to Jim in the next room telling lies to his daughter on the phone. She felt so alone. Jim didn't understand her obsession over Halle and the deaths of her sister and her family. He'd told her: "You need to let go and move on from this . . ."

"*Move on to what?*" she'd wanted to ask. "*What else have I got?*"

She certainly didn't have him.

There was just her dead sister and her slaughtered family—and so many unanswered questions about a woman named Halle Driscoll.

Stephanie couldn't let go of it. She wouldn't.

There was nothing else to hold on to.

Chapter Seven

L acee Roth didn't have a good feeling about this date. For starters, he was ten minutes late—and counting.

She sat at a small café table at a Starbucks in the lower level of the Long Wharf Marriott on the harbor. The place was practically empty at this odd hour: a couple at the window counter, a nerdy-looking guy on his laptop at another table, and a thirtysomething woman across from her in an easy chair, reading *The School of Essential Ingredients*. After walking there in the cold, steady drizzle, Lacee found the Starbucks kind of cozy. She had her hot chocolate, and Eartha Kitt was singing "Santa Baby" over the sound system. Still, Lacee was getting restless and impatient.

She didn't have many opportunities to meet single men at her job—in the Fine China and Silverware Departments at Macy's downtown. Mostly, she met engaged women and their friends or their mothers—picking out items for their bridal registry. Many of those brides were a lot younger than she was.

Lacee was 33—and pretty, with blue eyes and wavy, shoulder-length auburn hair. She'd lied about her weight in the form she'd filled out for Datamate.com a few months ago. She was about ten pounds heavier than she wanted to be. But then, some major weight gain was expected after going off crystal meth. Some people she knew in recovery had really ballooned. On her dates, she didn't talk about her past problems or about ex-friends or family members who were still mad at her. So far, she'd had her share of rejection—and rejects. She'd figured out early on to meet them for coffee in the afternoon, never dinner. A meal with a boring guy could be intolerably long—and pricey if she ended up with some tightwad who wanted to split the check.

Ray, whose Datamate.com moniker was "New2 Boston17," was 34 and never married. He worked out, loved all sorts of music, and wanted to "explore the city with a sensitive, smart, and sexy native as my guide. Let's get together and see what happens!" From his photo, he looked like he might be second-generation Eastern European or Russian. He had wavy, dark brown hair, and his eyes were intense, brooding, and soulful. Overall: lots of cute potential.

Too bad he hadn't shown up yet.

"Are you waiting for a blind date?"

Lacee turned to gape at the woman with the book in a nearby easy chair. She let out a startled little laugh. "Is it that obvious?"

The woman closed the book and let it drop into her lap. She wore glasses, and her tawny auburn hair was pulled back in a ponytail. It was almost exactly the same color as Lacee's hair. She wore a bulky black sweater and jeans. Lacee guessed she was in her early thirties, too.

"You keep looking at your watch and then over at the door," the woman whispered. Lacee figured she was born in Boston, because she had the accent. "I know exactly what you're going through. I've been in your spot—way too often." She rolled her eyes. "Oh, do I have some bad blind date stories. Do you have someone lined up to call you with an 'emergency' in case he's a creep?"

"I'm not sure what you mean," Lacee said.

"Don't you have an escape plan?" She shifted in the chair, leaning toward her. "You have a girlfriend call your cell about fifteen minutes into your date. If things are going well, you say you'll phone her back later. If the guy's a total loser, you act like the call's a big emergency, and you tell the guy you have to leave."

Lacee nodded. "Oh, yeah, I've heard of that."

"Well, do you have a friend who's calling?"

"Afraid not," Lacee admitted. She glanced over toward the door again. "Maybe I should have thought of that. I don't have a lot of faith in this guy. He's fifteen minutes late already."

"My maximum waiting time is twenty," the woman said. "Listen, do you want me to be the friend who calls you?"

"Really? You'd do that for me?"

"Hey, I've got your back," the woman said. "Tell you what, if you don't like him, just clear your throat and say—say, ah—'when you stop to analyze it.' That'll be your signal for me to call. I'll make a subtle retreat and phone you. Then you can tell him you've got an emergency. Your Aunt Sonya suddenly croaked or whatever."

"When you stop to analyze it," Lacee repeated.

The woman nodded and took out her iPhone. "What's your number?"

Lacee told her. The woman punched it into her phone. "So —once you ditch him, come meet me up-stairs in the hotel lobby," she said. "I've got nothing going on. I'm just here waiting for the rain to let up. My friend canceled on me, the rat. So you and me, we can go for a drink someplace. We'll swap bad date sto-ries. What do you say?"

Lacee shrugged. "Sure, I guess. Why not?"

"By the way, my name's Jill. What's yours?"

"Lacee."

Jill winked at her. "Well, we girls have to stick to-gether, Lacee." She glanced over toward the entrance. "Heads up, do you think this is him?"

Lacee turned to see her date wander in. Ray had lied on his profile. If that shrimp was six feet tall, she was Kate Moss. She guessed he was about 5'6", with a very slight build. His jacket looked dirty, and it seemed to just hang on him. The photo must have been old or re-touched—or maybe it wasn't even him. His wavy brown hair was flat and receding badly. Those dark, intense eyes just looked tired and baggy. He moseyed up to Jill, who had her nose in her book. "Are you Lacee?" he asked.

She looked up and shook her head.

Lacee waved to him. He glanced her way and did absolutely nothing to conceal his disappointment.

Frowning, he nodded and stepped toward her table. "I thought she was you," he said, plopping down in the chair across from her. "She looks like your picture more than you do, though I'm thinking she's younger. You said you were thirty-three, right?"

"Right," Lacee replied. She stole a glance over at Jill, who rolled her eyes.

In her head, Lacee was repeating the phrase, "when you stop to analyze it." If this dismal start was any indication of how the date would go, she'd be uttering those words in about five minutes.

"Too bad about your aunt," he said. Still in his chair, he was looking up at her as she put on her coat.

"Yes, well, she'd been sick for a long time," Lacee lied. "Anyway I really need to head over to my parents' house and be with them."

"Y'know, something like this always happens to screw up my dates," he said. "The last time, the woman's sister had an appendicitis attack."

Lacee buttoned up her coat and told herself not to feel guilty. The guy was a jerk. He never apologized for being late. He just complained about the parking. And then he complained about all the other women he'd met through Datamate. Not once did he show any interest in her or ask her anything—except at the beginning when he'd asked about her age.

"Well, it was nice meeting you, Ray," she lied. She grabbed her purse. "Sorry it didn't work out."

"I guess you want me to walk you to your car," he said, still in the chair.

"That's okay, I'm parked pretty close. You stay and finish your latte. Bye, now."

Lacee made a hasty retreat out the door—and up the escalator to the lobby, where Jill was waiting for her.

"God, he was so creepy!" Jill said, a few minutes later as they walked down State Street together. The rain had stopped for a while. The red brick sidewalk was wet and slippery. "He looked like one of those guys you'd see on TV who's been arrested for dismembering his mother or something. I don't know how you stuck it out with him for ten whole minutes. I thought you'd never give me the signal!"

They passed the Harborside Inn—with a Christmas wreath in each one of the tall, arched windows in front. "Let's go in here," Jill said, grabbing her hand and pulling her to the next doorway—into the Harborside's café and lounge.

The place had Bruce Springsteen belting out "Santa Claus is Coming to Town" at full volume, and people sang along. The front counter of the bar was illuminated with pink neon. Beams cut across the ceiling with multicolored lights. The furnishings were art deco meets *A Clockwork Orange*. As she and Jill threaded through the mob, Lacee noticed it was mostly a twentysomething crowd. She felt ancient among them. But Jill seemed unfazed. She found them a spot at the end of a long sofa against the wall. The waiter came by as they were taking off their coats. Jill ordered a round of Pussycats. "Okay, now," she said, turning to Lacee. "I need a blow-by-blow account of everything that happened after I left to phone you."

Lacee told her what she'd missed—including Ray's

admission that his last date had ditched him, claiming her sister had had a sudden appendicitis attack. She and Jill got a case of the giggles over it. "By the way," Lacee said, still chuckling. "The drinks are on me. I owe you, big-time. I'd still be stuck there in Starbucks talking to him if weren't for you."

Despite the young crowd and the deafening din, she was feeling more relaxed by the time the waiter came back with their drinks. He asked if they'd like to start a tab. Lacee smiled at him "Sure—"

"No, thanks," Jill suddenly piped up, digging into her purse. "We can't stay . . ."

"What?" Lacee murmured.

Jill pulled out a twenty and a five and impatiently shook the bills at the waiter. "Go ahead and keep the change."

He took the money and nodded. "Um, thank you . . ."

Lacee waited until the waiter moved away. "What's going on?" she asked.

Jill grabbed her glass and guzzled down half of her drink. "We can't stay here."

"Why not?" Lacee laughed. "Did your Aunt Sonya suddenly die or something?"

"He's here," she whispered. "Your date, he just walked in a minute ago. He's seen us . . ."

"Oh, no. Where is he?"

"The street entrance," Jill said, struggling to put on her coat without standing up.

"In this crowd? Are you sure it was him?"

"Positive. He was staring right at us. And he looked pissed off, too. I don't want to deal with him. He— well, he gives me the creeps. Let's just get out of here."

She nodded toward the doors to the hotel lobby. "That's our best bet over there . . ."

Lacee didn't know if making a run for it was a smart idea. What if he started after them? Jill was right about one thing. There was something dangerous about that odd, wiry little man. A hand over her heart, Lacee glanced toward the swarm of people in the bar area. "Where is he now?"

"Over there, can't you see?" Jill said with an edge to her voice. "Goddamn it, Lacee, are you coming with me or not?"

Lacee grabbed her coat. As she stood up, her legs felt wobbly. She thought she heard someone yell out over the music and chatter: "Where do you think you're going, bitch?" But then there was a wave of laughter, which drowned him out after that.

Was it him?

She threw on her coat and followed Jill. Weaving through the crowd toward the lobby doors, she was afraid to look over her shoulder, thinking he might be right behind her. She imagined tonight was the last straw in a string of dates who had dumped him. Now that he'd seen her here with Jill, he knew she'd lied to him. He had to be furious.

She burst through the doors—into the hotel's lobby, past a couple of luggage carriers and a conversation area with love seats and a coffee table. Ahead of her, Jill rushed toward the door to the street. "Where are you parked?" she asked, not looking back.

Lacee couldn't quite get her breath. "75 State, the garage," she panted. Any minute now, she expected

Ray What's-his-name to come up behind her and grab her by the hair.

"I'm closer," Jill said. "I'm parked on the street. C'mon, hurry . . ." She ducked outside.

A blast of cold, damp air hit Lacee as she rushed out the door. She caught up with Jill, and they ran down the sidewalk—coming up to the lounge again. Through the window in the door, she saw the crowd, and she heard the muffled noise. It seemed stupid and risky to pass right in front of the place. If he was still inside the bar, he might see them out here.

As she raced past, Lacee glimpsed someone stepping out of the lounge. Was it him? She was running so fast, she didn't even see if it was a man or a woman. Jill grabbed her arm and pulled her down a side street.

"I'm sorry," Jill gasped, not breaking her stride. "I never should have stuck my nose in your business. I didn't think he'd follow us into the bar, for God's sake. There's something wrong with that guy . . ."

Lacee glanced over her shoulder at State Street. On the brick sidewalk, she saw the shadow of someone approaching. It loomed larger and larger.

"C'mon, this way . . ." Jill led her toward an alley.

Lacee saw a man and woman cross the street at the end of the block. It was their shadow she'd noticed. She was still peeking over her shoulder—when all of a sudden her feet went out from under her.

Helpless, Lacee felt herself falling. She landed on her ass—on the hard, wet pavement. She got the wind knocked out of her. For a moment, she couldn't see anything. But she heard Jill's voice: "Oh, shit, are you okay? My God . . . get up . . . you've got to get up . . ."

Lacee was more stunned than hurt. She blinked, and then noticed the manhole cover she'd slipped on. Her purse was on the pavement. Jill was frantically gathering up all the items that had spilled out of it: her lipstick, compact, sunglasses, and wallet.

"Please, for Christ's sake, we need to keep moving," Jill muttered. She grabbed her by the arm and pulled her up. Then she handed her the purse. "C'mon . . ."

Lacee finally got her breath, but still felt shaky. She glanced back toward State Street. There was no sign of anyone. "Jill, I don't think he's following us . . ."

"Damn it, I saw him just after you fell. Now, please . . ." She pulled her toward the alley.

Lacee balked when she saw where they were headed. In the alleyway, several Dumpsters and recycling bins lined the backs of the buildings. A black SUV was parked about halfway down there. Though well lit, the alley had several shadowy alcoves and doorways. And this close to the water, God only knew how many rats were lurking around.

"That's my car right there," Jill said.

Lacee didn't budge. She still felt rickety—and confused. "You—you parked in an alley?"

"I do it all the time, and they've never given me a ticket. Now, c'mon, move your ass." She pulled her toward the SUV, stopping only for a moment to reach into her purse and pull out her keys. She pressed the lock device on her key ring. The SUV's lights flashed as they zeroed in on it. "Get in, get in," Jill urged her.

Lacee opened the front passenger door, but glanced back toward the end of the alley. There was no one. This whole time, she hadn't seen Ray What's-his-name at all, not since she left the Starbucks. Was Jill overreacting, or paranoid—or what?

"Lacee, get in, for God's sake," Jill said, hurrying around the front of the car.

She climbed inside and shut her door. A moment later, the driver's door opened and Jill scooted behind the wheel. She closed the door and pressed something on the driver's side that made all the doors lock. Then she turned the key in the ignition. But they didn't move. With a hand on her forehead, Jill just sat there for a moment and caught her breath.

At last, she let out a sigh. "Well, what the fuck are you waiting for?"

Lacee didn't understand—until she peered into the rearview mirror. Jill wasn't talking to her. She was addressing the man in the backseat.

Lacee hadn't seen Ray since she'd ditched him at Starbucks.

But she was looking at him now.

All at once, he lunged forward. He slapped a rag soaked with something over her mouth and nose. Lacee struggled and clawed at him, but it didn't do any good. His gloved hands were almost crushing her head. The chemical smell on the rag was overpowering. Everything went out of focus.

She could hear the window humming as it descended on the driver's side. She realized her new friend, "Jill," didn't want to get a whiff of the stuff they were using on her.

"Just breathe in, Lacee," she heard the woman say. "It'll be easier for you . . ."

CHAPTER EIGHT

His cell phone rang. Ryan rolled his eyes. "I'll bet it's her again."

He had the phone on the table, beside the pizza pan. There was one corner piece left. In Ryan's opinion, the Nite N' Gale had the best thin crust pizza around. He and Billy ate there practically every weekend—and always the same order: two Cokes and one large sausage and cheese. They were usually the last ones to leave. Tonight, they'd scored a window table—looking out at the parking lot and the train station. A few drops of rain slashed across the window. Some brief flashes of lightning were followed by the rumblings of distant thunder.

Ryan glanced at his caller ID, and nodded. "Yep, it's her," he muttered. He set the phone back down, and the ringing stopped.

"Why the hell does she keep hanging up?" Billy

asked. He had a piece of pizza in his hand. "You'd think she'd at least leave a message."

"Beats me," Ryan said. "She pulled this same shit on me two nights ago." He pointed to the last piece on the pan. "Do you want this?"

" 'Chow down, wide load,' " Billy said, quoting from one of their favorite movies, *Stand by Me*. "Did you ever figure out what it was about?"

Ryan shook his head. "No clue." He bit into his pizza.

She'd called and hung up without leaving a message at least six times on Thursday night. It was bizarre. He didn't phone her back. He figured if his dad's new wife really wanted to talk with him or if it was an emergency, she would have left a message. Still, he told his grandmother the next morning, and she phoned home to find out if anything was the matter. "I guess it was some kind of mixup," his grandmother had reported. "She said she was awfully sorry. Between you and me, I think she's a bit ditsy."

Now, here his father's new wife was pulling the same routine again tonight. As he ate the last piece of pizza, Ryan stared at the phone.

"Why don't you just switch it off?" Billy suggested.

"Are you kidding? What if Emily calls? I don't want to miss her."

"I hate to tell you, but Emily Cantrell isn't going to call," Billy said. "She did this same thing to you last weekend."

Billy was right. Last weekend, Emily had told him she'd call if she got off early from babysitting. That left him practically catatonic and panting by the phone until one in the morning. He really liked her, but she was kind of jerking him around. And they hadn't even had a date yet.

"She's babysitting again tonight, and said *maybe* she'll phone, right?" Billy asked. "Well, it's ten-thirty, and the only person calling you is your stepmother. I rest my case."

"Don't call her my stepmother," Ryan muttered.

"Well, maybe you should finally arrange a meeting with her," Billy said. "Then we could come up with an appropriate nickname for her. You don't even know what she looks like, do you?"

Ryan shook his head. Apparently, she hated having her picture taken. With her iPhone, Ashley had snapped a shot of her and his dad at their quickie, little wedding ceremony—just Ryan's brother, sister, and grandmother, the bride and groom, and a minister in attendance. The bride's family hadn't come. Ryan hadn't been invited. Ashley had sent the photo to him on her phone. Ryan could hardly see the bride's face in the shot. She was turned toward his dad, kissing his cheek. All he could see of her was the wavy auburn hair, a small bouquet in her hand, and a tight blue dress that showed she had a nice rack.

A bright flash of lightning seemed to make the lights in the restaurant flicker. One of the other customers in the place let out a startled "Whoa!" A few people laughed. Gazing out the window, Billy shifted in his chair. "Boy, looks like it's going to get nasty out." A few more drops hit the windowpane.

The cell phone rang again. Ryan grabbed it and checked the caller ID again:

FARRELL, LACEE
847-555-1939

"Is it her again?" Billy asked.

Ryan nodded.

"Listen, if you're in no mood to talk with her, why don't I pick it up?"

"What?" Ryan murmured.

"I'm curious as hell to find out why she keeps calling." Billy grabbed the phone. "I'll pretend I'm you. She doesn't know what you sound like. She's never talked to you, and your voice mail greeting isn't you. She'll never know the difference. How about it?"

Ryan crunched up his napkin and tossed it on the empty pizza pan. "Knock yourself out."

Billy clicked on the phone. "Yo, this is Ryan!" he announced—in a husky, dumb-macho voice.

Chuckling, Ryan shook his head and flipped him the bird.

Across the table, Billy grinned at him. "Yeah?" he said into the phone. "Yeah . . ." The smile ran away from his face. "What?" he asked in his normal voice. "Wait a minute . . . wait . . ."

Ryan leaned forward. "What's going on?" he whispered. He wondered if something had happened to his brother or sister.

Billy was still holding the cell phone to his ear. "Um, Lacee, could you just—just—"

He fell silent. Gaping at Ryan, he shook his head.

"What is it?" he asked, louder.

"Hold on," Billy said into the phone. "I'm not—"

Ryan reached for the phone in his friend's hand.

Billy surrendered it to him. "She hung up," he murmured.

There was another flash of lightning outside.

"What did she say?"

Billy shrugged. "She—she said your dad was in a lot of trouble, and talking crazy. She said the only person who could help him was you. She wants you to come over—right away. She was whispering the whole time and sounded really scared . . ."

A deafening clap of thunder seemed to shake the restaurant's foundation.

"Jesus," Billy murmured.

Ryan looked down at the cell phone in his hand. He clicked on the options, and stared at the "last call return" option. He hesitated before pressing it. "What kind of trouble is my father supposed to be in?"

"I don't know."

"Well, did she mention anything about Ashley and Keith?"

Billy nodded. "She said they were safe—for now."

" 'Safe for now'? What's that supposed to mean?"

"I don't know, man. I tried to tell her I wasn't you, but she wouldn't let me get a word in edgewise. The last thing she said was 'Please come, we need you here.' Then she hung up."

Billy nodded at the phone in Ryan's hand. "So what are you waiting for? Call her back."

Frowning, Ryan clicked on the "last call return" option. It rang and rang—then finally went to what sounded like an automated voice mail greeting from the service provider.

"Hi, this is Ryan," he said, after the beep. "I think

we got cut off. Call me back, okay? I—I don't know about driving over there right now," he glanced out the window, "what with the weather and everything. Anyway, call me back as soon as you can. Bye."

He clicked off.

Billy stared at him. "What are you going to do?"

There was another rumble of thunder.

Ryan took a deep breath, and then he waved at their waitress. "Can I get the check, please?" he called.

Ryan could hardly see a damn thing. Even with the wipers on full speed, a curtain of heavy rain cascaded down the windshield. Every few seconds he got a mere peek at the wet, tree-lined road ahead—and then it was all a watery blur again. The speedometer was only at 30 miles an hour, but Ryan sat hunched forward with his hands white-knuckled on the steering wheel. He used to think he could drive the fifteen-minute route between Billy's house and what used to be his home blindfolded—but not tonight. He'd already dodged several fallen branches on Waukegan Road. And his usual shortcut side street was under about two inches of water. He'd skidded and slid most of the way to the next road.

Billy had volunteered to go with him, but Ryan had insisted on dropping him off. He figured if he had to deal with his father—after six months of chilly silence between them—bringing along Billy wasn't such a good idea. Plus he didn't want Billy stuck there while this family drama unfolded.

He listened to the rain beating on the roof of his VW

bug. He'd switched on the radio for some comforting background noise, but static kept interrupting the music—along with frequent bulletins: "There is a severe weather alert for Lake and Cook counties—thunderstorms with heavy winds and rain. Expect flooding in some areas. If you're home right now, stay put. It's not a night to be out on the road . . ."

He'd tried to phone Lacee again, but had gotten the same generic voice mail as last time. He'd called Ashley, but it had just rung and rung. He'd even dared to call the home line—at the risk of getting his father—but again, no answer.

Biting his lip, he turned down another street. Puddles splashed and hissed as he drove through them, and he felt the car weave again.

He wondered what kind of "trouble" his father was in—and how his going over there was going to help matters any. Could this have anything to do with his mom's suicide?

He remembered that evening five months ago, and how devastated everyone had been. His father and he had hugged and cried on each other's shoulders. He figured the old man's tough-guy "men don't cry" attitude—along with this whole blowup between them—was suddenly a thing of the past. He figured the family would need to stick together if they expected to get through this. His kid sister and brother needed him. They needed their grandmother, too. Their dad wanted her to spend the night. So Ryan drove his grandmother back to her house so that she could pack some overnight things. Ryan started packing, too—his big suitcase. He decided it was time to move back home.

He hadn't quite finished packing when he heard a car pull up in front of the house. Peeking outside the bedroom window, he saw his dad's BMW parked in the driveway. There was a light snow. In the backseat, Keith had his window down and his arm stuck out to catch some flakes.

Just then, the phone rang. His grandmother answered it in her bedroom. Ryan could hear her whispering angrily. Baffled, he headed out to the hallway.

"I thought you two just made up," his grandmother was saying. "He's in his room right now packing his bags. I can't believe this. Brent, I am so disappointed in you. Sharon would be disappointed, too . . . You don't know why she did what she did . . . Well, I wouldn't be so quick to pin the blame on someone else—what with the way you've been behaving lately . . ."

Numbly, Ryan treaded down the stairs to the tall window beside the front door. He brushed aside the sheer curtain and stared out at the car. He could see his father in the front seat on his cell phone. Both Ashley and Keith were in back.

"Yes, I know they need me," he heard his grandmother crying. "But they need their big brother even more. And he needs them . . . No! I'm not leaving him here alone—not after what he's seen today. How could you do that to him? What kind of father are you? I'll tell you what, you leave Ashley and Keith here with us. Then you can go home, and be the one left to grieve all alone. . ."

Her voice dropped back to a whisper, and Ryan couldn't hear her anymore. Both his brother and sister waved at him from the backseat of the car. Ryan just put his hand up to acknowledge them. He knew they couldn't see the tears in his eyes.

After another moment, the BMW backed out of the driveway. He heard his grandmother sobbing in her bedroom.

He started upstairs, but stopped and sank down on a step halfway up. His grandmother came down to sit two steps above him. "I guess you heard," she muttered, sniffling.

"He couldn't even step out of the car and come inside to face me," Ryan said.

She squeezed his shoulder. "People who are grieving do all sorts of crazy, awful things," she sighed. "Sometimes they hurt people close to them. I'm so sorry, honey . . ."

"Keith and Ashley need you there," he said.

His grandmother refused to leave him alone. So Ryan got Billy to stay for the night. He and Billy drove his grandmother back to the house so she could be with Ashley and Keith. Billy helped her with her bag and walked her to the front door.

Ryan remembered waiting alone in Billy's car, watching the gentle snowfall—and what used to be his home. He'd gazed at his old bedroom's dark windows. He'd told himself right then, he'd never go back into that house again if his father was there.

Now, here he was, driving through monsoon conditions to help the old man. His father was in some kind of trouble. Ryan wondered if this was all just a ploy on Lacee's part to lure him over there. Maybe she thought if she got them together, he and his dad would make peace. If that was the case, she'd sure picked one hell of an awful night for it.

He didn't know much about Lacee except for what his brother and sister had told him. She was pretty—but nowhere near as pretty as their mom. She'd moved here from Boston and had been working at a temp agency when she'd met his dad. They'd hailed a taxi on Michigan Avenue at the same time, argued about whose cab it was, and then shared the ride. By the time Lacee had reached her destination, his dad had gotten her phone number. Ashley had thought the story incredibly romantic, because it had happened around Valentine's Day. But hearing about it had made Ryan want to puke.

He hadn't been too surprised when he'd found out his dad and Lacee were dating. The old man had sure bounced back quickly from Ryan's mom's suicide. Then, of course, he'd needed someone to cook, clean, and look after his kids. Until Lacee started running the household, Ryan's grandmother had gone over there several times a week to help out. She also had Ashley and Keith over to dinner every Thursday night so Ryan could spend time with them. They still did that every week—without their dad and his bride.

Both Ashley and Keith liked her well enough. She basically let them do whatever they wanted and eat whatever they wanted. The kitchen cupboards were well stocked with chips and store-bought cookies. She ordered out a lot or she made them microwave dinners, which were eaten in front of the TV. Keith's favorite "home cooked" dinner became Stouffer's lasagna.

Keith thought Lacee smelled nice, "kind of like

Febreze." He was fascinated with the machine she turned on at night to help her sleep with its rain forest sounds, including a croaking frog. Ashley let it be known that Lacee dyed her hair, because she'd seen a Clairol Nice 'n Easy kit labeled *Natural Light Auburn* along with all those packages of cookies and the microwave dinners in her grocery bag after a trip to Sunset Foods. Ryan's grandmother surmised that her 33-year-old daughter-in-law must be prematurely gray.

Despite all the cookies and ice cream she bought, Lacee wasn't much for desserts herself. According to Ashley, her stepmother liked having a couple of Frangelico liqueur cordials after dinner. Ryan's sister had a hard time pronouncing "Frangelico" when she told him about it. She said the stuff came in a funny-shaped bottle, which Keith had mistaken one weekend morning for the Mrs. Butterworth's syrup. He'd drowned his Eggos in it, and ended up getting sick to his stomach after only a few forkfuls. "The dumb-head kept eating it," Ashley said. "You'd think he'd catch on after one bite. God knows why he thought the Mrs. Butterworth's was suddenly where Dad keeps the booze." Apparently, at first, Lacee had been furious he'd wasted so much of her after-dinner libation, but then later, everyone had gotten a good laugh out of it.

It was sort of a family joke now. But Ryan wasn't in on it. He wasn't a part of it at all.

A huge branch had fallen and now blocked one side of his old street. Avoiding it, Ryan had to drive through a puddle so deep it spread over the curb and half the parkway. In the heavy rain, its surface looked like a thousand little explosions. As Ryan neared the house, he didn't see any lights on in the front. That was odd, since Lacee had been so adamant about his coming over. He thought she would have left some lights on for him—especially in this weather. Except for the chandelier in the front hallway, the house looked dark. Then again, the family room and his dad's study were in the back of the house.

His heart was racing as he pulled into the driveway. He hadn't been by in weeks. He thought how right Billy was about the old Victorian house looking like something out of a horror movie. Tonight it looked sinister, dark, and still—while the trees and bushes all around it flailed wildly in the storm.

A bright flash of lightning almost blinded him, and for a moment, the whole house lit up. Then an earsplitting crack of thunder seemed to make the earth shake. A couple of car alarms went off. The thunder came right after the lightning. When he was a kid, his dad had taught him to count between the lightning and the clap of thunder that succeeded it. The seconds that passed were supposed to tell you how many miles away the center of the storm was—one mile for every five seconds. *One one-thousand, two one-thousand, three one-thousand* . . . There had been barely a second between the flash and the boom of thunder just now. Ryan knew he was in the center of the storm.

He sat in the idling car, the wipers madly fanning across the windshield in front of him. After driving all this way, he suddenly didn't want to go inside that house. It wasn't his home anymore. And if Lacee or his father had really wanted him to come over, one of them should have left an outside light on for him.

Ryan took a deep breath, and then shifted into reverse. He started to back out of the driveway.

Past the static-laced radio, the car alarms, and the rain drumming on the roof of his VW, he couldn't hear anything else.

Ryan couldn't hear the screams and the shots fired inside the house that used to be his home.

"Brent, what are you doing calling at this hour?"

"Dennis, as my lawyer, I thought you should know. I wanted to set the record straight—"

"What the hell are you talking about? Are you okay, Brent?"

"I wanted to set the record straight," he repeated. "I'll be sending you an e-mail within the hour. Read it carefully. I'm sorry about all this. Please, don't call me back. Just wait for the e-mail."

"What's going on? Brent, you don't sound right. What—"

Brent hung up the phone. He sat in the swivel chair at his desk. The window curtains in his study were drawn.

One section of the paneled room had been in transition for several months. In the built-in bookcase, the framed photos of Ryan playing football had been removed. However, Ryan was still in some of the family pictures on display. Recently, the framed photographs of Brent's first wife, Sharon, had been put away, too. So—like Ryan, she remained only in group-family shots. Brent had nothing to replace those photos of his dead wife, because his current spouse didn't like having her picture taken. He'd also done away with several pieces of Notre Dame memorabilia. So the bookcases of Brent Farrell's carefully appointed study had several empty gaps—and though completely unintentional on Brent's part, each one of those gaps represented something once cherished that he had lost.

In front of him was a piece of notebook paper with words scribbled on it—a script of exactly what he'd just said to his lawyer, Dennis Meeks.

Brent was dressed in a white T-shirt and sweatpants. The father who had taught his son early on that "real men don't cry" had tears streaming down his face. He also had a gun pressed to the side of his head.

A crack of thunder made him flinch. "Okay," he said, sobbing. One shaky hand still clutched the phone receiver. "I've done what you've told me to. Now what?"

The woman behind him moved the gun barrel—so it poked into the flesh that had gone soft under his chin.

Trembling, Brent closed his eyes. "For Christ's sake, what do you want?"

He felt her leaning forward. Her lips brushed against his ear.

"Tell me you're sorry," she whispered.

CHAPTER NINE

S tephanie had never crashed a funeral before.

It had been a stupid mistake to wear the black suit she'd bought on Thanksgiving weekend for Scott and the kids' funeral. The material was thick, and now she was roasting as she stood in the hot midday sun by the crypt in St. Mary Cemetery. Though the outside temperature reading on her rental car was 77 degrees, the humidity level made it seem more like August than May. Her forehead was damp with perspiration, and she was beginning to feel the effects of taking the red-eye to O'Hare this morning. Except for a nap on the plane, she hadn't gotten any real sleep in thirty hours.

Stephanie was pretty sure she'd spotted Ryan Farrell and his grandmother with a priest, leading the way for the extended family into the mausoleum-like structure. With the three caskets laying in wait, there wasn't much room for the mourners. At least a hundred people stood outside the stone edifice. Most of them were high-school age or younger—children mourning their dead classmates. It reminded her of the crowd at the funeral for Scott, CC, and Ernie.

Two TV news vans were parked outside the cemetery gate. Several reporters and photographers had gathered there. Someone from the funeral home had kept them from going any farther. This was national news. Stephanie had seen the headline on page three of the *Seattle Times* four days ago while in the food court between planes at Sea-Tac:

FOUR DEAD IN CHICAGO AREA MURDER-SUICIDE
"The Money's All Gone"
Financier E-mails Attorney About Fraud Scheme
Before Shooting Wife, Children, Self

According to the article, after embezzling $350,000 of his company's funds—and then losing it only God knew where—a Lake Forest man named Brent H. Farrell e-mailed a full confession to his lawyer. It was written late Saturday night during a severe thunderstorm. In his P.S., he stated:

> "I drugged the children, put them to bed, and
> while they slept, I shot them both. I have shot
> my wife, too. I pray they are at peace. I am
> now about to join them. God forgive me."

Stephanie might not have read any more of the grisly story if it hadn't mentioned in the fourth paragraph that Farrell, a widower, had married his second wife just six weeks earlier. Lacee Roth Farrell had been found on their bedroom floor, shot in the face.

The fifth paragraph had been only one sentence. But when she'd read it, Stephanie made up her mind right then that she needed to fly to Chicago and talk with the surviving son and his grandmother:

> Farrell's first wife, Sharon Heppner Farrell, 43, committed suicide in their home last November 29.

Two photos accompanied the article. One snapshot showed the two children: a girl, twelve, and a boy, nine—both smiling for the camera at a baseball game. The little boy had a Cubs hat on. The other photo was of Lacee and Brent Farrell at their wedding. Her face was slightly obscured as she kissed her new husband on the cheek. For Stephanie, that photo was the clincher. It made her recall the picture CC had e-mailed her of Scott and Halle. Halle's face had been half-hidden in nearly the same way. It was as if both women had struck the same pose.

Staring at Brent and Lacee's wedding photo, Stephanie had wondered why the newspapers had used this one— when the woman's face was only partially visible. Weren't there any better photos of her? What bride in her right mind would settle for a wedding photo in which her face was hardly seen?

The suicide of wife number one, the quick courtship and marriage with wife number two, and just weeks later, the family shot to death. It was too much of a coincidence.

Jim said she was crazy. The killers of her sister's family had been caught. The police had even gotten a confession out of the two teenagers. They'd found Scott's abandoned car somewhere in New Jersey. But none of Rebecca's things had been recovered yet. Stephanie couldn't help thinking the police had lumped the murder of her sister's family in with all those commuter neighborhood robberies. They could have coerced a confession from those two boys—intimidating them or depriving them of sleep. She'd heard of things like that happening. They still hadn't gone to trial yet. That was set for July.

She'd probably alienated the police, badgering them about where Scott's money had gone. They kept telling her it had nothing to do with their investigation into the murders. Everyone was getting fed up with her. Again and again, Jim said, "Why don't you accept the fact that the money's all gone?"

Perhaps eventually she might have—if she hadn't read about Brent Farrell shooting everyone in his family—before putting a bullet in his own head. The $350,000 he'd embezzled—that money was all gone, too.

Stephanie hadn't been able to get away until last night, so she'd missed the wake yesterday. Lacee Farrell's body was being flown back to her native Boston this morning—for a memorial service and burial there. Stephanie figured the body was probably being loaded on a departing flight just as she was arriving at O'Hare. A lot of people didn't realize it was common practice to have a dead body or two in cargo aboard any given commercial flight. "Low-maintenance customers," one of her fellow pilots liked to say.

She'd phoned J. B. Church to ask if he could attend Lacee Farrell's memorial in Boston, and find out what he could about her. There wasn't much about Lacee on-line, and no photographs—except the one from the wedding. The detective said he was wrapping up an-other case today, but promised to get on it first thing in the morning. She had a feeling J. B. Church, like everyone else, thought she was crazy.

Her room hadn't been ready when she'd arrived at the hotel this morning, so Stephanie had changed clothes in the bathroom at the Hilton Garden Inn in Lake Forest. She'd come to the cemetery with photos of Halle and a carefully worded letter to Ryan and his grandmother, Mrs. Farrell—in case they didn't have the time or desire to talk with her. In the letter, she'd written down a link to a news article about the Thanks-giving night murders. She also had her contact infor-mation on there. She was bound to come across as a nutcase, and had to approach them as discreetly and delicately as possible.

The close family members started to file out of the crypt, several of them crying. Ryan and his grand-mother were dry-eyed, but they looked so tired and be-wildered. Stephanie stayed back, watching as different people came up to talk with them and shake their hands or hug them. Down by the gate, the photogra-phers and reporters suddenly seemed restless—as if they were on alert. Stephanie felt like one of them, ready to pounce on Ryan or his grandmother once the crowd thinned out.

A handful of mourners still hovered around Ryan and Mrs. Farrell as they made their way toward an idling limousine. One of the group—a tall, slender young Asian American man—stuck close to them both.

Stephanie took a deep breath and walked over to them. Along with his navy blazer and gray pants, Ryan wore a dark tie that needed to be readjusted. His grandmother was a well preserved seventysomething matron with ash-auburn hair.

"Ryan? Mrs. Farrell?" she called gently.

They stopped to stare at her.

"You don't know me," Stephanie said. "But I'm so sorry for your loss . . ."

Ryan nodded politely and reached out to shake her hand. He seemed to be doing it by rote.

"Thank you," the grandmother murmured. Then she ducked into the limo.

"My name's Stephanie Coburn." She shook Ryan's hand. "I—I know what you're going through. Last year around this time, my sister—my only sister, Rebecca— she killed herself. Just a few months later, her husband remarried, and very shortly after that, the whole family was killed. My sister had two children—around your brother's and sister's ages. Someone broke into their house, tied them up, and shot them . . ."

Ryan stole a look at his friend, and then he shook his head at her. "Um, I'm really sorry . . ."

She pulled the letter and photographs out of her purse. "It happened just outside New York on Thanksgiving night. Maybe you read about it. The police think it was a routine robbery gone haywire. But I think it had something to do with the woman who took my sister's place—the woman who married my brother-in-law . . ."

"Ryan?" Mrs. Farrell called from inside the limo.

He glanced distractedly back at his grandmother, and then turned to her. "I'm really sorry. I—"

"Listen, my brother-in-law was very good with money," Stephanie cut in. "But once he married this woman, all of his savings just vanished. Your father, I'm guessing he was an honest businessman—with an excellent reputation—until he married this woman. He was probably a wonderful father, too . . ."

Ryan seemed to flinch. Stephanie could tell she was losing him.

"I never met the woman who married my brother-in-law," she said, a quaver in her throat. "How well did you know Lacee Roth?" She shoved one of the photos of Halle into his hand. "The hair is different, but did she look anything like this woman?

Frowning, he barely glimpsed at the picture. "I never met Lacee . . ." He looked like he was about to hand the photo back to her, but he hesitated and turned toward the limo. He ducked his head in and whispered something to his grandmother in the backseat.

Stephanie turned to Ryan's friend. "I'm really sorry to be so pushy. I know this is a terrible time . . ."

The young man shrugged. "They need to be at some brunch thing . . ."

Ryan straightened up, turned, and gave her back the photograph of Halle. "My grandmother met Lacee on several occasions, and she says this isn't her. I'm sorry I can't help you."

Stephanie tried to give him the letter she'd written. "Please, if you could just read this—"

But Ryan shook his head and climbed into the limo.

"I'll be right behind you," Ryan's friend said. "Meet you at the Deerpath Inn." He shut Ryan's door and waved as the limo drove off. Then he gave Stephanie a contrite smile. "Well, nice meeting you," he said. He started toward another car parked along the winding road within the cemetery. It was a beat-up old Honda Accord.

Stephanie noticed the reporters and photographers eagerly hovering around the limo as it crawled through the open gates.

"You must think I'm horrible—or crazy," she said, trailing after Ryan's friend.

The young man stopped in front of his car door, and he frowned at her. "Ryan's had a lot of people calling or trying to see him—well-meaning friends, reporters, wackos, you name it. People have even been ringing his grandmother's doorbell or driving by the house, just to get a look at him . . ."

Stephanie gave the young man a weary, half-smile. "Well, this particular wacko flew on a redeye from Portland last night, because—well, I thought what happened to both our families is just too similar to be a coincidence." She held out her letter. "For the record, I'm not crazy. I really did lose my sister's family on Thanksgiving. I wrote down a link to the news article here. Could you—could you ask Ryan to take a look at it? My contact information is on there. I'm staying at the Hilton Garden Inn tonight—and going back to Portland in the morning."

He hesitated, then took the letter. "I'll give it to Ryan," he muttered. "But I can't guarantee he'll read it or get back to you."

"Thank you."

He just nodded, then climbed inside his car and started up the engine.

Sweating in the black suit, Stephanie stepped back and watched the car move toward the cemetery gates.

The reporters and photographers by the entrance gate at St. Mary Cemetery had started to disperse. There was nothing left for them to see—or report on. But one man was still on the job. None of the other reporters had ever seen him before. The short, wiry, thirtysomething man with the receding brown hair lingered outside the fence, a camera phone in his hand. He'd just snapped a photo of one of the mourners. Now he was sending it to his cohort with the following text:

L%k who's @ d cemetery rght nw. She wz jst talkin 2 #1 son. I told U DIS btch wud b trouble.

He didn't have to wait long for a response. His cell rang within moments. He answered it: "Yeah?"

"How long were they talking?" asked the woman on the other end of the line. She didn't sound alarmed, just slightly annoyed.

"About two minutes, max," he replied. Behind him, one of the TV news vans was pulling away. He covered his other ear to block out the noise. "But get this. After Number One Son and grandma left, she gave a piece of paper to his friend, the Asian kid. What the hell are we going to do about her?"

"Relax. Whatever she thinks she knows, we're about five steps ahead of her."

"She's here—at the funeral. So she's got something

figured out. I'm looking at her right now. I can take care of this tonight."

"Leave her alone for now. I mean it."

With a sigh, he retreated toward his rented Chevy Impala. He glanced over his shoulder at the woman standing outside the crypt.

"If anything happened to her now," his cohort told him, "it would just give Joe Quarterback a reason to think whatever she told him might have some—legitimacy. Right now, he's in the news and attracting a lot of crazies. He probably thinks she's one of them. Let's not give him a reason to suspect otherwise. We have her Portland address—or we'll catch her on the road."

He ducked into the car and shut the door. "I guess," he muttered.

"Oh, you're just itching to get at her, aren't you?" she said, with a laugh. "I feel the same way about Number One Son, especially since we almost had him the other night. Anyway, about this sister-in-law, have patience, my pet. We'll be in Seattle soon, and she'll be just three hours away. You'll get to scratch that itch in a little while. And our pretty lady in black, well, the next funeral she attends will be her own."

Sitting in his car with the phone to his ear, the man didn't say anything.

But he was smiling.

"Don't be afraid," Ryan Farrell told her. "C'mon in . . ."

Dressed in his dark blue blazer and the slightly crooked tie, he held open the crypt door for her.

"But I'm not really with the immediate family," Stephanie whispered. She felt like she was intruding.

"It's okay," he said. "You know you're welcome here."

Shyly, Stephanie just nodded a thank-you. As she passed by him into the crypt, he bowed and whispered to her—like a maître d' in a restaurant: "The veal marsala is excellent tonight."

All at once, she realized she was in Nelo's—with the red and white checkered tablecloths and the big map of Italy behind the bar. She knew her parents were sitting at one of the tables, but she couldn't find them. She hadn't realized there were so many hallways and hidden alcoves to the little restaurant. She searched and searched. It was all she could do to keep from crying out for them.

Pulling aside the curtain to another niche, she found her sister, Rebecca, sitting at the glass-top kitchen table from Rebecca and Scott's place in Portland. Stephanie sank down in the chair across from her. She was exhausted from the search for her parents, and it took her a while to catch her breath. "God, I've missed you so much, sis," she said finally. "I thought you were dead. I thought you'd committed suicide . . ."

Rebecca laughed and shook her head. "I didn't commit suicide. That's crazy. I'd have left you a note or something."

Stephanie looked down at the place setting in front of her: knife, spoon, fork, and napkin. Across the table, Rebecca had no place setting—just their grandfather's old straight razor. There was blood on it.

"Look at my other smile, Steffi," she heard her sister say. "See it?"

She glanced up at Rebecca, whose eyes suddenly looked dead. Her mouth yawned open and then her head tipped back, revealing a crimson slit across her throat. The blood started running down her neck.

Stephanie screamed.

She bolted up, and found herself on top of a bed. Her heart pounded furiously. For a few moments, she didn't know where she was. Had she screamed out loud? She wasn't sure.

She felt cold, and realized she hadn't covered herself with a blanket or anything. She wore a T-shirt and sweatpants. She remembered putting them on to go work out at the hotel gym. But then she'd decided to lie down for just five minutes. Rubbing her eyes, Stephanie numbly stared at the swirly-patterned, brown bedspread, and then at the matching curtains, which were closed across the window. Finally, she looked at the digital clock on the nightstand. It was 6:47, and she was in her room at the Hilton Garden Inn in Lake Forest. She'd been asleep for over two hours.

She thought of the horrible dream, and a sad, aching emptiness swelled inside her. From time to time, she got depressed on the road, alone in some hotel room. It was especially rough since Rebecca's death last year. She really didn't feel connected to anyone—except in her dreams. Yes, there was Jim, but too often she couldn't depend on him.

Stephanie was trying to talk herself into getting up when her cell phone rang. She grabbed it off the night-stand and blinked a few times to focus on the caller ID:

HAMNER, MARLENE
973-555-4398

She clicked on the phone. "Hello, Marlene?"

"Hi, Stephanie, I got your message," said Scott's mother. "That name you gave me . . . Brent . . ."

"Brent Farrell," she interjected.

"Yes, well, it doesn't ring a bell," she said. "At least, I don't remember Scott mentioning him."

"He didn't go to Chicago on business much, did he?"

"Not that I know of," Marlene said with a sigh.

She could tell Scott's mother was getting a bit tired of her calling up every other week with some question or new theory about what had happened to Scott, Halle, and the kids. "I know Scott was born in Pittsburgh," Stephanie continued. "You didn't live in the Chicago area at any time, did you?"

"Well, we lived in Green Bay, Wisconsin, for six years, and Scott was in high school during some of that time. He used to spend a month every summer in Winnetka. You know, in the north suburbs—along the lake? My best friend growing up, Gloria Ingalls—she was Scott's godmother. Her son, Dick, became pals with Scott. He used to stay with them . . ."

Stephanie grabbed a pen off the nightstand and scribbled on the Hilton notepad:

Dick Ingalls—Winnetka

"About what year was this?" she asked.

"Well, it would have been between 1983 and '86. Scott used to love those visits. But he never went back after high school. Gloria invited him several times, but he was always too busy. I don't think he and Dick ever saw each other again."

"Do you have any idea how I might be able to get ahold of this Dick Ingalls?" Stephanie asked.

"Oh, he passed away about three or four years ago," Marlene said. "It was so sad. He lost his wife, and then remarried. Gloria said he and the kids were so happy. It was like a fresh start. But they were all killed while they were on vacation in Lake Geneva—a house fire. Dick, his new wife and the three kids, all gone. Such a tragedy . . ."

"You said he lost his first wife. How? She didn't kill herself, did she?"

"No." She heard Mrs. Hamner click her tongue against her teeth. "No, Stephanie. She had some kind of stroke or aneurism. It was a sudden thing. The poor girl, she was only in her thirties. Gloria was heartbroken. She adored her. I don't think she ever got to meet the second wife. In fact, I remember her telling me in one of our last conversations. Gloria was living in Vero Beach at the time. It was about a year after the first wife died. She said Dick had a whirlwind romance with this woman. After they got married, Dick was going to fly Gloria up to Chicago to meet the new wife. They were living in Glencoe. I think. Anyway, it never happened. The family died in the fire a week or two before Gloria was supposed to visit."

Stephanie was still scribbling on the pad:

*1983-1986 . . . First wife dead
(stroke—in her 30's?) . . . "whirlwind*

romance" & marriage to Wife #2 . . .
Did anyone get to know Wife #2?
Photos of her?

The whole family (3 kids) dead . . .
house fire . . .

It seemed part of the same pattern.

Stephanie got up from the bed and started pacing around the hotel room. "Marlene, would it be all right if I called your friend?"

Mrs. Hamner hesitated. "Oh, well, you can't. She passed away about two years ago. That last time we talked was several months before she died. I didn't even know she was sick. It was cancer."

"Is Mr. Ingalls still alive?"

"No, he passed away about twenty years ago."

Stephanie frowned. "Listen, are you certain Scott and—and this Dick Ingalls never met up again?"

"Well, I'm not absolutely positive. But when I telephoned Scott to tell him about Dick and his family getting killed in the fire, he—ah, well, he seemed to feel bad. But he wasn't exactly devastated. I remember him mentioning he hadn't seen Dick Ingalls in twenty-five years. Then when I suggested he send some flowers or a note to Gloria, he seemed reluctant. He said something like, 'I'm not good at that. Rebecca handles that kind of thing' . . ."

"It sounds like he and Dick Ingalls had some sort of falling-out," Stephanie said.

"I always suspected as much," Mrs. Hamner replied. "And before you ask, I have no idea what it was about.

Considering how old they were, they probably fought over a football game or some girl. Anyway—in answer to your question earlier, I'm pretty certain those two were finished with each other before they even finished high school . . ."

Stephanie wondered if there was any connection to Brent Farrell.

"Is this any help to you?" Scott's mother asked.

"It might be," Stephanie replied. "I'm not sure yet. But either way, I appreciate it, Marlene. I know you must be pretty fed up with my calling every week or so."

"I'm not 'fed up' with you, dear," she said quietly. "It just hurts to keep dwelling on this. You've been picking at a scab. After six months, I think it's time you leave it alone and let it heal."

"I'm sorry, Marlene," she murmured.

Scott's mother sighed. "So—I guess I'll probably be talking to you in a week or two."

"Probably," Stephanie admitted. "Thanks, Marlene."

Twenty minutes after hanging up with Scott's mother, Stephanie was taking advantage of her room's free Wi-Fi. She found an article in the *Chicago Tribune*'s online archives, dated August 9, 2009:

GLENCOE FAMILY PERISHES IN BLAZE
Five Dead After Lake Geneva Summer Home Catches Fire

According to the article, everyone died in their beds— the children of smoke inhalation. As for the two adults, they were burned beyond recognition. Authorities were still investigating the cause of the fire. They suspected it was faulty wiring in the old house.

Accompanying the piece was a photo of the Ingalls family, which included the new wife and stepmother, Vanessa. They were posed in front of someone's yacht at a marina. Squinting in the sun, the two teenagers looked a bit bored, but the younger boy was smiling gleefully. Behind them was Dick, looking handsome in his Izod sport shirt and baseball cap. His bride was beside him, clinging to his arm. Her hair was blowing in the wind. She was laughing—and quite hard to recognize in those big sunglasses.

But she didn't look anything like Halle—or Lacee Farrell—in that wedding photo.

There was frustratingly little in the article about Vanessa Black Ingalls, except that she was from Toledo, and she'd been married to Richard for only three weeks. Stephanie tried to find images of her on Google. But she kept coming up with photos of an actress, Vanessa Hudgens, and people on Facebook who didn't resemble Dick Ingalls's wife at all.

Her cell phone rang, startling her. Stephanie snatched it off the desktop and checked the caller ID:

FARRELL, RYAN
847-555-1751

She clicked on the phone. "Hello?"

"Stephanie Coburn?"

"Speaking. Is this Ryan?"

"Yeah, hi. My friend, Billy, said you came all the way from Portland to talk to me. So I figured I owed you a phone call at least."

"Well, that's very nice of you. I'm sorry I bothered you today. I know my timing was terrible, but I wasn't sure if I'd have another chance to see you."

"That's okay," he said. "So—listen, I checked out the link you wrote down in your note. And I'm—well, first off, I'm very sorry about your sister and her family. I guess there are some similarities, but I really don't think what happened there has anything to do with me or my family. Plus I checked online for any follow-up stories to that link. And I'm sure you already know—a couple of guys have already confessed to those murders."

"Yes," Stephanie said. "But I think the police forced a confession out of them, because those two teenagers were responsible for a bunch of other robberies in the area."

"Even so, what happened to my family was totally different."

"Not if you look at the whole picture," Stephanie pointed out. With the phone to her ear, she got up from the hotel desk and walked over to the window. She could see the traffic on the Tri-State Tollway below. "First, there was my sister's suicide. Then in less than half a year, my brother-in-law was married again—to some stranger. I didn't even get a chance to meet her. No one did. Just weeks after the wedding, my sister's family was killed, wiped out—"

"I know," Ryan said quietly. "Like I told you, I read the article."

"I'm sorry if this seems—tactless, but when your mother . . ." Stephanie hesitated. "Well, did she leave any kind of note?"

There was silence on the other end of the line.

"The reason I'm asking is because my sister and I were very close. She would have told me if she had a problem so serious that she'd take her own life. This was a total shock. The only kind of note she left behind was a couple of words scribbled on the bathroom mirror to my brother-in-law. It just never made sense to me. And then this woman took her place, and in short order, she went through my brother-in-law's money— all of it. No one knows where it went."

"I don't get what you're saying."

"The three hundred and fifty thousand your father supposedly embezzled, that disappeared, too." Stephanie sighed. "Don't you see? It's almost too much of a coincidence. Your mother's suicide, the hasty remarriage . . ."

"If you think the woman who married your brother-in-law is the same woman who married my dad, then you're wrong. I already told you that today. The lady in that picture you showed me wasn't Lacee. And as for my mom's suicide . . ." His voice trembled a bit. "She didn't leave any note. But if my father made her anywhere near as miserable as he made me, then I kind of understand why she hung herself . . ."

Biting her lip, Stephanie listened to his voice become shakier. She could tell he was crying.

"Listen, I need to hang up now," he murmured.

"Please, just one more thing," she said. "My brother-in-law's name was Scott Hamner. Did—"

"I know. I told you, I read the article," he said impatiently.

"Does that name sound familiar at all? Do you think your father could have known him—maybe in high school? Scott Hamner or another man, Dick Ingalls—could you run those names past your grandmother? Dick Ingalls is dead, too. He and his family were killed in a house fire. If there's a chance they knew your dad—"

"I'm sorry," he interrupted. "I really don't want to have this discussion anymore. I thought I owed you a call at least. But I'm done talking with you. If I seem rude, it's because I buried my father along with my kid sister and brother this morning. Understand? So please, just leave me alone, okay?"

"Ryan, I'm sorry—"

She heard a click on the other end of the line.

"Shit," Stephanie muttered, switching off the phone. Tears came to her eyes. She couldn't blame Ryan Farrell for hanging up on her. In her desperation, she'd become pushy and tactless with the poor kid.

She stared out her window at the traffic on the Tri-State below.

It was eight o'clock on a Saturday night. She was alone in another hotel room, feeling connected to absolutely no one.

The Philadelphia Story on Turner Classic Movies and a room-service chicken Caesar with a half carafe of Cabernet didn't quite lift Stephanie from her doldrums, but the combination made things more bearable for an hour.

Scott's mother wanted her to stop "picking at the scab," but she couldn't. What had happened to Rebecca and her family was on Stephanie's mind constantly. Of course, it didn't help that she was alone so much. Some nights on the road, a good movie on TV was her only distraction.

Around 9:15, she heard someone take away the room service tray outside her door. Stephanie was only halfway through the Cabernet—and the film. She was struggling to stay awake in the comfy easy chair. Her eyes kept fluttering.

The hotel room telephone rang, startling her.

Jumping to her feet, she snatched up the phone on the second ring. "Hello?"

"Hello, Ms. Coburn," said the man on the other end. "This is Jason at the front desk. I'm sorry to disturb you. The room below yours seems to have a leak in the bathroom, and we're sending a maintenance man up to double-check that it's not coming from your toilet tank."

"Now?" she asked.

"Yes. We're very sorry for the inconvenience. Please accept our apologies. I'm leaving a voucher for you here at the front desk for a free breakfast in our café tomorrow morning."

"Well, that's not necessary, but thanks."

"If we end up having to move you to another room, we'll upgrade you to a suite. The maintenance man will be there shortly. Thanks so much for your cooperation."

"That's all right," she said.

After she hung up, Stephanie glanced in the mirror above the dresser. She looked like a slob in her black cardigan, T-shirt, and sweats. But she didn't see any point in changing unless she had to switch rooms.

Smoothing back her hair, she stepped into the bathroom and switched on the light. She stared down at the floor by the toilet. It looked dry. The tank wasn't making any noise. She hoped they wouldn't have to move her. The notion of having some fancy suite did nothing for her. This late at night, she just wanted to wind down and go to bed.

She buttoned up her cardigan and wandered back to the room. With the remote, she turned down the volume on the movie.

Even though she was expecting it, the knock on her door still made her jump. She knew it was the maintenance man, but checked the peephole out of habit. On the other side of the door, the wiry man in the blue workman's uniform was glancing over his shoulder—at the hallway. The glass in the spy-hole distorted everything slightly.

Stephanie reached for the door handle, but hesitated. She checked the peephole again. Now the man was looking over his other shoulder.

Stephanie instinctively stepped back from the door. All she could think was that he seemed to be making sure no one else was in the hallway. She hadn't been able to see if he was wearing a tool belt or carrying a bag.

He knocked again. "Maintenance!" he called.

The door handle rattled.

Stephanie backed away toward the bed and grabbed

the phone. "Just a minute!" she answered in a shaky voice. She dialed the front desk, and anxiously counted three ringtones.

"Front desk," the woman answered.

"This is Stephanie Coburn in room 216," she whispered into the phone. She cupped her hand over her mouth and the receiver. "Did someone there just call me—someone named Jason—about sending up a maintenance man?"

There was silence on the other end of the line.

"Hello?" she said under her breath. "Are you still there?"

"Yes, Ms. Coburn. Ah, we don't have anyone named Jason working the front desk—"

"Then someone's trying to break into my room," she said, cutting her off. "He's outside my door right now, dressed as a maintenance man."

There was no response.

"Hello?" Stephanie said again.

"Keep your door locked," the woman told her. "Don't answer it. I'm sending our security man up there right now. I want you to stay on the line with me."

"I'm not going anywhere," Stephanie murmured, staring at the security latch on the door. She'd set it in place earlier. That was another thing she did out of habit during her hotel stays. Right now, the latch seemed to be moving ever so slightly—as if someone were putting pressure against the door. The handle kept twitching.

"Stephanie?" the desk clerk said. "Stephanie, our security man, Dave Marsh, is on his way up. Don't open the door for anybody but him."

Standing by the bed, Stephanie kept telling herself

to breathe. "What's your name?" she whispered into the phone.

"Lynne Davis," the woman answered.

"Thank you for your help, Lynne," she said, her eyes still riveted to the door. The handle was perfectly still now.

All at once, he pounded on the door.

Recoiling, Stephanie almost dropped the phone.

"Ms. Coburn? This is Dave Marsh with security. Are you all right?"

"It's your security man," she said into the phone. "I'm going to set you down for a second . . ." She put the receiver on the bed, and then went to check the peephole.

On the other side of the door stood a stocky, fifty-something man. He wore a blue suit. He had a cell phone to his ear, and in his other hand, he held up an ID card for her to see.

Stephanie unfastened the security latch and opened the door. "I'm okay," she said. Her heart was still racing. "Did you see him?"

Stashing the ID badge back inside his suit coat, the security man shook his head. "He must have taken off," he said. For a moment, Stephanie couldn't tell if he was talking to her or to someone on the phone. But he was looking right at her. He seemed like he was out of breath. "This guy won't get out of here without us seeing him," he continued. "We have cameras by all the exits. I'll check the stairwells and the other wing. You said he was dressed like a maintenance man?"

Stephanie nodded. "He had on a blue uniform. He was short, slight build, with—with thinning dark hair."

"All right," the man said. "Please, stay in your room with the door bolted."

She nodded and let out a skittish laugh, "Yes, of course, gladly."

She did as she was told, then got back on the phone with the desk clerk, Lynne. She thanked her again.

They didn't find the bogus maintenance man. The police were called, and Stephanie ended up having to file a report. She talked to two uniformed cops for a half hour. One of them kept glancing over at her half-carafe of wine. For a while, Stephanie wondered if they doubted her story or thought she was drunk. But the hotel operator had a record of someone calling Stephanie's room from inside the hotel at 9:17.

What worried Stephanie most was that this "Jason" who claimed to be at the front desk had addressed her by name. This hadn't been anything random. Someone had deliberately targeted her.

The hotel moved her into a different room. Unlike what "Jason" had promised, it wasn't an upgrade. The room was one floor up and in a different wing. But it was an exact duplicate of the room she'd vacated. It had the same furniture. The bed was the same, too.

And in it, she didn't sleep a wink that night.

CHAPTER TEN

"Oh, crap," groaned 16-year-old Alison Metcalf. Sitting with her friend at a picnic table by the high school's parking lot, she'd just pulled something from her lunch bag. Now she was grimacing at it. "I grabbed the wrong bag. I got my brother's lunch. Gag me, Lunchables . . ."

It dawned on Alison that her poor 9-year-old brother, Danny, had it far worse off, stuck with her carrot sticks, low-cal yogurt dip, and a Special K bar. She was always dieting, even though her parents insisted she was too skinny. With blue eyes and corkscrew-curly, shoulder-length tawny brown hair, she knew she was pretty. But she wished her breasts were bigger, and she didn't like her long neck. And the occasional pimple made her feel utterly hideous.

"I'll take your applesauce if you don't want it," said her best friend, Cate. She had a perfect, milky complexion, bobbed jet black hair, a stud in her right nostril, and a killer body.

"No way," Alison replied. "The applesauce is the only thing in here I'll touch. But you're welcome to build your own cal fest with my processed ham discs, lardy Ritz crackers, and petroleum-based cheese-food-product slices. I'm sure they spell it C-H-E-Z-E for legal reasons . . ." She spoke a bit louder than normal, just in case the cool group at the neighboring picnic table had noticed her. Some of the girls among them were nice, but others were total bitches. For them, Alison hoped to come off as clever and sophisticated about the dorky packet of Lunchables in her bag.

She and Cate had a strategic spot for watching Shane Camper, George White, and their pals executing all sorts of awesome moves on their skateboards. Alison had had a little crush on Shane ever since the pouty-lipped, blond-haired dreamboat offered her a stick of Trident in the hallway between classes two weeks ago. He'd already smiled at her twice while zooming by on his skateboard.

The sky was gray, and it looked like rain, but Alison would be damned if she went inside now. She planned to stay out here as long as Shane did.

"Hey, isn't that your mom?" she heard Cate ask.

Alison glanced over toward the street, and was horrified to spot her mother in the family car, a 1972 Oldsmobile Vista Cruiser, tan with fake wood paneling. Alison's dad loved tacky old cars, and claimed this one was in "pristine condition." He'd fixed the interior to include a new sound system, GPS, and all the updates. Alison's mother drove the old heap around for everything—much to Alison's chagrin. She wondered why her parents couldn't be normal.

The car was idling, just beyond where the guys skateboarded. Her mother poked her blond head out the car window and squinted toward the school.

"What do you think she wants?" Cate asked.

Alison's first thought was that her mother had discovered the lunch bag snafu and come by to switch lunches back. She imagined her mother getting out of the car, trotting around Shane and George's crew on their boards, and then delivering her lunch to her—in front of God and everyone. If that happened, Alison figured she'd have to change her name and switch schools.

Shoving the Lunchables package back into the lunch bag, Alison got to her feet. On her way to the Vista Cruiser, she dodged the skateboarders and felt her face turning red. It dawned on her that maybe something serious had happened—either to Danny at school or their dad at the TV station, where he was the anchorman on the local five, six, and eleven o'clock news.

As she approached the car, Alison saw her mother wave and even smile a bit. So much for coming about a family emergency. Wide-eyed, Alison stared at her. "What's going on?" she asked.

Her mother looked up at her through the open window. "I'm sorry, honey. I didn't mean to cramp your style. I was hoping no one would see me . . ."

"*Everyone* can see you." Alison whispered. She had a hand on the Vista Cruiser's windowed roof. "What are you doing here?"

Her mom shrugged. "I just wanted to make sure you were okay . . ."

"Well, I was until you showed up!" Alison said. "Why? What's going on? Was there something on the news, another school shooting?"

Her mother shook her head. "No, I just had a feeling something was wrong, a premonition. So—well, I started worrying, and I decided to check on you . . ."

"God, Mom, are you insane? Everyone can see us. What am I supposed to tell people? You came here because you had a *premonition*? This is so humiliating!" Alison figured she'd have to make up some story about a relative dying to explain why her mother had dropped by school.

"I was just concerned about you, that's all," her mother sighed. "You want humiliation? I can always get out of this car, put my cardigan on your shoulders and give you a sloppy kiss on the cheek. How would you like that?"

"Huh, you might as well," Alison shot back. "I couldn't be more embarrassed. Is that all? Can I go back to my friends now?"

"Go ahead." Her mother smiled wistfully. "And I'm sorry I humiliated you."

Alison rolled her eyes. "Yeah, right. It's like that's your job lately." She swiveled around, and flounced back toward the picnic table—staying out of the way of the skateboarders. She didn't look over her shoulder, and prayed her mother was quietly driving away.

"What was that about?" Cate asked.

Alison tossed the lunch bag in the garbage. "Oh, my mother is a psycho, that's all," she muttered, plopping down beside her friend. She looked past the guys on the skateboards, and noticed the clunky Vista Cruiser wasn't there on the street anymore.

She felt relieved.

"Anyway, don't be surprised if our daughter won't talk to me for the next week," Dina Metcalf said, while watching the road ahead. It was raining lightly, and she had the wipers on low. Beside her on the passenger floor were three grocery bags and two twelve-packs of Diet Coke.

"How did you know where she'd be having lunch?" her husband, Mark, asked over the speakerphone.

"Oh, she's gaga for that skateboarder kid, Shane," Dina said. "So I just looked for where those idiots congregate on their skateboards—and there she was. I only wanted to check to make sure she was okay. I was hoping she wouldn't see me . . ."

"Well, Danny's okay, I'm okay, and Alison's okay, though psychologically scarred for life. Are you satisfied now?"

"Sure, I guess," Dina lied.

"I should scoot," Mark said. "On the show tonight, I'm wearing the striped tie you gave me. Love you, hon."

"I love you, sweetie," she said. She reached over and switched off the speakerphone.

No one else took her premonitions very seriously. But she'd awoken this morning with an awful sensation that her family was in danger. Dina couldn't ignore it. Something like this had happened years ago, shortly after she'd gotten married. She'd been on a plane, coming back from a business trip, and an inexplicable, deep anguish had overcome her. She had no idea what it was about, but she retreated into the coach cabin's restroom and burst into tears. She stayed in there sobbing for so long that the flight attendant had knocked on the door, asking if she was okay. Once the plane had landed, she immediately phoned Mark to ask if he was all right. He told her he was fine. By the time she'd gotten home, they received the news that her father had keeled over dead from a heart attack.

Not every premonition was so catastrophic, or accurate. But her track record was good enough that Dina trusted her gut instincts. She was only half-satisfied after checking in on Mark and the kids just now. She knew the clenched feeling in her stomach wouldn't go away until late into the night—when everyone else in the house was asleep and this day was over.

She turned onto their block, which wound through some woods down to the shoreline in West Seattle. Their house, which Mark described as a Frank Lloyd Wright wannabe, was partially on stilts. It looked over the treetops at Puget Sound and Vashon Island. Pulling into the driveway, Dina reached for the device on the car's sun visor and pressed the button to open the garage door.

She maneuvered the car inside. It was a two-car garage, but crammed with so many garden tools and boxes of junk that they only had room for the Vista Cruiser. Mark parked his 1968 Mustang in a little bay to the right of the driveway.

The garage door groaned with a mechanical hum as it made its descent. Dina stepped out of the car and squeezed through the narrow clearance between the front bumper and the garage wall. She reached for the passenger door, but instantly froze when she heard something behind her. It was a strange, scraping noise.

Danny had said last week that he'd seen a rat in the garage—or "maybe a really big mouse." They'd set out a few traps, but hadn't caught anything yet. Still, ever since Danny's alleged rat sighting, Dina had been a bit leery whenever she set foot in the garage.

She swiveled around and warily gazed down around the cement floor. Some of the storage boxes were stacked up to six feet tall. They cast heavy shadows on the floor and garage walls. Dina peered down at the dark crevices between the boxes. If she saw a rodent, she'd probably bolt into the house, and leave the groceries in the car. She looked toward the last stack of boxes over by the big garage door. Her eyes were still downcast—so before anything else, she saw the man's feet.

Dina gasped and glanced up.

Staring back at her was a scrawny-looking stranger with thin, brown hair. He wore a dark shirt and black slacks. He had a gun in one hand and a bottle of bourbon in the other. With a tiny smirk, he raised the bottle. "Why don't you have a drink?" he asked.

"Do what he says, Dina," she heard a woman say—from another part of the garage.

Just as Dina looked over toward her, the ceiling light shut off automatically. All at once, they were swallowed up in darkness. A dim light still filtered through the garage window, so Dina could see the woman in silhouette. She emerged from the shadowy alcove by the family's second refrigerator.

Dina almost forgot about the keys in her trembling hand—and the button for the car alarm. She pressed it.

The shrill, earsplitting siren reverberated within the garage walls. Dina ran toward the door to the house—and the switch to the automatic door. But, suddenly, the man grabbed her from behind.

"Don't rough her up!" the woman yelled over the noise.

Dina screamed and screamed until he clasped his hand over her mouth. She struggled, but he was too strong for her. He managed to pry the car keys from her hand. Then he turned off the car alarm.

In the abrupt silence, Dina heard the bourbon bottle rolling on the cement floor. And she heard him gasping as his arms imprisoned her. She felt his warm breath against the back of her neck. He smelled of stale cigarettes. One hand pulled back for just a moment. Then she sensed the gun moving up her back—until the muzzle was tangled in her hair. The cold steel barrel tickled her below the ear.

He turned her around so that she was facing the big garage door—and his accomplice. The woman had moved from near the front of the car around the back fender to where her partner had been hiding. She had long, auburn hair and wore a dark gray trench coat. Her face was still in the shadows.

The bourbon bottle was now in the woman's grasp. "Do what he says, Dina," she whispered. "Have a drink, have a few drinks . . ."

Slowly he took his hand away from Dina's mouth. "What—do you want?" she asked. She could hardly get the words out. Her whole body was shaking.

"I just want to make this as easy as possible for you," the woman said. "It's not your fault that you're married to a son of a bitch. I have no quarrel with you. In fact, don't worry about your groceries. I'll take them into the house. I need to get a feel for the layout anyway. Now, c'mon, do as the man says. There's no use in struggling or screaming. Just relax, and have a drink or two. It'll make the whole thing painless. Like I say, I'm trying to help you."

She opened up the bourbon bottle, and held it up for a moment—as if toasting her. "We girls have to stick together . . ."

Alison frowned at the two twelve-packs of Diet Coke on the counter.

Setting her backpack on one of the kitchen bar stools, she wondered what her mother was up to now. The big cartons of soft drinks always went into the garage refrigerator—and then got moved into the kitchen fridge three or four cans at a time. Why the hell had her mother lugged them into the house? Alison was the only one who drank Diet Coke. Was her mother making some kind of statement?

She could hear the TV down in the family room. Danny was watching cartoons. She didn't hear anything else.

"Mom?" she called. "Mom, are you home?" She wondered if her mother would even bother answering.

Alison realized she'd been pretty much of a pill when her mother had come by school today.

She headed downstairs to the family room. There was a fireplace, a minibar, and a big-screen TV. Hanging from the wall was a giant poster from the racing movie *Grand Prix*, with James Garner. It was her dad's favorite movie. Danny sat on the sectional sofa, watching some outer space cartoon and wolfing down a bowl of Trix. He was skinny with a cute face and a wavy mop of pale blond hair. He had his stocking feet up on the coffee table, near the cereal box. Behind him was a picture window with a panoramic view of the trees.

"Is Mom home?" Alison asked.

"Haven't seen her," he replied with his mouth full.

She frowned at him. "God, look at you. Pig out much?"

"I'm starving! I didn't have anything for lunch except your stupid carrot sticks!"

"Sorry," Alison muttered. She retreated upstairs and wandered back into the kitchen. She pulled a cold Diet Coke from the fridge, and counted two more cans in there. She opened the soda and took a swig. Grabbing one of the twelve-packs, she cradled it under her arm and headed down the little hallway that led to the garage. There was just a bench in there—and some coat hooks. Alison opened the garage door.

She stepped right into a wall of exhaust fumes. Dropping the twelve-pack of soda, she staggered back. The cans spilled out of the package with a clatter. But through the haze, she couldn't see where they went. Alison immediately covered her mouth with her arm. But a noxious gassy smell was still in her nostrils. She blindly reached around and felt for the button to open the big door. Jabbing it, she heard the garage door hum as it began to ascend. An old blanket was caught on the inside door handle for a few moments, and then it fell to the ground. The ceiling light went on, but the place was wall-to-wall smog. She realized her mother must have left the motor running, but she didn't hear it now. Had the car overheated and died? Alison could barely make out the Vista Cruiser through all the exhaust.

But with the big door open, the toxic fog started to dissipate. She could see a tiny, red, blinking glow within the vehicle—a light on the dashboard. She thought she saw someone in the front seat.

She'd heard of people killing themselves by sitting in the car and leaving it running inside the garage. They usually put something along the bottom of the garage door to keep the exhaust from seeping out.

She suddenly realized what that blanket was for.

"No!" Alison screamed. All at once, she started to choke and cough. She quickly buried her nose and mouth in the crook of her arm again. Then she hurried toward the Vista Cruiser. Almost tripping on a soda can, she fell against the side of the car. She'd let her arm down from her face for a moment, and started choking on the fumes once more. This close, she could see the car's front and back windows were open. Frantically, she tugged at the passenger door handle.

The Vista Cruiser's interior light went on as she opened the door. Through the smoke, she could see the empty bourbon bottle on the passenger seat—along with a prescription vial that looked like her mother's sleeping pills. Her mother's purse lay on its side on the car floor. The red "check engine" light kept blinking on the dashboard.

Her mother was slumped behind the wheel with her face pressed against the car window. With her eyes closed, and her mouth open slightly, she could have been asleep. Her complexion was rosy and healthy-looking—only she wasn't breathing.

"Mom!" she screamed. She started coughing uncontrollably. Every time she caught a breath, she cried out to her mother again. Alison tugged at her sleeve and shook her lifeless arm. She knew her mother was dead. Yet a part of her kept hoping she'd wake up.

Alison would later tell herself that it couldn't have been a suicide. Despite everything to the contrary, it had to be some kind of bizarre accident.

Her mother had had a bad premonition earlier that day.

And the last person she'd thought about was herself.

CHAPTER ELEVEN

Stephanie hadn't noticed the man at the table beside her until he abruptly got up and left. She sat at a small dinette-style table at the Beaverton Bakery Café by the ticketing area. The bakery had red-and-white-striped awnings over the service counter. The floor was black-and-white checkerboard tile. Their croissants and European blend coffees were a regular guilty pleasure for Stephanie before she started one of her jaunts. She still had fifteen minutes before she had to report for her flight.

She'd already eaten most of her chocolate croissant and was starting on a coffee refill. She was on her cell phone with the private detective, J. B. Church. At times, she might have talked at full volume to compete with all the airport announcements. Was she one of those obnoxiously loud cell phone talkers? Maybe that was why the man had left in such a huff. Or maybe he'd just had a plane to catch.

The discussion with her private detective was pretty discouraging. He'd already e-mailed her last week about attending Lacee Roth's memorial service in Boston. Lacee's friends and family members had lost touch with her over three years ago—long before Lacee moved to Chicago and married Brent Farrell. She'd been a crystal meth addict, and gone through all her money. She'd also borrowed or stolen a great deal of cash from family and friends. By the time she got out of recovery for the second time, even her immediate family members were keeping their distance. However, she seemed to be getting her life back on track around the time she moved to Chicago. She'd always been a bit impulsive and rash. So no one had been particularly surprised that she'd suddenly moved to a different city—or that she'd married a guy who turned out to be an embezzler.

"Anyway, you've had over a week to review this stuff," J. B. Church was telling her on the phone. "And I think you'll agree with me, there are some similarities to Halle Driscoll's history, but not really. You can make a lot of conjecture about Halle suddenly and quite uncharacteristically throwing her life away on crystal meth. And you can make assumptions about Lacee possibly going back to her old ways once she married Brent Farrell. But there's no proof to back that up. There's really no connection between these two women—or the two cases. You saw the photos I sent of Lacee. She doesn't look at all like Halle . . ."

"But what about—"

"Excuse me?" someone said. "Excuse me . . ."

Stephanie looked up at the pretty brunette in her

early thirties. Hovering by the table, she wore sleek designer glasses and a trench coat. She looked nervous.

"Just a second, J.B.," Stephanie said into the phone. She gazed up at the woman. "Yes?"

"I'm sorry to interrupt, but did you notice the man sitting next to you who just left?"

Stephanie shook her head. "Not really. At least, I didn't see his face . . ."

"Well, from my table, it looked like he might have reached into your purse and taken something."

Stephanie grabbed her bag off the chair, opened it, and looked inside. "J.B., let me call you back, okay?" she said into her cell. She didn't even wait for a response before clicking off.

"I thought you should check to see if anything's missing before he gets too far away," she heard the woman say.

Searching through her purse, Stephanie didn't look up. She nodded, "Yes, thank you."

"He seemed kind of suspicious . . ."

Stephanie found her wallet and pulled it out. She was only halfway relieved. She checked that her cash and credit cards were there. They were, thank God. Then for extra measure, she made sure her keys were in her purse, too. She let out a grateful little laugh once she had them in her hand. She suddenly remembered her carry-on bag on the other side of her chair, and checked to make sure that was okay, too. "I don't think he took anything," she said, finally looking up at the woman again.

"Well, I'm glad. You can never be too sure."

"Thanks very much." Stephanie tucked her keys and

wallet back in her bag. "It was nice of you to look out for me."

The woman smiled. "Well, we girls have to stick together. Have a nice trip."

Then she turned and walked toward the security gates.

Stephanie lost track of her in the crowd. With a sigh, she set her purse in her lap. She sipped some coffee and then phoned her private detective back. "I'm sorry about that," she explained. "I had a little false alarm emergency here."

"Well, I'm afraid this whole venture has been a false alarm of sorts," J.B. said on the other end. "I made a few calls to Toledo about this Vanessa Black Ingalls, who died in the fire in Lake Geneva. Her parents are dead, no siblings. She left behind some friends in Toledo, but stayed in touch with them after she moved to Chicago. You saw the photo I sent. She doesn't look like the other two. And the situation is different. One basis for your trying to connect these cases is that the widowers got married again P-D-Q. Well, Dick Ingalls waited well over a year before he married Vanessa. And his first wife's death wasn't a suicide. The death certificate showed she was done in by a cerebrovascular accident—or in layman's terms, a stroke. The details of these cases aren't even similar."

Stephanie gulped down some more coffee. It was lukewarm. "Well, I'd like you to keep digging, and find out more about this Vanessa person."

"I'm sorry. I'm not going to waste any more of my time or your money traveling to Toledo to chase down some ghost. I know you think you're on to something.

You may even think your life's in danger. Maybe you're a little paranoid after that incident you told me about— you know, with the guy trying to break into your hotel room two weeks ago?"

"Now, wait a minute—"

"I don't blame you," he said, cutting her off. "It would've scared the crap out of me, too. But you shouldn't let it validate the notion that you've stumbled upon some kind of *conspiracy*. It's probably just an isolated incident."

"So—you're done working for me, is that it?"

"In a nutshell, yeah," he sighed. "Listen, you hired me to find evidence that Halle Driscoll or someone she knew was responsible for those murders on Thanksgiving night. I'm sorry I just wasn't able to come up with the goods."

"So am I," Stephanie said. She took another swig of coffee.

"You're trying to connect what happened to your sister's family to these other unrelated deaths, and it's just not—"

"Not completely unrelated," she cut in. "My brother-in-law was friends with Dick Ingalls back in high school. They both ended up widowers and—"

"And both ended up dead—along with the new wife and children," he interjected. "Yes, I know. But try telling that to the police. Two scumbag punks with criminal records have already confessed to killing Halle Driscoll and your sister's family in New York. A house fire in a Wisconsin resort town took the life of Dick Ingalls and his family. And in suburban Chicago, Brent Farrell embezzled and lost a small fortune—so he killed his family and himself. He even e-mailed a suicide note to his lawyer. All of these cases are closed—*closed*, Stephanie, resolved as far as the authorities are concerned. Maybe there are some similarities. But these are different situations, different states, and different jurisdictions. I'm sorry, but you're grasping at straws. And I can't keep taking your money."

Rubbing her forehead as she listened to him, Stephanie slumped back in her café chair. Another announcement came over the airport's public address system, but it sounded a bit fuzzy. Stephanie couldn't make out the words. Then again, she wasn't really listening anyway.

It seemed J. B. Church was just one more person who had become sick and tired of her. She'd succeeded in totally alienating Ryan Farrell the night of his family's funeral two weeks ago. Earlier this week, she'd been on the phone with Scott's mother and asked her something about Dick Ingalls and Scott. Marlene had started crying. "You need to stop," she'd said in her broken voice. "Please, Stephanie. I can't do this anymore . . ."

Jim was fed up, too. He was seeing less of her, because of family demands and business trips. He called her from the road, and whenever she started talking about Rebecca or her family, he'd get impatient and give some excuse for hanging up. Sometimes, she wondered if he was really out of town during those conversations. Or was he just pretending to be on the road as he did while at her place talking with his daughter?

"You still there?" J.B. asked.

"Yes," she sighed.

"I'm sorry I can't be more help to you," he said.

"Me, too. You can e-mail me your bill, and I'll send you a check as soon as I get back from this rotation. That's next Thursday." Stephanie started to sip her coffee again, but it had gotten cold, so she set it back down. "Thanks for trying," she said.

Then she clicked off the phone. "Shit," she muttered.

Stephanie tossed the phone into her purse and stood up. She suddenly felt dizzy. Her chair tipped over with a clatter. She told herself she'd just gotten up too fast. A few people were staring at her. Did they think she was drunk or something?

Taking a deep breath, she bent down to pick up the chair and set it upright again. She tossed out her coffee, napkin, and the last few bites of her croissant. She'd lost her appetite.

She checked her bags through the express security gate for airline personnel, and then reported in. She smiled at all the usual people and made the usual chitchat. But all the while, she felt this vague panic. Her heart seemed to be pounding furiously, and a part of her just wanted to sit down and cry.

She tried to keep her mind on her work as she did her customary walk-around inspection of the Bombardier Q400. She felt better, stepping outside for a few minutes. It was a beautiful spring morning. But just as she was looking at one of the propellers, she felt a crying jag coming on. Stephanie was terrified someone might see her—the plane's captain—sobbing uncontrollably out there on the tarmac. It seemed like something out of a Charles Addams cartoon, and the image in her head suddenly made her want to laugh and cry at the same time.

Once she was inside again, Stephanie managed to pull herself together. Passing through the Jetway, she kept a smile on her face and nodded to the passengers in line. Inside the plane, she said hello to the flight attendants, Chad and Claudia. But Chad frowned and squinted at her. "Are you doing okay?" he whispered.

"Of course," she said with a laugh. "I'm fine."

It didn't dawn on her until she settled into the cockpit that something might indeed be wrong with her. She suddenly felt claustrophobic, and that same vague panic swept through her again. This had never happened to her before. The controls, lights, and switches all seemed blurry for a few seconds.

Her co-pilot, John Manzuk, a pale, skinny redhead in his late twenties, climbed into the sheepskin-lined seat next to her. He immediately started talking about how he couldn't find a Harry Potter book for his daughter at the airport Powell's. John was a nice guy and a good pilot. But he was a bit of a chatterbox. Part of her wanted to tell him to shut the hell up.

With a shaky hand, she reached for her headset and put it on. Talking over him, she started the crosscheck.

Chad stepped into the cabin, and handed her a computerized printout. "Here's the manifest," he said. "We have sixty-six souls on board."

While she finished the crosscheck, she could hear Chad making the announcements: "Ladies and gents, this is Chad, along with the lovely and talented Claudia of your cabin crew. On behalf of Captains Stephanie Coburn and John Manzuk, welcome aboard Pacific

Cascade Skyways Flight 1284, with service to beautiful Spokane, Washington. Our flight time to Spokane is thirty-nine minutes . . ."

Stephanie was aware of the tower talking to her on the headset. Some of it seemed like gibberish. What was going on? The lights on the dashboard in front of her were suddenly so vivid and colorful. The instrument panel seemed to be breathing in and out. Closing her eyes for a moment, she kept a hand on the throttle, and told herself to calm down. She'd done this hundreds of times. They gave her the okay from the tower. That much she heard. She then carefully announced: "Cabin crew, please prepare for gate departure."

She told herself that whatever this was—a panic attack or the start of a nervous breakdown—she'd get through it. She could hang in there for 39 minutes or just under an hour from gate to gate. If she bailed now, there would be a huge delay and a lot of pissed-off passengers. Plus the airline would be furious. She was already strapped in, and the ground crew signalman was giving her the okay to back away from the gate.

"Cabin door's closed and secured," Chad announced.

John was repeating instructions from the tower. As she worked the wheel, throttle, and switches, it was all by rote. The plane started backing away from the gate, and she thought, *See, you can do this* . . . She kept her eyes fixed on the signalman. In his orange and yellow vest, he looked to her like a lobster, waving his claws in the air. Everything beyond the windshield seemed to be rippling, as if they were underwater.

"Stephanie, are you okay?" she heard John ask.

Part of her wanted to say no. Something was very definitely wrong. She had no idea what was going on. She kept thinking she had a job to do, which meant getting people to their destination on time—no matter what.

"Fine," she said. "I'm fine." As they taxied toward the runway, she tried to focus on the instructions from the tower—that little man jabbering inside her head.

"You don't look so hot," John was saying. "And you're shaking . . ."

She made an announcement, talking over him: "We are third for takeoff, and should be off the ground in about five minutes."

Her voice echoed—as if it were someone else speaking. All these voices were talking to her at once. The lines on the runway were weaving. Nothing like this had ever happened to her before. She felt like she'd been drugged.

Then she remembered that man at the table beside her who had left in such a hurry. Had he put something in her coffee?

She could almost hear J. B. Church talking above all those other voices: "You're a little paranoid . . ."

Maybe it was some kind of panic attack. All she had to do was breathe. If she could just get them off the ground, then she could go to autopilot. "Cabin crew," she announced, hating the little tremor in her voice. "Prepare for takeoff . . ."

"Stephanie, I'm concerned," her copilot said. "You look really out of it—"

"I'm fine, goddamn it!" she snapped. But she knew she wasn't. She never talked like that to a coworker.

The black box was picking that up. What was she doing? Her judgment was off. This wasn't a panic attack. She was hallucinating, for God's sake.

All at once, she could see the brunette woman who had approached her in the café. Stephanie remembered the designer glasses and the friendly smile. "Have a nice trip," she'd said.

"Twelve eighty-four, you're next for takeoff," the tower told her.

"No, we're not, traffic control," Stephanie heard herself say. It felt like her heart was about to burst out of her chest. "Ah, we—we need to turn around."

With tears in her eyes, she looked at her copilot. "John, can you get us back to the gate?"

They would tell her later it was the last thing she said that made any sense.

CHAPTER TWELVE

"Would it be okay if I looked at your yearbook?" his grandmother asked sheepishly.

Ryan sat in a tall director's chair at the kitchen's butcher-block counter bar, eating the grilled cheese sandwich she'd just made for him. "Of course," he said. He pushed the book across the counter toward her. "You don't have to ask, Grandma."

"Well, I just wanted to make sure." She put on the glasses that hung from a silver chain around her neck. She opened the book's royal blue and gold cover. "I mean, one of your friends could have written something very personal in here."

"Except for several cheerleaders thanking me for all the great sex this year, there really isn't anything too personal in there." A part of him loved shocking his grandmother.

She clicked her tongue against her teeth and shook

her head. "Funny man . . ." She started paging through the book.

His grandmother's kitchen was cozy. She had modern stainless-steel appliances—and a fondness for roosters. There was a framed poster of a rooster on the wall, a rooster napkin holder, cookie jar, trivet, salt and pepper set, and rooster dish towels. "Every time I step into your grandmother's kitchen, I have to stifle all the cock jokes that come to mind," Billy once said.

At the end of the counter, a small TV had *The Ellen DeGeneres Show* on at a low volume. With her nose in the yearbook, his grandmother settled in the director's chair across from him. Ryan gratefully ate his grilled cheese. He was hungry. It had been the last day of school, and he'd skipped lunch to meet with his teachers about taking makeup exams for the time he'd missed after his family was killed. During one of his free periods, he'd also talked with the principal, who wasn't sure Ryan could return to school next year, since he'd no longer be living in the Lake Forest School District. The coach was trying to figure out a way for him to stay on so the school wouldn't lose its star quarterback.

Meanwhile, all Ryan's classmates were pumped about the start of summer vacation. Many of them had caught him in the hallway between classes, asking if he was coming to this party or that party tonight. Ryan had told them all he wasn't sure. They'd asked him to sign their yearbooks. He'd obliged, but hadn't invited anyone to return the favor. What were they going to write? "Sorry you had such a shitty year" or "Maybe I'll see you next year . . . maybe not . . ."

So the yearbook his grandmother was now looking at had no inscriptions in it. And Ryan had no plans for tonight—except to study for his makeup exams.

"My goodness," his grandmother declared, gaping at the back of the yearbook. "Look at all the page numbers after your name in the index. Your parents would be so proud—well, they are, I know they are. You're the spitting image of your dad in these pictures. I feel like I'm looking at his yearbook from nearly thirty years ago."

Ryan didn't exactly welcome comparisons to the old man. But he'd seen photos of his dad from late college, and he'd had a ruggedly handsome look to him, like a young Harrison Ford. Ryan was curious if they really looked that much alike when his dad had been in high school. But he didn't say anything. Finishing up his sandwich, he wiped his mouth, crumpled up his napkin, and tossed it on his plate.

"If you don't believe me, just check out his old yearbooks down in the basement. They're in a box in the storage room . . ."

"It's okay, I believe you," Ryan said, working up a smile.

Five hours later, he was in the basement storage room, trying to find his father's high school yearbooks.

He was alone in the house. His grandmother had gone to her book club's potluck dinner. He'd practically had to push her out the door, because she'd been reluctant about leaving him alone. She was pretty active and usually had something going on two or three nights a week. It was never a problem. He never went hungry, and he liked having the house to himself. Why she'd been worried about him tonight in particular was beyond him.

He must have been sending out some kind of vibe, because Billy had called, telling him that he shouldn't be alone tonight. "Now, if you're over there by yourself having a porn marathon, then fine, go for it," Billy had said. "But you're *studying* on a Friday night, the first night of summer vacation? I don't know why you feel like you have to punish yourself tonight . . ."

"God, you and that stupid psych class," Ryan had lamented.

"I'm just worried about you, man."

"I know. Listen, I'm not going to off myself, if that's what you're thinking. Okay? I wouldn't do that to my grandmother—or you."

He couldn't really blame his grandmother and Billy for being cautious. First, his mom had hanged herself. Then his dad had shot everyone in the family, and put the last bullet through his own head. To Ryan, his father's actions—to avoid scandal and jail—seemed so typically selfish and hotheaded. But while his mom must have had a bellyful of the old man, her suicide six months earlier had been so unlike her. She wouldn't have done that to him or Ashley or Keith. It just didn't make sense.

Before saying good-bye to Billy, he reassured him they would get together tomorrow night. He polished off the rest of a chicken casserole his grandmother had made two nights ago. Then he tried to study.

But maybe part of him had been procrastinating, because suddenly he'd wanted to see his dad's high school yearbook photos.

Even with all the lights on down there, his grandmother's basement was still creepy as hell. A maze of
pipes ran along the low ceiling of the main room. Near
the washer and dryer and the big sink, garment bags
hung from one of the pipes. A shelf along one wall
held dozens of jars of homemade pickled vegetables
and fruits. Those glass containers always reminded
Ryan of an old *Alfred Hitchcock Presents* he'd seen on
Nickelodeon in which some guy put his wife's head in
a jar.

The basement also had an outside entrance, accessible by a cement stairwell along the side of the house.
No one except a burglar or serial killer would ever use
it. And the door had a stupid window in it—almost like
it was just asking someone to break in. There was a
flimsy chain lock across the bottom of that door, but one
quick, forceful kick could take care of that in a matter of
seconds. Sometimes, when Ryan heard noises downstairs late at night, he'd think about that stupid basement
door.

Off this room was a storage room that held folding
chairs, boxed Christmas decorations, old paint cans,
tools, stacks of old vinyl records, and containers full of
odds and ends. That included two large Marshall
Field's boxes with "Brent" scribbled on them in laundry marker.

He set one box on the floor, opened it, and the first
thing he pulled out was a beer mug with the Notre
Dame logo on it. "Huh, wouldn't you know?" Ryan
muttered to himself.

He took out a bobblehead Cubs figure, and then
kept digging. He found several plaques and framed ci-

tations for his father's athletic achievements in high school. There were framed photographs taken during football games and track meets. Two yearbooks were near the bottom of the box: *New Trier Echoes—1987* and *Echoes New Trier High School 1986.*

He opened up the 1986 edition and started to go to the index.

Suddenly he heard a noise upstairs. It sounded like the floorboards creaking. Ryan remained perfectly still for a moment. He looked out toward the shadowy furnace room—and the basement door. He didn't see anything, but wondered what he'd do if he spotted a man on the other side of it, staring back at him through the window.

The noise upstairs stopped. He told himself it was just the house settling. Why was he so jumpy tonight? He fearlessly confronted all sorts of intimidating hulks on the football field. Yet there was something scary about being down here while alone in the house at night. He came down to this basement for stuff while his grandmother was home, and it never bothered him. Did he think his 73-year-old grandmother was going to protect him or something?

"Screw this," he muttered. He dumped everything back in the box—except for the yearbooks. Switching off the storage room light, he took one more wary glance at the basement door as he headed for the stairs.

Once upstairs, he shut the basement door, locked it, and set the yearbooks down on the breakfast bar. He stopped and listened for a moment—to make sure he didn't hear that creaking again. There wasn't a sound.

Now it was too quiet.

He switched on the small TV for background noise. *Diners, Drive-Ins and Dives* was on the Food Network. Ryan sat in one of the director's chairs with his back to the TV. He looked up his father in the 1986 yearbook's index. He took some satisfaction seeing that his dad had only five page numbers after his name—compared to the eight page numbers after his own.

On page 31, there was an individual portrait of his dad for some club called Tri-Ship—and indeed, there was a resemblance. Ryan had a hard time locating his father in a group picture of the varsity football team on page 44. So he scanned the names listed in the caption:

(third row) M. Freeman, B. Riddle, P. O'Leary,
C. Jans, K. Konradt, R. Ingalls, B. Farrell . . .

He finally spotted his father in his jersey and shoulder pads. Squinting in the sun, he sat on the third bleacher bench up—with his helmet in his lap.

In the next group photo on page 49, the faces of the guys on the track team were slightly blurry. Ryan thought he recognized his dad among the group, all in their sweats, lined up in front of a track. He double-checked the names of the guys in the back row:

(second row) J. Martin, A. McMurray,
G. Donnellan, M. Scanlin, P. Joyce, R. Ingalls,
B. Farrell . . .

Ryan found himself studying the smug-looking, shaggy-blond-haired guy standing next to his dad near the end of the second row. Wasn't he sitting next to his dad in the football's team photo? R. Ingalls, why did that name seem familiar?

Flipping back to the football page, Ryan noticed that the same smug blond jock was indeed beside his dad. They must have been friends. But Ryan didn't recall his father ever mentioning this Ingalls guy— and the old man had talked about his high school athletic exploits plenty of times during all those football-tossing sessions.

Ryan kept wondering why he knew that name.

In his head, Ryan could hear the voice of that crazy woman from Portland over the phone: "Do you think your father could have known him—maybe in high school?" She'd mentioned her dead brother-in-law ". . . or Dick Ingalls . . . Dick Ingalls is dead, too. He and his family were killed in a house fire . . ."

Ryan quickly paged back to the index and looked up *R. Ingalls*. He found the guy's individual portrait on the same page as his dad's, for Tri-Ship and Intramurals. They were on the same teams and in the same clubs. They had to be buddies.

Classmates' notes and signatures were plastered all over the inside covers of the yearbook. It took Ryan a while, but he found the one he was looking for:

Brent—you are a righteous dude!
Keep on Truckin', man.
—Dick

He tried to remember the name of the Portland woman: *Stephanie* something. Out of politeness, he'd called her the night of the burial. But then he'd ended up asking her to lose his number and leave him alone. During the following week, she'd phoned and hung up twice, leaving no message. His caller ID had caught the number—with the Portland area code. Was it 503? He'd scribbled down the number someplace so he could block it if that crazy woman ever tried to phone him again. But she never called back. The number was still on a Post-it note somewhere upstairs in his desk drawer.

In the cemetery, she'd given Billy a note to pass on to him. It had a link to a newspaper story about her sister's family in New York. They'd been shot to death last Thanksgiving. He wasn't sure if he'd thrown the note away or if he'd stashed it in his desk drawer, too.

His grandmother had a little writing nook near the door to the basement. Her old desktop computer almost sounded like a cement mixer every time it started up. Ryan moved over to the desk—and sat down in the chair, which had a rooster dish towel draped over the back of it. While the computer wheezed and clicked, he went onto Google. He typed in the words: Family Murdered, Thanksgiving, New York.

Hunched close to the monitor, he clicked on the first search result link. Over the monitor came an article with the headline:

FAMILY OF 4 SLAIN IN CROTON HOUSE BREAK-IN
A Community in Terror
Grisly Thanksgiving Night Shooting
Claims Lives of 2 Children, 2 Adults

He remembered reading all the horrifying details four weeks ago—the night after he'd buried his own family. But he couldn't remember the woman's brother-in-law's name. He found it in the second paragraph: "Scott Hamner, 43."

He was the same age as Ryan's dad.

Ryan almost tipped over his chair when he got up and hurried back to the yearbook on the counter. He flipped back to the index and anxiously searched the H's. Hamner wasn't in the list.

Ryan reached for the other yearbook and opened it. Several loose photos and yellowed news clippings fluttered out from between the pages. Ryan ignored them. He kept thinking that perhaps Scott Hamner had been a new student during his dad's senior year. But he couldn't find a Hamner listed in the 1987 yearbook index, either.

"Damn," he said under his breath.

In the second yearbook, he checked the pages for both his father and Dick Ingalls to see what they'd been up to in 1987. He definitely saw a resemblance between himself and his dad at this age. In his portrait, Ingalls had his blond hair combed and parted down the middle. He looked like a handsome cocky creep, very full of himself.

Ryan noticed his father and Ingalls were no longer next to each other in their football and track team photos. He flipped to the inside covers of the book and scanned the inscriptions and signatures. He didn't find one from Dick Ingalls.

Had something happened between them during their senior year that had soured the friendship?

Ryan began to collect the photos and clippings that

had fallen from inside the yearbook. The clippings were from *The Winnetka Talk*, with reports on various football games or track meets in which Brent Farrell had shone. Among the photos, he found a photo booth series of his dad and some brunette mugging for the camera. She had kinky-looking hair, raccoon eye makeup, and what looked like shoulder pads beneath her blouse. Ryan wondered if she'd been one of his dad's first girlfriends.

There were a few more snapshots, but the one that really caught his eye showed his dad as a teenager—with three other guys. Their arms slung over each other's shoulders, they stood in front of a chain-link fence that had a green tarp on the other side of it. His dad was at the far right, and the kid beside him was unmistakably Dick Ingalls. Next to Dick stood a skinny guy in a dorky-looking, ill-fitting white short-sleeve shirt. Beside him on the far left was a dark-haired guy in a red Izod shirt, flexing his arm to make a muscle.

Ryan took the picture over to his grandmother's desk. The Croton murder story was still on the monitor. With the mouse, he scrolled down the newspaper article until he found three photos. Two were school portraits of the kids, Celia "CC" and Ernest Hamner. The third picture was of a blonde in a purple dress nestled against a guy with a healthy tan and a Jason Statham buzz-cut. This was Halle and Scott Hamner.

Just take away the shaggy dark hair, and that kid flexing his arm muscle in the foursome shot bore a strong resemblance to the dead man.

Ryan studied the old snapshot again. If that was indeed Scott Hamner on the far left, then three of those four young men were now dead. And their families were killed along with them.

What were the odds?

Maybe that Stephanie woman from Portland wasn't so crazy after all.

CHAPTER THIRTEEN

I read about you in the newspapers and it turned my
stomach. It also brought up bad memories of a personal
tragedy. I don't care what kind of personal problems you
have. That's no excuse for being so careless with so many
people's lives. I read there were 66 people on that plane.
Someone like you belongs in jail. I hope they throw the
book at you. My daughter-in-law was hit and killed by a
drunk driver. As far as I'm concerned, you're no better than
that careless drunk man. In fact you're worse, 66 times
worse.

Sincerely,
Dorothy Bochner

Sitting at her desk in the study niche off her living
room, Stephanie stared at the computer monitor. At
least this e-mail was more articulate than most of the
others. She was tempted to answer it. She would have

explained to Dorothy that she'd been set up, and told her she was very sorry about her daughter-in-law.

But Stephanie had learned that it only made matters worse if she tried to explain her innocence. How so many people had gotten her e-mail address after the story broke was a mystery to her. But for the first couple of days, she'd averaged about twenty e-mails a day.

That was nothing. The first week, someone had spray-painted "BITCH" on her front door. On two occasions, rocks were thrown through the French doors in the living room. People threw trash and bottles out of their car windows onto her lawn. They yelled out hateful things as they drove by. At least that had subsided. But the e-mails were still trickling in—about two or three daily now.

"If you answer them, you just end up getting into a pissing contest with them," Jim had told her, after the first wave of e-mails. As a congressman, he knew what it was like to receive hate mail. "I have it down to a system. The absolute crazies don't get anything back. The other complaints get a boilerplate response from me."

That was the last bit of advice she'd received from Jim, who felt they should "cool it" for a while after the news story hit the local papers:

DRUGGED AIRLINE PILOT
ABORTS FLIGHT SECONDS BEFORE TAKEOFF
Pacific Cascade Captain Had Traces of LSD
In System While in Command of Passenger Plane

How could she blame him for wanting to distance himself? It would be political suicide if it got out that he'd been involved with this negligent, drugged-up, "lady pilot"—as several of the e-mails referred to her. But Jim knew she was innocent. So—yes, she did blame the son of a bitch. He should have stuck by her.

He knew she'd been set up. Worse than set up, someone or some group was trying to kill her—and it didn't matter to them that they also might have killed her sixty-six passengers and the three people on the flight crew. To whoever was behind all this, those sixty-nine innocent lives were just collateral damage.

She'd tried to tell this to the doctors who had examined her that day. They thought she was paranoid, a side effect of the drugs in her system. She also told it to the lawyer the airline had assigned to her case. She was certain the man sitting at the next table in the café that morning had drugged her coffee. Or perhaps it was the woman. Maybe they were both in on the scheme. And it was no coincidence, happening just two weeks after that man had tried to break into her hotel room in Lake Forest. Someone wanted her dead. Stephanie was sure this was connected to the murder of her sister's family.

The airline's lawyer wanted to use that tragedy to gain sympathy for her, but he didn't think there was a chance in hell FAA investigators would buy her conspiracy theories. The police in New York considered her a pain-in-the-ass nutcase, and the lawyer didn't want the aviation review board thinking the same thing about her. He hoped her impeccable record up until now—along with her claim that someone had laced her morning coffee with windowpane—might be her best defense when the FAA hearing came up in July. Until then, she was on suspension with reduced pay.

The last two weeks had been stagnant and incredibly

frustrating—without one good lead in her investigation into the deaths of Scott and the kids. She'd phoned Ryan Farrell twice, but had hung up when the calls went to voice mail. She'd managed to get in touch with the mothers of the accused killers, Ronald Mady and Calvin Davis. Stephanie thought they could help prove their teenage sons had been coerced into confessing to the Thanksgiving night slayings. Maybe she could get the press on their side, and they could persuade the police to reopen their investigation into the murders. Ronald's mother was unresponsive. She'd obviously given up on her son a long time ago. But Stephanie thought she'd been getting through to Mrs. Davis.

The latest e-mail from Calvin's mother had come earlier today. Stephanie hadn't known how to respond to it. She'd been reading it again when she'd noticed the new e-mail in her box—Dorothy Bochner's diatribe.

Staring at Dorothy's denunciation on the monitor, Stephanie hit the Delete option. Then she finished off the last gulp of Cabernet in her glass. She wasn't much of a drinker, but she'd gone through a few bottles of wine during this leave of absence.

She sat back and clicked on Mrs. Davis's e-mail again:

Dear Ms. Coburn,

As I mentioned in my last note, Calvin & Ronald were hauled into police headquarters for questioning on Sunday 12/2 at 6 in the evening. They were held there overnight without any lawyer present. They were badgered & threatened, deprived of sleep & food. The detectives questioned the boys separately & played them against each other. Calvin told me later that they told him he could go home if he just signed a confession saying he was guilty of the commuter town robberies. He was so scared & tired, he believed them.

I got the impression from your last e-mail that you believe Calvin committed those robberies, but was unjustly accused of the murders on Thanksgiving night in Croton. Calvin did not commit those murders & he did not commit those robberies. I think this is a case of guilt by association, because he sometimes hung out with Ronald Mady, who has been a bad influence on him.

I appreciate you wanting to help prove Calvin didn't kill anyone. But you don't seem to understand that he is wrongly accused of breaking into those other homes, too. My son is innocent.

I spoke with Calvin's lawyer about you. He told me that you were in the news recently for using drugs while about to fly a plane full of passengers. He doesn't think having you on our side will be very helpful. In fact, he believes it will hurt us.

With this in mind, I ask that you address all future correspondence to him. His contact information is listed below.

Yours Truly,
Tatyana Davis

Stephanie jotted down the attorney's e-mail and phone number. Obviously, Calvin's mother was in deep denial about her son, and it would end up hurting him if they went with Mrs. Davis's strategy. Stephanie had read

every police report she could get her hands on regarding
the case. Calvin's culpability in the commuter town robberies was a slam dunk. He'd been caught with some of
the stolen property and the gun that was used. One robbery victim identified his voice and another remembered his jacket and sneakers. But the police didn't have
anything implicating Calvin in the murder of Rebecca's
family. That was where the "guilt by association" came
in. Without Calvin and his friend confessing to those
killings the police wouldn't have had a murder case.

Hunched over her desk, Stephanie wanted to explain
all this to Calvin Davis's mother and the lawyer. But
suddenly, it all seemed so pointless.

Getting to her feet, she took her wineglass into the
kitchen. She refilled it, and then checked the refrigerator and freezer. She still hadn't eaten dinner yet. She
decided to order Chinese. With the wineglass in her
hand, she treaded back to her computer to look up the
number for Fu Jin. Maybe they delivered.

As she sat down, Stephanie noticed a new e-mail—
with an attachment. "Oh, goody, another fan letter,"
she mumbled. "Somebody else wants to tell me what a
terrible person I am." She didn't recognize the sender:

5/31/13   Ryeguy66@comcas   Question for You

She clicked on it. The warning came up about
whether or not she knew the sender. Because of the attachment, Stephanie hesitated. But then she figured,
she had virus protection. She went ahead and clicked
on it once more:

Dear Stephanie,

I think you asked me if my father knew someone named
Dick Ingalls in high school. Well, it turns out he did. My
grandmother says they were friends while they were at
New Trier High School. They were in the same graduating
class in 1987.

Inside his old yearbook, I found this (attached) photo of
them with 2 other guys. I showed the photo to my
grandmother and she only recognized my father and
Ingalls. I asked if she ever heard my father mention Scott
Hamner, and she said no. But I think the guy in the red shirt
who is making a muscle kind of looks like your brother-in-
law (except with more hair than he had in the recent
newspaper photos).

I don't know who the other guy in the photo is. I looked at
the graduation class photos in the yearbook, and saw a few
guys who sort of look like him, but nothing really definite.

Anyway, I'm sorry if I wasn't more of a help to you when we
last talked. I hope this is some help now.

Please let me know if the guy in the red shirt is your
brother-in-law or if you recognize the fourth guy.

Thanks,
Ryan Farrell
847-555-1751

Holding her breath, Stephanie clicked on the attachment and then downloaded it.

The color photo emerged one section at a time—

until she saw the full image. It showed four high-school boys with their arms slung over each other's shoulders. Squinting in the sun and smiling, they stood in front of a chain-link fence.

The first person she recognized was Scott. It was him—back when he had hair. He and Rebecca had married right out of college. So this photo must have been taken just five or six years before then. Stephanie remembered when he looked like that shaggy-haired boy in the red shirt, mugging for the camera.

From studying photos of them as adults—which ran alongside the news articles about their untimely deaths—Stephanie figured the boy on the far right was Brent Farrell and the handsome blond one next to him was Scott's friend, Dick Ingalls. The photo must have been taken somewhere in the north suburbs of Chicago when Scott was in town visiting for the summer.

Stephanie had no idea who the fourth young man was.

It was 10:20 in Chicago, but she knew Ryan Farrell was still awake. She grabbed the phone and dialed his number. It rang once, and then he picked up.

"I was hoping this was you," he said. "Is that your brother-in-law in the picture?"

"Yes," she said, a little breathless.

"Do you know who the fourth guy is?"

"No. But you realize—"

"At least three of the four guys in that picture are dead," he cut in.

"That's exactly what I was thinking. All three knew each other. They were all widowers. And shortly after they got remarried, they were killed—along with their families."

"So—what do we do now?" he asked. "Should we go to the police?"

"I'm not sure," Stephanie sighed. "I talked over that possibility with a private detective. He pointed out that we're dealing with three different states, three different jurisdictions, and three cases that the police consider closed. For my sister's family, they've even got a couple of confessed killers. Which you pointed out yourself, remember?"

"I'm sorry about that," he muttered.

"Forget it. I picked a lousy time to approach you. Anyway, I think it'll be tough convincing the police they're wrong about these deaths—especially if we don't have any proof. All we can give them right now is that photo, and the fact that three out of four of them are dead. After that, it's just a lot of conjecture."

"So what's your—your *conjecture* about all this?"

"I'm almost positive it has something to do with the new wife. The deaths of the families seem to have been set up—made to look like a robbery gone haywire . . . or a man who killed his family . . . or a house fire. I think it's quite possible that my sister didn't kill herself—and neither did your mother."

"Jesus," Ryan whispered.

"You said in your e-mail that you didn't see anyone in your father's yearbook who looked like the fourth young man in the photo. We need to find out who he is. If he isn't already dead, he could be next. Maybe his wife just committed suicide. Plans could already be in motion to murder him and his family. Or who knows? He could be the person behind everything that's happening. Whatever, right now, he's all we have to go on."

She paused. "Listen, Ryan, do you want to work on this with me?"

"Yes, of course," he said.

"Well, I'll be up front with you. I have a feeling whoever is behind these killings—well, they're on to me. The night of your family's funeral, someone tried to break into my hotel room there in Lake Forest. And two weeks ago, somebody drugged me. I'm an airline pilot. At the airport, they slipped LSD into my coffee just minutes before I climbed into the cockpit of a passenger plane. I started to—hallucinate on the runway. But I still had enough sense to abort the takeoff. Anyway, it was national news. Maybe you've read about it . . ."

"No," he murmured. "No, I haven't."

"Well, it's one more reason I'm not sure we should go to the police yet. I don't have a lot of credibility right now. In fact, most people think I'm a horrible person. I'm considered a drug addict or paranoid or crazy—or all of the above. So do you still want to work with me?"

There was a long pause on the other end.

Stephanie held the phone against her ear and said nothing.

"Where do we start?" he finally asked.

Chapter Fourteen

"Sure, I guess," said Jenny Ballatore. "This is awfully nice of you."

She recited her phone number for the brunette at the nearby café table at Peet's Coffee in the Emeryville Public Market. The woman punched it into her iPhone.

The vast food court was noisy and crowded. Neon signs advertised all the little eateries, and so did the delicious aromas—everything from crepes cooking to Philadelphia cheesesteaks sizzling. Most everyone was eating dinner, which made Peet's a good meeting place for a blind date. It would be easy for them to find each other amid the empty tables. Right now there was only one other customer: the woman who had just offered to come to her rescue should Jenny's date be a total drip.

He wasn't here yet. Ten minutes late, not a good start.

When the other woman had first sat down near her, Jenny had worried her date would get confused, finding two thin brunettes in their early thirties at neighboring tables. The other brunette said her name was Lacee. She'd come to the mall to see a movie, which was sold out; so she'd stopped by Peet's to figure out a backup plan for the night.

Jenny wondered if "SanFran Man27" from Great Connections would prefer Lacee to her. After all, why would he want the brunette with the prominent scar that ran across her right cheek? The mark was two years old, just recent enough that Jenny was still self-conscious about it.

She must have had a tentative look to her, because Lacee had her pegged right away as someone waiting for a blind date. Then Lacee had suggested her escape plan, the old emergency phone call routine. Jenny figured it was as painless a way as any to bail on a bad date. So she decided to go along with the scheme.

"Just scratch the end of your nose and that'll be our signal," Lacee said, leaning toward her. "And after you ditch him, we can meet up and go for a drink. The Hilton has a decent bar—or there's Trader Vic's. We can swap bad date stories over Cosmos."

Jenny shrugged. "Maybe I can get a rain check. If this date doesn't pan out, I think I'll just grab some takeout here, then go home, curl up with my cat, and watch *House Hunters*."

Her new friend frowned. "Well, you're no fun."

"I know," Jenny sighed. "That's what I hear from a lot of the guys I've met through this dating service. They don't seem to understand that some people just aren't into recreational, semi-anonymous sex."

The woman laughed. "Hey, honey, all I wanted was a drink or two."

Jenny worked up a smile. "Well, let's see how I feel about that drink in ten minutes. It's how much longer I'm giving this guy to show up."

"Either way, I've got your back," her new friend said. "We girls have to stick together."

Jenny sipped the decaf she'd ordered fifteen minutes ago, back when she'd been operating under the delusion that her date would show up on time. The coffee was cold now.

She hadn't been very lucky in love—or in life. She'd spent the last three years caring for her Alzheimer's-afflicted mother in Walnut Creek. She was a Web site designer, and had managed to work out of her mother's home without it hurting her business. But what that arrangement had done to her social life was another story. Her married friend, Carroll, in San Francisco, was her lifeline to sanity. Jenny talked with her at least twice a week, and Carroll drove out to Walnut Creek to visit every month or so.

Of course, dating anyone was out of the question. No help was the accident. While pouring herself some orange juice, her mother had broken the glass. She went into a panic, and started screaming. Her hand was bleeding, and yet she clung to the glass with its sharp, jagged edge. When Jenny tried to take it away, her mother slashed her across the face with it.

By the time the ambulance arrived, Jenny had gone through two dish towels trying to stop the bleeding. But she'd gotten the glass away from her mother. Nineteen stitches. The doctor said she was lucky none of the muscles in her face were affected.

After that, Jenny wished she had a dollar for every time her mom asked what had happened to her face. It was just as well she didn't remember.

Her mother had died five months ago. With the sale of the house and what she'd inherited, Jenny had thought about buying a place in San Francisco. But the prices were outrageous, so she decided to rent an apartment in a new high-rise here in Emeryville. It had a beautiful view of the San Francisco–Oakland Bay Bridge. And all the advertisements for the place seemed geared toward thirtysomething singles like herself.

She'd been duped. Most of the occupants of the Bay Vista Apartments were senior citizens. Yes, there were some young married couples—along with a very few thirtysomething singles who had also fallen for the complex's marketing strategy. On the plus side, it was a terrific one-bedroom with all the modern amenities, a gas fireplace in the living room, and that killer view. But neighbor-wise, she may as well have still been at her mother's bungalow house in Walnut Creek. Jenny often found herself picking up mail and watering plants for elderly neighbors during their hospital stays. For the last three weeks, she'd been buying groceries for Sono, the feisty 90-year-old Japanese American woman who lived in the unit above her. Sono was just recently showing signs of slowing down. Every morning, Jenny also helped Sono put on the therapeutic stockings the doctor had recently prescribed to keep her legs from swelling.

Jenny's cat—named Simon, after the kid who got

killed in *Lord of the Flies*—was a swell companion, but Jenny told herself she deserved more. So for $99.00, she'd joined Great Connections. She'd debated whether or not to use a photo of herself that showed the scar. Why not just get it out there so the guy knew about it up front? Then again, there were some strange men out there who thought a scar like that was hot. But she wasn't interested in those kinds of men. The photo she ran— taken by an elderly neighbor—was a three-quarter profile that didn't show the scar.

So far, Jenny had suffered through about a dozen disastrous dates, courtesy of Great Connections. She wasn't completely sure if the scar was to blame, because several of those men had wanted to sleep with her. Unfortunately, none of them had seemed interested in her beyond that. Out of loneliness, she had sex with a couple of those guys, but didn't feel too good about it. She contemplated demanding a refund from Great Connections.

And right now she was ready to give up on SanFran-Man27. He was 25 minutes late. She turned to her new friend and worked up a smile. "Well, I think it's time to cut my losses and call it a day."

"It's not too late to turn this into a fun night," the woman said. "My offer still stands. And they know me at Trader Vic's. We probably won't even have to pay for our drinks."

Jenny got to her feet and picked up her purse. "Some other time," she said, "maybe this weekend. You've got my number. Give me a call, okay?"

The woman stood up, too. "You sure? C'mon, don't be a party pooper. I'll bet the guy who stood you up was a total loser. We'll have our pick of men at Trader Vic's. They'll be all over you, Jen. Let's go, *one drink*. What do you say?"

"Thanks anyway," Jenny said. "I'm just going to head home."

"I thought you were getting takeout."

"Oh, I have some Lean Cuisine in the freezer that I can nuke," Jenny replied. A part of her wanted to get away from this Lacee person. She seemed full of good intentions, but she was awfully pushy, too. "Anyway, it was nice meeting you, Lacee. Thanks for keeping me company."

She turned to walk away. But her new friend came up beside her and put a hand on her arm. "Listen, Jen, could you do me a favor? Could you walk with me to my car? I've heard some scary stories about the parking lot here after it gets dark. There's safety in numbers. And once we get to my car, I can drive you to yours."

Jenny figured Lacee had been ready to help out with her blind date situation. She couldn't very well refuse. She nodded. "Sure, of course."

They started walking, and the woman linked her arm with Jenny's. "Thanks, you're a lifesaver. It's like I said, we girls have to stick together . . ."

When Jenny woke up, everything was black. She couldn't move.

Tape sealed her mouth shut. Her hands were tied behind her, and she could feel something tight around both ankles. It almost cut off the circulation to her feet.

She realized she was in a compartment of some moving vehicle. She could feel the bumps in the road. The motor hummed, and someone had country and western music on the radio. She heard other cars, too, whooshing past. She figured they must be on a highway somewhere.

The compartment felt like a coffin. It was hot and stuffy. A rancid, sick smell filled her nostrils every time she breathed. When she tried to shift around into another position, the back of her head throbbed horribly, making her nauseous. Had someone hit her?

Jenny tried to remember what had happened. How had she ended up here?

Her last memory was of walking with her new friend across the Public Market's parking lot. She'd thought it odd that Lacee was so concerned about someone attacking her there, and yet she'd parked her SUV at the edge of the lot in a poorly lit area by some railroad tracks. It was all by itself, too. The nearest car was several rows away. And the nearest person she could see was over by the mall, at least a block away.

"You're really out in the boondocks," Jenny said, with a nervous laugh. "Why in the world did you—"

"Don't worry, I'll give you a lift to your car," Lacee interrupted. She pressed the device on her key ring, and the SUV's headlights flickered. "Get in . . ."

Jenny stopped a few feet short of the vehicle. Something wasn't right.

"Oh, my God!" Lacee gasped. She was staring at something over Jenny's shoulder, and she seemed terrified. "Jesus, get in! Get in the car! *Now!*"

Glancing back, Jenny didn't see anything. But

Lacee's command had been so urgent that she automatically hurried to the passenger side of the SUV and opened the door. All the while, she was digging into her purse for her pepper spray. Just as she jumped into the front seat, she found the little canister. She quickly closed the car door with her other hand.

In an instant, Lacee was behind the steering wheel. She shut her door, and then reached for something on the armrest. The car door locks clicked. Jenny frantically looked outside for their would-be attacker. She didn't see a soul nearby. The closest person was still about a block away.

Lacee was catching her breath and glaring at her. "You conniving bitch," she growled. "Your photo on Great Connections doesn't show that ugly scar. How am I supposed to duplicate that?"

"What?" Jenny asked.

All at once, someone grabbed her from behind. A rubber-gloved hand went around her throat, almost choking her. She saw part of a man's face in the rearview mirror. His grip was so powerful. He yanked her back against the seat's headrest. Another gloved hand came around on her right side. He started to put a washcloth over her mouth. She could smell some chemical on it.

Jenny blindly waved the small canister over her shoulder and pressed the nozzle.

"Fuck!" the man wailed—over the pepper spray's hiss. He dropped the washcloth and let go of her.

With her eyes squeezed shut, Jenny tried not to breathe in any of the noxious fumes as she fumbled for the door handle.

The man was still cursing and howling in the back-seat.

"Goddamn it to hell!" she heard the woman snap. "Stupid! Where's the washcloth? Shut up, and crack a window before you pass out!"

At last, Jenny found the door handle. She yanked at it, but the door wouldn't open.

Suddenly, something hard hit her on the back of the head. Stunned, she slumped against the car window. She couldn't move or open her eyes. She heard a humming noise. It must have been the other windows descending, because she felt the cool night air. But it didn't revive her any.

She could hear the man in back still groaning in agony. Every other word out of his mouth was an expletive. The woman who called herself Lacee shifted around in the driver's seat and kept barking instructions at him. Jenny only caught snippets of their conversation. Their voices seemed to fade in and out.

"Get the washcloth, for God's sakes . . . She's still not completely out . . . Hurry . . ."

". . . fucking blind . . . can't find anything . . . how am I supposed to see to drive?"

"Take my Evian . . . splash it on your eyes . . . the washcloth . . . it's by her seat belt . . ."

"I say we kill the bitch right now . . ."

"C'mon, quit dawdling . . . Soak it in the chloroform again. I don't want her waking up . . ."

". . . like to cram this rag down her throat and choke her . . ."

"That's no way to talk about your plaything for the next three or four months."

Helpless, Jenny felt something covering her mouth and nose. She was too weak to struggle. She couldn't even lift a hand to defend herself. With the cloth over half her face, she thought they were trying to suffocate her. Every time she tried to take a breath, she slipped away a little further.

". . . won't have to worry about any marks on her," she heard the woman say. "I think we might burn them this time."

That had been the last thing she'd heard—until now.

Another car zoomed by. But the vehicle carrying her seemed to have slowed down. From the sound of the motor and the whir of the tires, Jenny guessed it was a camper or an RV. The compartment was too warm to be the trunk of a regular car. And she didn't detect any exhaust smell. The horrible stench that repulsed her was nothing like car emissions. It was more like death.

Jenny had a feeling someone had been in this compartment before her. Either they'd died in here, or puked, or shit themselves. Whatever it was, the smell lingered.

Though her head pounded every time she moved, Jenny managed to roll over within the confines of the compartment. For a few moments, all her weight was on her hands tied behind her—and it hurt like hell. But the pinched skin and crackling wrist bones were nothing compared to how her head felt. Rolling over seemed to take forever, too, yet all the struggling was worthwhile. She was facing the other way now, and could see a thin strip of muted light on this side. Amid the blackness, it was a welcome sight.

Jenny realized a few minutes had passed since she'd

heard another car. The road was rougher now, too. Pebbles crunched under the tires. The country and western radio station was breaking up. That wasn't a good sign. They had to be someplace pretty remote. On a long drive, when nothing else was on the car radio, she could always count on picking up some C&W station, clear as a bell.

Where were they? She waited and listened for the DJ to name the city they were broadcasting from, but he hadn't mentioned it yet.

Were they taking her someplace in the mountains or the desert to kill her?

No, she'd heard the woman: ". . . that's no way to talk about your plaything for the next three or four months."

It felt like the vehicle was turning. The ride became even choppier—and she could feel every pothole in the road. It sounded like a hailstorm as gravel ricocheted against the underside of the chassis.

With a squeal, the vehicle came to a stop. The music got shut off. But the motor was still going. She heard footsteps—inside. They grew louder and closer. After a few moments, she could see a break in the line of light. He was standing right in front of the compartment.

Jenny started to shake.

Suddenly, there was a loud bang. She blinked furiously as dust and bits of debris swarmed around her. He must have kicked the side of the compartment. "Welcome to Nevada!" he announced. She heard a click, and then he let out a grunt. Jenny felt the compartment move. Wheels squeaked, and she realized she was inside some kind of tall storage drawer. Though the room was dim, it still took her eyes a few moments to adjust to the light.

They'd stuck her in a drawer—under a bed. The beige and maroon dust ruffle and spread lapped over one end of the open drawer. She was in the bedroom of an RV. Jenny could see the compact quarters, the ersatz-wood cabinets, and a small TV attached to the wall by brackets.

The man standing over her had his back to the light, and she couldn't see his face. "Well, aren't you the little contortionist, getting yourself turned around in there? I'll have to keep my eye on you. So—listen up. There's nobody within a mile of here. You can yell your head off, and no one will hear you. But I don't want you screaming, because it annoys the shit out of me. So if I take the tape off your mouth, are you going to scream?"

Gaping up at him, Jenny shook her head.

He bent over and quickly ripped off the tape. It hurt so much she almost shrieked, but she managed to hold back. Tears welled in her eyes.

At the same time, it felt good to breathe through her mouth again. And the air wasn't quite so stale and foul. "Listen to me," she rasped, her throat parched. "I don't have a lot of money. I don't come from a rich family. My parents are dead—"

"Shut the fuck up," he said, folding his arms. "We know all about you. We've been watching you, too. We just didn't get close enough to see that hideous scar. Somebody sure did a number on you . . ."

"You've been watching me?" she asked.

"Hell, I've been through your underwear drawer, sweetie. While you were out, I was in your apartment—three times. I had a real close call the other night when you came back from the store. You almost caught me in there. You've even written to me, some real intimate shit, too—about how you like long walks, and how you're looking for a compassionate man . . ."

Jenny stared up at him, and realized he was San-FranMan27. He'd used someone else's photo. He and that woman had set her up. But why? If they weren't after money, what did they want?

"You were looking for someone who likes cats," he said. "Well, I don't. So if you're not in the mood to co-operate with me, then that cat of yours . . . What's his name again?"

"Simon," she said.

"I won't have any problem killing Simon, and giving you his head as a souvenir. Do we understand each other?"

"Yes," she murmured. "Please, I need to go to the bathroom—and I'm so thirsty. I promise I won't try anything. If you'll just—"

"Question, first," he cut in. "Who knows about this date tonight? Did you tell anyone?"

"No," she said. "Wait a minute, that's not quite true. I mentioned it to my upstairs neighbor this morning. But she's ninety years old and starting to go senile. She can't remember my name half the time."

Jenny still couldn't quite see his face, but she could tell by his stance and the way he nodded that he seemed satisfied with the answer. She wasn't telling the entire truth. She'd also told her friend, Carroll Jordan, about the date yesterday. Carroll would probably be calling tomorrow to find out how it went. When

Jenny didn't get back to her, Carroll would know something was wrong.

"I'll get you some water," the man said. "But you won't get a sip until I have some numbers from you—starting with your ATM code, social security number, Internet server passwords, and phone codes. Then you can get water and make water. But don't expect any privacy while you're in the can, because I'll be right there watching you."

Biting her lip, Jenny tried to push that disgusting thought out of her mind.

"We've got a long trip ahead, and you'll be spending it in that box. I'll give you a shot so you can sleep through most of it. Believe me, honey, I'm doing you a favor. You don't want to be awake in there any longer than you have to. I'm putting you in some Depends, too—just in case you have an accident in your sleep . . ."

Jenny shook her head. So he had done this before, probably with several women.

She was also thinking about how—near the end—she'd regularly changed her mother's adult diapers.

She started to cry.

He leaned in close to her. She could see his face now and the red burn marks around his eyes from the pepper spray. "Look what you did to me, you bitch," he whispered. "It still stings, you know . . ."

"I'm sorry," she whimpered.

"I believe you are. But just the same, I owe you, Scarface."

He leaned in even closer until his mouth was just inches from hers. "And by the way, you belong to me now."

CHAPTER FIFTEEN

Thursday, June 6—5:33 P.M.
Lake Forest

Dear Ryan,

I was sorry to hear about your tragedy. I feel conflicted writing this e-mail. I regret to say that my experiences with your father in high school weren't pleasant. I suppose the less said about that, the better. But in your e-mail, you asked for comments. All I can say is that I hope, as he matured, Brent mellowed and became a nicer person.

Regarding the photo you sent, I recognize your father (far right) and Dick Ingalls (2nd right, and not one of my favorite people, either). The other two I don't know. From the background, it looks like the photo was taken in front of the tennis courts at New Trier High School. I hope that's some help.

Once again, I'm sorry for your loss.

Sincerely,
Joel Basinger

"Shit," Ryan said under his breath.

The underclassman girl at the library desk must have heard him. She was pale and skinny, with her brown hair in braids. She frowned at him.

They were the only two people in the place. School was out. But with summer classes about to start, everything was still open. Hardly anyone else was around. Ryan had passed only one person in the hallways on his way here. With half the lights shut off to save electricity, the empty corridors were a bit spooky. It was a gloomy, rainy day, too. He'd come to the library to study for his makeup exams. But for the last twenty minutes, he'd been on his iPhone, checking his e-mail.

In jeans, a black T-shirt, and sneakers, Ryan was slumped back in his chair at a long table. One of the books in front of him was his father's old yearbook. He'd brought it with him this afternoon, just in case he got another e-mail from one of his father's classmates. He wanted to put a face to each response.

He found Basinger, Joel L., among the senior class photos. The kid with the blond Flock of Seagulls hair looked wimpy and slightly effeminate. He was the only one wearing a bolo tie, which just seemed to be asking for attention—and trouble. Ryan imagined his father and Dick Ingalls making the kid's life a living hell.

With a sigh, he ran his hand over the yearbook page. Stephanie had asked him to scan and e-mail her this section with his dad's classmates' graduation photos. From the names and some research on Google, she'd managed to track down someone named Nancy Abbe on the alumni reunion committee. Then Ryan e-mailed Nancy, asking for contact information for all of his father's classmates. And oh, yes, if she had any updates about who was deceased among them, that would be helpful, too.

In a graduating class of 468 students, almost 20 were now dead. Stephanie started researching the casualties. A few of them were men who had died "after a long illness." "That used to be how they referred to it when someone died from AIDS," Stephanie explained to him.

Among the deceased class members, only his dad and Dick Ingalls had suffered untimely deaths along with their respective families. According to Ms. Abbe, the list was about a year old. So—Ryan and Stephanie couldn't be sure that some more recent casualties hadn't slipped under the radar.

While Stephanie had investigated the mortality cases, Ryan composed an e-mail to his father's classmates. In it, Ryan said he was creating a photo tribute to his late father. He had unearthed the attached snapshot of his father with Dick Ingalls and two other friends. Could anyone identify the other two? And did anyone have comments to share about his father?

Stephanie had thought it best that Ryan not mention that he knew the man in the red shirt was Scott Hamner. It was better to wait and see if someone else in the class knew him. Stephanie said they had to be careful. The person behind all the murders could very well have been in that graduating class. It could be someone settling an old score. Considering those boys didn't hang out together after high school, they probably knew their killer back then.

"Whoever this is," Stephanie said. "You don't want to tip them off that you know about my brother-in-law."

Four nights ago, Ryan had sent out the note in a mass e-mail.

Scores had come back right away: "MAILER-DAEMON . . . Returned Mail," or "Out of Office: Auto Reply." So far, he'd gotten about fifty personal responses. Most of them were polite. They gave their condolences. They said his father was "a good athlete," and "very handsome," and "quite popular." But no one said he was nice.

In fact, one woman commented, "He was a practical joker, and could get pretty mean and cruel sometimes. I'm sure he changed as he grew older." So Joel Basinger wasn't the only one who thought his father was a jerk.

Only one classmate recognized Stephanie's brother-in-law:

The one on the far left was named Scott. Sorry I can't remember the last name. I only met him once. He was a friend of Dick's from out of town. I don't know who the other guy is. It looks like the photo was snapped at the high school's tennis courts.

A few other people mentioned that the locale seemed to be outside New Trier's tennis courts. It struck Ryan as odd, because his dad didn't play tennis. Stephanie said that as far as she knew, her brother-in-law had never swung a racket in his life. Ryan went back to the yearbook and searched through the tennis teams—varsity and underclassmen. He scanned the faces in the group photos, looking for someone who resembled the skinny guy in the white shirt. But he didn't come up with anyone close.

He glanced at his iPhone again—at Joel Basinger's e-mail.

Suddenly, the phone rang. His ringtone of U2's "With or Without You" echoed in the near-empty library. Ryan glanced toward the desk, only to get the evil eye from the girl in the braids again. "Sorry!" he whispered to her. He clicked on the phone and hurried for the library door. He didn't even have a chance to check the caller ID. He stepped out to the dim, empty corridor. "Yes, hello?" he said into the phone.

"Ryan, it's me, Stephanie. Can you talk?"

She was always worried someone would catch on that they were communicating. She didn't even want his grandmother to know. She'd e-mailed him a photo of Lacee Roth taken before she'd met Ryan's dad. Stephanie had asked him to show it to his grandmother to confirm this was her daughter-in-law. "Just say somebody sent it to you, but you don't know who," Stephanie had told him. A lot of good it had done. His grandmother had studied the photograph, and then handed it back to him. "Well, it sure looks like Lacee. But it's not the best picture of her. You have no idea who sent you this? You sure it wasn't that horrible woman from the funeral?"

Ryan had shrugged and said he had no idea.

Stephanie had asked him again just yesterday. "No one knows you've been talking with me, right?"

He assured her that he hadn't told a soul. But that was a lie. He'd blabbed to Billy, who thought they were both crazy not to go to the police. Ryan had tried to tell him about the lack of hard evidence and the different jurisdictions involved.

"Oh, shit, I can tell right now," Billy had said. "This is not going to end well."

Still, Ryan knew his friend would keep it a secret.

He leaned against one of the lockers in the row along the corridor. "It's okay, Stephanie," he said into the phone. "I can talk. There's absolutely no one else around."

"Well, I wanted to give you a heads-up," she said. "I'm going to be on the news tonight, CNN and one of the networks. My attorney let me know. One of the other airlines had an emergency landing, because the co-pilot suffered some kind of blackout. It happened this morning in Phoenix. Anyway, they're running a clip of me from two weeks ago, lumping both stories together as part of a—a recent bad trend in aviation or something. Must be a slow news day. This interview with me was right after I came down from the drug. According to my attorney, the way I'm talking in the clip, it sounds like paranoid gibberish."

"Okay," Ryan said tentatively. He wasn't sure what any of this had to do with him.

"I just thought you should know," she explained. "I don't want you seeing me on the news and thinking you're in cahoots with a major loon. Plus, if your grandmother or any of your friends see it, you can't tell them what we're doing—"

"I know that," he said. "We already talked about that, Stephanie. And don't worry, I haven't told anyone." He felt bad lying to her.

"Good. That's why I haven't come there to work with you. Whoever is behind this, they've figured out I'm on to them. There have already been two attempts on my life—and one of them while I was staying in your hometown. If they find out we're working together, you and your grandmother could be in danger. I've put you in enough potential hot water by having you send that e-mail to your father's graduating class—"

"Hey, that was my idea, don't forget," Ryan cut in.

"I'm sorry. It's just that back on Thanksgiving night, when I wasn't sure what was happening to my sister's family, I sent a neighbor girl over to their house. If the killers had still been there—well . . ." She sighed. "It was reckless of me. This poor girl was the one who found them dead. I keep thinking I'm doing the same thing all over again with you. I'm putting you in harm's way so I can figure out what happened to my sister and her family . . ."

"My family got killed, too," Ryan whispered. "You're not forcing me to do anything, Stephanie. So quit apologizing. In fact, your timing's pretty good. I just got another response from one of my father's classmates."

"Did they tell you anything? Anything new?"

"Well, he made it pretty clear he thought my father and Dick Ingalls were a couple of a-holes. I'm inclined to believe him."

"Forward the e-mail to me. Anyone with a bone to pick—justified or not—is a suspect."

"Will do," Ryan replied. "Anyway, the guy couldn't identify anyone in the photo except for my dad and Dick. He said he thought the picture was taken by New Trier's tennis courts." Ryan glanced down the dim hallway and sighed. "You'd think at least one of these people could identify that skinny guy in the white shirt. Do you suppose he was from out of town—like your brother-in-law?"

There was no response on the other end.

"Stephanie?"

"My God," she said. "I'm so stupid. Everyone's telling us this is the tennis court at the high school. But Scott visited the Ingalls only during the summers . . ."

"So—why would they be at the school?"

"Exactly," she said. "This picture was taken in the summer. Do you think it's at a public tennis court?"

"Well, Dick Ingalls wasn't on the tennis team. And we know my dad and your brother-in-law didn't play tennis. Why would they—"

"They're at a country club," she interrupted. "They're not on the tennis court. They're just standing outside it—probably by the club's pool or the refreshment stand."

Ryan thought of the photograph—so embedded in his brain. "You're right. It's got to be at some country club. The guy's goofy white shirt, it's part of his uniform. He wasn't someone from the high school—or any school nearby. That's why no one recognized him."

"The three friends were all from pretty well-to-do families," Stephanie said. "And here's this kid working at a country club, taking orders from them and their fathers. He could have built up a lot of resentment . . ."

Ryan was thinking about the e-mail from Joel Basinger. He wondered if there were any more like him. How many classmates hadn't e-mailed, figuring if they didn't have anything nice to say about his dad and Dick Ingalls, why respond at all?

"He's smiling in the picture," Ryan said. "Do you think it's possible he was part of their clique?"

"Maybe."

"Or maybe he secretly hated their guts."

"I guess we shouldn't jump to any conclusions about him just yet," she said.

"But he knew them at the time when they were hanging out together," Ryan pointed out. "You talked about someone settling an old score. Well, maybe my dad, your brother-in-law, and Dick did something to really piss somebody off. They all stopped being friends by the end of senior year, we know that much. If something did happen, it was over that summer—when this guy knew them."

For a moment, she didn't say anything. "Listen," she said at last. "Find out from your grandmother if they belonged to a country club or if Brent ever spent time at a country club with Dick. I'll see if Scott's mother knows anything. If we can figure out which country club it is, we might be able to find out from their employee records about who this kid was. Maybe we can track him down."

"Okay, but we—" Ryan hesitated. "We need to consider a possibility . . ."

"That he's already dead?"

"Yeah."

"Well, dead or alive, right now, he's all we have to go on."

After Ryan hung up, he wandered back into the library to collect his books.

"Oh, there you are," the girl behind the desk said. "I wasn't sure if you were coming back or not. We're about to close."

Ryan nodded. "Sorry, didn't mean to hold you up."

"You didn't," she said.

He gathered his books. "Well, thanks a lot. Have a nice night."

She gave him a shy smile. "You're nice."

Ryan let out a surprised little chuckle. "Well, thanks, so are you."

"No, I mean it," the girl said. "You're a big football jock. You don't have to be nice to people, but you are."

He smiled and shrugged. "Thank you. Are you going to be okay closing up here by yourself? It's kind of creepy out there in the hallways. I can wait for you."

"That's all right. My older brother's coming to pick me up."

"Well, good night, then."

"Good night, Ryan," she said.

He didn't know her name, but she knew his. That was the way it was with him and a lot of people in school. He gave her a wave and stepped out to the hallway.

As he walked down the shadowy corridor, Ryan thought about his father. Fifty classmates had commented on him. And no one had called him nice. In fact, there was every indication that he was a terrible bully. Maybe Dick Ingalls and Scott Hamner were just like him.

Ryan couldn't help wondering just what they'd done to deserve the punishments they'd gotten.

CHAPTER SIXTEEN

She woke up freezing.

Her teeth chattered behind the tape that sealed her mouth shut. She rubbed her bare arms and legs, trying to bring some warmth to her cold, prickly skin. In her semiconscious fog, Jenny suddenly realized she was moving her arms and legs. Her hands were free. The cord binding her ankles together was gone. But the rope burn was still there.

She sat up—too suddenly. Her head started throbbing, and she felt so dizzy and nauseous, she thought she might be sick. With a shaky hand, she pulled the tape off her mouth, a little section at a time. Slow or fast, it was still torture. Once she pried the tape off, Jenny gratefully breathed through her mouth.

How long had she been asleep? She vaguely recalled two different times when her captor had opened that drawer under the bed and given her an injection. But she had no idea how many hours had passed between those shots.

He'd stripped her down to nothing but a bulky pair of Depends. Even in the summer, Jenny needed to wear a T-shirt and have a sheet or light blanket over her while she slept. No wonder she was so cold. Did he have the air conditioner in the RV cranked up?

She glanced down at the bare mattress—with a plaid blanket folded in one corner. She grabbed the blanket and threw it around her shoulders. It was scratchy against her skin, but warm.

Sitting on the edge of the bed, Jenny numbly looked at her surroundings. A dim, strange, flickering light was all she had to see by. He'd moved her from the RV. This new place had no windows. Corrugated metal walls arched over her. The floor—a laminated wood parquet—had what looked like two trapdoors cut into it. Across from her was a set of bunk beds. Just beyond them, against the arched wall, was a kitchenette with a mini-fridge, a microwave, a sink, some cabinets, and a desk.

Jenny got to her feet, and almost collapsed. She braced herself against the wall. After lying in the same position inside that drawer, her legs weren't working right. She readjusted the blanket around her shoulders and hobbled along the cold floor to the sink.

She was so thirsty, she felt dehydrated. She turned the cold water valve, but nothing came out of the faucet. The hot water didn't work, either. She opened the mini-fridge. There was no light inside, but she spotted two bottled waters. They were lukewarm, but she opened one and guzzled down half of it.

Catching her breath, she turned and looked at the chocolate brown, ribbed imitation-velvet sofa—and the small TV bracketed to the corrugated wall. The flickering light came from the TV, tuned to some televangelist show. The sound was off, thank God. Jenny figured if she could find a different station, maybe the local news, she might be able to figure out the day, time, and where she was. She glanced around for a remote, but didn't see one. She tried to find something along the side of the TV that worked the volume or the channel changer. But none of the buttons on the side of the TV worked. They'd been glued or soldered in place.

The tunnel-like room had doors on either end. Jenny realized it was a bomb shelter or underground bunker. One of the doors had a big wheel crank on it. She tugged at the wheel, but it didn't budge. She made her way to the other door. A stationary bike was right beside it. She started to teeter on her feet again, and grabbed the handlebar to keep from falling.

Taking a few deep breaths, Jenny opened the second door. An automatic light went on above the shower stall. The tiny bathroom smelled moldy. She tried the valves to the sink and shower. Nothing. The toilet wasn't working, either. There was no water in the bowl.

"Hi, Jen!"

She swiveled around and stepped back into the main room. Jenny recognized the voice—coming from a speaker somewhere above. It was her friend, Carroll Jordan. It sounded like a recording.

"I'm just checking in to see how your blind date went. I didn't hear from you Tuesday night. I'm not sure if that's a good sign or bad . . ."

Jenny looked up at the ceiling, just inches beyond her reach. She spotted the recessed box, which had to be a speaker. She also noticed two more recessed compartments—each with a small green light in it. On her tiptoes, she could see the camera in each one of them. Someone was watching her every move.

"Maybe the two of you have already eloped and you're honeymooning in Barcelona," Carroll said. It was obviously recorded off her voice mail.

Jenny remembered telling her abductor the only person who knew about their date was the ninety-year-old woman who lived upstairs. Now he wanted her to know that he'd caught her in a lie.

"Anyway, give me a call," Carroll continued. "Jimmy's out of town on business, and Suzy has a cold. So I'm going crazy here. Adios!" The beep sounded, and then the recording started to play again: "Hi, Jen! I'm just checking in to see how your blind date went . . ."

Jenny stood in the middle of the bunker with the blanket wrapped around her. The sound of her friend's voice brought her to tears. She longed to be back in her apartment with her cat. Who was looking after Simon? Her captor had threatened to give her Simon's head "as a souvenir" if she didn't cooperate.

Her friend's message, now repeating for a third time, seemed to taunt her about her lie. She wondered if her abductor would make good his threat.

Jenny rubbed her forehead. "I'm sorry!" she said loudly, hoping to be heard over the recording. "I forgot I told my friend about our date. It was an honest mistake, okay? All the codes and passwords I gave you are correct, aren't they?"

She imagined him and that woman tapping into her checking and savings, draining both accounts until there was nothing left—including the money she'd inherited from her mother. The most they could get was about sixty-five thousand dollars. That was a lot of money for her. But for a couple of kidnappers, it probably wasn't much.

The recording abruptly stopped.

"Why are you doing this?" Jenny screamed. The shrill words seemed to reverberate inside the bunker.

There was no answer. In the long silence, she could make out a train in the distance.

"Over in the desk," he said at last, "there's a pen and paper in the drawer . . ."

Jenny headed toward the small desk with a chair—near the big door. She opened one of the drawers. She found a Bic pen and a yellow legal pad. Pulling them out of the drawer, she turned around and looked up at the closest camera on the ceiling. She showed him that she had the pen and paper in her hand.

"You're not going to lie to me again, are you?"

She adamantly shook her head. "No, that was an oversight. I'm sorry."

"I want you to be comfortable here. Tomorrow, I'll turn on the electricity, ventilation, and water. You'll have sheets for the bed, clothes, soap, shampoo, toothpaste. I'll furnish you with a remote for the TV, food, soft drinks, snacks—you name it. But that'll have to wait until tomorrow, because you lied to me. Meanwhile, you'll find out just how cold it gets down there at night—and how hot and stuffy it becomes during the daytime. After twenty-four hours, you'll have a hard time breathing in there, too."

Clutching the pen and legal pad, Jenny defiantly

stared up at the camera. She tried to keep from shaking. "What am I supposed to do with this? Write, "I'm sorry" a thousand times?"

"Twenty things you cherish," he replied. "Write down twenty things from your place that you can't live without. I'll make sure you have them."

Jenny couldn't help shaking her head. It was such a bizarre request. The reason behind it made no sense, considering the brutal way she'd been treated so far. Why would they go to the trouble of bringing her the things she missed most?

She kept gazing up at that little green dot in the recessed box in the ceiling. She tried to swallow, but she couldn't. Her mouth was dry again. "What about my cat?" she asked. "What have you done with him?"

"It's here with me now. It was in the Winnebago with us all the time."

"Is he alive?"

There was a pause. "I'll let you know tomorrow. You work on that list. And take it easy. This is going to be the longest twenty-four hours you've ever lived."

"Why are you doing this?" she demanded to know. "Why did you pick me?"

She heard a click. And somehow she knew he'd turned off the speaker.

The image on the TV monitor wasn't exactly high-definition. With the murky, grainy color picture, he felt like he was watching an old bootlegged video on a defective VCR. The lighting was so dim down there in the bunker right now. Still, he could see her seated at the desk, clutching the blanket around her as she wrote on the legal pad.

He was at his own desk, in the back room on the third floor of an old white stucco house. The rest of the floor was empty, except for some broken furniture and trash. But this room was his control center. One section of his L-shaped desk held his computer keyboard and a big, HD monitor. On the other half he had the surveillance monitor, speakers, a control panel, and the mic, which allowed him to talk to the woman in the underground bunker. Right now, the mic and the sound were shut off. She couldn't hear him. He couldn't hear her.

From the window, he looked down at the backyard and its neglected, overgrown lawn. On the other side of a high chain-link fence ran the railroad tracks. The big elm tree in the middle of the yard had a thick, braided rope dangling from one of the branches. The rope lazily swayed in the morning breeze.

Amid the shrubs along the side of the yard stood a dilapidated, 4 x 6 green and white fiberglass shed. Rust streaks bled from every bolt and screw in it. But the foundation was firm. A padlock secured the door. Anyone who broke inside would find a bunch of old garden tools. The mat covering the floor was filthy. He had to put on gloves every time he lifted it. The trapdoor was under there—along with a ladder, which went seven feet underground to the bunker.

It amused him to look outside and know she was down there beneath that unkempt lawn.

His cell phone rang.

He snatched it off his desk. "Yeah?" he said into the phone.

"Did you see the news last night?"

"Yeah," he grunted. "I had a feeling the sister-in-law would be trouble. I know I said this before, but I still can't believe with the dose you gave her she had enough smarts to abort the flight. Hell, I wasn't sure she'd even make it onto the plane . . ."

"She probably didn't finish the coffee. Anyway, we didn't exactly get the result we wanted—"

"Yeah, some result you were after, the whole plane kaput," he cut in, chuckling. "You are a cold cookie, aren't you? Or was that the idea of the guy you're working with?"

"Let's leave him out of this."

"I'd still like to know who he is."

"You make out okay. Why ask questions?"

"Well, let me ask you this," he said. "What are we going to do about our lady pilot? She's on TV, talking about a conspiracy. All she has to do is mention the Farrell job in Lake Forest, and people will start connecting the dots. And we know she's onto us there, because—"

"Yes, yes, I'm aware of that," she interrupted. "That's why I'm calling. How soon can you go to Portland and take care of this once and for all?"

"Tomorrow afternoon. I need to get this new one settled into her quarters."

"And how is our guest?" the woman asked.

"She'll have to go 'without' until tomorrow morning," he said. "I told her it's her punishment for lying to me. At the moment, she's writing her wish list . . ."

"Good. I'll collect the stuff tomorrow. I don't want

to be going in and out of her apartment any more than I have to. One of her neighbors from down the hall spotted me last night."

"Did they see you up close?"

"It was some old guy, probably with cataracts. He started chatting me up halfway down the hall. I gave him the brush-off before he got too close. I don't think he noticed any difference. But I don't want to keep pushing my luck. This painted-on scar looks phony. Anyway, get her list to me in the morning."

"Check," he said.

Somewhere in one of his desk drawers, he had the "wish lists" the others had made up—those things they couldn't live without. The stupid women never got any of the items they'd missed. The stuff was removed from their apartments—so friends and family wouldn't be too suspicious: "Why, Lacee never would have left behind her precious china elephant!" It was amazing the shit some of these women considered valuable. In Lacee's case, the china elephant was found in the master bedroom, not too far from her corpse, at the house in Lake Forest where Brent Farrell supposedly shot his family and himself.

That was where all their things from their wish lists ended up. The stuff they couldn't live without went to the crime scenes.

He thought about the list Jenny Ballatore was now composing. She would never see any of that crap again—except possibly in the last few minutes of her life.

"All right then," his cohort said on the other end of

the line. "Make your reservation for Portland. I'll talk to you tomorrow morning before you leave. Let's nip this sister-in-law situation in the bud."

"I'll take care of it," he said. "Third time's a charm."

"Good," she said. Then she hung up.

He clicked off the line, slouched back, and stared at the monitor. His guest was still writing her wish list. At least that stuff would be with her in the end—when they found her without a face.

He glanced back over his shoulder toward the hallway. "Kitty?" he called. "Hey, kitty, kitty . . ."

–Photo albums (bottom shelf living room bookcase)
–The coffee mug with "Jenny" on it.
–Scarab bracelet (in jewelry drawer, not worth much, but it was my mother's)
–iPod classic (in kitchen, recharging).
–The Sword of Shannara Trilogy by Terry Brooks (on top of bookcase in bedroom).
–Silver Platter with parents' names on it (wedding gift from 1976—on display in living room)
–Jade Clock (was my grandmother's—living room)
–Journals (about 8 of them—in bottom drawer of desk)
–Portfolio of design work (front closet—big gray folder)
–Photo of parents in silver frame (living room)
–Blue Teakettle (on stove—was my mother's)
–Night guard (in container on nightstand)

Jenny looked over her "wish list." The items went from sentimental to practical to just plain silly.

Every morning for the last eight years, she'd had her coffee out of that tacky mug her father had given her. There was a cartoon of a San Francisco cable car on it. She liked the feel of it in her hand, and she liked how the mug always made her think of her dad. The silver platter, the jade clock, and the silver frame were all worth something—and so was her mother's scarab bracelet, another lie she was telling him. But her sentimental attachment to those things far outweighed their monetary value. Still, her captor would only care how much he could get for them. So she wasn't likely to see any of those items again. Nevertheless, she decided to ask for them—especially the bracelet. She'd loved it ever since she was a kid.

The practical side of her wanted the iPod classic, so that she could listen to some music down here. It had over nine hundred songs on it. The Terry Brooks trilogy was 1,200 pages long. It would help the time go by faster in her little prison. She wanted her journals for the same reason. Besides, she hated knowing that creepy man had unlimited access to all her private thoughts for the last several years.

The son of a bitch had been right. It was the longest twenty-four hours she'd ever experienced—even with the naps. Time moved "like molasses in January," as her mother used to say. He'd been right about the heat, too. Without any ventilation, the bunker became humid and stuffy. Yet for modesty's sake, she still kept herself wrapped in the itchy wool blanket. Jenny couldn't believe she'd been so cold in this place just hours before. How many hours, she wasn't sure.

She would have killed for a clock—or a cool breeze or

a Diet Coke or a sandwich. She remembered the smells in the Emeryville Public Market's food court: crepes, coffee, pho, cookies, and cheesesteaks. Her stomach hurt. She had no idea when she'd last eaten. Was it two days ago—or three?

Jenny searched every drawer and every cabinet in the place. Maybe he'd accidentally left some food behind from the last time he'd locked a woman down here. He'd obviously done this before. She just didn't know why. Though the camera was watching, she checked for possible escape routes, too. The trapdoors in the floor were locked, and the big wheel on the door to the bunker didn't budge.

She found a bit of paper sandwiched between the wall and a loose piece of brown plastic baseboard. Jenny pried out the folded paper and opened it up. Her heart sank when she read what was scribbled on it:

If you find this message, please CONTACT THE POLICE. My name is Karla Bowman. I'm from Minneapolis. I believe someone has assumed my identity. I'm a prisoner in an underground bunker near a railroad track. I believe this bunker is in the backyard of a man who drives a Winnebago. I have been here since May 27. This man has raped me countless times. He is 5' 5", brown hair, brown eyes, olive complexion. I don't think I will leave this place alive. PLEASE GIVE THIS NOTE TO THE POLICE immediately! Thank you.

Jenny was unsure how her predecessor had hoped to get this note outside. Perhaps by putting it in the trash and praying someone might find it after her captor took out the garbage? She couldn't think of any other way. Tears stung her eyes as she wondered what had happened to this woman imprisoned here at least a year ago.

Jenny began to cry for herself, too.

She awoke facedown on the brown sofa. She was naked. She heard the humming sounds of a refrigerator and air pouring through a vent. The lights were on.

Sitting up, she rubbed her eyes and managed to focus on the boxes in the aisle between the sofa and the kitchen counter. One was an assortment of snack packs from Costco: Cheetos, chips, Fritos, and pretzels. Another was a plain brown box with "Food Packs" stamped on it. There was a twelve-can-pack of Diet Coke and another of 7Up. There was even a huge eight-pound bag of "Fun-Size" Milky Ways, Three Musketeers, Nestlé Crunch, and 100 Grand bars. On the bed, she saw neat stacks of folded sheets, clothes, and towels. There were even a few paperback books.

"I want you to be comfortable here," he'd promised.

She found the blanket on the floor—along with the adult diapers she'd been wearing.

Jenny wrapped the blanket around her. She managed to climb off the sofa and stagger to the kitchenette sink. Bracing herself against the counter, she gave the valve a twist. There was a loud yawn, and then water shot out of the faucet. She bowed over the sink and gulped from the stream.

She grabbed the big bag of candy, and bit on one corner to rip it open. She dug out the first thing she could—a Milky Way. She tore it open and devoured it.

The blanket fell off her shoulders, and she was naked for a few moments.

She wouldn't have cared—only as she eagerly unwrapped another candy bar she glanced down and noticed the blood on her thighs.

Horrified, she started to choke on the second candy bar. Bending over the sink, she spit it out. She wanted to cry. But she was so dehydrated no tears came.

She couldn't believe she'd been so eager for him to bring her all these things. She should have known it would all come with a heavy price. If Karla Bowman's note was any indication, this was just the start.

Jenny picked up the blanket, and wrapped it around herself. She hobbled toward the little bathroom. She was hoping the shower worked so she could clean herself up.

But at the last moment, she thought of the list he'd wanted her to compose. She turned and staggered over to the desk. She saw there were two more legal pads and several more pens.

He'd taken away her wish list.

Jenny thought of all the cherished items she'd written down. And she wondered if she'd ever see any of them again.

CHAPTER SEVENTEEN

Monday, June 10—7:48 P.M.
Portland

"**D**o you know how hard it is for me to get away at the last minute like this?" Jim asked.

"Yes, I know better than anyone else," Stephanie answered.

He was late. For the last twenty minutes, Stephanie had been waiting for him in the bar at Hotel Lucia. In a black cocktail dress, she sipped her Cabernet at a table for two in the corner. Beside her chair was a Macy's bag.

Standing in front of her, Jim looked handsome in his suit and tie. He also looked slightly annoyed. He kissed her on the cheek. "Sorry, rough day," he said, sitting down across from her. "You look beautiful."

The waitress came by, and Jim ordered a martini. When she asked if she should start a tab, Stephanie piped up: "No, thanks, we won't be long. We'll take the check with his drink."

He waited until the waitress walked away. "So—what's this about?" he asked.

She sipped her wine. "Well, it's been two weeks since you said we should 'cool it' for a while. I figured if that's your way of breaking up with me, I deserve better. I mean, for over three years now, I've been—for lack of a better word—your *mistress*, and I think if we're—"

"Oh, Jesus Christ," he grumbled. "Stephanie—"

"I think if we're breaking up," she continued, "it ought to be face-to-face and over a drink. And it ought to be definite, not this vague, 'let's take a break' routine."

"Stephanie, I meant what I said. We both have a lot on our plates right now. I simply think we should give it a rest for a bit. But I don't want to break up with you."

She slowly shook her head. "No, Jim. I'm breaking up with you."

He rolled his eyes. "For God's sake, Stephanie . . ."

"I always knew I couldn't really depend on you, and that was okay for a while," she shrugged, "but not anymore. What's 'on my plate right now' is that I've lost my family. Somebody tried to kill me—twice. They've set it up so I'm a national disgrace. I still have people writing me every day, telling me what a scumbag I am. You know all this. And yet you pick this time to tell me we should 'give it a rest for a bit.' That not only makes you a lousy boyfriend. It makes you a coward."

Jim stared at her with his mouth open. He leaned in to say something, but the waitress arrived with his martini and the check. So he clammed up, gave the woman a fake smile, and nodded. He waited until the waitress moved away from the table. Then he turned to Stephanie again. "I was honest with you from the start about my situation," he whispered. He reached for his martini glass. "You know how important my daughter and my work are to me—"

"My family and my work are important to me, too," Stephanie said. "Or at least, they were. You were important to me, too." She shook her head again. "But I don't want to do this anymore."

"So— that's it?" he asked.

"There's this," Stephanie said. She reached down for the Macy's bag, and moved it closer to him. "Here's everything of yours that I could find at my house—a shirt and tie, a couple of T-shirts, toiletries, your *Best of Van Morrison* CD, your copy of *Goodfellas*, and the rubber ball thingy with the face on it that you squeeze when you're stressed out." She finished off the last of her wine and sighed. "I guess I shouldn't have been surprised. Still, after three years, I thought I would have accumulated more."

"I can't believe you're doing this," he grumbled. He drained half of his martini glass. Then he sat back and fingered the top of the Macy's bag. He gazed at its contents. "This is silly. You know you'll change your mind in a couple of weeks—"

"No, I won't," she said, standing up. She grabbed her purse. "In fact, you can do us both a big favor . . ."

Even though she spoke quietly, a few people at nearby tables were staring. She could tell the attention made Jim uncomfortable as hell. She came up beside him. She stared down at the top of his head—and his wavy, tousled black hair. "When I finally find out whoever killed my sister and her family, and the airline clears me of all these charges, when people suddenly change their minds about me, do us both a favor and don't come asking me to take you back . . ." She patted him on the shoulder, "Because I'm liable to punch you in the face."

She eyed the bar's exit, and started toward it. "So long, Jim," she said. And she didn't look back.

Pulling into her driveway, Stephanie reached up to the sun visor and pressed the button on the garage door opener. While she waited for the door to lift, she wiped her eyes and blew her nose again. On her way home, her cell phone had rung once. It had been him. He'd hung up without leaving a message.

She maneuvered her Lexus into the garage. All the while, she kept thinking how much she wanted to call Rebecca and tell her what she'd done. This would have been at least a ninety-minute conversation, with Rebecca giving her an "Atta girl, I'm proud of you," at every right moment. They might have even had a few laughs about it. They would have started planning their next visit. "You and the kids haven't been here in almost a year," she imagined herself saying.

Climbing out of the car, Stephanie thought about getting away for a couple of days this week, maybe to her friends', Erica and Ben's, cabin outside Spokane. She had a standing invitation to use the place whenever she wanted. She knew where they hid the key. They didn't have any Internet or Wi-Fi, and cell phone service was pretty iffy. That meant no nasty e-mails, no calls or hang-ups from Jim—just the woods, a good book, and some DVDs.

As she put the key in the door to the house, she heard something shift behind her. She turned and looked around the garage. Leaning against the wall was a big plastic kiddy pool that CC and Ernie used to play in when they were kids. The thing was filthy with dust. She'd been meaning to get rid of it for years. Right now, it was teetering slightly.

Stephanie couldn't take her eyes off it. "Who's there?" she said.

The kiddy pool stopped wobbling.

She told herself it was just the car coming in that made the big plastic pool flutter a little. Still, she walked over and gave it a tap with her foot to make sure no one was hiding behind it.

The ridge of the plastic pool made a scraping sound on the cement floor.

All of the sudden, the automatic garage door mechanism switched on overhead. Startled, Stephanie clutched a hand over her heart and let out a little laugh. As the big door made its noisy descent, she hurried to the other door—connected to the house—and unlocked it. Stepping inside, she bolted the door behind her. She headed through a little hallway, past the basement stairs, and into the kitchen. She set down her purse and keys on the counter and made a beeline to the wine cabinet. It was definitely a two-glass Cabernet night, maybe even three.

Pouring a glass, Stephanie took it into the living room and sat down in front of her computer. She realized she couldn't use Erica and Ben's cabin this week, not even for a couple of days. How would Ryan Farrell be able to get ahold of her? The poor kid was doing her work for her, trying to identify the fourth young man in the old photograph.

Stephanie had asked Scott's mother if Scott ever mentioned going to a specific country club during his summer visits with Dick Ingalls. Marlene couldn't remember the name of any club. But it seemed like the boys were always golfing or swimming.

Ryan's grandmother thought the Ingallses might have been members at Skokie Country Club in Glencoe. So for the last couple of days, Ryan had been sneaking into the clubhouse and hanging around the pro shop, trying to talk to some of the older employees about the skinny young man in the photograph. So far, all he'd gotten was a polite escort off the grounds—twice.

Meanwhile, Stephanie was getting frustrated—in fact, downright irritated—with Calvin Davis's mother. The kid was a lowlife armed robber with a criminal history since age eleven. He and his worthless buddy had beaten up two of their victims—in front of their families, no less. And here, Mrs. Davis was worried about associating with the likes of *her*.

Sipping her wine, Stephanie checked her e-mail to see if there was something new from Ryan. There was just one e-mail, and the address didn't look familiar. The subject line was blank. She clicked on it:

Your going to hell. Jail isn't good enuff for a bitch like you. You ought to be shot. Women have no business being airline pilots anyway. You probably think you . . .

Stephanie didn't read any more. She quickly deleted it. Then she took another hit of Cabernet. She told herself that if this chauvinist idiot couldn't spell "enough" and didn't know the difference between "you're" and "your," then the hell with him.

Switching off the computer, she took her wineglass upstairs. She stepped out of her black dress, and then put on a T-shirt and sweatpants. It was warm enough to go barefoot. She was hanging her dress back in the closet when she heard a noise downstairs.

Stephanie froze and listened for a few moments. Nothing.

Still wary, she crept out to the hallway and over to the top of the stairs. She didn't see any movement down on the first floor. She stood there, and after a few seconds, she heard the noise again. It sounded like a floorboard creaking. She told herself it was probably just the house settling—at least, that was what she hoped it was. After another minute or two, all was quiet down there.

"Shit," she muttered, retreating to the bedroom. Yes, definitely a three-Cabernet night. She took another sip from her glass before ducking into the bathroom. In the mirror she noticed her eyes were bloodshot from crying. She pinned back her hair, then washed her face and patted it dry.

By the time Stephanie headed down the stairs again, her wineglass was almost empty. She went into the kitchen to refill it, but suddenly stopped in her tracks. She heard another noise, a trickling sound this time. She thought it might be the toilet tank upstairs, refilling. But then she remembered she hadn't used the toilet upstairs.

She put down her wineglass and crept over to the

basement door. The hinges squeaked as she opened it. She could hear the trickling sound more clearly now. It sounded like the water in the laundry-room sink was on. Or was something leaking down there?

Her basement was one big unfinished room with a bare cement floor, pipes running along the ceiling, a furnace and hot water heater. She didn't have anything down there, except the washer, dryer, and some stuff in boxes.

She switched on the light at the top of the stairs. The steps leading down there were wood plank. She didn't see anything—at least, not yet.

She couldn't help thinking that someone had already tried to kill her twice. Was this some sort of trap to lure her down there? The neighbors were less likely to hear her screams from the basement.

Biting her lip, Stephanie turned around and grabbed her car keys and cell phone. She shoved them into the pocket of her sweatpants. Then she opened the kitchen drawer and pulled out a butcher knife. In her bare feet, she tiptoed back to the top of the stairs. She couldn't hear anything but the water trickling.

The staircase creaked as she took two steps down. She had a better view of the basement now. She spotted a shadow on the wall. It was moving slightly. At first, she couldn't tell what it was. But then she could see the shadow of a rope swaying from one of the pipes along the ceiling. The rope was fashioned into a noose.

For a moment, she couldn't move—or breathe. She realized her death was going to look like a suicide.

Just like her sister, just like Ryan's mother . . .

Clutching the knife in her hand, she half-turned on

the rickety staircase and quietly took a step back up, and then another. She kept listening for a sound below—besides the water dribbling. She kept looking down toward the basement.

She watched another shadow—bulkier this time—sweeping across the cement floor. Someone was coming toward the stairs.

Stephanie spun around and ran toward the door to the garage. She almost dropped the knife fumbling with the lock. Behind her, she heard footsteps clamoring up the basement steps.

She flung open the door to the garage and slammed it shut after her. Frantically digging into her sweatpants pocket for the car key, she dropped the knife. It hit the garage floor with a hollow ding—and just missed her bare foot. She clicked on the device to unlock the car. The headlights flashed. Leaving the knife on the floor, she ducked inside the car and quickly locked the doors.

"God, please . . . please," she whispered, jamming the car key into the ignition. She started up the engine, then hit the automatic door opener. With the mechanics churning above, the garage door started to lift.

Anxiously peering in the rearview mirror, Stephanie shifted into reverse.

The garage door opened only halfway before it stopped. Then it started to descend again.

That was when she saw a man in a ski mask, standing in the doorway to the house. He had one hand on the manual button that operated the big door. The other hand held a gun.

Stephanie pressed down on the horn. The ear-piercing blare echoed within the garage. Beyond the resounding

wail, she could hear the neighbors' dogs suddenly barking. She switched on her brights, blinding the man for a
few seconds. He shielded his eyes.

She hit the remote again. The big door started to
open once more. Stephanie stepped on the gas. The car
lurched back, and she heard a loud scraping noise as
the edge of the garage door caught on the Lexus's roof.
She shot back toward the driveway.

She pressed on the horn again, and saw lights going
on in neighboring homes. Across the street, someone
had stepped outside their door.

Her high-beams spotlighted the man in the ski
mask. He ducked inside her house.

The car's tires screeched as she slammed on the
brake past the end of the driveway. Then she shifted
into drive, and sped up the block. At the first intersection, Stephanie pulled over. With a shaky hand, she
pulled out her cell phone and dialed 9-1-1.

While she waited for the police emergency operator
to answer, Stephanie wondered what the man in the ski
mask was doing inside her house right now.

Nothing was missing or out of place.

The police couldn't find any initial evidence of
forced entry.

In the basement, there was no hangman's rope dangling from a pipe overhead.

Stephanie realized how it must have looked to them.
Here was this hysterical, barefoot woman with alcohol
on her breath. She'd damaged both the garage door and

her car roof. She'd also disturbed half the neighborhood.

When the police asked where she'd been earlier when this "alleged culprit" might have broken into the house, Stephanie said she'd been having a drink with a friend. She didn't elaborate. She didn't want to drag Jim into this.

Wasn't she the same woman who was under investigation with the FAA for getting high right before piloting a plane full of passengers?

They didn't ask, but Stephanie was sure they had to know. She told them about the two previous attempts on her life. She wanted to tell them more—about her sister, Scott and the kids, and about the similar killing pattern with Scott's friends from high school. But Stephanie figured she'd only come across as even more unbalanced.

The cops were very polite, accommodating, and thorough. But she could tell they didn't quite believe her story.

The only person who would believe it, the only person who understood, was a teenage boy, two thousand miles away.

CHAPTER EIGHTEEN

Friday, June 14—1:43 P.M.
Wilmette, Illinois

He parked his VW on the street, about a block away from the main entrance to Lake Ridge Country Club. None of his friends' parents were members, so he couldn't count on getting in as someone's guest. So far—with a little help from his friends—he'd been able to talk to employees at Northmoor and Old Elm country clubs, as well as Onwentsia Golf Club. He'd shown the old photo of his father and his three buddies to caddy masters, locker room attendants, waiters, and the guys who ran the pro shops at these places. But he'd come up with nothing. Nobody recognized anyone in the picture. He'd sneaked into Skokie Country Club and Sunset Ridge to question the employees there. Again, no one recognized the guys in the picture. And after talking with a few workers at those clubs, he was tossed out on his ear. Both times, they told him he was lucky they didn't call the police and have him arrested for trespassing.

So Ryan decided to try another tack. This time around, he parked on the street so he didn't have to deal with the club valet. The fewer hurdles he had to jump over, the better. He was dressed in a white shirt, a tie, and khakis. He carried a manila envelope with "James Munchel, Pro Shop" scribbled on the front. Ryan had phoned ahead to find out the name of the guy.

Stephanie had told him that someone had broken into her home, and might have looked at her computer. They could know she was e-mailing him. She'd warned him to watch his back and not take any chances. The person or persons behind all these murders could be affiliated with the country club where that photo had been taken twenty-seven years ago.

Ryan thought about that as he walked up the club's driveway. The sun beat down on his face. He was already sweating, and he hadn't even made it to the front door yet. Off to his right was a high chain-link fence with a green tarp behind it—just like in the photograph. Of course, it couldn't have been the same tarp, but it was the same setup for sure. On the other side of it, he could hear the sound of rackets smacking tennis balls and feet scrambling around the courts.

Ahead, the driveway curved around to the entrance of the sprawling clubhouse. A couple of cars whooshed past him. Ryan managed to time it so that when he approached the front of the place, the valet was busy parking cars. He'd gotten past the first hurdle.

At the big double-door entrance—with potted palm trees on either side—he almost slipped past the doorman by coming in right after three women who had just gotten out of a Mercedes. He nodded and murmured a thank-you.

"Excuse me," the doorman said. He was a tall, thin black man with a wizened face. He wore a blue suit with epaulets on the jacket's shoulders. "Can I help you?"

Ryan stopped in the doorway and showed him the envelope. "Hi. I need to deliver this to James Munchel in the pro shop."

The doorman held out his hand. "I'll take it to him."

Ryan shook his head. "Oh, well, thanks, but I need to deliver it to him in person and get his signature. Can you tell me how to get to the pro shop from here?"

The doorman frowned and raised his index finger— as if to tell him to hold on for a minute. He pulled a whistle from his jacket pocket and blew into it. The sound was short and shrill. All Ryan could think was that the doorman was summoning a security guy—or maybe it was a signal for someone to call the police. Maybe the people at Skokie and Sunset Ridge had issued an alert about some teenager snooping around, bothering different country club employees with questions. His first instinct was to make a run for it. But he stayed. "What was that for?" he asked.

"Just stay put," the doorman said, tucking the whistle back in his pocket. Then he set his hand on Ryan's arm. "Someone's coming to take care of you."

Ryan didn't say anything. The ominous way the doorman put it, he might have been talking about a mob hit: "Someone's coming to take care of you." Ryan really wished the guy would let go of his arm. He tried to keep a pleasant smile plastered on his face. He could feel the beads of sweat on his forehead.

In the distance, he heard water splashing, and kids laughing and screaming. He figured the pool was close by, but he couldn't see it from here.

He stood in the doorway with a view into the grand foyer. A huge crystal chandelier hovered over a big, round mahogany table. The carpet had a rich, swirly gray-and-maroon pattern. The furniture was like something out of the White House—swanky, expensive-looking antique stuff.

A stocky, fiftyish balding man came out of one of the rooms off the foyer. He wore a dark blue business suit and a conservative tie. He also had a flower in his lapel, which Ryan thought looked kind of corny. Walking toward them with a brisk gait, he seemed annoyed. "What's the problem?" he asked.

"Sorry, Mr. Harvey," the doorman said. "He has something for Jim in the pro shop that needs a signature."

Mr. Harvey held out his hand. "What is it?"

"Excuse me," Ryan said, finally yanking his arm free from the doorman's grasp. He clutched the envelope against his stomach. "I don't know what's in here, sir," he said steadily. "My name's Ryan. I'm with Fleet Messenger Service. And I wouldn't have this job much longer if I made a habit of peeking inside the envelopes I deliver—or if I let anyone else besides the addressees view the contents." He was proud of himself for this little speech—and the way *addressees* just tripped off his tongue. And how he'd said it didn't sound pissy at all. Instead, he came across as a guy just trying to do his job.

As for the contents of the envelope, the only thing in

there was a slightly faded photograph from 1986, showing four friends posing outside the tennis courts that may very well be the courts here at Lake Ridge Country Club.

"Sir, I have to hand-deliver this and get a signature," he continued. "So—is there a James Munchel in the pro shop here? If not, I'll move on. I have other deliveries to make today."

The stocky man frowned. "All right," he sighed. He nodded toward the foyer. "Take a right and you'll see the stairs. That will take you to the Men's Grill. Go out the glass door to the patio and take another right for the pro shop. Check in with Isaiah here when you leave."

Ryan nodded to both of them. "Thank you."

His heart racing, he headed through the grand foyer. This was turning into a major hassle. He probably would have been better off sneaking in through the employee entrance and taking his chances—like he'd done at Skokie and Sunset Ridge. He hurried down the carpeted stairs to a richly paneled room that looked like an upscale restaurant-bar. The place was busy with customers—all men. A Cubs game was on the big TV behind the bar. Overhead fans were whirling. One wall was all windows, looking out at the golf course. The glass door was open.

Ryan studied the bartender and the waiters. None of them looked old enough to be working at the club twenty-seven years ago. To his left, the door to the men's locker room was open. Ryan poked his head in the doorway and spotted a dumpy old man in a towel shuffling down the aisle between the lockers. Over to the side of the door was a blackboard with tee-off times posted. He scanned down the list and picked out the guys who had teed off at 9:30: Gunderson, Wagner & Guests. He figured they had probably finished their game by now.

Tucking the envelope under his arm, Ryan headed for the door. Outside was a small patio—and to the right, the pro shop. There were two mannequins in the window—a male and female in golf clothes—with clubs poised in their fake hands. A bell rang as he opened the door. They had the air-conditioning cranked up. The place smelled like new leather—probably from all the golf bags and golf shoes. There were racks of men's and women's clothes, and Ryan noticed on the wall, near the counter, a big mirror that had "Golf Digest" written across the top of it—and "Golfer of the Year" along the bottom.

"Can I help you?" the lean, white-haired man behind the counter asked. His face was slightly sunburned, and he wore a bright green polo shirt and white and green plaid slacks. Ryan guessed he was about sixty.

"Hi, how's it going?" Ryan said, approaching the counter. He reached inside the envelope and took out the photograph. "My dad's here as a guest of Mr. Gunderson. They were golfing earlier today. Last time he was at this club was way back in the eighties. He can't remember who he was here with, but he has this picture . . ." Ryan handed him the photo. "Anyway, he and Mr. Gunderson were talking about it, and Mr. Gunderson said, 'Show the picture to Jim Munchel in the pro shop, he might know.' So—they sent me here."

The man studied the photograph, and set it on the

glass-top counter. "Well, that's your father, no mistaking it," he said, pointing to Ryan's dad.

"You knew my father?" he murmured.

The man laughed. "No, but I can tell, just by looking at you—and then at this kid in the picture. You're the spitting image of him."

"Oh, yeah, I guess," Ryan said, disappointed.

"This other kid is Dick Ingalls . . ."

Ryan stared at him. His mouth dropped open.

"The Ingallses were members up until the early nineties, when Dick Senior died. I don't know this other guy—in the red shirt." He pointed to Stephanie's brother-in-law. "And this one, he was a valet here for a couple of summers . . ."

"Do you remember his name?" Ryan asked. "It's important—my dad said."

He frowned. "I'll be damned. I'm drawing a blank . . ." He turned and called into the back room. "Javier, come check this out . . ."

Ryan nervously drummed his fingers on the countertop.

A muscular, fiftyish, Latino man swaggered out from the back room. He wore khakis and a tight-fitting polo shirt. "I'm trying to get caddies lined up for the Konradt-Reynolds foursome," he said with a slight accent. "What's going on?"

"You were here in the eighties," Munchel said to him. "Take a look at this picture. That's Dick Ingalls on the end . . ."

The man, whom Ryan assumed was the caddy master, squinted at the photograph and grinned. "Huh, Tricky Dick," he said. "Did that kid get around or what? Remember when they caught him and that chick going at it on the ninth green? He did more banging around here than a screen door in a cyclone—"

"Hey . . ." the pro shop man murmured, giving his friend a cautioning look. He nodded at Ryan. "This is the son of a guest of Mr. Gunderson's. We're trying to figure out the name of this one." He pointed to the skinny young man in the white shirt—at the far left of the foursome in the photo. "He worked here a couple of summers, nice kid. He was a valet . . ."

"Oh, yeah," the caddy master nodded. "I remember him. He was here when we had the tournament—and when that waitress disappeared. What was her name? She was gorgeous, but dumb as shit. C'mon, you know. Her old man was the groundskeeper, squirrelly old guy . . ."

"Jane something," Munchel said. "No, Jayne was the last name. Selena Jayne . . ."

"That's it!" the caddy master exclaimed. "What a mess that caused, and with the tournament going on at the same time, too. Did they ever find out what happened to her?"

Munchel cleared his throat. "No, I don't think they did," he muttered. "Anyway, about the kid in this photo . . ."

Ryan could tell the pro shop man didn't want to talk in front of some guest's son about a scandal that had happened at the club twenty-seven years ago. Impatiently tapping his foot, Ryan was glad they were back on topic. He pushed the photo across the glass—closer to the men. "Um, if you can't recall his name, do you think maybe someone else here might?"

He just wanted to get the guy's name and get out of

there. This was what he'd been working toward for days. He'd finally found the country club where this picture was taken. But he didn't have much time. Upstairs, that Mr. Harvey guy and the doorman were probably wondering where the hell he was.

"It was Mike or Mitch," the caddy master said finally.

"No, it was Matt," the pro shop man replied. "I'm almost certain now."

"Almost?" Ryan asked.

Leaning over the counter, the pro shop man smiled. "Tell you what—"

The phone rang.

"Sorry," he said, reaching for it. "Just a sec . . ."

Biting his lip, Ryan nodded. He wondered if the call was from Mr. Harvey or Isaiah, asking about the kid from Fleet Messenger Service.

"Pro Shop, this is Jim," he said into the phone. "No . . . No, I haven't signed for anything . . ."

Ryan looked down at the photo on the countertop. He wanted to grab it and get the hell out of there.

"No, not yet," Munchel was saying into the phone. "Well, I was waiting for that shipment for two weeks, and they sent me the wrong set of clubs. I wasn't going to sign for something I didn't want . . ."

Ryan let out a sigh of relief and leaned against the counter.

"Yeah, well, I'll need them by Tuesday, okay?" the pro shop man continued. "Good. Thanks . . . Right . . . Well, listen, I gotta go . . . Okay, bye." He clicked off the line. "One more sec," he said to Ryan. Then he dialed a number—four digits.

Tapping his foot again, Ryan once more thought about those two guys up by the front entrance.

"Hello, Doreen, it's Jim down in the pro shop," he said into the phone. "How is my favorite accountant?" He chuckled. "No, I do not sweet-talk you every time I want a favor. But did I ever tell you that you have beautiful eyes?"

The caddy master leaned over the counter toward Ryan. "The old bag's eighty if she's a day," he whispered.

"No, this isn't for me," Munchel said. "It's for a guest of Mr. Gunderson's. We're trying to remember the name of a kid who was a valet here for a couple of summers back in the mid-eighties. His first name was Matt . . ."

"It was Mike!" the caddy master chimed in.

"Do you have payroll records from back then?" the pro shop man said into the phone, ignoring his friend. "It was the same year we had the tournament—"

"Ask her if she remembers the name of Selena Jayne's old man," the caddy master interrupted.

"Yeah, if you could look it up now, that would be great," Munchel said, speaking over his friend. "I've got Mr. Gunderson's guest here . . . Yeah, I'll wait. Thanks, Doreen, you're a sweetheart." He covered the mouthpiece and looked at the caddy master. "Barton . . . Barton Jayne. She could hear your big mouth yapping. Doreen says he retired eleven years ago . . ."

The phone's other line rang.

Munchel nodded to his coworker. "Can you pick that up on the other extension?"

The caddy master retreated to the back room. Ryan

couldn't see him anymore, but he could hear him: "Pro Shop, Javier speaking."

With the phone to his ear, Munchel smiled at Ryan. "So—who won the game this morning, Mr. Gunderson or Mr. Wagner?"

Ryan hesitated.

"Jim! It's Mr. Harvey on line two!" the caddy master called from the back room.

"Tell him I'll call him right back," he replied, over his shoulder.

Ryan could hear the man in the other room mumbling into the phone. But he couldn't make out what he was saying. Why were they still talking? He wondered if Mr. Harvey was right now describing the Fleet Messenger Service kid to the caddy master.

Hang up, he thought, *hang up already.*

"Yeah, I'm still here," Munchel was saying on his line. "Oh, yeah, Mark Metcalf . . ."

Ryan grabbed a pen from near the cash register and scribbled it down on the envelope. "Does she have a last known address?" he asked.

"Do you have his address there, Doreen?" He covered the mouthpiece, and gave Ryan a dubious look. "You know, it's going to be from when he was in high school—almost thirty years ago. There isn't a snowball's chance in hell he'll still be there."

"Well, it's a starting point," Ryan answered. "My dad's trying to track him down. He owes the guy some money."

"Hey . . ." the caddy master said, emerging from the back room. He stopped in the doorway and folded his big arms. He was scowling at Ryan. "Did you tell the guys upstairs at the front door that you were with some kind of messenger service?"

Still on the phone, Munchel shushed him. "1107 Terry Lane . . . Evanston . . ." he said. "Okay, thanks, Doreen. I owe you one." He hung up.

Ryan quickly scribbled the address down on the envelope. "Thanks so much, you guys," he said. He put down the pen, and then grabbed the photo and the envelope. He backed toward the door.

The caddy master started to come around the counter. "Hold on there, kid. What's your name?"

"I'll be sure to tell Mr. Gunderson how much help you guys were," he said with a tremor in his voice.

The bell rang as he pushed open the door with his back. "Thanks again!"

He wanted so badly to bolt out of there, but he forced himself to walk. He figured if he ran, they'd just chase after him. Still, he went at a fast clip—and in the opposite direction of the Men's Grill. He didn't dare risk going through there again, not if those guys upstairs were looking for him. He had no idea where he was headed, but saw a gate on the other side of the pro shop. He pushed it open, and discovered a sidewalk and a little strip of choppy, unkempt lawn. A couple of old patio chairs were on the grass. Ahead was another section of the building with a door marked STAFF ONLY. A blond kid not much older than him was standing beside the entrance, talking on his cell phone. He wore a busboy's uniform and smoked a cigarette. He barely looked up as Ryan hurried past him and opened the door.

Ducking inside, he found himself in what seemed

like a basement area—with gray walls and a cement floor. Overhead, the fluorescent lights couldn't keep the place from looking gloomy. Somewhere close by, a water heater or air conditioner churned out a loud racket. Ryan passed some man with a big pushcart full of bundled towels that had "Lake Ridge Country Club" on them. He figured the guy must have unloaded the towels from a delivery truck. So he headed in the direction the deliveryman had come from. He hoped he'd find an exit, and prayed no one would be outside waiting for him.

He heard some women laughing, and turned the corner to see two cute girls in waitress uniforms. One of them was punching a time clock. They weren't much older than him. Farther down the hallway, Ryan spotted a green exit sign over a door that was propped open.

Clutching the envelope close to his chest, he passed the two girls and nodded at them.

"Hey, good-looking, where are you going in such a hurry?" one of them called out.

The other girl laughed. "I get off at eleven!" she yelled.

His face turning red, Ryan retreated outside. He stopped and peeked around the laundry delivery truck. He didn't see anyone in the driveway, which was obviously for deliveries and employees. As he hurried toward the street, he passed another tall chain-link fence shrouded with a tarp on the interior. Again, he heard tennis balls getting smacked back and forth. Stopping for a moment, he caught his breath. Ryan realized he was on the other side of the tennis courts—and maybe it was on this exact spot that the photograph had been taken twenty-seven summers ago.

From what he could tell, it was the last summer his father and his three buddies had hung out together. The guy from the pro shop had said Mark Metcalf was a nice kid. No one had described his father or Dick Ingalls that way. So—what was Metcalf doing hanging out with them? As he hurried up the driveway toward the street, he kept replaying in his head something else those two men in the pro shop had said about Mark Metcalf and that summer:

"He was here when we had the tournament—and when that waitress disappeared."

"Did they ever find out what happened to her?"

Ryan ran down the block to where he'd parked his VW bug. He jumped inside the car, and dug a pen out of the glove compartment. With a shaky hand, he scribbled on the envelope:

Selena Jane—or Jayne?
Father—Burton? Barton?
GOOGLE!

The note to himself was written right beside that other name: Mark Metcalf.

Ryan was still catching his breath when he pulled his cell phone from his pants pocket and speed-dialed a number. It rang twice before someone answered.

"Ryan?" she said.

"Hi, Stephanie, I got it," he said. "The guy was a valet here at Lake Ridge Country Club. And his name's

Mark Metcalf. He lived in Evanston at the time. That's why none of my father's classmates recognized him. He was in a different school district . . ."

"Mark Metcalf," she repeated—as if she were jotting it down. "I wonder if he's still alive. I'll start looking him up on the Internet. Ryan, you're amazing. Good job. What's the name of the country club again?"

"Lake Ridge Country Club," he said. "It's in Wilmette. And listen, Stephanie, remember how we figured if something happened with these four guys, it happened over the summer the picture was taken?"

"Yes . . ."

"Well, I think it happened here—at the country club. And I think it might have something to do with a girl disappearing . . ."

CHAPTER NINETEEN

Friday, June 14—3:40 P.M.
Seattle

"Hey, Mark," said the head newswriter, Jesse Moritz. He leaned back in his chair. "I'm printing up tonight's lead stories right now."

There were two big desks in the newsroom. One belonged to Jesse, and the other to the associate producer. The rest of the staff were stuck in work cubicles—with dividing walls short enough so everyone could see the five, six, and eleven o'clock news on the big flat-screen TV on the wall.

Jesse's desk was always a mess—as was Jesse. He had glasses, a goatee and unruly, long, dark brown hair. He dressed like a slob. No one would ever guess the guy had three local Emmys. Today, he wore a Mariners T-shirt that had a hole in the shoulder, plaid shorts, and sandals.

"I can see you're pushing the casual Fridays policy to the limit again, Jess," Mark said, drolly. He watched the printer spit out the last page of the lead stories.

"I would have worn my thong, but it's at the cleaners," Jesse said, handing him the pages. "Here you go. I threw some three-syllable words in there today just to screw with you."

Mark cracked a smile. "Well, they better have them written phonetically on the teleprompter or somebody's ass is going to be in a sling." He patted Jesse on the shoulder, and headed to his office. Mark, his co-anchor, Debi Donahue, and the producer were the only ones with their own offices. The rooms were small, with windows that looked out to the newsroom.

Unlike his writer friend, Mark Metcalf always dressed impeccably. One of the benefits of being a news anchor was that they gave him a budget for his on-the-air wardrobe. He also had a local Emmy, but just one. However, he'd recently made *Seattle* magazine's list of Top Ten Best Dressed Men in Seattle. The people in the newsroom got a chuckle out of it. They blew up the page from the magazine, framed it, and hung it in his office. His co-anchor, Debi, said he looked like the dapper dad in a Macy's catalog: "Mr. Square-jaw with his perfect brown hair and the touch of gray at the temples, so handsome, no wonder you get more fan letters than I do."

His mail was in a basket attached to the outside of his office door. There were about a dozen envelopes today, which Mark set on his desk—along with the lead news stories. He took off his dark blue blazer and carefully placed it on a hanger so it wouldn't be wrinkled for the broadcast in a little over an hour. He hung the hanger on a coatrack behind his desk, sat down, and started opening his mail. A lot of it was the usual junk mail. But he came across a card with a lily on the front of it. "With Deepest Sympathy," it said.

Mark let out a sigh, and opened the card. There were six or seven printed lines— something about loss and healing. He glanced over the lines, and read the personal message at the bottom:

So sorry to hear about your wife's passing. I will pray for you & your family. You are my favorite newscaster. Debi is nice too! I never miss your 5 o'clock news. However, I'm not sure I care for the new sports-caster. He seems smarmy. But that's just my opinion.

Once again, my deepest condolences to you.

Sincerely,
Sylvia Hartman

He glanced at the framed photo on his desk—of Dina, Alison, Danny, and him, taken in front of the doughnut sculpture at Volunteer Park last year. They all looked so happy, but in reality, the kids had been fighting and ready to kill each other. At one point between poses for their photographer friend, Dina turned to Mark and whispered, "Can we just ditch these monsters after this and go for a drink someplace? Wait. I'm a horrible mother, aren't I?"

He looked at her, smiling in the photo, and wished he could tell her now that she was a wonderful mother—and the love of his life.

They had buried Dina nearly a month ago. He was

still getting sympathy cards. He hadn't thought that his TV audience knew about his wife's death. But apparently they did. The news services didn't pick up the story, and in the *Seattle Times* obituary, Dina's suicide was referred to as "an accident in their home." However, some local bloggers and tweeters (probably Alison's classmates) got wind of the real story, so it wasn't that much of a secret. His producer had wanted Debi to make a discreet announcement on the news—just to explain Mark's absence that week. But Mark asked them not to.

When he came back to work, he was tempted to say a quick on-the-air thank-you to viewers for their support. But he just didn't want people Googling Dina's name for information about how she'd died. The official report was so vague. It only inspired people to keep digging until they found some blog that said Dina Metcalf had asphyxiated herself in an old Vista Cruiser. He was ashamed of it. He was ashamed of the stupid old car he had her driving. He'd gone on Craigslist and sold the damn thing for cheap last week. Catalytic converters in cars had long ago put an end to that type of suicide.

Instead of making an on-air announcement, he answered every e-mail and every sympathy card. He still had about eighty cards left from a box of five hundred the funeral parlor had printed up. He would send one of those—with a personal note on the back—to Sylvia Hartman.

He wasn't the only one ashamed about Dina's suicide. Poor Alison was devastated. She assumed all the blame, too. The morning of the funeral, she didn't even want to come out of her room. Mark went in there, sat on her four-poster bed, and held her in his arms while she sobbed. "It's because of me that she killed herself," Alison lamented. "I was so mean to her when she stopped by school that afternoon. She was worried about me. She just wanted to make sure I was okay. And I was such a nasty bitch to her . . ."

He stroked her curly, brown hair. "Alison, honey, that kind of stuff bounced right off your mom. We talked on the phone minutes after she left the school, and she was joking about it. I'm not saying she didn't take you seriously when it mattered. But she was your age once, and she remembered how it was with her mother, the arguments and flare-ups. She knew you loved her. There's no way you could have caused her to—to do what she did."

Alison gently pulled away from him and wiped her eyes. "Then why? Why did she kill herself?" she asked in a raspy, broken voice.

Mark shook his head. "I really wish I knew, sweetheart."

It still haunted him. He'd asked Dina's parents, her sister and two brothers, her close friends, and even her doctor—and none of them could come up with a single reason why Dina would have taken her own life. Mark figured it had to be something he'd done, only he was just too goddamn stupid to realize how much he'd hurt her. That was what shamed him most of all.

He pushed Sylvia's sympathy card to one side, and opened up the rest of his mail. The last piece looked like it might be another sympathy note. But when Mark pulled it out of the envelope, he found a card with a color-tinted photo of a baby's hand wrapped around a man's index finger. "For My Father . . ." it said under the picture.

"Oh, Jesus, no," he murmured, warily opening up the card.

There was a twelve-line printed poem that he barely glanced at. What mattered most to him was that under the words, "Happy Father's Day," there was no signature.

Friday, June 14—3:55 P.M.

Jenny knew where she was now and what day it was. From the local TV newscasts, she had to be in Cedar Rapids or somewhere nearby. She figured her captor was staying in a house and this fallout shelter was in his backyard. She often listened for voices overhead. She thought she heard someone laughing once, but the sound was so far off, it could have been anything. A train roared by four times every day, but she didn't hear any cars.

Right now she was sitting on the ugly brown sofa, watching *The Sandpiper* with Elizabeth Taylor and Richard Burton—on Encore. The movie had been shot in Big Sur. On the screen right now, Liz and Dick were on a beach, with a blazing orange sunset in the background.

She missed sunsets. She missed the sky, and cool breezes off the water. She longed to be outside again. The movie wasn't helping, but it was the closest she could get to what it was like up there—beyond several feet of dirt.

She'd been in this underground bunker for eight days. It seemed like an eternity. Routines helped the time go by—the TV, books, those bland packaged meals, sessions on the stationary bike, her daily shower, and bed. Despite these temporary distractions, there was no getting past that she was stuck there, utterly trapped—and for how long, she didn't know. Nor did she have any idea how this imprisonment would end.

The electricity and utilities were on a timer. Everything shut down at 11:30 nightly—and came back on at 6:30 in the morning. That included the heat. There was only a dim blue light in the bathroom that she could see by at night. Sometimes, when she couldn't sleep, she wrapped herself up in a blanket and took a book in there to read.

The two tiny green lights on the cameras overhead never went out. She knew he was watching her. Yet, she couldn't help feeling he'd gone away and left her there all alone. The last time he'd spoken to her had been on that first day, before he'd switched on the power and given her the food and supplies—before he'd violated her. There was no way in hell she missed the son of a bitch. But she needed him.

Where was he? Was he already in some other city, looking for the next woman? He and his partner had probably gone through all her money by now. It had been over a week since he'd taken her "wish list." And of course, she hadn't seen any of those items yet. She wondered what that was all about.

Four nights ago, she'd snuck out of bed and managed to unscrew the little light over the desk. She hid it, wedging it between the wall and the side of her mattress. She decided if he ever came back to have his way with her again, she'd grab that lightbulb and stab him in the throat with it.

Two nights ago, she'd faked a seizure, thrashing around the room for several minutes and then collapsing on the floor—right by the bed. She had the lightbulb within her reach. She lay on the cold floor for three hours. Every once in a while she opened her eyes just enough to see the green pinpoint lights above her. He never came down. He didn't speak to her over the sound system. She was almost sure no one had witnessed her little skit.

The notion that she was all alone terrified Jenny. As much as she hated him, that creep was her lifeline. With him gone, she was even more helpless and vulnerable. What if a storm knocked the power out? She'd slowly suffocate in this little prison. She imagined him and his partner getting into an accident. If they were killed, no one would ever know she was down here.

Jenny tried to focus on the movie. But while Liz and Dick made out on the beach, she started thinking about her cat again. She wondered what they'd done with him.

Certainly her friend Carroll had figured out by now that something was wrong. Were the police looking for her? Even if they'd started searching for her, how long before the Oakland police detectives put it together that she was buried in someone's backyard in Cedar Rapids, Iowa? They would never find her.

On the TV, Richard Burton's wife, played by Eva Marie Saint, had just figured out that he was sleeping with Liz. She was crying and screaming at him.

In the background, Jenny thought she heard children laughing.

She immediately grabbed the remote and muted the TV. The children's voices were still there. They were above her. They must have been cutting through his yard.

If she could hear them, they might be able to hear her.

"HELP!" she screamed. She leapt to her feet. "HELP! I'M DOWN HERE—UNDER THE GROUND! HELP ME!" She banged on the corrugated wall again and again—until her hand hurt. "CAN YOU HEAR ME? THERE'S SOMEONE DOWN HERE! CALL THE PO-LICE!"

She paused, and listened. One of the kids was squealing.

"Wait, shut up!" another one said. Jenny couldn't tell if it was a boy or a girl. The voice was so faint and far away. "Did you hear that?"

Jenny started pounding on the wall again. "I'M DOWN HERE!" she yelled. "PLEASE . . ."

But she trailed off at the sound of a distant rumble. She knew they couldn't hear her, because the train was passing by. She couldn't hear them, either.

As the roar of the train faded, she started banging on the wall again—with her other hand this time. "ARE YOU STILL THERE?" she called, her voice getting hoarse. "CAN YOU HEAR ME? IS ANYONE THERE? HELP ME!"

She fell quiet for a moment, and just listened. She didn't hear a thing.

The children had moved on.

"PLEASE, HELP ME!" she cried out desperately. Tears streamed down her face. "GOD, DON'T LEAVE ME HERE! IS ANYONE UP THERE? CAN ANY-ONE HEAR ME?"

Jenny staggered back and collapsed on the ugly brown sofa. She rubbed her sore hand.

"Please, help me," she whispered—to no one.

Friday, June 14—11:33 P.M.
Seattle

The staff members in the newsroom broke into applause and whistled when Mark emerged from the studio after the eleven o'clock broadcast. Debi was in the doorway ahead of him, and she made a big, sweeping gesture with her hand—as if presenting him to the others. The phones were ringing. With a grin on his face, Jesse came up and shook his hand. "That was classic, Mark," he said. "And listen to those phones! I'll bet this goes viral . . ."

"Thanks, thanks a lot, everybody," he muttered, trying to work up a smile.

In his last segment of tonight's news broadcast, he had made reference to the "Seattle Shitty Council." He quickly corrected the flub, but Debi got a case of giggles. She was enough of a pro that she quickly recovered. As for Mark, he managed to wrap up the broadcast with a smile on his face and a few shreds of his dignity still intact.

Ordinarily, he'd have had a terrific laugh over it with the newsroom gang. But tonight, he just didn't have it in him. When he'd gotten that Father's Day card earlier today, it had knocked the sense of humor right out of him. He felt his face getting red with embarrassment as his coworkers cheered and laughed.

"You've got to answer one of these phone calls," Jesse said. "You've just got to . . ."

But Mark shook his head and started toward his office. He tried to keep a smile plastered on his face. "Oh, I've had enough humiliation for one night, thank you."

With a little wave, he ducked into his office. The phone was ringing in there, too. He ignored it.

Before the newscast, he'd swung by Quality Food Center for some essentials— nothing perishable. He was doing most of the grocery shopping now—and he still wasn't very good at it. He was about to reach for the two QFC bags when Jesse stepped inside thc office.

"Hey, are you okay?" he whispered.

"Just a bad day," Mark said with a shrug. "I'll snap out of it. Sorry to be such a downer."

"Feeling shitty, huh?" Cracking a smile, Jesse shook his head. "Sorry, I couldn't resist. Seriously, want to go out for a drink and unload?"

"Thanks anyway, Jesse. Think I'll head home."

"Well, be careful driving across town. Even at this hour, the inner-shitty traffic can be pretty nuts."

Mark patted him on the shoulder. "You can't give it up, can you?"

"Nope, sorry. Take care tonight, okay? Don't forget to wash your makeup off."

Mark nodded. "Thanks."

He watched Jesse slink back into the newsroom and murmur something to Debi and another coworker, who both seemed concerned. Grabbing the grocery bags, Mark switched off his office light with his elbow and stepped out of the office. "Good night, all!" he called over his shoulder.

He heard several people say good night—loudly, to be heard over the phones that were still ringing. He continued toward the exit, not looking back. He took the stairs instead of the elevator. It was only one flight down. The station was housed in a two-story sixties-style building near the Space Needle and Seattle Center.

In the gloomy stairwell with its beige cinderblock walls, Mark hurried down the steps. He thought about that Father's Day card again. It had unnerved him. Somehow, he'd managed to get through the five and six o'clock news broadcasts without flubbing. But reading his lines off the teleprompter, he couldn't think of anything else but that damn card.

Every Father's Day week for the last four years, he'd gotten an anonymous card—with no return address and an out-of-state postmark. But this time, the sender had mailed the cryptic card from "Seattle, WA 98122."

The person behind those cards was now close by. Maybe he or she had been around for a while now. Mark wondered if this had anything to do with Dina's suicide. Had this mystery person talked with her that afternoon last month?

Dina had known about the first Father's Day card. The day he'd gotten it at the station, he'd phoned home and asked if she'd sent it—or if she'd had a friend out-of-state send it as some kind of prank.

"Now why in God's name would I do that?" Dina had laughed. "Hey, you know what this means, don't you? It means you could have a child somewhere out there you don't know about. It must have been from before you knew me, because you've certainly never been unfaithful to me."

She was right. He hadn't been with another woman since meeting her.

"You know, I'll bet some crazy fan sent it," Dina said. "Or maybe someone just got their envelopes mixed up. Somewhere, someone's dad has a fan letter to you."

Dina didn't seem to think anything of it. But it gnawed away at Mark. It didn't make any sense. He was never much of a lothario. He'd only been with five women before Dina: three he'd dated for a while, one was a fling, and another was a mistake. Except for the one he regretted, he'd kept in touch with all of them long enough after the fact to know he hadn't gotten any of them pregnant.

That left the woman who was a mistake, the woman he'd spent most of his adult life trying to forget. But the notion that she'd gotten pregnant seemed next to impossible.

Dina didn't know about her—unless, of course, someone had gotten to her and told her. Was that what had happened on the afternoon Dina killed herself? Was that the explanation? He wondered if Dina would have committed suicide over that. Maybe. Maybe she was that utterly disappointed in him.

He wanted to get home to his kids. He usually drove back and had dinner with them between the six and eleven o'clock broadcasts. Alison's best friend, Cate, was spending the night. When Mark had left them, they were eating popcorn and watching TV. Danny was in bed reading. Having another person in the house, even if she was just a kid, somehow made him feel better.

Shifting around the grocery bags for a moment, Mark pulled the door open and stepped outside. It was a cool, clear evening. He headed to his vintage blue Mustang in the parking lot. This close to the Space Needle and the Seattle Center, there were always people around. He wasn't paying much attention to anyone when the woman approached him.

"Excuse me, someone's following me," she whispered. "Do you mind if I stand here and talk to you like I know you? It'll only be for a couple of minutes . . ."

Dumbfounded, he stared at the pretty, thirtysomething brunette. She was thin, with a denim jacket over a casual pink dress. "Um, sure," he said.

"It's that husky guy back there in the brown jacket," she said. "See him—with the dark hair?"

Mark looked over her shoulder and saw the man she described. He must have just turned around, because his back was to them. He was walking away—in the other direction, toward the Space Needle. "I think he got discouraged," Mark said.

"Not him," the woman sighed. "I'm pretty sure it's the same guy who's been outside my hotel room window a couple of nights this week. I was hoping when I moved here from the Bay Area that I'd make some new friends, but he's not what I had in mind." She touched Mark's arm. "Listen, thank you so much. I just want to make sure he doesn't come back. I still have five more blocks to my hotel. Do you mind if we stand here for another couple of minutes? I hope those groceries aren't too heavy."

"It's no problem, really," he said.

She cocked her head to one side and seemed to study his face. "Do you mind if I ask you something?"

He shrugged. "Shoot."

"This is kind of tactless, but since we'll probably never see each other again, I just have to ask. Are you wearing makeup?"

Mark laughed. "Oh, yeah, I forgot I had it on. I'm an anchorman on the news." He nodded toward the building—with the station call letters and logo illuminated by the doors. On the side of the building was a small billboard with him, Debi, and the rest of the on-air news team. "I just finished a broadcast," he explained.

She covered her mouth. "Of course! I thought you looked familiar. I've been watching your news show practically every night since I got into town two weeks ago. Mike Metcalf, right?"

"Mark," he said.

"Oh, yeah, Mark, sorry." Suddenly, she seemed a bit nervous. It was kind of charming. "Anyway, I—I'm sorry I missed your show tonight."

"Well, I'm not. I made a big flub on the air. It'll probably be on YouTube tomorrow."

"I'll have to check it out." She touched his arm again. "Listen, I've bothered you enough. I think I'll be okay getting to the hotel from here. Thanks for coming to my rescue."

"This is silly," he said. "Why don't I give you a lift there?"

She hesitated, and then smiled. "Ordinarily, I'd say that I don't accept rides from strangers, but I already know who you are. Only you don't know me . . ." She flicked back her long, dark brown hair and held out her hand.

Mark put down one of the grocery bags and gave her hand a shake.

"It's nice to meet you, Mark," she said. "My name's Jenny Ballatore."

CHAPTER TWENTY

Tuesday, June 18—1:17 P.M.
Portland

The guys at the body shop had changed the radio station in her car. It was churning out rap music—instead of the classic rock 'n' roll from her usual oldies station. She was trying to drive and fiddle with the tuner at the same time. Stephanie could fly a commercial airliner, but she still couldn't figure out how to select and save a radio station on her Lexus. At every red light between the auto body shop and home, she tried to find her station.

This was only one of life's many frustrations this week. At least the car roof looked like new—at a cost of $703.89. The garage door damaged that night last week had also been fixed. She'd had her locks replaced—and a new security system installed. And she'd applied for a gun permit. Each task had been a major pain in the neck to complete.

But none of them were quite as exasperating as trying to track down Mark Metcalf.

How stupid she'd been to assume finding him would be easy. Google was full of Mark Metcalfs. Most of the Web, image, and news searches took her to the actor Mark Metcalf, who was in everything from *Animal House* to *Buffy the Vampire Slayer* to *Seinfeld*.

Of the four young men posing by the tennis court in that photo, Metcalf's face was the most out of focus. Stephanie couldn't match his likeness with any of the scores of images she'd studied on Google. She'd varied the spelling: Marc Metcalf, Mark Metcalfe, Mark Medcaff. And she'd tried different search key words: Mark Metcalf; Chicago and Mark Metcalf; Lake Ridge Country Club; and Mark Metcalf, Death. She still couldn't find anyone who might be him.

Since Friday, Ryan had paid three visits to Mark Metcalf's former address in Evanston. But no one had answered the door at 1107 Terry Lane.

Stephanie didn't want Ryan going off on his own investigation. "I'm just afraid you might end up asking the wrong person if they knew Mark Metcalf," she'd told him when they'd talked on Sunday. "You're digging around his old neighborhood. And we've pretty much figured out this killer must have known him in high school. Chances are this could all be tied in with an event that happened back in 1986 when these four boys knew each other. I don't care how clever you are or what kind of cover story you give, the killer will still know you on sight—because, like it or not, Ryan, you look a hell of a lot like your father when he was your age."

Stephanie was worried about him and his grandmother. Ryan kept assuring her they were fine—no break-in attempts, no strange cars parked on their block, no signs of trouble. But Stephanie still felt they were on borrowed time. How soon before the killers targeted them the way they'd been after her? Like her, they were loose ends.

Her only hope was that while she'd been calling it quits with Jim at the Hotel Lucia last week, the intruder in her home hadn't looked at the e-mails on her computer. Then again, maybe the killers were so confident in the way they'd eliminated Brent Farrell's family they couldn't imagine Ryan or his grandmother ever doubting the official police findings.

Perhaps right now, she was the only loose end they cared about.

Either way, Ryan seemed to be pushing his luck. He'd told her when they'd spoken on Sunday: "I want to go back to that country club and talk to some more employees about this Metcalf guy and Selena Jayne. Maybe they were dating or something. If I could talk to the payroll lady, Doreen, I might be able to get a current address for Selena's father. I could—"

"No," she cut him off. "I don't want you going back there. They'll be on the lookout for you. Just lay low for a while. Let me do what I can from here, okay?"

"But everything's *here*," he argued.

"All right, then I'll fly out there if I have to. But for now, just don't do anything. Keep a low profile, and watch your back. You should be focusing on your makeup exams anyway. That's important, Ryan."

"God, you sound just like my mom."

"Sorry," she murmured.

"No, it's okay, I like it."

Unfortunately, for all her talk about carrying on the investigation, she hadn't gotten very far. They still didn't know if Mark Metcalf was alive or dead, a potential victim or the person behind all these killings. It was possible he simply had been in a photo with these three guys and he had nothing to do with any of this. Perhaps she and Ryan should be looking for the person who snapped that photograph.

She'd been searching for Mark Metcalf for the last four days.

And hell, right now, she couldn't even find her station on the car radio. Exasperated, she shut off the radio and turned down her block.

Stephanie figured maybe it was time to put Mark Metcalf on the back burner, and switch tacks in her investigation.

Pulling into her driveway, she pressed the device to open the garage door. The big door ascended, and Stephanie smiled a little. It felt good to park in her garage and have everything working again.

When she opened the door to the house, the incessant beep of the new home security alarm was reassuring. Stephanie rushed to the code box in her kitchen, and punched in the numbers to disarm it. Pouring herself a glass of water, she took it to her study nook off the living room. She switched on the computer, and then typed in her password. She used to leave her computer on—and let the monitor go into sleep mode. She'd never bothered with her password before. But all that had changed since last week.

With her fingers racing over the keys, she pulled up

an article she'd downloaded three days ago from the *Chicago Tribune* online archives.

She'd already read the article and sent it to Ryan. It was just a small piece with one photo, showing a pretty young blonde with bangs. The girl looked like a Vanna White wannabe. The date of the article was Friday, August 29, 1986:

STILL NO CLUES IN EVANSTON GIRL'S DISAPPEARANCE
"It's My Worst Nightmare,"
Says Widower Father

EVANSTON: The search continues for Selena Jayne, 17, who was last seen leaving her Evanston home on Wednesday evening, August 20. Ms. Jayne told her younger sister that she was taking a bus to see a movie at the Wilmette Theater. It is unclear whether or not Ms. Jayne was meeting anyone there.

Police interviewed employees at the theater, but no one recalled seeing anybody matching Ms. Jayne's description at either the 7:00 or 9:15 shows.

Selena Jayne had been working as a waitress at Lake Ridge Country Club in Wilmette. Wednesday was her night off.

Selena's father, a widower, Barton Jayne, 49, is the groundskeeper at the country club. "We're praying for her safe return," he said. "But every day we don't hear from her, I feel a little less hope. It's my worst nightmare. Selena has always been a good girl, a hard worker, and very responsible." Ms. Jayne attended Evanston Township High School until her mother's death in 1985. According to her father, Selena dropped out of school to help raise her younger sister.

SELENA MARIE JAYNE
Date of Birth: 1/27/1969
Hair: Blond
Eyes: Brown
Height: 5' 4"
Weight: 120 lbs.
Complexion: Fair

Anyone with information regarding Selena Jayne's whereabouts is urged to contact the Evanston Police Department.

Stephanie figured if the father wasn't dead, he was seventy-six now. She hadn't been able to track him through Google, and Ryan couldn't find anything in local phone books or directory assistance.

After talking with Ryan on Sunday night, she'd looked up a phone number and jotted it down. Now Stephanie took out her cell phone and dialed the number.

"Lake Ridge Country Club," a woman answered. "How may I help you?"

"Hi, can you connect me to Doreen in Payroll, please?" Stephanie asked.

"That extension is four-oh-five-eight. I'm connecting you now."

With the phone to her ear, Stephanie counted four rings. She thought it might go to voice mail. But then someone answered, a woman with a gruff voice: "This is Doreen."

"Hello, is this the payroll department?"

"Yes, Doreen speaking. Who's this?"

"My name's Stephanie, and I'm calling about a former employee there, my uncle. His name's Barton Jayne. J-A-Y-N-E. I understand he worked there . . ."

"Well, that's funny. You're the second person this week asking about him. Barton hasn't worked here for years. What's this about?"

"My Uncle Bart and my mother were estranged for a long, long time. She just passed away on Sunday. I thought he might want to know. The family lawyer said I should find him. I don't have any idea how to reach him. I was hoping you have a current address for him."

"I'm sorry," the woman replied. "I don't give out that kind of information."

"I understand," Stephanie said, working a little quaver into her voice. "I'm sorry—I'm sorry to bother you like this. I don't know how I'm going to find him. I'm ready to give up. And I think my mom would really want him to know—she wasn't mad at him in the end. I'm sorry. I told myself I wasn't going to cry . . ." Stephanie had started out faking it. She hadn't expected real tears to come, but they did.

"Let me see what I have here," Doreen said. "I got a Christmas card from Barton after he left. I may have written down the address. Last I heard he was the groundskeeper at a church in Glenview. I think he told me he was living above the garage by the rectory. Ah, okay, here it is. Do you have a pen and paper?"

"Yes, please, go ahead," she said, wiping her eyes.

"St. Paul's Episcopal Church, 1947 Harms Road in Glenview," she said. "Got that?"

"Yes, thank you."

"That's from 2007. I don't have a current address for the daughter."

"The daughter?" Stephanie echoed. "You mean Selena?"

"No, oh, no. I'm talking about Nicole. She worked here, too, for a couple of summers."

"When?"

"Oh, it was 1992 or '93," the woman answered. "About five years after Selena disappeared. But then, I suppose you already know all about that."

"Only what I've heard from my mother, which wasn't much," Stephanie said.

"There isn't much to tell. They never did find her. She was a sweet girl, beautiful, but strange, too."

"Strange in what way?" Stephanie asked. "I—I never met my cousin."

"Well, she was just very naïve—and not too mature for her age. Her mother had been sick for so many years. Your uncle was an excellent groundskeeper, but I don't think he knew much about raising two girls on his own. Anyway, I hope I was some help."

"You were. Thank you very much."

"I'm sorry for your loss," the woman said. Then she hung up.

Stephanie clicked off the line. She almost speed-dialed Ryan's number to tell him of her find, but she hesitated. That was all he needed. Within an hour, he'd be in his car, driving to Glenview and knocking on St. Paul's rectory door. She didn't want him taking any chances.

Getting to her feet, she took her water glass and started upstairs. She wanted to change her clothes and get comfortable. She still had some calls to make—starting with the rectory. There was a chance Mr. Jayne had moved on to another job or he could have passed away. She needed to confirm that he was still working there.

As she stepped into her bedroom, Stephanie started to pull the polo shirt over her head. She was about to toss the shirt on her bed when she noticed something on the nightstand.

It hadn't been there this morning. In fact, it had never been in her house at all.

Ever since her parents had died, it had been in Rebecca's house.

The Royal Doulton figurine of an old lady selling balloons was one of the items she'd reported missing from the house after her sister's family was slaughtered.

Now it was on her nightstand.

Someone wanted her to know that they'd gotten away with murder.

They also wanted her to know they'd made it past all the extra new security added to her house.

And they were coming back.

Tuesday—4:40 P.M.
Evanston, Illinois

Number 1107 on Terry Lane was a Cape Cod style house with gray shingles and white trim. It seemed modest in comparison with all the other, somewhat stately homes on the cul-de-sac. Ryan went ahead and parked his old VW in their driveway. The last three times he'd come by, he'd parked on the street. He hadn't wanted to block anybody going in or out. But no one had been home any of those times, so he figured, *Why the hell not park in their stupid driveway?* They probably weren't home anyway. Why be so timid and overly polite with people who probably weren't even there?

Dressed in a yellow Izod shirt and jeans, he rang the bell. The forty-five-minute drive here—including stop-and-go traffic on Edens Expressway—now seemed like a huge waste of his time. As if the people living here now were any relation to Mark Metcalf or knew anything about him. It had been twenty-seven years since the guy had lived in this house.

He rang again, and then knocked.

It seemed so pointless. It was a hot, muggy afternoon. He could have gone swimming or something—instead of this. He knocked on the door again, loudly this time.

"All right already, I'm coming!" someone called from inside the house.

Ryan couldn't believe it. Someone was actually home.

"Who is it?" the woman yelled. "Who's there?" It sounded like she was on the other side of the door now. And she sounded pissed off.

"My name's Ryan!" he called. He figured she was looking right at him through the peephole. "I'm sorry to bother you. I'm looking for someone who used to live in this house."

He heard the chain lock rattling. Then the door opened a couple of inches—as far as the chain allowed. A frumpy-looking, thirtyish blonde glared at him

through the crack. "If you're really looking for someone who *used* to live here, then they wouldn't be here
now, would they?"

Ryan tried to smile. "Um, that's a good point. I was
hoping you might know how I could get ahold of them.
The family who lived here was named Metcalf. This
was back in the eighties."

She quickly shook her head. "I have no idea who
you're talking about." It looked like she was about to
shut the door.

"Hey, wait a minute, okay?" Ryan said. "Is there
someone on the cul-de-sac who's lived here for a
while—someone who might have known them?"

She rolled her eyes. "Try the Sperrys—1123." She
shut the door in his face.

"Okay, thanks a lot!" Ryan called in his best wiseass
manner. "It was really great talking to you! Bye!"

He turned away, and retreated to his car. "What an
asshole," he muttered.

After only a few minutes parked in the driveway, the
VW was already baking inside. Backing out of the driveway, he turned around and started looking for the address.

The house at 1123 was a graceful old Tudor with a
beautifully maintained lawn. There were two cars in
the driveway. That was a good sign. Ryan parked on
the street. On his way to the front door, he said a little
prayer these people would be home and a little nicer
than their skanky neighbor down the block. He rang
the bell.

He heard some activity inside—muted voices, then
footsteps. The door was opened by a man in his mid-

forties with receding sandy-colored hair. His eyes had dark circles under them. He wore shorts and an oxford shirt with the sleeves rolled up. "Can I help you?" he asked.

"Hi, my name's Ryan, and I was wondering if Mr. or Mrs. Sperry is home."

"Mr. Sperry passed away six years ago," he said, scratching his chin. "And Mrs. Sperry—well, she can't come to the door. I'm her son-in-law. Is there something I can help you with?"

"Um, I was hoping Mrs. Sperry could tell me something about a family that used to live in the gray house down the block. Their name was Metcalf."

"Who is it, Jeff?" someone called from inside the house.

He glanced over his shoulder, and then nodded at Ryan. "Come on in," he said. "And just wait right here for a minute, okay? You can leave the door open . . ."

As soon as Ryan stepped over the threshold, a rank smell hit him. It was like rotten fruit. At least they had the air-conditioning cranked up. He waited in the foyer—as he was told. He couldn't quite see into the living room, where he heard people murmuring. But there was a mirror on one wall, allowing him a glimpse of what was going on just around the corner. A hospital bed was set up in the living room. An old woman was in the bed, surrounded by a small group of people— some sitting, some standing. Ryan noticed the man who had answered the door. He whispered something to a red-haired woman in a sleeveless blouse and shorts. She nodded, patted his shoulder, and then stepped away. Ryan couldn't see her in the mirror anymore.

After a moment, she came around the corner with her purse slung over her shoulder. She was pretty, and about the same age as the man, who was probably her husband. "Hi, I'm Gretchen, Mrs. Sperry's daughter," she said. "My mom, she—well, she's sick. Actually, she's dying. My family's been keeping a vigil for the last two days. C'mon, let's go outside . . ."

Ryan followed her out to the front stoop. It felt good to breathe fresh air again. He realized the awful smell inside the house had been death.

Gretchen dug into her purse and took out a pack of Virginia Slims. "Look at me," she said, lighting her cigarette. "I'm sneaking a smoke while my mother lies in there dying of cancer."

"I'm really sorry," Ryan said. "And I—I apologize for my timing, too. It really sucks."

She let out a tired laugh. "Don't worry about it. They'll give me a yell if there's any change. I was looking for an excuse to step outside for a few minutes." She leaned against the doorframe and puffed on her cigarette. "So—my husband told me. Your name is Ryan, and you want to know about the Metcalfs."

"Yeah, Mark Metcalf was a friend of my father's, and I'm trying to track him down—Mark, that is."

She sighed and exhaled some smoke. "Well, I'm not sure if I can be any help. The last time I saw Mark was at his mother's funeral, which was in '95 or '96. He had a girl with him. I think she was his fiancée. He was a sportscaster for some TV station in Oklahoma City. Or maybe he was the weatherman, I forget. Anyway, he was on the local news there. I'm afraid that's all I know—and that was almost twenty years ago."

"Does he have any brothers or sisters?" Ryan asked.

Gretchen shook her head. "No. After Mrs. Metcalf died, Mark's dad moved to Florida. I'm not sure whether or not he's still alive."

"Did you know Mark well? Did you know any of his friends?"

"No, he was a few years older than me. I have to admit, I hardly noticed him. He always had some sort of job. I think he worked at a country club for a while—"

"Lake Ridge Country Club," Ryan said.

"That sounds right," Gretchen said, shrugging. "Like I said, I didn't pay much attention to him. I can't tell you anything about the crowd he hung out with—or if he even had a crowd. He was a real nice guy, but kind of nerdy, you know? Then he hit college and wow, something happened, because he came back for summer vacation looking really good." She smiled wistfully. "I remember when he was still gawky-looking, my mom used to say, 'That Metcalf boy is going to be a real heartbreaker when he gets a little older.' And she was right."

She took one last drag of her cigarette, dropped it on the stoop, and ground it out underneath her sandal. She nudged it off the front stoop with her foot. "Anyway, I should get back inside," she said. "I'm not sure I was much help."

"You were," Ryan said. "Thanks a lot. And I'm— I'm really sorry about your mom."

Gretchen opened the door, but then she turned to smile at him. She had tears in her eyes. "Let me give you a little bit of advice, Ryan," she said with a tremor in her voice. "They might drive you crazy once in a while. But cherish the time you have with your folks while they're still around. Okay?"

Ryan felt his throat tighten. He decided not to tell her it was too late for him.

He managed to work up a smile, and nodded. "Okay," he whispered.

Tuesday—5:47 P.M.
Portland

"So—I Googled 'Mark Metcalf, TV News,' and of course, I got all these stupid links about the actor again. But I finally found something—a Web site for the KIXY TV news team in Seattle. That's right by you, isn't it?"

"It's about a three-and-a-half-hour drive," she said, "or fifty-three minutes from gate to gate if you're flying."

Stephanie was on her cell phone, standing by the window in her room at the Airport Executive Inn. She'd shut the drapes earlier, but now parted one curtain back to look out at the parking lot. She was pretty sure no one had followed her here.

After finding the Royal Doulton figurine in her bedroom, she'd packed in a hurry. That included the figurine of the old woman selling balloons. Even though it seemed slightly tainted now that these killers had handled it, the piece still had sentimental value. She'd thought about calling the police, but it seemed pointless. Her credibility with them was next to zero. She'd reported the piece as stolen from her sister's house in Croton back in November, and now it was in her home.

How could she explain it to them? Would they believe that the killers of her sister's family were terrorizing her?

The cops wouldn't buy it at all.

So Stephanie had packed her suitcase. She'd deleted all the e-mails to and from Ryan in her desktop computer, and then unplugged the thing. After setting her home security alarm, she hurried to her car in the garage and drove all over Portland. Once she was sure no one was following her, she checked into the Airport Executive Inn—a mere four miles from her house. She had enough points accrued from all her travels to stay there for free. She registered under her own name, and parked close to the back where no one could see her car from the street.

She'd been contemplating a trip to Chicago so she could talk with Selena Jayne's father in person. She'd also planned to ask about Mark Metcalf at his old address in Evanston.

But Ryan had beaten her to the punch in the hunt for Mark Metcalf. Apparently, Lake Ridge Country Club's former valet wasn't in Chicago anymore. He was just fifty-three minutes away.

"They have his picture on the KIXY TV Web site," Ryan continued. "The neighbor on Terry Lane said he got better looking as he got older, but I still recognized him from the 1986 photo. They had his bio on the Web site, too," Ryan continued. "Born in St. Louis, went to college at the University of Colorado, got his start at a TV station in Oklahoma City. They never mentioned Chicago. Maybe that's because he'd just as soon forget about it."

"Did they say if he was married or not?" Stephanie asked.

"I was just getting to that. The bio said he has a wife and two kids. So—then I went online and googled 'Mark Metcalf, KIXY TV News.' There's a video of him on YouTube, flubbing a line and accidentally saying 'shit' on the air. It's pretty funny. But more important, there's a *Seattle Times* obituary for his wife, Dina. She died a month ago."

"How?"

" 'An accident in the home,' the article said, which sounded like bullshit to me. I mean, if she broke her neck falling off a ladder or tripping down a flight of stairs, why not just say so? But that 'accident' business was the official story they gave. So I went looking on the blogs, and found something. Dina Metcalf died of carbon monoxide poisoning after parking her vintage Oldsmobile in the family garage and leaving the motor on. Looks like suicide."

"The key words here are *looks like*," Stephanie said.

"So if the suicide was staged, that pretty much means my mom and your sister didn't kill themselves, right?"

"That's what I was thinking," Stephanie said. "It never made any sense to me that Rebecca committed suicide. But in a strange, twisted way, it makes sense that she was murdered. It's all part of a pattern. They do away with the wife, staging it like a suicide. The husband is left confused, vulnerable, feeling guilty. Then he meets some woman who builds him up again . . ."

"Only so that they can kill him—along with the new wife and the kids," Ryan said.

Stephanie realized he was right. They didn't kill any of these husbands while they were still grieving. They waited until their lives seemed back on track again. It was like waiting until a sick prisoner got well before executing him.

"So do you suppose this Metcalf guy has met his future Mrs. yet?" Ryan asked.

"That's the key, the new wife," Stephanie said. "She's part of this. I don't know how they're getting these women to cooperate. Obviously, these women are going in on these schemes not knowing they'll end up dead—and disfigured."

Stephanie glanced at her wristwatch, and grabbed the little leather folder from on top of the TV. She'd stayed in enough hotels throughout the Pacific Northwest to know that some of the dish companies in other cities carried Seattle stations in their lineup.

There it was amid the TV stations listed in the channel guide: KIXY Channel 15 (Seattle).

With the remote, she switched on the TV, muted it, and set the channel to 15. There was a commercial for toilet paper with a cartoon bear.

"Do you think this is at all tied to that waitress disappearing back in 1986?" Ryan asked.

"Possibly," Stephanie said, still eyeing the TV. "That reminds me. I have an address for the father. Mr. Jayne's working at an Episcopal church in Glenview. I confirmed it with someone there. He lives in the garage apartment behind the rectory."

"That's fantastic. What's the address?"

"No—no, forget it. I don't want you taking any chances. So far, they seem to think you've accepted the official story about what happened to your family. You don't want to tip them off you know something. Right now it's up for grabs how involved Barton Jayne is in any of this."

"Stephanie, I'll just go talk to him. He's there right by a church. What can happen? Besides, I can handle a guy in his seventies."

"Forget it. I'll fly out there and talk to him in a couple of days. If he's connected to these killers or being watched by them, it won't matter that I'm paying him a visit. They already have it in for me."

She had nightmares of reading online about a deadly fire at Rosanne Farrell's Highland Park home, claiming the lives of Ryan and his grandmother. Or perhaps it would look as if a burglar had killed them. Or maybe it would appear as if Ryan had copied his father in some sort of murder-suicide ritual.

"Let me handle things with Mr. Jayne," she said, looking at the TV again. It was another commercial, this time for fabric softener. "But first, I'm going to talk to Mark Metcalf."

"So what am I supposed to do, just sit here?" Ryan asked.

Stephanie saw the news come on the TV, and turned up the volume.

The two news anchors were an attractive blonde and a handsome man with a hint of gray at his temples. He wore a tan blazer and a blue striped tie. In him, Stephanie recognized the kid from the photo. He was announcing the lead story about a five-car pileup on Interstate 5, near the City Center.

Stephanie turned up the volume a bit louder. "Do

you hear that, Ryan?" she asked. "It's Mark Metcalf. I'm looking at him on TV right now . . ."

And he was just fifty-three minutes away.

Tuesday—6:31 P.M.
Seattle

"Mark, I've got a woman on line two," said Gail. The twentysomething associate producer had quietly stepped into the studio at the tail end of the broadcast. They'd just gone off the air. Mark and Debi were still at their news desk. "She won't give her name," Gail said, leaning on the desk. "But she's been on hold for the last five minutes. She insists on talking to you."

Mark got to his feet. "Could you take a message? Tell her I'm in a meeting with a news emergency, anything to get rid of her. Please?"

She sighed. "I'll try." Then she retreated into the darkness beyond the studio lights.

Mark just wanted to go home. He'd been getting a lot of calls and e-mails since his on-the-air flub last Friday night. It was a current YouTube favorite. No doubt that was why the woman had been holding for five minutes to talk with him.

He should have had Gail just tell the woman the truth. His emergency was a nine-year-old son at home with the stomach flu. He'd been with Danny while the boy threw up all morning. Mark had gotten some chicken soup and Saltines in him before leaving for the five o'clock broadcast. Alison had given up a night out with friends to babysit.

Ducking into the restroom, Mark took off his jacket,

tie, and shirt. At the sink, he washed off his makeup. It was just a light base, but he didn't like wearing it in the daylight when people might notice.

He dried his face with a paper towel. He was thinking if he got home before seven, Alison could still go out with her friends and be back by ten o'clock—in time to babysit again, so he could take off to do the eleven o'clock broadcast. At least Alison would have a couple of hours to unwind with friends. She was in summer school during the day with driver's ed, and repeating a chemistry class she'd failed last year. Then she had to be home to babysit her kid brother by four, so that he could make the five o'clock broadcast. She could have bitched and moaned and played the martyr about it, but she didn't. He wanted to give her a little break tonight.

His coworker, Jesse, stepped into the washroom. Today he wore plaid shorts and a T-shirt with Rocky and Bullwinkle on it. "Gail sent me in," he said. "You know that woman she had on hold earlier? Well, she ain't giving up. She's called back and she's holding again. She wants to talk to you, and get this—she has identified herself. She's Stephanie Coburn, and she wants to give you an exclusive interview."

Putting his shirt back on, Mark squinted at him. "Who's Stephanie Coburn?"

"Don't you remember anything I write down for you to read?" Jesse asked. "She's the dipshit pilot with Pacific Cascade Skyways, you know, the one who decided right before takeoff that hallucinogenic substances and flying a commercial jet full of passengers might not be a good mix."

"Oh, her," Mark said, buttoning up his shirt. "That happened when I was off for the week, remember?" They'd buried Dina that week.

Jesse sighed. "Sorry, Mark."

"Forget it," he said. "Anyway, I have no desire to talk with her."

"Well, she's offering an exclusive interview. And she's news."

"Yeah, well, the Kardashians are news, too. And I don't want to talk to any of them, either."

"It's an exclusive, Mark. It could go national. Gail's a sweetie, but she's got a big mouth. It's bound to get to the powers that be you passed on this. It's too soon after 'Seattle Shitty Council' to make another major blunder. They took that one pretty well, but you don't want to tick them off by turning down a high-profile story. You should at least hear her out."

"Okay, okay, I'll talk to her," Mark sighed. He grabbed his coat and tie.

"She's on line one."

Mark decided to take the call in his office.

Hanging up his coat and tie, he sat on the edge of his desk and reached for the phone. He pressed line one. "Hello, this is Mark Metcalf."

"Hi, my name's Stephanie Coburn," she said. "But then, I guess they already told you that. I'm sorry to bother you. I didn't really call to offer you an interview. I called because—well, my brother-in-law was Scott Hamner. Does that name mean anything to you?"

Mark didn't say anything. But for a few seconds he couldn't breathe.

"He was friends with Dick Ingalls—and Brent Farrell. Do you remember them?"

"Um, yes, I remember Dick Ingalls," he admitted. "He and his family were members at a country club where I worked for a couple of summers, back when I was in high school. But I didn't know him very well."

"You weren't friends with him?"

"Not really," he said. "We didn't even go to the same school. I worked as a valet at the club. I may have parked the Ingallses' car a few times. As for the other two, I'm sorry, I don't remember them."

"I came upon a picture of the four of you together," she said. "And I think it was taken at the club."

"Well, you're going back almost thirty years, so I won't refute you."

"If you weren't friends with them, why were you posing in this picture with them?"

"Lady—um, Stephanie, listen . . ." He got up and paced back and forth in front of the desk, stretching the phone cord. "I ended up in a lot of photos when I was working at that place—usually after someone asked me to snap a group shot. They'd turn around and tell me, 'Now you get in the picture,' and I'd end up posing with a bunch of strangers. I think it was people's way of being nice to the help. Anyway, I'm not surprised I'm in a photo from back then with some guys I hardly knew."

She didn't say anything.

Mark let out a long sigh. "If I was friends with these guys, I'd tell you. Now, what's this about?"

"All three of them are dead," she said.

Mark stopped pacing. He'd heard about Brent Far-rell killing his family and himself after some embezzling scheme had gone awry. He didn't know about the others.

"Their families were killed, too," she continued. "And in each case, it had something to do with their second wives. All of these men were widowers. Dick's first wife had a stroke. My sister—Scott's wife—slashed her throat. Brent's first wife hung herself. Two suicides. Do you see a pattern here? Didn't your wife kill herself?"

"My wife's death was an accident," he said steadily.

"I'm sorry," she said. "But you must believe me. I'm trying to help you. I think you and your family are in danger. Whoever's behind these deaths, they know I'm getting closer to finding the truth. They've been after me. They've tried to kill me. They drugged me before I got on the plane that day. Listen, you can check my background. I have an excellent flight record—and absolutely nothing in my history about drug or alcohol abuse. I'm in hiding right now, because these people want me dead."

"If you . . ." Mark hesitated, and chose his words carefully. "If you truly feel your life's in danger, you should contact the police. I'm sorry, I can't help you."

"Does the name Selena Jayne mean anything to you?"

Mark felt as if someone had just slugged him in the gut. "No, not really," he said.

"She was a waitress at the club the same time you were there."

"I didn't really mix with the waitstaff," he said. "I

was out front parking cars. They were inside serving food."

"She disappeared in August of 1986. Do you remember that?"

Mark hesitated. "That sounds familiar now. Yes, I—I recall hearing something about that. I really wasn't acquainted with her. Do you know if they ever found her?"

"No," she answered. "You're the only one from that photograph who's still alive. Can you think of any reason why someone would want to kill the others—and their families?"

"Well, since I hardly knew them, no, I can't think of a reason. I'm sorry I can't help you. Now, I'm extremely busy. I hope—you'll be all right. Good-bye."

Mark hung up the phone, and then rubbed his forehead with a shaky hand. He felt sick to his stomach. He grabbed his coat and tie, and hurried out of his office. He almost ran right into Jesse.

"Whoa, what happened?" Jesse asked, stepping back. "Do you get an exclusive?"

Mark quickly shook his head. "No. She's—she was after something else. She's crazy. If she calls again, I don't want to talk to her. Got that? Tell Gail to hang up on her."

He didn't wait for Jesse to respond. He hurried toward the stairwell and ran down the steps. *This can't be happening*, he thought. Were the others really dead? Was that Stephanie Coburn person on the level? Or had someone put her up to the call? He wondered if this had anything to do with those Father's Day cards he'd received every year.

Once he got home, he'd go online and look up what

had happened to the other guys. Could it really be true that Brent's and Scott's first wives had killed themselves? "I think you and your family are in danger," the woman had said. He hoped to God she was indeed crazy.

Mark rushed through the lobby and pushed open the glass door. It was a cool, cloudy night. He started for the parking lot.

"Mark?"

He stopped in his tracks and turned to gape at his new friend. "Hey, Jenny," he said, a little out of breath.

Smiling, she held up a bag that had "Top Pot Doughnuts" printed on it. "You ran right past me," she said. "I got you and your kids some breakfast treats for tomorrow morning."

He managed to smile back at her. "Well, thanks, that's awfully nice of you. But really, you shouldn't have, especially after the wine yesterday . . ."

She handed him the bag. "I hope you don't think I'm a stalker or anything."

"Well, if you are, you're a perfectly nice one."

When they'd met the other night, they'd ended up parked in front of her hotel, talking in his car for forty-five minutes. She'd noticed his wedding ring. "So—I guess you're off the market," she'd said.

He'd told her about Dina, and said he would probably be off the market for quite a while. He'd walked her to the hotel lobby door. She'd thanked him, kissed him on the cheek, and ducked inside.

Mark had been a tiny bit smitten. And he felt horrible about it. But he told himself he would never see her again.

Then to his surprise, she'd been waiting for him outside the station after the eleven o'clock show last night. She had a bottle of wine for him. "It's a thank-you present for coming to my rescue," she explained.

He offered to give her a ride back to the hotel, but she declined. Somehow, he wound up giving her a ride anyway, and sitting in the car with her for another twenty minutes—until Alison called saying Danny wasn't feeling well. She wanted to know when he was coming home.

It was kind of a reality check. Saying good-bye to her at the hotel lobby door, he'd shaken her hand. No kiss on the cheek.

He really hadn't expected her to turn up again tonight.

"You look like you're in a hurry," she said. "I won't keep you."

"Yes, my son's stomachache took a turn for the worse this morning. I need to get back home and make sure he's okay."

"Well, I guess doughnuts are about the last thing he needs right now." She let out a pitiful little laugh. "Good call, Jenny."

"He'll probably bounce back and be fighting his sister for them in the morning." Mark hoisted the bag up. "Anyway, thanks."

She started to walk alongside him to the car. "Let me know if you need a helping hand," she said. "I practically qualify as a nurse. I looked after my sick mother for two years. Plus the place I lived in in the Bay Area was full of senior citizens. Somehow they always came to me with their aches and pains. So—I'm pretty good in a crisis, Mark."

"You're sweet," he said, stopping in front of his Mustang. "Can I give you a lift back to the hotel?"

"No, thanks," she said, fishing into her purse. "It's a nice night and early yet. I'd like to walk. There are a lot of people out. I'll be all right." She pulled out a card and handed it to him. "I mean it about calling me if you need anything—help around the house, someone to babysit, you name it." She shrugged and glanced down at the pavement. "You'd be helping me out, too. Living at a hotel in a new city can be kind of lonely."

Mark glanced at the card with an arrow logo in beautiful colors:

JENNY BALLATORE
Website Design & Graphics
www.jennygraphics.com
510-555-2286

He tucked the card into his pocket, and then took out his car keys. "I may just take you up on that. Thanks again. G'night, Jenny."

Mark ducked inside his car. He felt bad for not sticking around to make sure she got back to the hotel all right. But it was still light out. Besides, he was too distracted and unnerved by that phone call to be decent company to anybody.

He started up the engine, waved at her, and then pulled out of the lot.

As he headed down the street, he could see her in his rearview mirror.

She was standing just where he'd left her, watching his car.

CHAPTER TWENTY-ONE

Tuesday, June 18—7:07 P.M.
Seattle

When traffic wasn't atrocious like tonight, he usually made it from the TV station to his house in West Seattle in about fifteen minutes. It was eight miles on the odometer, and yet home seemed so far away right now.

Mark nervously drummed his fingers on the steering wheel. He had to remind himself that even after he got home, hugged Alison, and checked in on Danny, it wouldn't change things. He would still have a woman out there asking questions about something he'd done twenty-seven years ago.

Merging onto the West Seattle Bridge, Mark thought back to when he was seventeen, and working as a valet at the Lake Ridge Country Club. He used to ride his bike to and from the club every day. That was an eight-mile trek, too. But it was worth it. On a busy day, he'd end up with over a hundred bucks in tips in his pocket. Some members there were premier snobs, and treated him like a peon. But most seemed to appreciate how he busted his ass for them.

"That Mark is a good kid. He's one hard worker. The way he's always on the go and running around, he's like shit at a pony show. He's all over the place."

That strange, albeit high praise came from one of the club's most influential members, Mr. Ingalls. Dick used to imitate his mogul lawyer dad and repeat the quote to Mark just to tease him. Mark didn't mind one bit. A letter of recommendation from Richard F. Ingalls could help get him into a good college—just as long as Mr. Ingalls didn't use that "shit at a pony show" reference. Dick's dad encouraged him and Dick to hang out together. Apparently, he thought Mark might be a good influence on his son.

"You weren't friends with him?" Stephanie Coburn had asked.

"Not really. We didn't even go to the same school."

But that summer of 1986, they weren't in school. And Dick didn't work, so he was at the club nearly every day—swimming in the pool, golfing, and getting into trouble. He was a cocky, good-looking guy with a rich and powerful dad. So people forgave him pretty easily—whether it was for driving a golf cart into a pond or for getting caught skinny-dipping with a girl after-hours in the club pool. And then there was that time he was discovered—once again with his pants off—on the golf course at midnight with a waitress from the club.

Dick would bring his pal, Brent Farrell, and a friend from Wisconsin, Scott Hamner, as his guests to golf or swim. They became the club's brat pack. Once Mark finished work, they'd invite him out with them. They'd take Mr. Ingalls's boat out, or they'd pool hop. There were drag races down Sheridan Road and impromptu late-night beer and bong parties down at Wilmette beach. For Mark, those were dangerous, giddy adventures. Most of the time, he was terrified they'd get in trouble, but he kept his mouth shut. Those summer nights partying with Dick and his friends sure beat pedaling home on his bike to a dinner his mother heated up for him.

Dick was a charmer. But he had a reputation for sleeping with a girl once or twice, and then wanting nothing to do with her. Even though they knew he was no good, girls at the club still gazed at him with adoring puppy eyes.

Mark knew what it was like to have an impossible crush. He looked at Selena Jayne the exact same way.

She had an angelic face and the body of a centerfold. The buttons along the top front of her waitress uniform always seemed ready to bust. She was so pretty, and so naively sexy—whenever she walked into a room, guys just stared.

Mark fantasized about her. But he kind of felt sorry for her, too. It seemed like she didn't have a very happy life.

Occasionally he was summoned into the dining room if a member needed something from their car. On these occasions, he'd see Selena waiting tables. He'd see the men leering and snickering. The wives would shake their heads and give their husbands a poke with their elbow. They all looked down on her or laughed at her. And sweet, trusting Selena just didn't get it.

Mark knew her enough to say hello. He lived for those rare moments they'd pass each other in or around the club. She always gave him a big smile and said hello back to him. After that, he'd get so tongue-tied, he couldn't say anything else.

One afternoon in mid-August, she said hello to him as he was punching in at the time clock. He managed to stammer a hello back.

"Your name is Mark, isn't it?" she said. "I asked around . . ."

"Yeah, hi, you're Selena, right?"

"Right." She touched his arm. "Hey, you seem like a really nice guy. And I hear you're friends with Dick Ingalls, too. Do you think you could introduce me to him sometime? Because I think he's super-cute . . ."

Mark did his damnedest to act like he hadn't just been shot through the heart. "Well, I—I guess so. If I get a chance to introduce you to him, I will. But I should warn you, Dick is kind of a love 'em and leave 'em guy. He's not what girls call *boyfriend material*."

That didn't discourage Selena, who introduced herself to Dick later that week.

"She asked me to take her to the movies on her night off," Dick told him. "I just need to make sure my old man doesn't hear about it—or her old man."

Dick's dad had chewed him out for having sex with that waitress on the ninth green. The girl even got fired for it. So although Dick used to joke about how much he wanted to lay Selena, he didn't want to push his luck going after another waitress from the club. Besides, Selena's groundskeeper father was a stern, scary, holy roller. Anyone messing around with his innocent little daughter was asking for trouble.

But when Selena asked him out, he just couldn't say no.

"Well, I hope you treat her nice," Mark said.

"You've got it bad for her, don't you?" Dick laughed. "Okay, I tell you what, I'll let you have her. She's yours. The two of us will take her out, maybe get her a little drunk, and then I'll split. You can take over from there." He poked his finger on Mark's chest several times. "But if you don't bang her, I'll be so pissed off. She's one fine piece of ass, and I'm giving her to you. Don't blow it, man."

Dick Ingalls was his hero for a few days. Mark didn't take him seriously about having to "bang" Selena. Mark didn't plan on that happening. And he certainly didn't want to take advantage of her while she was drunk. Besides, he was a virgin. He told himself he'd be happy to have a quiet talk with her and maybe they could neck a little.

Oh, who was he kidding? He really wanted her.

But he also wanted it to be special.

Dick had gotten Selena to agree to meet the two of them at a bus stop in Winnetka. Mark took it as an encouraging sign that she'd welcomed having him along on the date.

But when they pulled up to the bus stop in Dick's red Toyota Celica convertible, Mark was horrified to see Brent had shown up there in his mother's station wagon—with Scott in tow. They were flirting with Selena, and she was laughing. But she seemed uncomfortable, too. She looked pretty in her sleeveless, pale blue dress and sandals.

Brent announced they had two bottles of Jack Daniel's, a bottle of Annie Green Springs wine, and two six packs of Old Style.

Dick insisted they take a bottle of Jack Daniel's, "and Annie Green Springs for the lady." They cruised around for a while, with Selena sitting on Mark's lap in the front seat. He didn't mind that arrangement at all. Dick talked about losing Brent and Scott, who stayed on their tail. He sped up a few times, which seemed to get Selena pretty excited. She looked so beautiful with her hair blowing in the wind. Laughing and squirming, she kept her arms around him. She also took several gulps of the cheap wine, spilling some on him. Mark didn't mind that, either. But every once in a while, she'd reach over and touch Dick's shoulder. At one point, she even put her fingers through his hair and sighed.

That was when Mark started to feel like she was squishing him.

They never did lose the station wagon. Eventually, Selena announced she was starving. Dick gave the other two some money and sent them to Mustard's Last Stand. He was paranoid about being seen with a waitress from the club, even if she was on Mark's lap. So they parked in a church lot nearby and waited. It seemed odd he was worried about someone spotting them, and yet he drove all over with the convertible's top down. Then again, it was a beautiful warm night. And Dick drove fast. No one could have recognized Selena in the car while they were actually driving.

So many details about that night would later gnaw away at Mark. He would try to remember exactly where they'd gone, and wonder who might have seen them.

They ate at a picnic table at a deserted park near Tower Road Beach. Once they were out of the car and Selena was off his lap, Mark watched her latch onto Dick. And his friend did nothing to discourage her.

Dick was the one who suggested they go swimming. He knew a private beach in Glencoe, and said they'd have the place all to themselves.

As they were about to go back to their cars and head north to Glencoe, Selena broke away from Dick and walked over to Mark. He could tell she was a little tipsy. She gave him a shy smile, and kissed him on the cheek. "You're such a nice guy," she whispered. "Would you mind going in the station wagon—so I can be alone with Dick? You know how I feel about him . . ."

He didn't even try to smile back at her. "Sure, no problem," he murmured.

At that point, he was so tempted to ditch them, walk the mile to Green Bay Road, catch a bus to the club and then pedal home on his bike.

Instead, he'd climbed into the backseat of the station wagon and downed a few gulps of Jack Daniel's.

If only he'd ditched them.

Mark thought if there was one moment in his past he could take back, that would be it.

He tried to block it out of his mind as he headed down his street in West Seattle. He reached into the Mustang's console for the garage door opener. He pressed the button, and turned into his driveway. As the garage door opened, he carefully steered his Mustang into the very spot where Dina had killed herself.

"All three of them are dead," Stephanie Coburn had told him. "Their families were killed, too . . . All of these men were widowers . . . Didn't your wife kill herself?"

Grabbing the bag of doughnuts Jenny had given him, he climbed out of the car and let himself into the house. He locked the door behind him, though it somehow seemed so futile. He wished he could just turn a latch and forget the past. It was catching up with him.

All he could do for now was try to keep his kids safe.

He was home at last, but nothing had really changed. He still had a feeling of dread in the pit of his stomach. It was how Dina used to describe her premonitions.

And too many times, those premonitions had come true.

Tuesday—9:14 P.M.
Glenview, Illinois

Ryan pulled over in front of St. Paul's Episcopal Church on Harms Road. Stephanie hadn't given him the address, but it wasn't too tough looking up Episcopal churches in Glenview, and calling both of them to find out which one had a caretaker named Barton Jayne.

The church was an old stone edifice with a steeple. The red double doors were a fresh, bright contrast to the dull, dark backsides of the stained glass windows and all that gray stone. Along one side of the church was a small cemetery. With dusk hovering over the landscape, it looked a bit foreboding.

Ryan glanced toward the other side of the church— at a large Tudor house with a long driveway. An SUV and a sedan were parked there in the turnaround area. The garage was Tudor style, too, with a second-floor apartment. The lights were on in the windows.

Ryan climbed out of the VW. He was about to start down the driveway when he spotted an old man with an armload of flowers heading into the church by a side door. He was skinny with a full head of white hair. In his denim shirt and baggy, flat-butt jeans, he sure looked like a caretaker.

Hurrying toward the church, Ryan followed the man through the side door. Inside, it was dark and cool. Only a couple of low-watt spotlights were looming over the two sections of pews. Another dim light barely illuminated the altar. The old man was up there, changing the flowers in a pair of tall ornate vases on each side of the altar table.

The door clicked shut behind Ryan, and the sound seemed to echo in the cavernous church. With a bunch of flowers in his hand, the caretaker swiveled around to stare at him.

Ryan came up to the altar rail. "Excuse me," he said. Suddenly, he felt like he was talking too loud. "Um, are you Mr. Jayne?" he asked in a quieter voice.

The old man didn't nod or shake his head. "Who are you?"

"My name's Mark," Ryan lied. He noticed a bunch of old lilies on a towel, laid out on the stone-tiled floor. The caretaker had already replaced the flowers in one vase, and was about to fill the other. "My dad is Mark Metcalf . . ."

"That name doesn't mean anything to me," the man said. Then he went back to his work as if Ryan weren't there.

"Well, if you're Barton Jayne, I think my father might have known your daughter, Selena," Ryan said. "They worked together at Lake Ridge Country Club about thirty years ago. I guess you worked there, too."

Frowning, the old man impatiently pushed the flowers around in the vase in a clumsy attempt to arrange them. "The name still doesn't mean anything to me," he said. "But yes, I'm Barton Jayne, and I worked at that club for thirty-three years."

"Well, Dad was only there for a couple of summers. He was a valet, parking cars."

"I saw to it the grass was cut and minded my own business. I never got chummy with the summer help."

"Well, my dad knew your daughter," Ryan explained. "He didn't say as much, but I think he might have even gone out with her a couple of times."

"Selena didn't go out on dates," Mr. Jayne said. He bent down and carefully wrapped the old lilies in the towel. "She was busy working and looking after her little sister. She didn't have time for that nonsense. My daughter didn't go chasing after boys."

"But I understand she was very pretty. I'll bet the boys were chasing after her—I mean, even though Selena wasn't interested."

Mr. Jayne carried the bunch of old flowers in the towel as if he were holding a swaddled infant. Brushing past Ryan, he scowled at him. He had cold, dark brown eyes under white, bushy brows. "That's a filthy thing to say," he muttered. "Selena was a good girl."

"I'm sure she was," Ryan said, trailing after him toward the side door. "I'm sorry. I didn't mean to imply—"

"I don't see the point in dredging up this old sad business," Mr. Jayne said. "What do you want anyway?"

Ryan dashed in front of Selena's father and opened the door for him.

Mr. Jayne stepped outside and walked around the front of the church. Ryan caught up with him. "Sir, ever since my father told me about Selena and how she disappeared, I've been really interested in the case. I was wondering if they ever found out what happened."

"Nope," he said, looking straight ahead. He kept walking—toward the little cemetery.

As they passed through the open gates to the graveyard, Ryan could tell he wouldn't get anything from Selena's father. "Does—uh, does your other daughter live around here?"

He wove around the headstones. "Nope, Nicole's in Las Vegas. She works in a real estate office there."

"Would it be okay if I talked to her?"

"That's up to Nicole," he answered, coming to a stop at the last row of headstones near the graveyard's edge.

"Well, could I ask you for her phone number or e-mail address?"

"I'm not giving you my daughter's phone number," he grumbled. "You got a pencil and paper on you?"

Ryan shrugged and shook his head.

Mr. Jayne clicked his tongue against his teeth. "Here," he said, handing him the lilies wrapped in the towel. "Careful with these . . ." He pulled a pencil out of his shirt pocket. It was a short pencil, the kind golfers use to keep score. Ryan wondered if Mr. Jayne had helped himself to a supply from the country club. Jayne fished an old receipt out of his pants pocket. "What's your number? I'll give it to my daughter next time she calls. If she wants to get in touch with you, she will. Or maybe she won't. Like I said, it's up to her."

Awkwardly holding the smelly old flowers, Ryan dictated his cell phone number—slowly, so the old man could write it down on the little receipt in the palm of his bony, callused hand. Mr. Jayne was still scribbling when Ryan noticed it was starting to get dark out. He also noticed the dead gladiolas in a vase on the grave in front of him. Then he saw what was written on the tombstone:

SELENA MARIE JAYNE
1969–1986
Loving Daughter and Sister, Watch Over Us

"My God," he murmured. He nodded at the grave site. "So they—they found her body?"

Tucking the receipt back into his pocket, Mr. Jayne frowned at him. "The grave's empty," he said. "But I wanted her to have a piece of land—with a marker. They let me put this one here ten years ago." He took the flowers from Ryan. Then he knelt down, and pulled the dead gladiolas from the vase. Tossing them aside, he put the slightly wilted lilies in their place. Then he fussed with the flowers. He was probably trying to make them look like new.

Instead, they just looked sad.

"Can you make sure Nicole gets my phone number?" Ryan asked. "I'd really appreciate it."

"Yeah, sure," Mr. Jayne grunted, still rearranging the lilies.

"Thank you for your time, Mr. Jayne," he said, backing away.

Ryan turned and headed toward the cemetery gates. He took one last look over his shoulder at Mr. Jayne.

The mean old man looked so pathetic, setting wilted flowers on his daughter's empty grave.

Tuesday—8:10 P.M.
Seattle

Danny was feeling better. Sitting on the sofa, he ate his dinner off a TV table and watched his DVD of *Captain America* for the third time. Mark had made him a peanut butter and jelly sandwich and tomato soup.

Danny's older sister had been thrilled to get out of the house for a couple of hours. Mark told himself that she would be okay with her friends. One of them, with her mother driving, had swung by and picked up Alison about thirty minutes ago.

Mark had managed to squeeze in some Internet time in his study, enough to confirm what Stephanie Coburn had told him about the deaths of his three former friends. He'd known about Brent Farrell's death, but learning about the other two was a shock. Everything Stephanie Coburn had told him seemed to be true.

He hadn't had time to dig too deeply into how all

their first wives had died. But he was inclined to believe what Stephanie Coburn had said: a stroke and two suicides. Dina made it three suicides. Or were they really suicides? Was someone making them all widowers? Dick's wife had apparently died of natural causes. And his family was the first to die. Was it just a coincidence that Dick Ingalls was the one Selena had really liked? Was that the start of a pattern in which all of the others had to be widowers, too?

"I'm trying to help you," Stephanie Coburn had said. "I think you and your family are in danger."

Mark was now kicking himself for letting Alison go out. But her ride had arrived just as he'd sat down in front of his computer. He hadn't realized then just how credible the threat was.

For now, he stuck close to Danny. He didn't make himself any dinner. He couldn't eat a thing. He contemplated calling the station and reporting in sick. He didn't want to leave the kids alone tonight.

Getting up from the sofa, he walked up to the big picture window. He gazed out over the tops of trees at the Sound. The waning sunset reflected off the water's rippling surface. The beach was down there, but he couldn't see it from here.

Mark thought of that private beach in Glencoe, the one Dick Ingalls had known about. He remembered the drive there. He remembered taking a few gulps of Jack Daniel's in the backseat of Brent's mother's station wagon. In the front, Brent and Scott had Peter Gabriel's "Sledgehammer" blasting on the radio. They followed Dick and Selena in the convertible.

The private beach was on a secluded, tree-lined, dead-end street. Along the block, big, beautiful old homes were spaced far apart and set back from the road.

Dick parked halfway down the block. "I don't want to tip off any cops patrolling the area that we're using the beach," he explained when Brent pulled up along-side him. "Park in front of me, okay?"

Brent pulled the station wagon in front of them and switched off the engine. Mark got out of the car, and after a couple of tentative steps, he realized he was a bit drunk.

On foot, Dick and Selena led the way toward the end of the road. She was weaving slightly, too, and clinging to her half-empty bottle of Annie Green Springs. Meanwhile, Dick clung to her, copping a feel of her breasts as they headed toward a long driveway.

Trailing after them, Mark glimpsed a mansion be-yond the bushes and trees. He wished he were a little drunker, because he could still hear Selena giggling. He also heard Brent telling Scott, "I don't care if I have to settle for Dick's sloppy seconds, I'm getting some of that tonight."

Mark wasn't sure if he gave a damn anymore what they did. Maybe Dick would get her to take off her clothes, and at least then he'd see her naked. At this point, he figured he wasn't much better than the other guys.

A few steps into the driveway, Dick and Selena turned and cut through some hedges. "This is scary!" Selena declared over the sounds of twigs snapping and bushes rustling.

Mark followed them through the hedge to a crude path that wove downhill around trees and shrubs. It was so dark Mark could barely see where they were going. But he could smell the lake and hear the waves gently lapping on the shore.

"Lions and tigers and bears, oh my!" Selena sang out. Dick shushed her.

Blindly making his way down the slope, Mark kept thinking that at any minute, he could trip and fall into a ditch. His stomach was in knots. If this turned into a night of skinny-dipping, he didn't care about the guys. They'd had several bare-ass moonlight swims this summer. But he was nervous about getting naked in front of Selena. What if he got hard in front of her—and no one else did? How uncool would that be? And then there was cold-water shrinkage, which never seemed to affect Dick, damn him.

He forged on through the woods. Gradually, the trees thinned out, and he could see Dick and Selena ahead, arm in arm. He could see the lake. The ground beneath his feet had gone from rocky dirt to sand.

Selena let out a gleeful squeal. Mark emerged from the trees in time to see her kick off her sandals and run toward the water. Her blue dress and blond hair were blowing in the light breeze. The small waves washed over her feet, and she took another swig of Annie Green Springs.

Dick came up behind her, and grabbed the bottle. "Hey, that's enough," he said. "Save those lips for me . . ." Then he kissed her—a long, open-mouth, wet kiss.

Mark stared at them, and thought, *Hey, Dick, just curious. When exactly were you planning to take off and leave her alone with me?* Apparently, his friend had forgotten his magnanimous plans to set them up.

And where did he get that awful line? "Save those lips for me." Whatever, the cornball come-on sure worked like a charm on Selena. She was all over him.

At this section of the beach, there was just a narrow strip of dry sand between the wooded hill and the lake. But farther down, the shoreline grew wider, and an old, slightly lopsided concrete pier jutted into the water. Mark didn't see anyone else around.

He glared at Dick and Selena, still making out. He paid no attention to Brent and Scott, behind him. They were muttering to each other and cackling. He heard rustling sounds. Suddenly, both Brent and Scott ran past him naked.

Selena saw them and let out another shriek. Wide-eyed, she covered her mouth.

They both scurried into the water and dove in under the surface.

Mark plopped down in the sand and sat there.

Selena was giggling. Dick kissed her again, then broke away, and set the wine bottle in the sand. "C'mon!" he called to her. He shucked off his shirt, shorts, and briefs. He had one of those perfect bodies, with perfect tan lines.

Selena let out another little shriek as Dick strutted past her. In the water, he turned around and splashed her. She laughed, covered her eyes, and backed away. "You're a scandal!" she cried.

"Come on in," Dick urged her. "The water's fantastic! If you're shy, we'll close our eyes . . ."

"Well, you're certainly not shy!" she said.

The other two chimed in, trying to coax her into the lake. Dick turned to grin at him. "C'mon, Metcalf, get your ass in the water!"

"Mark's the only one here with any sense!" Selena said. "We're all going to get arrested!"

Frowning, Mark got to his feet, and stripped down to his boxer shorts. He didn't want to be with them, so he walked down the shoreline a ways, closer to the pier. At the last minute, he took off his boxers, and then ran into the water.

It didn't warrant a scream from Selena.

She was too busy taking off her dress, and making a big production out of it. "No peeking!" she called.

Mark swam out to deeper water. Cool and refreshing, it sobered him up a bit. His ears were clogged, so he couldn't quite hear what Selena was saying. But she was down to her white bra and blue panties. She seemed all nervous and fluttery while the guys encouraged her to take everything off.

Mark treaded water and watched as she turned her back to them and shed her bra. She tossed it aside. Covering her breasts, she turned around again—to wolf whistles and applause from the guys. She reached down for the Annie Green Springs, and took a gulp of courage. Mark got a glimpse of her breasts when she did this. Keeping his head above water and his eyes on Selena, he swam in a little closer to them.

He felt a little short of breath as he watched her wiggle out of her pale blue panties. She looked so beautiful in the moonlight. She let go with another scream, and then scampered into the lake. She started splashing Dick and the others. Brent dove underwater and did something to make her squeal again and recoil. But she was laughing.

After a while, Dick took her in his arms and kissed

her again. He felt her up, and she seemed to like it. The other two stood by and watched.

Dick handed her off to Scott, who kissed her. Then Brent got behind her and started rubbing against her. Suddenly, it got quiet, and they took turns kissing and fondling her. Selena seemed to enjoy all the attention.

After a few minutes, Dick turned toward him. "Well, get in here! What are you waiting for?" he called. "Isn't this what you wanted?"

It wasn't what he'd wanted. Yet Mark was turned on. He watched her hungrily kiss Dick Ingalls. Her breasts rubbed against his chest.

Mark slowly swam closer to them. He could hear her moaning now. Dick gently broke away from her and steered her toward him. Selena sort of glided into his arms. Her skin was taut, silky, and wet. Her nipples brushed against his chest as she wrapped her arms around him. This was the furthest he'd ever gone with a girl, bare skin touching bare skin. Under the water's surface, his cock was brushing against her thighs. He'd never had these sensations before. He couldn't believe it was really happening. Selena seemed a little out of it. But she kissed him. His lips parted against hers, and for a moment, Mark could pretend they were alone.

Then she pulled back and reached for Dick Ingalls again. He kissed her, and whispered something in her ear. He smirked at Mark and the other two. "Why don't you guys stay here and practice holding your breath underwater or something?" He and Selena started swimming toward the pier. "I'll give you a holler in a few minutes!" he called.

"Shit, I knew he'd get to her first," Brent muttered.

Mark swam toward deeper water again. He watched as Dick and Selena made their way to the shoreline. He could see them in the distance as they staggered onto the beach. Selena dropped onto the wet sand, and Dick climbed on top of her.

To his annoyance, Brent and Scott swam out near him.

After a few minutes, they heard her cry out.

"Shit, you don't think she's a virgin, do you?" Brent said, treading water.

"Well, if she was, she isn't anymore," Scott replied.

"I just got to have a piece of that . . ."

"Would you look at them go at it?"

Mark didn't want to look any more. And he didn't want to listen to these jerks. He ducked his head under the lake's surface and started swimming toward the beach. He wobbled over a few stones in the soft, wet sand as he made his way onto the shore. Shivering, he rubbed his arms to fight the chill. He shook off as much water as he could, and then went hunting for where he'd left his boxer shorts.

By the time he found the shorts and put them back on, he noticed Selena and Dick had moved to the pier. He wandered back to where he'd left the rest of his clothes. He found the Jack Daniel's bottle, which Brent or Scott must have brought along. It was about half full. Mark took a gulp, and it warmed him. He still had water in one ear and tried to shake it out.

So much for sex on the beach being really hot, he thought. He just felt cold, damp, and grubby with sand.

Scott emerged from the lake, looking sort of silly—

naked, tottering over the stones along the shore. "Where's the Annie Green Springs?" he asked, out of breath.

Mark wordlessly pointed to where Dick had set down the bottle. Then he glanced over at the pier again. It looked like Brent was on top of her now. Dick stood nearby watching them for a minute, and then he dove off the pier.

"Goddamn it," Mark said under his breath. He could almost forgive her for letting Dick do what he wanted with her. After all, she had a crush on him. But Brent? Sure, he was good-looking. Still, Mark had thought Selena was better than that. He was so disappointed in her. He wondered if she was doing it with Brent at Dick's urging. Was she really that anxious to please him?

Collecting the wine and some of his clothes, Scott headed toward the pier. He didn't bother putting anything on.

That was when Mark realized Scott was probably next. He'd be bragging about this to his friends in Wisconsin next week.

Brent wouldn't be bragging to anyone—unless it was about how quick he was. He looked like he'd finished after only a couple of minutes. He walked down to the shore and washed himself off with lake water.

Scott moved in on her. Selena sat up for a moment and drank some of the cheap wine. Then she was lying down again, and Scott maneuvered on top of her.

Mark plopped down on the sand and took another swig of Jack Daniel's. He heard water splashing and looked over to see Dick coming up from under the lake's surface. He shook water from his shaggy blond hair and swaggered toward Mark. "Let me have a snort of that," he said, holding out his hand for the whiskey bottle.

Dick's unshrinkable penis was right at eye level. Rolling his eyes, Mark turned his head away as he passed him the bottle. Dick took a drink, and then sat down on the sand beside him. "You're next," he said, slapping a wet hand on Mark's shoulder. "She's saving the best for last."

"I really don't think I'm up for it," he admitted. "This night didn't exactly turn out like I thought it would." He glanced over toward the pier again. Scott and Selena were still going at it. About halfway down the beach, Brent was standing naked and peeing into the bushes.

"I told her that you liked her—a lot," Dick said.

"When did you tell her that? Right after you screwed her?"

"No, stupid, I told her in the car. She was happy to hear it, too. I shit you not. She thinks you're a *real gentleman*."

"So what?" Mark grumbled. He picked up a stone and hurled it into the lake. "You're the one she's hot for. She's probably doing all this just to please you."

"Yeah, well, I'm not interested in her anymore. I mean, been there, done that." He took another swig of whiskey and shrugged. "So I guess it's up to you to help her get over me."

He nodded toward the pier.

Mark followed his gaze and noticed Scott was standing up now, signaling him. "C'mon, Mark! She's asking for you!" he called.

Mark turned to Dick, who was grinning at him. "You heard the man. She wants you . . ."

Getting to his feet, he gathered up his clothes—along with Selena's blue dress, her bra, and her panties. Heading toward the pier, he passed Brent Farrell, going in the opposite direction. Brent said something to him. Mark tuned him out.

Dick's friend from Wisconsin was at the shore end of the pier, in his briefs and a T-shirt. His jeans were tucked under his arm. As they passed each other, Scott slapped him on the back.

Mark ignored him and continued down toward the end of the pier, where Selena lay naked. He had every intention of being the *gentleman* she thought he was. But almost involuntarily, he stopped and stared at the beautiful contours of her body, the round breasts and the subtle movement of her flat stomach as she breathed in and out. Trembling, she gazed up at the starlit sky—and then at him. This close, Mark could see her eyes lacked focus. She didn't look like she was having a good time at all. He imagined the concrete beneath her had been rough and cold.

"Are you okay, Selena?" he whispered. He dropped his own clothes, and then showed the dress to her. He swept some of the sand off it. "I brought you your things. You can get dressed if you want. I—I just want you to know, I'm not like those other guys. I really liked you—I still do. And I want to be with you," he shook his head, "only not this way."

She sat up, and took another swig of the wine.

Getting down on one knee beside her, Mark tried to hand her the bra and panties. But she didn't take them.

Her hand moved to the center of his chest. It was cold and scratchy with sand. Her fingers traced a line down to his navel, then beyond. She tugged at the front of his shorts and kissed him on the mouth.

Mark shuddered gratefully at her touch. She pulled him on top of her. "Are you okay?" he whispered. "Am I squishing you?"

She didn't say anything. Her hands moved up and down his back. She squeezed his buttocks.

He kissed her face while she guided him inside her.

Mark couldn't stop shaking. He hadn't expected this to happen. He was scared—and at the same time, incredibly turned on. "Is this okay?" he whispered in her ear.

She didn't respond. But he thought he heard her crying.

He pulled back to look at her face. She had tears in her eyes, and she was grimacing.

"Are you all right?" he asked. "Selena?"

Mark heard someone snicker. He glanced over toward the shore end of the pier and saw Brent Farrell—with his clothes back on. He stood there, watching them. "That's it, nail her, man," he said.

Mark was about to scream at him to get lost. But suddenly something smacked him along the side of his head. It hurt like hell, and he saw spots. Stunned, Mark tumbled off Selena.

Past a loud ringing in his ear, he could hear her crying again. He realized she'd hit him.

"I'm sorry!" he said automatically. He pulled up his boxer shorts. "Did I hurt you? Are you okay?"

"What the hell's going on?" someone yelled.

Mark reached out for her, but Selena slapped his hand away and started screaming. She leapt to her feet, but lost her balance and fell.

The other three were running down to the end of the pier. Dick had put on his briefs, and he was in front of the other two. "What happened?" he yelled, out of breath. "Selena?"

"Leave me alone!" she shrieked, standing up again. She must have found a small stone on the pier. She hurled it at him. "Stay away!"

"Ah, fuck!" Dick growled, recoiling. He brought his hand up to his forehead.

"What the hell?" Brent yelled. He lunged toward her. He and Scott tried to grab her arms. Naked, she frantically fought them off. She was like a crazy person.

"You're scaring her!" Mark cried. "Just leave her alone!" He tried to pull Brent away from her.

All at once, Selena reeled back and fell off the pier.

Mark heard the splash as her body hit the lake—and almost at the same time, a dull thud.

One of the guys—either Brent or Scott—started laughing. "What the fuck, man?"

Mark bolted to the edge of the pier and gaped down at the water. He didn't see her. A small concrete shelf jutted out from that side of the pier. Mark wondered if she'd hit her head on it. "Selena?" he called. His heart pounded furiously.

He thought he saw some air bubbles come to the lake's silver-black surface. He dove in. It was too dark to see anything underwater, but he hoped maybe her body was white enough that he'd spot her. He blindly swam around under the surface until he couldn't hold his breath any longer. He came up and gasped for air.

From the pier's edge, his three friends numbly stared down at him.

"Do you see her?" Mark yelled, still trying to get a breath.

Scott shook his head. The other two just stood there.

"Jesus, what's wrong with you guys? Help me!" He plunged under the surface again, swimming around the concrete jetty. He thought maybe she'd been knocked unconscious and ended up under the little ledge.

There was a loud splash. Mark came up for air again, and saw Dick had joined in the search. "What happened? What did you do?" Dick asked, treading water.

"Nothing!" Mark cried. "She just freaked out on me . . ." He anxiously looked around. He kept thinking it was way too long for her to stay underwater. She was drowning—if she wasn't dead already. *Please, God*, he thought, *please, let her be okay . . .*

Dick ducked his head back under the water and swam around the pier. He finally popped up again. "This is fucking impossible," he gasped. "Where'd she go?"

Mark kept hoping against hope they'd hear her giggling, and she'd be on the other side of the jetty. He looked up at the other two. "Do you guys see her *anywhere*?"

Scott shook his head.

"Listen, go up to one of those houses and bang on the door. Get them to call the police—an ambulance."

But neither of them budged. "Jesus, we're screwed," Brent whispered.

Dick kept searching in the water.

"Would one of you idiots go call the police, for God's sake?" Mark yelled. Then he dove under the surface again. With his hands, he felt around the sides of the pier, trying to find a crevice or niche in which she'd been caught. He felt rough concrete, slimy seaweed, and barnacles. Somehow he knew the search was in vain.

He kept having to stop and bob up for air. On the fifth time up, he swallowed some water and went into a coughing fit. He thought he was going to choke to death. His arms suddenly felt like lead. He tried to stay afloat, but it felt as if something were dragging him down.

Suddenly Dick grabbed him and pulled him toward the shore. "Give it up, man," he said, panting. "We're never gonna find her . . ."

Mark was still coughing when they reached shallow water. Though he still felt shaky, he managed to stand up. Dick repeatedly slapped him on the back until his lungs cleared and the hacking stopped.

He nodded to his friend, "Thanks." Then he spotted Brent and Scott waiting for them on the shore. Mark couldn't believe neither one of them had gone for help yet. "We gotta call the police," he said, as soon as he caught his breath.

Dick shook his head. "We can't. How's it going to look?"

"I don't care how it looks! There's still a chance—"

"If she's in the lake, she's dead. No one could last underwater that long."

"That's exactly why we have to get the police . . ."

"Calling the cops right now isn't going to save her, Mark. What the cops will find is a dead girl all of us just screwed. They'll figure that out when they examine her body, and they'll think we raped her. They'll think we raped her and killed her. That crazy old man of hers is going to insist we did . . ."

"Let's get out of here, for Christ's sake!" Scott called from the shore.

"We can't just leave," Mark said.

"Yes, we can," Brent shot back. "No one's going to miss her."

Mark couldn't fathom how callous he was. "Good God, what's wrong with you people?"

"Listen to me," Dick said, grabbing his arm and pulling him toward the shore. "We could all end up in jail for this. Going to the cops is not an option. Even if, by some miracle, they don't think we raped her, this is going to be news. This is the kind of shit that will follow us around the rest of our lives . . ."

Mark kept shaking his head. It wasn't right. They couldn't shrug off responsibility for this. Talk about the rest of their lives. This thing would be hanging over their heads forever. How could they expect to live with themselves knowing they didn't do anything?

He and Dick staggered ashore. Scott handed Dick his clothes. "Why'd she go nuts like that?" he asked.

"She was having a good time until Metcalf started pounding away at her," Brent said.

Mark suddenly lost all control. He flew into a rage. "You asshole!" he screamed, lunging at Brent.

Dick grabbed him from behind before he could get a punch in. Still, Brent fell down on his ass. "Stupid son of a bitch," Brent bellowed, kicking sand at him. "What the hell is wrong with you?"

Everyone started yelling and talking over one another. Mark had tears in his eyes. He wanted so much to punch Brent's face in. Dick was still holding him back.

"Shut up, all of you!" Dick hissed finally. "You're making so much noise, we won't have to call the cops. Somebody's gonna call them for us. Now, chill out. Brent, take Scott back to my place, will ya?" He turned to his friend from Wisconsin. "You got the house key, right?"

Scott had the key. He picked up Dick's clothes, and handed them to him again. He asked about the bottles of booze and Selena's things.

"We'll take care of it," Dick said, finally letting go of Mark. "You guys get out of here, and keep your mouths shut. Don't let anyone see you leaving. Keep your headlights off while you're going down the block. Wait until you hit Sheridan Road to turn them on. Scott, if anyone's awake at home, and they ask where I am, I'm dropping off Mark. And we all went to Eden's theater and saw *The Untouchables* tonight. Got that?"

Once Brent and Scott had ducked into the thicket and started up the trail, Dick got dressed. He gathered up Mark's clothes and handed them to him. "C'mon, snap out of it. You look like a goddamn zombie. We need to get out of here . . ."

While Mark put on his clothes, he kept looking out at the lake for some sign of Selena. He didn't want to leave until they found her.

Dick went to work collecting the Jack Daniel's and

Annie Green Springs bottles. He said they should leave Selena's sandals where she left them. They would leave her dress, bra, and panties there on the pier, too. Once her body was discovered, they'd find the clothes nearby and maybe assume it was an accidental drowning. None of the clothes were torn. It would look like she'd undressed herself. And after all, she had.

Dick was already talking about how they needed to make sure their asses were covered. He said Selena had sworn to him she hadn't told a soul about their date. And while they'd cruised around the neighborhoods, no one would have been able to identify Selena as the blond in the car with them. They could say it was some bimbo they'd picked up hitchhiking. No one had seen them in the church lot or the deserted park. And no one had seen them coming down here.

Mark was impressed at how Dick had taken control of things earlier. He seemed to be so sharp in his thinking, too. But it was all self-preservation. There didn't seem to be a single thought about the poor, simple, lovesick girl who had just wanted to go on a date with him.

Mark tried once again to convince him that calling the police was the right thing to do—even if it got them into deeper trouble.

"No way, man," Dick said, clutching the booze bottles to his chest. "Ever stop to think that from the look of it, what Brent said is true? You're the one she freaked out on. I'm not saying you did anything. I know you couldn't have. But that's how it happened. And that's what all three of us will have to tell the cops."

"She freaked out on you, too," Mark muttered. "Remember? In fact, your forehead's still bleeding."

Dick winced as he touched his temple along the hairline, where Selena had thrown the rock at him. "Listen," he sighed. "There's still a chance—a decent chance—she swam to the shore without any of us noticing and she's hiding in those woods somewhere right now, just waiting for us to go. Let's face it, she's a strange girl. I wouldn't put it past her. That's another reason not to call the police. If she's hiding there somewhere, do you think she wants that? With that crazy old man of hers, do you know what kind of trouble you could get her into if the cops were in on this?"

Mark wanted to believe him. He wanted to think that tomorrow he'd see Selena punching the time clock at the club, and she'd be so embarrassed. She'd show him the bruise on her elbow from when she'd hit the concrete shelf that jutted out from the pier. And she'd say how drunk she must have been to act that crazy.

"C'mon, let's get out of here," Dick said, nodding toward the path in the woods.

Mark took one last look at the small beach. "Selena!" he called.

Dick shushed him. "Goddamn it, Mark," he whispered.

He waited and listened for an answer. But all he heard was the waves gently lapping on the shore. In the distance, he noticed some movement on the pier. But it was just Selena's blue dress, fluttering slightly in the breeze.

They hardly said a word to each other in the car. He and Dick rode with the top up. On the floor of the passenger side, he found a little coin purse that belonged to Selena. Dick said he would get rid of it.

Dick dropped him off at the club. Mark didn't go home. Instead, he pedaled seven miles north, back to that private beach in Glencoe. He made his way down the dark, wooded trail to the lake. He didn't know what he'd expected to find.

What he didn't find were Selena's sandals. There was no sign of her dress, bra, or panties, either. He searched all along the shore—in case the wind had blown them into the water. Someone or something had taken her things away. He prayed Dick was right. Maybe she'd been hiding from them all along.

He never fell asleep that night. At work the next day, he was dead tired and slightly hung over. The only thing that kept him going was the hope he'd see Selena there. But she never showed up for work. Two days later, the police interviewed some people at the club about her disappearance. They didn't talk to Mark.

They didn't talk to Dick, either. He'd phoned Mark that Saturday to tell him he hadn't heard anything and no one had asked him anything. "So please, keep your mouth shut, okay?"

"Did you go back to the beach that night?" Mark asked him, thinking he might have made off with Selena's things.

"No. Why? Did you?"

"No," Mark lied.

That was the last time Dick ever called him. Mark didn't see him again, except in passing at the club. Then they just nodded politely at each other—and after a while, not even that. He never saw Brent or Scott again. The club's brat pack had dissolved.

There was an article in the *Chicago Tribune* about

Selena's disappearance, and some talk at the club that she'd run away. Her body was never found. The sad, strange thing was that Brent had been right with his callous remark.

No one really seemed to miss her.

Mark saw his own reflection as he gazed out his living room window. The sun was setting over Puget Sound. He had to leave for the station in about an hour.

With the remote, Danny put *Captain America* on pause. "Hey, Dad," he said, glancing over his shoulder at him. "Could I have one of those doughnuts now?"

Working up a smile, he moved back to the sofa and sat down next to him. He mussed his son's hair. "Better not push your luck, kiddo," he said. "You could still have a little bit of that stomach bug. Wait until morning, okay?"

Danny sighed, and then squinted at him. "That lady who bought us the doughnuts, is she your girlfriend?"

"No, she's just a very nice lady," Mark said.

Danny pressed the remote, and the DVD started again.

Mark couldn't focus on the movie. He was still thinking about Dick Ingalls, Brent Farrell, and Scott Hamner—and that night on the beach twenty-seven years ago. He was the only one left alive from that night. But then he thought of Selena, and wondered.

Maybe he wasn't the only one still alive after all.

CHAPTER TWENTY-TWO

Parked across the street from Stephanie Coburn's hotel, he sat at the wheel and dined on a Whopper, fries, and a Coke. The lady pilot had thought she'd given him the slip this afternoon. But he'd stayed on her tail—all the way to the Airport Executive Inn. He even knew what room she was in: 149. Right now, she had the curtains closed, but he could still see a sliver of light between them.

He really wasn't paying too much attention to the hotel right now. His iPhone was propped up on the rental car's console. It had a live feed from the cameras in the bunker. He was watching his captive in her quarters buried beneath the earth, nineteen hundred miles away.

Though the picture quality wasn't worth shit, he still got a little thrill whenever she changed her clothes or took a shower. Right now, she was sitting on the sofa, watching TV. But in about ten minutes, it would be lights-out, and she'd be getting ready for bed. She'd dropped some of her initial shyness, and often seemed to forget about the cameras. He'd seen her peel down to nothing for her shower or to change into her flannel nightgown. But once in a while she'd seem to remember she was being watched. Then she'd grab something to cover herself, and flip him the bird. He always got a kick out of that.

He had a feeling he was going to miss this one when her time was up. Scarface was a feisty little bitch— smart, too. She seemed to know she was all alone there. She'd faked a seizure a while back, and he'd almost fallen for it. Had he been at the Cedar Rapids house at the time—and not here in Portland—he might have gone down to the bunker to investigate. She was quite the little actress.

He wasn't worried about her escaping. There was no escape. Only one of the five women imprisoned down there had gotten out ahead of schedule. She was the first. Her name was Karla, a very hot-looking redhead. It was hard not taking advantage of that, which he did several times. She'd been in the bunker for five weeks while the new Karla prepared to meet her future husband.

They had a camera in the bunker's bathroom, but the steam from the shower always made it pretty useless after a couple of minutes. One day after he'd gone down into the bunker, knocked her out, and did what he wanted, Karla killed herself. She'd gone into the restroom to take a shower. He wasn't watching when a wet, naked Karla managed to unscrew the light above the shower stall and stick her finger in the socket.

His partner had been furious. They had to start all over again, and find another girl to take Karla's place. That was Vanessa, the one they killed in the Lake Geneva house fire.

He nibbled on a fry and watched his current prisoner, who was still curled up on the sofa. He imagined she missed having her cat in her lap while she watched TV. That lousy cat had the run of the Cedar Rapids house right now. It had enough food and water to last for several days. He'd grown fond of the little stinker— an orange tabby with a thick red plastic collar, probably for fleas or something.

When it came time for Jenny to die, he would tell his partner he wanted to keep the cat. If they were torching the family house this time, did they really need a charred cat in there with all the other bodies?

It was about a minute before lights-out in the bunker. He watched as Jenny finally climbed off the couch. She pulled her long-sleeve T-shirt over her head.

He stopped eating his Whopper for a moment to watch her.

The phone rang.

"Damn it," he muttered. Grabbing the iPhone, he switched modes. "Yeah, what's going on?" he said.

"I'm calling to ask you the same thing," she replied. "How's our lady pilot doing? Still breathing?"

"Not for long," he said. He reached for another French fry and ate it. "I'm taking care of her tonight. I stole the key card from one of the maids this afternoon. So breaking in should be a cinch, unless she's got the dead bolt on the door. She'll go just like her sister.

They'll find her in the tub. I even got the pack of razor blade cartridges from her closet at home. I just need to crack it open and get the blade out."

"And what if she has the dead bolt on the door?"

"Then it's Plan B. I got her Lexus wired to blow when she starts it. The house is set up the same way. I hid all the charges this afternoon when she was out picking up the car. I went back two hours ago and set the motion detectors by the doors and front French windows. The next person to walk through one of those doors will trigger it. So if she goes home, she *goes*." He chuckled. "Of course, I'm banking on Plan A. It's more the hands-on type of work I like. If I pull it off, it'll only take about five minutes to unwire the car—and maybe twenty to unwire the house. All that stuff's expensive, and I know how you hate to waste good equipment. So—we're covered."

"Fine," she said. "Once she's out of the way, I need you to head back to Cedar Rapids and get our package ready for extraditing. Things will be reaching their conclusion within the next few days. I'm moving into the house tomorrow night."

"That's fast work. Don't you usually marry them first?"

"Not this time. Something's come up. We have to accelerate things. How soon do you think you can get her to Seattle?"

"I need to make sure the Winnebago's up for the trip. Can you give me three days?"

"Yeah, that'll work," she said. "Just take care of our pilot friend tonight, once and for all, okay? Then you can fly back to Iowa in the morning."

"Consider it done."

"Talk to you tomorrow," she said. Then she hung up.

He clicked off, and then switched over to the live feed from the bunker in Cedar Rapids. It had changed over to the infrareds, so he could still see her in the dark. The image was in heavy gray-green hues and slightly blurred. She was already in bed—damn it.

He finished up his Whopper and fries and shoved the wrappers back in the Burger King bag. With the straw, he sipped the last of his Coke—until it started to make that rattling vacuum noise with the ice. He tossed the debris out his window, giving it a good arc so it went out toward the middle of the road. Then he reached for a lidded ice bucket on the floor in front of the passenger seat. He'd stolen it from the housecleaning room when he'd lifted the key card. Inside the ice bucket were several mini-bottles of booze, the kind airlines use. There was also a container of over-the-counter sleeping pills.

From beneath his seat, he took out a gun. He tucked it inside the waist of his jeans and pulled his shirttail down to cover it.

Stepping out of the car, he carried the ice bucket across the street and cut through the Airport Executive Inn's parking lot. He used a side door into the hotel.

He had it all planned. He would let himself into her room and pull the gun on her before she had a chance to do anything. He'd force her to take the sedatives, swallowing them down with the booze. Once she was sufficiently out of it, he'd undress her, carry her to the tub, and slash open her wrists. Or maybe he'd just go for the throat—like he did with her sister. It was quicker. He'd decide later, depending on how sedated she was and how long he felt like sticking around.

He passed a large, gray-haired woman—obviously a hotel guest—in the corridor. He smiled and nodded at her. With the bucket tucked under his arm, he looked like he was just stepping out of his room for some ice.

The hallway was dimly lit, with a beige and hunter-green carpet. Heading toward room 149, he fished the key card out of his pocket. Just then, a man in sweat-pants and a T-shirt stepped out of room 152. He had an ice bucket, too. "Hey, which way is it?"

"Thataway," he muttered, using his thumb to point down the hallway.

"Thanks," the man said, heading in that direction.

He kept moving, passing room 149 and ducking around a corner toward a stairwell. He waited a few minutes. The guy from 152 finally returned with his ice, stepped inside his room, and shut the door.

He listened to the lock click. Then he crept back toward room 149. He was banking on it being too early for her to have gone to bed. So chances were good she hadn't set the extra security lock yet.

He glanced up and down the hallway, and then slid the card into the lock. The little green light went on above the lever. He quietly opened the door, stashed the card back in his pocket, and reached for his gun. He didn't hear a sound in the room. The lights were on. Over on the bed, a pillow had been placed against the headboard—as if someone had been sitting there. A pizza box was on top of the wastebasket and a Diet Coke can sat on the desk. The room had been occupied, but no one was here now. There wasn't even any luggage. The bathroom door was open, and it was dark in there. He switched on the light, and checked behind the shower curtain—just to be sure.

He couldn't believe it. The bitch had given him the slip.

Tucking the gun back inside his pants, he skulked out the door, and then hurried down the hallway to the side exit. Her Lexus was still in the parking lot. Hell, he would have heard the blast if she'd tried to drive off in it.

Baffled, he shoved open the door and stepped out-side. Had she snuck out and caught a taxi down the road a piece? Or had she simply switched rooms?

He stood in the hotel parking lot with the ice bucket under his arm. He remembered one of the last things his partner had said to him before hanging up the phone several minutes ago: "Just take care of our pilot friend tonight, once and for all."

He was determined as hell not to let her down.

And there was always Plan B.

The hotel desk clerk was very apologetic when Stephanie called to report that she'd spotted a bedbug under her pillow. She'd insisted on switching to a room on the other side of the hotel. He'd been very accom-modating. When she came by the desk to pick up the key card for her new room, she saw that the clerk was a handsome, thirtysomething black man with a thin mus-tache. He suggested that rather than lug her bags to the opposite end of the hotel, she load up her car and drive around to the entrance on the north side.

Stephanie thanked him for the advice. But she really had no intention of moving her car. In case someone was watching the hotel, she didn't want to let on that she'd switched rooms. She'd decided while eating her pizza that after all her narrow escapes, maybe an unscheduled room switch would be a wise precaution.

She didn't tell any of this to the desk clerk. But she asked if he was working the front desk for the rest of the evening.

"Yes, ma'am," he nodded.

"Could you do me a favor? Please don't tell anyone I switched rooms." She took a twenty-dollar bill from her purse and set it on the counter. "If someone phones and asks for me, go ahead and put it through. But I won't be picking up. So—let it ring or offer to take a message, whatever you usually do. Just, please don't let on that I switched rooms." She slid the twenty toward him. "Okay?"

He smiled at her and pushed the bill back at her. "No problem, Ms. Coburn. I'll be happy to do that for you."

"Thank you," she said, stashing the twenty back in her purse. "Listen, if someone does call or they come in and ask for me, could you call my room, let it ring once, and then hang up?"

He nodded. "One ring . . . kind of a signal, right?"

"Exactly, then I'll know to call you back."

"Can I ask you something?"

Stephanie hesitated. She figured he was going to ask if someone was chasing her. "Sure," she said finally.

"Is the bedbug story really true?"

She sighed and shook her head. "I'm sorry. I just really needed to get out of that room."

He nodded and smiled. "I'm glad we don't have bedbugs. You can leave your key card in the old room when you leave."

In her new quarters, she unpacked a few things, but still didn't feel settled in. She doubted she could feel settled anywhere until all of this was over with.

She phoned Ryan, and told him about her frustrating discussion with Mark Metcalf. "He says he barely knew Dick Ingalls from the country club, and doesn't remember posing in that picture with him, your father, and my brother-in-law. As for knowing Selena Jayne, he claims he didn't mix with the waitstaff. And he was adamant that his wife's death was an accident."

"Yeah, she accidentally parked her car in the garage, shut the door, and left the motor running," Ryan said. "Right."

"He hung up on me," Stephanie said. "I called the station back a couple of times and got the royal brush-off from whoever's answering the phone. He's putting up walls. I think I'll fly to Seattle in the morning. Maybe I can get through to him if I can talk to him in person . . ."

"Yeah, after all, it worked like a charm on me." Ryan said.

"Wiseass," Stephanie said, cracking a smile, her first of the day. "So—did you talk to Mr. Jayne?"

"You told me not to."

"Yeah, but something tells me you went looking for him anyway. Am I right?"

"Okay, yeah, I talked to him," Ryan sighed. "He's a grumpy old fart, but kind of sad, too. I didn't get anything from the guy. I gave him my phone number and asked him to pass it along to Selena's sister."

"So—now he knows your name?" she asked, pacing around the hotel room.

"I told him I was Mark Metcalf, Junior. Anyway, I'm hoping the sister can tell me something."

"Nicole?"

"Yeah," Ryan said. "She's in Las Vegas."

"I wouldn't hold your breath waiting for her to call you."

"I know. So—in the meantime, tonight I started googling the hell out of Mark Metcalf, KIXY-TV News, and I found a photo of him that was from his daughter's Facebook: "Alison Metcalf, 16, West Seattle High School, Favorite Movie: *Perks of Being a Wallflower*, Favorite Book: *To Kill a Mockingbird*, Favorite Band: Fleet Foxes." She's currently taking driver's ed and repeating a chemistry class in summer school, and she hates it. She's very cute in her Facebook picture. I could nab one of those Travelocity bargain fares and meet you in Seattle. If you can't get through to her old man, maybe I could infiltrate from within the family."

"Are you crazy? We know Mark Metcalf is next on their list. That means right now they're probably keeping close tabs on him, his house, and his family. If they see you anywhere near his daughter, they'll know you're on to them. You'll be writing your own death sentence. You and your grandmother are reasonably safe right now, because they don't think you know anything. So just stay put, and don't rock the boat, okay?"

He sighed. "All right, I won't do anything."

"I can just see you within seconds after we hang up," Stephanie said. "You'll be online looking up cheap fares to Seattle. Listen, don't push your luck the way I did. You still have some family left with your grandmother, and you have your friend, Billy. You're not hiding in some hotel, constantly looking over your shoulder. I stuck my neck out and now look at me. I'm all alone here. I don't have any friends I can turn to—"

"I'm your friend," he said. "You're not alone."

Stephanie smiled and sat down on the edge of the bed. "Thanks," she said. "I needed to hear that. Thanks, Ryan . . ."

After they hung up, Stephanie switched on the TV for background noise and company. The hotel had a gym, but she didn't dare step outside her new room unless it was absolutely necessary. She didn't even want to go out for ice.

She double-checked the security bolt to make sure she'd put it in place, and then started to undress for a shower. She was down to her bra and panties when her room phone rang—just once.

She automatically put her blouse back on. Then went to the phone and dialed the front desk. He answered after two rings: "Front Desk, this is Jonah."

"Hi, Jonah, this is Stephanie in room 107."

"A man just phoned, asking if you'd checked out or switched rooms. I told him, 'not to my knowledge,' and offered to take a message. I hope I did all right . . ."

"Yes, thank you very much," she said, sitting down on the bed again. She told herself to breathe. She'd figured they might have managed to stay on her tail this afternoon. That was why she'd switched rooms. She'd prepared for this.

"Ms. Coburn?" he said. "Did you want to hear the message?"

"You mean he left one?" she murmured. "He didn't just hang up?"

"He said to tell you he was sorry he missed you . . ."

She let out a sad, little laugh.

"And he wanted me to be sure to tell you that Scott called." The desk clerk paused—as if he needed to read the next part, "And that 'he, Rebecca and the kids will see you real soon.' "

Stephanie felt her throat tighten up, and tears welled in her eyes.

"He had me read it back to him to make sure I got it right," the desk clerk said. "Is there anything else, Ms. Coburn?"

"Just if he calls back tonight," she said in a shaky voice, "please, tell him you weren't able to get ahold of me. Tell him I didn't get the message. Will you do that for me?"

"Certainly," he replied.

"Thank you very much," she said. Then she hung up the phone.

She had a feeling he wouldn't be calling back tonight.

She'd gotten his message. And the son of a bitch probably knew it.

The alarm went off at 4:15 A.M. Stephanie shut it off, and then sat up in bed.

She'd had an awful night of tossing and turning. The last time she'd looked at the clock radio on the hotel room nightstand, it had read 1:08 A.M. Rubbing her forehead, she threw back the sheets and staggered out of bed to the bathroom. As she brushed her teeth, Stephanie cringed at her pale, haggard reflection. She told herself at least she was still alive.

She figured they were watching the hotel and her car. So after getting dressed, she phoned for a taxi and asked them to pick her up at the side entrance to Midge's 24-Hour Steak & Pancake House, next door to the hotel. With her bag, she slipped out the side door and made her way through the parking lot to Midge's. Standing by the restaurant's employee entrance, she didn't have to wait long. Stephanie was pretty sure she hadn't been spotted by whoever was on her tail. Still, she asked the driver to loop around, park in front of the restaurant, and pop in for a coffee or soda to go. "Whichever you prefer," she said. "It's on me. And leave your taxi light on. I don't want anyone knowing you've picked up a fare."

The driver was around her age, and handsome, with tousled dark brown hair and a bit of beard stubble. "Do you mind me asking what gives?" he asked.

"I've got a husband who likes to knock me around. I'm finally leaving him."

"This ride's on me, lady."

She ducked down in the backseat, and stayed there while he was in the restaurant. When he returned with his coffee, Stephanie remained hidden.

"What's your name?" she asked the driver.

"Steve—Steve McKinney," he replied over his shoulder.

"Steve, could you drop me at the corner of Hilliard and 23rd?"

That was a block away from her house. She needed some things for the trip to Seattle. She'd left in such a hurry this afternoon, she'd forgotten her sunglasses and a few other essentials—including some decent clothes if she was going to call on Mark Metcalf at his TV station.

She remained crouched down in the backseat of the taxi until they were two blocks away from the hotel. Then she peeked out the rear window. No one else was on the road at this hour. It was easy to see nobody was following them.

She'd checked the bus schedules. There was a well-shaded stop down the street and around the corner from her house. She'd hide there until the bus showed up at 5:20. It went to the airport. It seemed less risky than having the cab wait for her. Whether it was at the end of her street or around the corner from her place, a parked cab would draw attention. Besides, they wouldn't be looking for her at a bus stop.

"Listen, Steve, you're saving my life," she told the driver, finally straightening up in the backseat. "You sure I can't pay you?"

"Your money's no good here this morning."

"Well, thank you," Stephanie said.

"Here's my card," he said, handing it to her over his shoulder. "When all this is done, could you call me, and let me know that you're okay?"

Stephanie stashed it in her purse. "Sure thing, Steve," she said. She felt a little guilty lying to him about her predicament. He seemed like a nice guy.

"If I don't hear back from you," he said, "I'll always wonder what happened to that pretty woman with the lousy husband."

"You'll hear from me," Stephanie said.

She looked at her watch: 4:50. He would be dropping her off in about five minutes. It was still dark out. She had that working in her favor. She would cut through a neighbor's yard to get to her back door. She'd have to keep the lights off in the house, too. Even then, it wouldn't take long to gather up what she needed. She'd be in and out of the house very quickly.

She glanced over her shoulder again, out the rear window. No one seemed to be following them. Stephanie told herself she was okay for now.

And it was only a matter of minutes before she'd be home.

CHAPTER TWENTY-THREE

"The moving walkway is now ending," said the recording. "Please look down . . ."

Under the stream of flashing multicolor neon, Ryan had just managed to edge past two idiots who stood side by side on the conveyor belt walkway. He was trying to get to United Concourse C for his Seattle flight, which left in forty minutes. He'd booked a one-way ticket for $97, with the provision he could be ready with three hours notice.

That had given him just enough time to pack and concoct a great cover story for his grandmother. He'd told her that he and Billy were driving up to Madison to check out the University of Wisconsin for the next two or three nights. He'd felt a little guilty lying to her, especially since she'd insisted on giving him eighty dollars for traveling money. He'd reminded her that he had over two thousand dollars saved in the bank from working as a clerk at Sunset Foods last summer. But she'd shoved the money in his shirt pocket anyway.

He'd phoned Billy to make sure he didn't blow his cover by impulsively coming over to the house anytime within the next few days. "You're really asking for trouble, aren't you?" Billy had said. "Like I told you, this isn't going to end well."

"I'll be fine," Ryan had told him.

Still, he remembered Stephanie warning him not to take this trip. "Don't push your luck," she'd said. A part of him was reluctant about leaving his grandmother alone and vulnerable. But if these people spotted him in Seattle, they'd go after him, not his grandmother in Highland Park. Besides, he couldn't just sit around and do nothing. He'd seen Alison Metcalf's photos on her Facebook page. Yes, she was cute. But the pictures of her and her kid brother were what really got to him. They reminded him of Ashley and Keith.

He didn't want Alison and her kid brother ending up dead, too. If he could do something to prevent that, he would. It was worth the risk.

He was about to step onto the escalator when his cell phone rang. He checked the caller ID:

JAYNE, NICOLE
702-555-0901

Ryan immediately moved aside, away from the crowded escalator. Then he clicked on the phone: "Hello?" he said.

"Hi. Is this Mark?" she asked.

It took him a moment to remember that he'd told Mr. Jayne his name was Mark Metcalf, Junior. "Um, yeah . . ." he said, setting his backpack on the floor. Over the airport speaker, they were making announcements; and that recording about the moving walkway kept repeating. He covered his other ear to block out the noise.

"My name's Nikki Jayne," she said. "I understand you paid a call on my dad last night, and you had some questions for him."

"Yes, that's right. Thanks so much for calling me."

"So how'd you like my dad? He's a million laughs, isn't he?"

"Well, I think I caught him off guard."

"If he was pious, crabby, or cantankerous, you caught him at his most charming," she said. "I understand your father worked with my older sister at Lake Ridge way back in the eighties. I'm sorry, but the name Metcalf doesn't ring a bell with me."

"Well, he was a valet there for a couple of summers, including the summer your sister . . ." He hesitated.

"The summer Selena disappeared?" she interjected. "It's okay. I'm not my father. I don't mind talking about it. I was only ten and a half when it happened. I mean, I was still counting half-years. That's how young I was at the time. What's your interest in this, if you don't mind my asking?"

"Well, my dad mentioned her recently, and I just got more and more curious."

"He probably had a thing for her. Selena was a knockout."

"I know, I looked up some articles on her disappearance and saw her picture."

"The photos didn't do her justice, believe me. She was even prettier in person. She looked like Marilyn Monroe—at least, I thought so when I was a kid. Anyway, about your interest in Selena . . ."

"Yes, well, I guess I just want to find out what happened to her," he said, struggling for an explanation.

"You and me both," she replied. "So—my father said you looked like you were in high school or college maybe. School's out for summer, so you can't be doing this for a term paper or anything. You sure you're not fronting for some tabloid or cheapie true crime rag? I mean, two weeks from now, I'm not going to open up a newspaper at the checkout stand and find myself quoted in a story about my sister, am I?"

"No," he murmured. "God, no."

"Okay, I've got about five minutes left on my cigarette break. What do you want to know?"

"Well, um, so you don't remember Selena ever talking about Mark Metcalf?"

"Nope, sorry. Like I told you, that name doesn't ring a bell—not even a distant bell."

"What about Brent Farrell or Scott Hamner?"

There was a pause. "I don't think so. The first guy sounds vaguely familiar, but I don't remember Selena ever mentioning him. I think I heard the name somewhere else, more recently . . ."

Ryan figured she must have read about his father and the "murder-suicide" six weeks ago. "What about Dick Ingalls?" he asked.

"Oh, my God, *Dick Ingalls*, that name's a blast from the past," she said. "Now, him I remember. Selena had a major crush on him. He was one of those rich, good-looking bad boys, always getting into trouble."

"Did Selena ever go out with him?" Ryan asked.

"Oh, I don't think he would have given Selena the time of day."

"Are you sure? I mean, you just said she looked like Marilyn Monroe."

"Yes, but none of those rich kids at Lake Ridge would be caught dead dating the help. Plus I would have heard about it if she'd ever gone out with Dick. She talked about him enough: 'Oh, I think he winked at me . . .' or 'He nodded at me, I'm sure he was flirting . . .' But the puppy love feelings she had for him were unrequited. Funny thing about Dick Ingalls, he peaked in high school. When I was a kid, I used to hang out with the employees at the club, and help with chores—whether it was in the snack shack or wherever. I remember Dick was very sexy, very cute—and he knew it, too. But by the time I was seventeen and working at the club myself—I wasn't a waitress, I worked in the ladies' room, a loathsome job—anyway, I spotted him there with his parents one night. Dick was only twenty-five or so, but he looked—*spent*, you know, rode hard and put away wet. Too much partying, I guess. That was the last time I saw him. I wonder whatever happened to him."

Ryan decided not to say anything about the fire that swept through Dick's Lake Geneva summer home. "The other three guys I mentioned," he said, "Brent, Scott, and my dad, Mark, they were all friends of Dick's. They hung out together that summer Selena disappeared. I can't help thinking maybe they were all somehow involved in—"

"So—wait a minute," she interrupted. "Do you think Dick, your dad, and these other two guys might have had something to do with what happened to Selena? Oh, honey, no . . ."

"What makes you so sure?"

"Because like I told you, if Dick had so much as said 'boo' to her, Selena would have told me about it—in detail. I was the last one to talk to her that night she went off to the movies by herself. If she was going on a date with Dick Ingalls, I would have known about it. Besides, the police interviewed a whole bunch of people at the club about Selena. No one from the club knew a thing—and believe me, everyone there was into everyone else's business. So if you're worried about your father being involved in my sister's disappearance, you can just relax."

"Are you positive?" he asked.

"I'll tell you what I think, and I know the police are pretty certain this is what went down. I think Selena met somebody at the movies and he offered her a ride home—and that was that. Selena was always so trusting. My guess is the guy did what he wanted to her, killed her, and buried her body someplace. I just hope—whoever it was—he got paid back in spades for what he did to my sister."

"Are you really that certain she's dead? I mean, isn't there a chance she could have run away?"

"She left the house in a blue sleeveless dress and

sandals. And all she was carrying was a tiny change purse. If you're going to run away, you pack a few things." She paused. "Besides, if Selena had skipped town, she would have let me know. She wouldn't have left me alone with our old man in that miserable house. She would have contacted me somehow. Selena wouldn't have ditched me. We were six and a half years apart, but we were very close. No, my sister didn't run away, honey. She's dead."

Ryan didn't know what to say. He wondered if it was true. Maybe his father and the other three guys in that photo hadn't had anything to do with Selena's disappearance.

"Listen, my break ended about five minutes ago," Nikki Jayne said. "I should skedaddle. Anyway, put your mind to rest about your dad and his pals having anything to do with my sister's disappearance. I'm sure he wouldn't have brought her up in conversation if he was hiding something from you. I mean, really, think about it."

"You're probably right," he said. "Thanks."

He did think about it—after they hung up. The truth was his father had never said anything to him about his three buddies or Lake Ridge Country Club or Selena Jayne. And Mark Metcalf had told Stephanie that he barely knew any of the others—including Selena.

So what were they hiding?

He still had twenty-five minutes left before his plane took off. Ryan didn't move from the dark alcove off to the side of the escalators and stairway. He wanted to tell Stephanie about this conversation with

Selena Jayne's surviving sister. He just hoped she wouldn't hear the airport announcements in the background. He didn't want her to know where he was—or to guess where he was headed. He speed-dialed her number.

He counted the ringtones. There were six of them before an automated voice from the service provider came on to tell him his party wasn't able to answer the phone. The beep sounded for him to leave a message.

Ryan hesitated. "Ah, hi, Stephanie. I just got finished talking with Nicole Jayne. I want to go over it with you and get your take on it. This is weird that I didn't get you or your regular voice mail. Give me a call as soon as you can, okay?"

Then he clicked off, picked up his bag, and headed up the escalator.

Wednesday, June 19—4:22 P.M.
Seattle

As she walked from her hotel toward the Seattle Center, the woman checked the text her cohort had just sent:

Our prob n Portland iz takN cAR of. Plan B wz a sukses. Our laD pilot & her home R both gone az of 5 DIS morn. She must have sneaked awA frm d hotel & takN a taxi. I defused her car n d hotel lot & shpd equip 2 mIslf. Jst touched dwn n Cedar Rapids. Shud hav d Winnebago checked & redE 2 transport our pkg 2moro morn. caL U s%n.

It only took the woman a moment to type and send her response: ☺

"God, Dad, I just said good-bye to you like an hour ago," Alison sighed on the other end of the line. "Danny and I are fine—except he's driving me crazy, as usual. Cate's coming over in a bit. If he starts to bug us, I may strangle him."

Mark sat at his desk with a news script in front of him. But he hadn't been able to focus on it. He kept thinking about Stephanie Coburn's warning that he and his family were in danger. He'd advised the kids this afternoon to be on their guard. He'd told them someone had threatened the TV news team and their families— something that actually happened from time to time. He told Alison and Danny not to wander off by themselves, and to keep a cell phone close by at all times. He didn't want them taking any chances.

This warning had, of course, prompted Danny to hide around corners and jump out to scare Alison at every opportunity possible.

What bothered Mark most was that if someone went after his kids, it wouldn't be too difficult for them to figure out when Alison and Danny had been left alone in the house. All they had to do was turn on the news to see he wasn't home. He really wished he had someone older there staying with the kids—just as extra insurance.

He never owned a gun, and hadn't known how to get one in a hurry. Then he'd remembered one of the news team reporters recently did an exposé about local gun shops flagrantly ignoring firearm-sales guidelines. The focus of the piece was one particular store owned and managed by a smug, oily sleazeball. The exposé had helped shut down the place. However, a lot of undercover footage had been shot at another negligent store, but never used on TV. The old owner had come across as sweet but clueless. It didn't make for very dramatic footage. Mark had called Jesse earlier and found out the name of that second store: Sportsman Pete's Gun & Ammo Supply.

Just an hour ago, Pete Junior, who was almost as dense as his sweet old dad, had sold Mark a Glock 19 handgun for $369.99. Mark had shown him the same badly forged gun permit they'd used in the exposé. He walked out of the store with the Glock and a box of bullets. He had them in his desk drawer now. He'd have to take some lessons on how to shoot the damn thing without blowing a finger off. And of course, that meant even more time away from home and the kids.

"I know you think I'm being overly cautious," he told his daughter on the phone. "But humor me on this. It's a lousy day out there anyway. Stay inside with the doors locked until I get back at a quarter to seven, okay?"

"All right, but how long are we going to be in lockdown mode here?" she asked.

"Until we're sure these threats aren't a genuine concern. Grin and bear it, honey. Love you. Now, put Danny on."

"DANNY!" she screamed, almost into the phone. "DAD WANTS TO TALK WITH YOU!"

After a few moments, his son got on the line. "Hi, Dad."

"Hi. Stop bothering your sister. Leave her and Cate alone, okay?"

"Okay . . ."

Mark looked up as Jesse stepped into the office with a sheet of paper in his hand. Mark figured it was a new story or something. Jesse's ensemble today was a Hawaiian shirt that clashed with his camouflage cargo shorts. His uncharacteristically somber expression didn't go with the outfit.

"Okay, I gotta scoot. I'll see you in a couple of hours. Love you."

"Bye, Dad," Danny said, and then he clicked off.

He hung up the phone, and squinted at Jesse. "What's going on?"

"This just came in from Portland," he said, still standing by the office door. He winced as he looked down at the page in his hand. "You know that woman from yesterday, Stephanie Coburn? She's dead."

Mark numbly stared at him. "What?" he whispered.

"A big explosion went off in her house at around five this morning . . ."

Mark shook his head.

"It blew out neighbors' windows and set off a whole bunch of car alarms. They're picking up debris two blocks away. The Portland police are still looking for her body in the rubble."

"My God," Mark murmured.

He remembered how scared Stephanie Coburn had sounded on the phone. "I'm trying to help you," she'd told him. "Whoever's behind these deaths, they know

I'm getting closer to finding the truth. They've been after me. They've tried to kill me . . ."

"Do they—do they know what happened?" he asked. "Is there an explanation?"

Jesse set the piece of paper on Mark's desk. "It's all here. The blast practically leveled the house. A neighbor spotted a Ford pickup speeding down the street right after the explosion. They gave the police a description—including a partial of the plate."

Mark scanned the news bulletin. It was all there as Jesse described. They mentioned that Stephanie Coburn was in the news recently for piloting a commercial airline jet while under the influence of a hallucinogen. "Coburn claimed someone had drugged her coffee," the article said. "Her case had been scheduled for the FAA Review Board in July."

"I'm writing the copy for it right now," Jesse said. "But I need to ask you, Mark—off the record, if you want—what exactly did she say to you yesterday?

The bulletin was shaking in his hand. Mark set it on his desk, and shrugged. "Nothing that made any sense to me," he lied. "The way she talked, I thought she was kind of crazy, paranoid."

Jesse's eyes narrowed at him. "Well, you ought to call the Portland police and let them know. Maybe she told you something important in all her paranoid talk."

Mark nodded. "You're right. I'll call them right after the five o'clock show."

"It'll be our lead story," Jesse said.

"Could we give the spot to Debi?"

Jesse raised an eyebrow. "Sure. We're on in twenty. Better start putting on the war paint."

"Thanks," Mark said. He watched Jesse head back into the newsroom.

It was too much for him to comprehend. Now the threat to his family seemed horribly real. He hated knowing the kids were alone in the house.

Of course, Jesse was right. He had to call the Portland police. But what would he tell them?

He kept wondering what he could have done to help Stephanie Coburn. This was the second time in his life he'd turned his back on a woman who desperately needed help—the second time he'd done nothing and let someone die.

The phone rang, and he almost jumped out of his skin.

Mark grabbed the receiver. "Hello?"

"Hi, Mark," said the associate producer, Gayle. She'd put Stephanie's call through to him last night. And he'd told Gayle to hang up on her after that.

"Yeah, Gayle, what is it?" he asked, rubbing his forehead.

"I have a call for you. It's kind of an emergency, she says . . ."

He immediately thought of Alison.

"Her name's Jenny Ballatore," Gayle continued.

"Oh, um, all right," Mark said. "Thanks, Gayle. You can put her through . . ."

There was a click, and then she came on the other end of the line: "Mark?"

"Yes, hi. What's going on?"

"I'm so sorry to call you—and you have to be on TV

in fifteen minutes. I didn't know who else to turn to. That guy who's been stalking me, he was in my hotel room this afternoon. I came back and caught him in there. He pushed me down and ran out—"

"My God, were you hurt?"

"I'm okay—"

"Did you call the police?" he asked.

"Yes. I've been with them for the last two hours. The hotel moved me to yet another room, but I just can't go back there . . ."

"Listen, Jenny, grab a taxi and come here to the station."

"I'm here," she said "I'm in the lobby."

"Well, come on up. You can wait in my office while I do the broadcasts."

"No, I can't. I don't want anyone to see me. I'm a mess. I've been crying. Could you—could you come down for just a couple of seconds?"

"Sure," he said. "Be right down."

Hanging up the phone, he hurried out of his office, through the newsroom and into the stairwell.

Mark found her down in the lobby. Her long chestnut hair was pulled back in a ponytail. Her face was flushed and her eyes looked bloodshot. She wore a blue T-shirt and jeans. Shaking her head at him, she seemed utterly embarrassed. "I'm so sorry to do this to you . . ."

"That's okay." He was about to put his arms around her, but hesitated.

She had no such hesitation. She wrapped her arms around him and pressed her face against his shoulder. "God, I'm going crazy," she cried. "I've been trying to find another hotel, and either they're booked or the rates are through the roof. I don't know what to do . . ."

He patted her back, and could feel her long, silky hair. "Listen, don't worry . . ."

She pulled back a little and gazed at him with tear-filled eyes. "I don't want to keep you. It's just that I hear there are some cheaper hotels on Aurora Boulevard. I was going to check online. If I find a decent place, would you mind driving me there—I mean, after you finish the six o'clock show? I hate to take up your time. I hate being this needy . . ."

"Don't be ridiculous. Listen, you can stay at my house. We have a guest room on the lower level. It's probably a little dusty, but the sheets are clean."

She wiped her eyes. "Oh, I couldn't impose on you . . ."

"Listen, you'd be doing me a favor," he said. "It would be nice to have another adult in the house for a change. In fact, you'd be like an answer to a prayer. Only . . ." He broke away from her and shook his head. "On second thought, it's not fair to you, not in my current situation."

"What do you mean?"

"You'd be going from the frying pan into the fire. It's a long story, but I have reason to believe my family could be in danger—maybe not right now, but possibly soon. It might be best if you—"

"Well, who's looking after your kids right now?" she asked.

"Nobody," he answered, suddenly very ashamed. "And I'm going crazy with worry."

"In that case, I accept your invitation," she said.

"You go do the news. I'll get my stuff from the hotel and meet you back here at six-thirty."

"Are you sure you want to do this? I mean, I could really use another adult around the house, but not at the risk of endangering you . . ."

She hugged him again. "There's safety in numbers. I'd really love the company, too. As for the bedroom, I don't mind a little dust. I promise I'll only stay a day or two. I don't want to outwear my welcome. You'd be saving my life, Mark . . ."

He wasn't so sure about that.

With that same uncertainty, he finally put his arms around her and returned the embrace.

She squeezed him tightly—as if she might never let go.

CHAPTER TWENTY-FOUR

Wednesday, June 19—5:54 P.M.

The hotel he was staying at in West Seattle reminded him of the Bates Motel in *Psycho*—only with two stories. Otherwise, it was the same late-fifties style, squat, rambling layout. All the rooms were accessible from the outside, which meant he had to step out for ice, and other guests passed by the window of his room on the second floor. He had a view of the parking lot.

Ryan had checked online and gotten hotel and bus information for West Seattle. He figured if Alison Metcalf went to summer school there, the Metcalfs' house couldn't be far away. The hotel, the Grove Inn, was practically the only game in that part of town. Actually, his room was nicely furnished and clean. Plus they had cable. And it was walking distance to a McDonald's. He could have done a lot worse.

Still, the place's resemblance to the Bates Motel had him dead-bolting the door and keeping his face toward the curtain while he showered. Ryan quickly dried off, and wrapped the towel around his waist. Wiping the steam from the bathroom mirror, he got a shocking reminder of what he'd done earlier that afternoon.

By the time he'd gotten to West Seattle, it had been too late to catch Alison Metcalf at the high school. On the plane, he'd been haunted by something Stephanie had said about looking so much like his father that his family's killers might recognize him. So with some time to spare, he stopped by Shear Perfection, a unisex hair salon. The stylist trimmed Ryan's unruly brown hair to a modified crew cut and then dyed it blond—really blond, platinum. Everyone in the salon thought he looked cool and edgy.

Staring at his reflection in the half-fogged mirror, Ryan thought he looked like a clown. But at least he didn't look like his father.

After getting dressed, he checked his phone. He was hoping Stephanie might have called while he was in the shower. He'd left her three messages today. He'd told her in the last one that he was in Seattle. He'd figured that would get a response out of her. But so far, nothing. And no one had left him a voice mail while he'd been showering.

He was worried about her. He hadn't spoken with her since last night. She'd been alone and hiding out in a Portland hotel—pretty much the same thing he was doing right now. She'd been thinking of coming to Seattle, too. Had she made it here?

Ryan figured he'd try her again after watching the news. He grabbed the remote and clicked on the TV.

He'd seen a billboard for the KIXY News Team while on the bus from the airport to West Seattle. He'd been getting his dorky haircut and dye-job when Mark Metcalf and his "teammates" were on at five o'clock. However, their six o'clock broadcast was just about to start. Ryan wanted to see what the only surviving kid from that old photograph looked like on live TV.

With the remote in his hand, he sat down on the end of the bed and watched as they showed a news teaser—with clips of a fire at a building in Pioneer Square, a drowning in Lake Sammamish, and a defeat for the Mariners. After a jazzy intro with all the graphics, they showed Mark Metcalf and his pretty blond co-anchor behind a desk.

Ryan thought back to the man from the country club's pro shop and the Metcalfs' former neighbor who both had said that Mark was a nice guy. Whether it was real or fake, the good-looking anchorman had that demeanor. He seemed nice, dependable, and reassuring. Ryan couldn't imagine the man on TV ever slapping his kid in front of God and everybody during a football game.

"Our top story tonight," announced his co-anchor. "An explosion ripped through the quiet Portland neighborhood of Hawthorne early this morning, leveling one home and blowing out windows of neighboring houses for a block. One person is assumed dead . . ."

"Probably some crystal meth lab thing," Ryan muttered to himself.

"The residence destroyed belonged to Stephanie Coburn, a pilot for Pacific Cascade Skyways. Coburn was in the news recently after allegedly piloting a commercial passenger plane while under the influence of LSD . . ."

"No," Ryan said, staring at the TV. He got to his feet. "Goddamn it, no . . ."

On the screen, they switched over to a reporter from a Portland affiliate station. The woman stood in front of the smoldering, blown-out remnants of someone's house—*Stephanie's house*. Into her handheld mic, the reporter explained that emergency responders were still searching for a body in the wreckage.

Now he knew why Stephanie hadn't returned any of his calls.

They showed blurry, rickety footage of the post-explosion fire, which someone had captured on their cell phone. The reporter said they were still unsure about the cause of the explosion, but a Ford pickup was spotted speeding away from the scene just moments after the blast.

With tears in his eyes, Ryan stood in front of the TV.

They switched to a clip of Stephanie, looking disoriented as she tried to explain that someone must have drugged her minutes before she'd strapped herself into the cockpit of that commercial jet. Ryan had seen the footage before. It was part of an interview she'd told him about, rerun nearly two weeks ago. "I don't want you seeing me on the news and thinking you're in cahoots with a major loon," she'd said.

She'd been right about how she'd come across—spacey, unreliable, and paranoid. But Ryan knew the truth.

On TV, they went back to the co-anchors at their news desk. Ryan studied the somber look on Mark Metcalf's face while his pretty partner wrapped up the news piece: "Portland police are tracking down the owners of that Ford pickup seen driving away from Coburn's home just after the explosion. Tune into KIXY News at eleven for all the latest developments on this story . . ."

Sinking down on the edge of the bed, Ryan told himself there was still a chance Stephanie was alive. They hadn't found her body yet. She'd given them the slip before. She could have done it again.

Still, he started sobbing. If she were alive, she would have called and let him know by now. If she were alive, he wouldn't feel this awful loss and hopelessness.

"A three-alarm fire broke out this afternoon at a Pioneer Square landmark . . ." Mark Metcalf announced.

But Ryan had stopped listening. He stared at the handsome news anchor and wondered how he could just sit there and act as if he had no connection to Stephanie Coburn whatsoever.

The son of a bitch had just spoken to her last night.

Wednesday—7:12 P.M.

"That's pretty."

"Oh, do you like it?" her dad's friend replied. The pretty brunette held out her hand to show off the scarab bracelet. "This was my mom's. It's always been one of my favorites." She went back to unpacking her suitcases, which were laid out on the guest room bed. She was only supposed to stay a night or two, but it looked like she was hunkering down to spend the rest of the summer. "How come you aren't wearing any jewelry?" she asked. "I figured you'd have inherited a bunch of stuff from your mother."

Leaning against the doorway, Alison shrugged. "Most of the really pricey stuff is in a safe-deposit box at the bank. I mean, what am I going to do with a string of pearls or my mom's engagement ring? I probably won't even see any of it until I'm twenty-one or married. I ended up with some less expensive stuff that's nice—not as nice as your bracelet. Anyway, I don't wear any jewelry unless I'm going out."

She certainly wasn't going out tonight. Her friend, Cate, was supposed to have come over and kept her company during "lockdown mode," as Alison called it. But now Cate and a bunch of other people were going to Pegasus Pizza. Then they'd be hanging out at Alki Beach. Alison's crush, Shane Camper, and some of his skateboarding friends were supposed to be there. Of course, it would go on past 10:30, maybe even past midnight. Cate said they'd come pick her up. Alison said not to bother. She had to babysit her stupid kid brother.

So she was friendless and homebound. Making matters worse, her dad had called between newscasts, asking her to make sure the house was presentable for company. He was bringing his friend, Jenny, home for dinner. "She's spending the night," he said. "So would you mind giving the guest room a quick dust? I'm pretty sure the sheets are clean . . ."

"Before I put a mint on her pillow, should I take Danny's geography project and all that other crap off the bed down there?" she asked, deadpan.

Her father was right about the clean sheets. Her Grandpa and Grandma Niebank had slept in the bed when they'd come in for the funeral last month. They'd stayed with them an extra week, and her grandmother had changed the sheets before they'd left. But in the last three weeks the room had become a catch-all storage area for a lot of things—including some winter clothes that needed to go to the cleaners, stacks of old magazines, and Danny's 40 x 20 homemade relief map of the United States. Her father acted like cleaning the room would take five minutes, but it was a major project.

"Who is this Jenny person anyway?" she pressed. "Is this the doughnut lady? What's going on with you guys? Is she your girlfriend or something?"

"No, she's not my girlfriend," her father replied. "Honey, I'm not going to be in the market for a girlfriend for quite some time. No, Jenny is just a really nice woman who happens to need a place to stay tonight. I'd like to help her out. Just do what you can to clear off the guest room bed. Make the place look a little presentable, and I'll owe you one. Okay?"

It was a major pain to move Danny's relief map to the corner of the room. It was made from flour, paste, and food dye. Crumbs remained on the bedspread, and the Florida panhandle broke off during the transfer. She tossed the bedspread in the washer, vacuumed the carpet, and opened the windows to air out the room. She browbeat Danny into loading up the dishwasher with all the dirty plates, flatware, and glasses that had been left out on the kitchen counter and everywhere else for that matter.

By the time her dad and the doughnut lady arrived, Alison had the house looking reasonably clean. And except for the bedspread in the dryer, the guest room was ready for occupancy.

The doughnut lady was a lot sexier and prettier than Alison had expected. Her black T-shirt and tight jeans showed off a killer body. Alison could tell by the way the woman talked and acted around her dad that she was on the make for him. She kept flicking her hair and touching him oh-so-casually. Maybe her dad thought they were just friends, but this lady had other ideas.

Along with two suitcases, she also had a big brown box of stuff she'd brought with her from the Bay Area and a bagful of groceries. Apparently, within the last hour, she'd rented the red Hyundai now in the drive-way, and then followed Alison's father here in it. She'd said she wanted to come and go without asking him to chauffeur her all over the place.

"Your father is an absolute lifesaver to put me up like this," she said, hanging up a dress in the closet. "You are, too, Alison. I can only imagine how weird it must seem to have this total stranger moving into your guest room—even just for a couple of nights." She started to unpack another dress, but stopped to look at her. "You know, your father didn't tell me how pretty you are. You're a knockout. If you don't mind my saying, a tiny bit of eyeliner would do wonders. You've got gorgeous eyes. You should accentuate them."

Alison felt herself blushing. "Well, thanks. I don't wear much makeup."

"You're lucky," she said. "For a while I had to wear gobs of makeup to cover this scar on my face. It was really awful. I finally went to this plastic surgeon and you can't see it anymore, thank God."

"Hey, you guys!" Alison's father called down to them. "What do you want on your pizza? We're getting one large sausage and cheese, and a big salad. The other pizza's up to you . . ."

The woman smiled at her. "It's your call," she said.

"I usually get just cheese," Alison said, shrugging.

"Make ours cheese, please!" she called.

Alison's cell phone rang. It was a text from Cate.

"Boyfriend?" Jenny asked.

"No, a friend-friend," Alison answered, frowning at the text. "She's bugging me to go out with her and some other friends tonight. They're having pizza, too, and then hanging out at the beach."

"Sounds like fun. What are you moping about?"

"Because I can't go," Alison said. "I have to babysit Danny while Dad goes back to the station for the eleven o'clock show."

"Well, I'm here. I can babysit. You're off the hook. Go out with your friends."

Alison worked up a smile. "Oh, that's nice of you. But Dad wouldn't want me dumping Danny on you. Plus we're in lockdown here, because he's worried about some wacko who's threatening people on the news team."

"Well, that's just silly. I'll be fine here with Danny, and you'll be with a whole bunch of people, right? Are any guys going to be there? Any guys you're interested in?"

Alison was a little embarrassed. She rolled her eyes. "Actually, there's this one guy I like, and he's supposed to show up . . ."

"Oh, then you're going," she said, reaching into her

suitcase. "That's all there is to it. I insist. Do you have a ride there and back?"

Alison nodded, but she didn't think her dad would let her go.

"Well, text your friend and tell her to come pick you up," she said. "Let me talk to your father. Don't worry."

"Are you sure? I mean, he just ordered a pizza for us."

"Oh, like cold pizza won't get eaten. Please." She plopped something in Alison's hand. "Here, go get dolled up."

Alison looked down at the tube of eyeliner in her hand.

"And here, wear this tonight. It might bring you luck." She unfastened the scarab bracelet from her wrist and gave it to her. "But if you lose it, I'll kill you. I'm going to talk to your dad now. You get ready . . ."

She patted Alison's shoulder as she headed out of the guest room.

In awe, Alison gazed at the scarab bracelet—and then at her father's friend. She felt like she suddenly had this cool big sister. "Jenny, listen, thank you."

She turned and smiled back at her. "No sweat. We girls have to stick together."

Thursday, June 20—1:44 A.M.

He couldn't sleep.

Mark had been lying in bed for the last hour, staring at the ceiling. Even with Dina gone, he still stayed on his side of the bed. Every once in a while, his hand strayed over to where she used to sleep, and he'd feel a sad little pang in his heart. "What's wrong, hon?" he could almost hear her asking. "Can't you sleep?"

If she were beside him right now, he would tell her everything.

He would tell her how he wished he hadn't hung up on Stephanie Coburn Tuesday night. It was yet another terrible moment he couldn't take back.

He would tell Dina that he felt like such a coward. He might have redeemed himself a little by coming clean to the police about Stephanie Coburn's phone call—and what it meant. Instead, all he could think about was protecting his family and his reputation.

After the five o'clock show, he'd asked to see the complete interview with Stephanie Coburn, the one from which they'd shown a brief snippet tonight. In the five-minute piece, she seemed confused and paranoid. She claimed someone had set her up, spiking her coffee with LSD. It was a conspiracy. Her sister had committed suicide, but she knew it wasn't really a suicide. Someone was out to get her.

With only fifteen minutes before they were on the air for the six o'clock show, Mark telephoned the Portland police, and told them Stephanie Coburn had called him on Tuesday night. "I don't know if this has anything to do with the explosion or not," he said. "But I figure I should let you know . . ."

They put him through to one of the detectives handling the case. When the man asked him what exactly Stephanie had said, Mark repeated phrases she'd used in the taped interview. He didn't say a damned thing about his three dead friends or Lake Ridge Country Club or Selena Jayne.

"Did she mention why she called you in particular?" the detective asked.

"I assumed it was because she might have seen me on TV," Mark lied. At the same time, he was thinking of the potential threat to his family. "She had a sister who committed suicide. She might have read somewhere that my wife killed herself. She died last month. Some blogger reported it was a suicide."

"And was it?"

"Yes, carbon monoxide poisoning," Mark admitted. "She pulled our vintage car into the garage and left the motor running." It killed him to say that out loud. He cleared his throat. "Anyway, Ms. Coburn seemed to think my family and I were in danger. She was calling to warn me. I thought she was a crank or crazy. I hung up on her. Of course, I wish I hadn't, now. After what happened to her this morning, I can't help thinking she might have been on to something. So I'm worried about my kids . . ."

The detective took down his contact information, and recommended that he phone the Seattle Police Department if he was concerned about his children's safety.

Mark wondered if they took him seriously at all. Or maybe they just didn't take Stephanie Coburn very seriously. According to the detective, about a week ago, she'd caused some sort of disturbance on her block, claiming she had an intruder in her home. But police hadn't been able to find any evidence of a break-in.

When Mark asked for an off-the-record update about the explosion, the detective said they still hadn't found a body or any body parts in the wreckage. "Her car isn't in the garage—or what's left of the garage," he said. "So it's quite possible she might not have been home when the place blew up. But we don't know for sure yet. Anyway, don't quote me on that . . ."

Mark figured the guy couldn't have been a very experienced detective, confiding something about a big story to a newsman and then saying, "Don't quote me."

He phoned the Seattle police, and asked them to beef up the patrols on his block. They'd obliged him before when there had been threats to him and people at the station. They didn't even ask for an explanation. They just said they'd do it.

He should have felt more secure with another adult in the house. But he kept thinking Jenny might have been better off in some hotel. Still, she seemed so grateful for the company. Mark guessed she'd been more lonely than scared. The kids certainly seemed to like her, especially Alison, who got a reprieve from babysitting tonight thanks to Jenny. He'd let Jenny talk him into allowing Alison to go out. She'd argued that Alison would be safe if she stuck close to her friends and had her cell phone with her. To Alison's credit, she was home before he'd returned from his eleven o'clock news spot. To Jenny's credit, he'd found Danny asleep in his bed and a kitchen that was spotless.

It was a relief to make it home—and lose whoever had followed him practically all the way from the station. He was convinced someone in a white Taurus had been on his tail. They'd stayed one or two cars behind him from the Seattle Center to I-5 to the West Seattle Bridge. At the intersection of Alaska and California, he'd run a yellow light to elude them.

He was starting to feel some of Stephanie Coburn's paranoia.

Several times tonight, he'd peered out the front windows to make sure no one was prowling around the house. He didn't see anybody. In fact, at one point, he spotted a police car drive by. That was reassuring.

Mark heard a noise downstairs, and quickly sat up in bed. It sounded like glasses clinking.

He quietly crawled out of bed and put on some sweatpants. He always slept in just his boxer shorts. He remembered the gun he'd purchased today. He'd smuggled it home tonight. It was in a shoebox on his closet shelf, not even loaded yet. He decided to leave it where it was, and crept out to the hallway. Pausing at the top of the stairs, he thought he heard a door close downstairs. He wondered if Jenny was still up. It was dark on the main level.

He skulked down the steps, and checked the front door—still double locked. The door off the kitchen to the garage was locked, too. He didn't hear anything except a steady drip from the kitchen sink. With a twist, he tightened the cold-water spigot, and the dripping stopped. He moved back to the hallway and the stairs to the lower level.

He heard murmuring. It sounded like Jenny was talking to someone.

He crept down the steps. As he rounded the corner, he saw the guest room door was closed. A sliver of light shone across the threshold. He couldn't make out what she was saying, but she was whispering to somebody. He figured she was on the phone.

"Jenny?" he called in a hushed voice.

The murmuring stopped.

He gently tapped on the door. "Jenny, are you okay?"

After a moment, the door opened. She stood at the threshold in a sleeveless yellow nightgown. The light behind her made the flimsy material almost transparent. He could see every curve of her body. Her long dark hair was down around her face and slightly mussed. She gazed at him. "Hi," she said. "I'm sorry. Was I making too much noise?"

"I thought I heard you talking to somebody," he said.

She gave him a shy smile, and then rolled her eyes. "Oh, you're going to think this is so corny, but I was praying."

"Well, I didn't mean to interrupt," he said.

"That's okay. Your ears must have been burning. I was thanking God for you." She touched his bare shoulder. "You really came through for me tonight, Mark. Thank you."

"No, listen, I should thank you," he said, moving his shoulder away. He crossed his arms in front of him. "I didn't invite you here to babysit and clean the kitchen. I mean, you're our guest, for Pete's sake."

"I like feeling useful," she said.

"Say, were you upstairs a few minutes ago?" he asked. "I thought I heard something . . ."

"Oh, I hope I didn't disturb you. I decided to go up and pour myself a nightcap . . ." She nodded toward a half-filled old-fashioned glass on her nightstand. "I didn't take any of your stuff. It was from the liquor I brought with me tonight. I left a couple of bottles on the cellaret."

"Please, you can help yourself to anything in the house," Mark said.

She smiled and flicked back her hair. "Maybe you'd like to join me—for a drink. If we have one in here, we won't wake up anyone."

Standing in her doorway, he stared at her in the sheer nightgown. She touched his shoulder again.

Mark felt himself starting to get hard. He took a step back. "No, thanks," he said. "I should get back to bed. See you in the morning. Sleep tight, okay?"

Before she could say anything else, he retreated up the stairs.

Once in his bedroom, Mark slipped back into the bed he used to share with his wife. Lying there alone, his heart was racing.

He knew sleep tonight would be a long time coming.

Thursday—5:57 A.M.
Cedar Rapids

A loud clank woke her up.

But Jenny didn't move. She just stayed there in her bed, kept still, and listened.

Earlier today, she'd thought she'd heard sounds above—a car, or maybe that Winnebago. She had a feeling he was back. A part of her was relieved. The lights had flickered a few times during the last several days. They were just little power surges, but still a nagging reminder of how vulnerable and helpless she was without him. Every once in a while, she realized the place smelled, too. She kept clean and washed her clothes in the sink. But the used food containers had piled up, and the two twist-tied plastic garbage bags in one corner of the bunker reeked. She was running out of food, too. He was the one person who knew where she was. She needed him.

At the same time, she dreaded his return. Was he going to knock her out and rape her again? Or had he found some other woman to take her place? Jenny kept thinking she'd never see the sky again. He'd kill her down here, and then bury her someplace else.

She could hear muted footsteps. They weren't from directly above, but on the other side of that big door with the wheel crank on it. He was coming down here.

Her eyes had long ago adjusted to the darkness after lights-out. She half-sat-up in the bed and stared at the wheel crank on that door. Her hand slid past her pillow toward the edge of the mattress in search of the light-bulb she'd stored there almost two weeks ago.

Jenny heard a hollow ding, and after a moment, the wheel started to turn.

Her heart was pounding. But she set her head back on the pillow. Her fingers slid across the smooth glass bulb, and then she grasped it in her hand.

There was a clang, which must have been the sound of the door unlocking.

Jenny's eyelids fluttered a bit as she feigned sleep. She could still see the big door at the end of the bunker. A light was behind it. She glimpsed her captor's scrawny silhouette as he crept around the big door. It looked like he had an iPhone in one hand. He appeared to be watching a movie of some kind. Was he picking up what the cameras recorded down here?

He stopped and slipped the phone in his pocket. Then he took out a plastic bag with something in it. He took a step closer, and she saw he had a mask covering his nose and mouth, the kind some people donned in public during an epidemic. He was wearing surgical gloves, too. He'd had them on when he'd first attacked her in the SUV outside the Emeryville Public Market. She realized he had a rag inside that plastic bag, and it was probably soaked with chloroform or whatever he'd used to knock her out the last time.

Had he come to take her out of here? Or did he want to knock her out so he could have his way with her again?

Jenny kept her face pressed to the pillow. Her eyes were practically shut now. She didn't dare open them any wider. He was just a blur, getting closer and closer until he hovered over the bed. She heard the muffled rustling of the plastic bag. Then she detected a slight chemical smell.

"You got a long trip ahead, Scarface," he whispered, "all the way to Seattle."

Jenny saw his hand coming up to her face.

She tightened her grip on the threaded base of the lightbulb. Then in one swift motion, she swung it toward his head and smashed the bulb against his jaw. She'd been aiming for his neck. Shards of glass sprayed all over. She heard him howl in pain.

With all her might, Jenny gave him a shove and raced down the aisle toward the open door. Pieces of broken glass cut her bare feet, but she kept running.

Past the door, she found herself in a little vestibule with a ladder. She grabbed onto the rungs and started climbing. She heard him groaning and grunting in the bunker.

But she could also smell the fresh night air.

"Goddamn it, you bitch!" he yelled.

Jenny scurried up the ladder to an open trapdoor. She poked her head out and realized the entryway to her corrugated prison was a small, old fiberglass shack full of tools. The door was open, and she got a glimpse of the sky for the first time in two weeks. Dawn was breaking.

All at once, she felt his hand around her ankle, tight as a vise. He yanked her down. Helpless, Jenny lost her grip. She banged her elbow against the steel ladder as she plummeted down and crashed to the ground. The wind was knocked out of her.

For a few seconds she couldn't breathe or see anything.

Then he came into focus. He stood over her. The blood on his face was streaming down the side of his neck.

He bent down, and Jenny saw his fist coming at her face.

She felt the hammer-like blow.

Then she didn't see a thing.

CHAPTER TWENTY-FIVE

"I can't believe it," her father announced, a glass of orange juice in his hand. "We're all having breakfast together, and it's not even a special occasion."

"But it is a special occasion, Dad," Danny piped up, his mouth full of Cap'n Crunch. "Jenny's here!"

Sitting next to Danny at the kitchen table, her father's friend was sipping out of a mug that had a cartoon cable car and "JENNY" written on it. She patted Danny's shoulder. "I think I love this guy."

"Give it another twenty-four hours, it'll pass," Alison said. She went back to eating her Honey Nut Cheerios.

It amused her how Jenny acted like it was a big deal to get breakfast ready for everybody. All they were having were toast and cereal. It wasn't like she'd whipped up eggs Benedict or something. Still, Alison liked her. After all, thanks to Jenny, she'd gotten out of the house last night and was able to hang out with her friends at Alki Beach. She didn't even mind so much that Shane pulled a no-show. When Alison came home, Jenny wanted to know everything that had happened, like they'd been confiding in each other for years or something. But Alison lapped up the attention. Jenny insisted she keep the scarab bracelet for the next day or two.

Alison was wearing the bracelet this morning. She planned to show it off at summer school. It gave her something to look forward to. Thursdays were always a drag, because they tacked on a two-hour chemistry lab in the afternoon.

Everyone else had something going on today. Danny had a birthday party to attend at 11:30. Meanwhile, her dad had to be at the station to film promos at 10:30. So he'd worked out some elaborate plan to drop off Danny at a friend's house, and they'd give him a ride to the party from there. But the friend's mother had just phoned minutes ago saying her little monster was sick with the flu. It had thrown her dad into a panic—for about thirty seconds.

Jenny came to the rescue, saying she'd stay with Danny, and drive him to and from the birthday party.

Her dad said he didn't expect her to be running errands and babysitting. But Jenny seemed eager to do it. As much as Alison liked her, she still felt their house-guest was on a major campaign to get in good with their dad. At least, that was what her friend, Cate, had thought last night, when she'd told her about Jenny.

"Watch out," Cate had said. "My wicked stepmother acted the same way when she started dating my father. There was nothing she couldn't do for us. Then she married my dad, and wham, she turned into a total bitch overnight. Still, that's a cool bracelet. So what does she look like anyway? Is she pretty?"

Alison glanced around the breakfast table. She reached for her purse, which was hanging off the back of her chair. Then she fished out her iPhone. "Hey, I'm getting a picture of this 'special occasion' and posting it on Facebook." In reality, she just wanted to get a shot of Jenny to show to Cate.

"Oh, no, not me," Jenny protested. "I'm a mess."

Alison snapped a couple of photos anyway—mostly of Jenny. It was light enough in the room that she didn't need a flash. "Oh, c'mon, you look gorgeous!" she said, getting to her feet. She stepped back from the table and raised the camera phone again. "Say cheese!"

"No!" Jenny said, putting a hand in front of her face. "I mean it, seriously!"

"Just one shot . . ."

"Alison," her father said. "I don't think—"

"You look great, Jenny," she said, snapping the photo. "What's the problem?"

"Damn it, no means no!" she snapped. She sprang up from the table, almost tipping over her chair. "When someone doesn't want their picture taken, you should respect that." She kept her hand in front of her face and bolted out of the kitchen.

"God," Alison murmured. She turned to her father. "Talk about touchy . . ."

"Nice going, Alison," Danny said.

"You should go apologize to her," her father whispered.

With a heavy sigh, she treaded out of the kitchen.

She still had the iPhone in her hand. She found Jenny standing by the stairs to the lower level.

"Alison, I'm sorry to fly off the handle like that," she said, touching her arm. "I don't know if your dad told you. But one reason I'm staying here is because I had this stalker guy bothering me at my hotel. The last thing I need is for someone to be posting my picture on Facebook. I don't want this creep tracking me down here. You understand, don't you?"

"God, yes, of course, I'm sorry," Alison murmured. He father had mentioned Jenny's stalker situation when he'd told her to get the place ready for company last night. She still felt Jenny had overreacted a bit. Alison had no intention of posting any breakfast table snapshots on Facebook. She just wanted her friend, Cate, to see what their houseguest looked like.

"Here," she said, showing Jenny the camera phone— and the photo of everyone at the table. Jenny had her hand blocking her face in the shot. She clicked the delete button. "Here, I'm deleting it, see?"

"Thanks, Alison." She stroked her arm. "Are we still friends?"

"Of course," Alison said. "Listen, I should get a move on. I don't want to be late for school."

She headed back into the kitchen with her iPhone.

She didn't tell Jenny there were still two shots of her in the camera phone.

Thursday—10:35 A.M.

From the outside, the high school looked like a huge, turn-of-the-century brownstone train station. In jeans and a black T-shirt, Ryan wandered the halls, carrying an envelope full of printouts of news articles. He asked one passerby after another, "Do you know where they teach the driver's ed classes?" It was Alison Metcalf's morning class. She'd mentioned it on her Facebook page.

Ryan asked six people, before one scrawny-looking kid with a red-and-white-striped shirt right out of *Where's Waldo?* gave him an answer. "That class let out about five minutes ago," he'd said, squinting a bit at Ryan's too-blond hair. "I know, because I'm taking it. A lot of the kids hang out afterward by the courtyard entrance. Do you know where that is?"

"Not a clue," Ryan said.

The kid pointed down the hall. "Just keep following those exit signs and they'll lead you to it. Is there somebody from the class you're looking for?"

"Alison Metcalf?" Ryan replied, but somehow it came out as more of a question.

The kid nodded. "Yeah, she's usually there."

"So what's the story on her? Is she nice?"

"Yeah, she's pretty cool."

"Thanks, man," Ryan said. "Thanks a lot."

As he wandered down the corridor—only marginally crowded with summer school students—Ryan couldn't ignore the sensation of something pressing against his chest. It was an anxious, shaky feeling that had been nagging him ever since last night when he found out about Stephanie. He was still hoping against hope that she was okay. He'd gone on the Internet this morning for an update on the explosion. The Portland police still hadn't found a body. So there was a reason to hope. They'd tracked down the owners of the Ford pickup seen speeding down the block as the blast occurred. The owners, a Beaverton couple, insisted they hadn't been anywhere near Stephanie's house at the time of the explosion. Apparently, after some grilling by police detectives, the wife finally confessed that her husband had gotten all riled up about the reckless, pill-popping lady pilot who had endangered a planeload of passengers. So they'd driven by Stephanie Coburn's house at five in the morning, and her husband hurled a brick through the front window. "It must have set something off, because the whole place went up," the woman told police.

Ryan kept reminding himself that Stephanie had been staying at a hotel last night. There was every possibility she hadn't been home when the place blew up. Still, why hadn't she gotten in touch with him to tell him she was all right? That awful pressure in his chest wouldn't go away. Only a phone call from Stephanie would get rid of it.

He kept following the exit signs as the *Where's Waldo?* kid had instructed. At last, he stepped outside and found himself near a courtyard by what looked like a new attachment to the turn-of-the-century building. The wing had blue and white tiles and big, modern-looking windows. Several park benches bordered the crowded quad. Some guys on skateboards were off to one side, zipping around, performing stunts.

It took Ryan a while before he spotted a cute girl who looked very much like Alison Metcalf in her Face-book photos. She had brown curly hair and wore a sleeveless white shirt with khaki shorts and sandals. She and a friend sat on top of the back to a bench— with their feet on the seat part. She was showing her friend her bracelet.

Ryan made his way over to her. The friend seemed to notice him first, and she elbowed Alison and nodded toward him. Alison locked eyes with him. He tried to smile. "Hey, how's it going?" he said. "Are you Alison Metcalf?"

"No, she's Angelina Jolie," her friend said. "But she's often mistaken for Alison Metcalf."

He worked up a chuckle. "Good one."

"I'm Alison," she said, banging her knee against her friend's. "Who are you?"

"My name's Ryan Farrell. Your dad is Mark Metcalf, the news guy, right?"

She gave him a wary look. "Why do you ask?"

He reached into his envelope for the 1986 photo of both their dads and the two other guys.

"Wait a minute," she said. "Have you been calling the news station?"

"Is this the wacko?" her friend asked. "Oh my God . . ."

"I don't know what you guys are talking about," Ryan said. He handed Alison the photo. "My father knew your father back in high school—in the Chicago suburbs. That's your dad in the white shirt, isn't it?"

Alison laughed. "Oh, my God, he looks like such a geek!"

"That's my father beside him on the right," Ryan said.

"He looks like you," she said, a bit more serious.

"Only without that ridiculous hair," her friend chimed in.

"Oh, you should talk, Miss Clairol Jet Black," Alison said, giving her friend another nudge. She studied the photo again, and looked at Ryan. "So—what's this all about?"

He looked over at her friend. "I probably don't know you well enough to ask you to get lost, but do you mind? I really need to talk to Alison alone."

Alison's pal glanced at her, and Alison nodded. The girl frowned at Ryan and pointed to another bench. "I'm going to be right over there, watching you two."

"Thanks," Ryan said. He sat down on the bench.

Alison climbed down from the top of the seatback and sat beside him. She looked at the picture again. "So—what's going on? What's the big secret?"

Ryan took a deep breath. "If one of the blogs I read is true, than we both have something in common—besides the fact that our dads knew each other in high school. You and I—we both discovered our mothers after they committed suicide."

Alison stared at him. "I don't think you're very funny."

"It's no joke." He pointed to the young men in the photo for her. "His first wife slit her throat. There was your mother in the garage with the car. And my mom hung herself. This guy on the end, his wife died of some kind of stroke. Each one of these guys met a woman and got married again. And shortly after that, the guy, the wife, and the whole family were killed. I lost my dad, my sister, and my brother six weeks ago. Everyone in that picture—except for your father—is dead. And their families died with them."

Alison shook her head and handed the picture back to him. "I don't want to hear any more."

She got to her feet.

"Has your dad met someone recently—a woman, a potential girlfriend?"

Alison turned to face him. Her hand went around the bracelet on her other wrist.

Then she sank back down beside him.

"Wait a minute," Alison said, studying the photo of Ryan's father and Lacee Roth. "This woman here, she looks a lot like Jenny, the woman staying at our house."

Sitting next to her on the bench in the school's courtyard, Ryan pulled out another shot of Lacee, an earlier photo Stephanie had found. "This is a better shot of her," he said.

Alison quickly shook her head. "She doesn't look like Jenny there. But in this shot with your dad, she does. It's the same thing with this Halle person. The hair's different and the makeup's different, but the bone structure's the same . . ." She handed him the pile of photos and stood up. "Let me show you. C'mon, follow me . . ."

She waved at her friend across the quad, and then led him into the building. "You said your grandmother met Lacee a few times?" she asked.

He had to hurry to keep up with her. "Yes."

"And you showed her that photo of Lacee from a couple of years ago—before she met your dad?"

"Right, and she said it sure looked like her."

"*Looked like*, yeah," Alison said. "But did she say it was positively her?"

Ryan remembered his grandmother had been a bit vague about it. She'd said it wasn't a very good picture.

Alison led him into a dim, windowless classroom with tiered seats. A big white screen was in front of the blackboard. She took the envelope from him. "Shut the door and pull the shade, will you?"

He obliged her. The place was so dark he could barely see her trotting up the stairs in the center aisle. The only lights he could go by were some illuminated exit signs. Alison disappeared in the shadows. He heard a click, then a humming sound. A light went on above—and it reflected on the big white screen. He could see Alison now, standing beside an overhead projector.

She put a photo on it. Ryan stared at the huge blowup of Lacee with his father. "I'm almost positive that's Jenny," she said, her voice echoing in the big room.

She switched the pictures on the overhead. He was now looking at Halle Driscoll and Scott Hamner. "That's Jenny, too."

"Are you sure?" Ryan asked.

"You and your friend," Alison said. "You never met her. You were just going by these photographs—and getting distracted by how much she made herself look like these other women. But I've met the woman in these photos. These two are her. They're the same woman . . ."

On the projector, she switched to the photo of Dick Ingalls and his second wife at a marina. "This one's not as clear. The sunglasses are covering a lot, but I can see Jenny in the mouth and chin."

"Damn, I wish we had a picture of this Jenny person," Ryan said.

She shut off the overhead projector, and the classroom went black.

"We do," he heard her say.

"Okay, Grandma, see where it says "Attachment?" Just double-click it. And when it asks if you want to download it, click on yes."

Watching him on the phone with his grandmother, Alison smiled. With everything he'd just dumped on her, the smile was fleeting. Still, for a brief moment, she thought about how cute he was. He was sweet, too. Among the photos he carried around, there were pictures of his dead sister and brother. Her heart broke for him.

They stood on the corner in front of the school. She'd called a taxi a few minutes ago, but it seemed to be taking forever to arrive. She hated knowing that woman was alone in the house with Danny right now. Ryan had told her that Danny was probably safe—for the time being. It wasn't part of the killing pattern to murder one child at a time. The families were all together when they were killed. Still, Alison was anxious to get home and make sure her brother was all right.

"Is it downloading?" Ryan asked his grandmother, long-distance to Highland Park, Illinois. He covered the phone and turned to her. "My grandmother's computer is ancient. We may be here all day waiting for it to download."

He'd e-mailed his grandmother the photo of Jenny that Alison had taken on the sly at the breakfast table this morning. He'd told her that some anonymous person had e-mailed him the photo.

Impatient, Alison took another look down the street, hoping she'd spot their cab.

"Okay, Grandma, so what do you think?" Ryan said into the phone. "Is it possible the woman in the picture is Lacee? I mean, the hair's different and all. But do you think it could be Lacee?"

Alison tried to read the expression on his face as he listened.

His mouth clenched a bit, and he sighed. "You sure?" He turned his face away. "No, like I told you, someone sent it to me, and I thought it might be a picture of Lacee's sister or something . . . No . . . I haven't talked with her since that time at the funeral, Grandma. Listen, I need to scram. You can just delete that photo, okay? Billy says hi . . . No, no, we have plenty of money . . . Okay . . . Yeah, I love you, too. Bye."

He clicked off the line and turned toward her again.

"Well?" Alison said.

He nodded. "A 'dead ringer,' she said."

"Her car's still there," Alison said as they rounded a curve in the street.

She'd asked the taxi driver to drop them off a block away from the house, and now they were on foot, sticking close to the woods along the side of the road. She needed to make sure her brother was safe, and she didn't want "Jenny" seeing them. Ryan kept saying the woman wouldn't harm Danny, not yet. She probably had every intention of driving him to the birthday party—and picking him up later. Alison figured Ryan was probably right. Just the same, she wasn't going to let her brother get into the red Hyundai with that bitch until she got a license plate number from it.

She figured once the house was empty, she and Ryan would check out the woman's stuff in the guest room. Obviously, this woman's real name wasn't Jenny Ballatore. It was probably a made-up name, or someone's identity she'd stolen. Last night, the woman had brought with her two suitcases and a big brown box. Among all that stuff, there had to be something that would give them a clue about her real identity.

Alison had told Ryan about how touchy "Jenny" had been about having her picture taken. Ryan said that according to his kid sister, Lacee had been extremely camera-shy. "Now we know why," he'd added. "Another thing about Lacee, she didn't do much cooking. With her running the house, my brother and sister lived off Lean Cuisine, Stouffer's, and takeout."

"That sounds about right," Alison said. "Jenny made a big deal out of the fact that she fed us breakfast this morning—and all she did was make toast and open some cereal boxes."

As they approached the driveway, Alison stopped and entered the Hyundai's license plate number into her iPhone notebook. Then she and Ryan swung around and cut through the neighbor's backyard to the side of the house. She'd seen Danny and his friend scale the stonework exterior to the balcony that jutted over the side of the hill. Their living and dining rooms each had a set of doors that opened up to that balcony. Thanks to their mother's green thumb, several still-thriving potted mini-trees and tall plants were on the veranda. Alison figured they'd provide some coverage while she was up there, spying on their houseguest.

"Give me a boost up," she whispered to Ryan. She tried to reach for one of the stones that stuck out farther than the others.

"What are you doing?" he said, hesitating.

"I'm going to climb up to the balcony and take a look inside the house," Alison explained in a hushed voice. "I want to see what she's doing when she thinks no one's around. For all I know, she could be poisoning our food or something. C'mon, please, give me a boost. Okay?"

Ryan seemed a bit reluctant as he squatted down and put his hands together.

Alison set her foot in his hands and he lifted her up. Her sandals were a little iffy on the stones. She thought about kicking them off to make the climb easier. But she was worried they might make too much noise when they hit the ground. Besides, as she grasped one stone after another to pull herself up, the rough edges scratched and hurt her hands. She found herself wincing with the pain every time she grasped another stone. She didn't want to do the same damage to her bare feet. She kept wondering how Danny and his friend had made it up here without killing themselves.

Just inches beneath the balcony, she made the mistake of glancing down at Ryan. He stood at least twenty feet below her, staring up. He looked terrified for her.

Alison froze. She started to tremble. Her grip on the jagged stone above her head seemed so fragile. Her shoulders ached and her limbs suddenly felt heavy and useless. She wasn't sure she could pull herself up any farther.

It occurred to her that just ninety minutes ago, she was bored to tears in her driver's ed class. Then Ryan had approached her. After realizing he was on the level with his story about families getting killed, and how their fathers had known each other, she'd gone into some kind of automatic pilot response. She suddenly needed to find out who Jenny really was. She needed to make sure Danny was okay. Everything up until now had been a knee-jerk response to what Ryan had told her.

But now, as she clung precariously to a piece of rough stone on the side of the house, it dawned on her that her mother had been murdered. And the woman her father had brought home to stay with them might have killed her —and set up that fake suicide. She may very well have murdered all those other people, too. And some of them were just children.

Alison glanced up at the scarab bracelet around her wrist, a gift from the murderess. With all the strength she could muster, she pushed herself up and swung that hand onto the edge of the balcony floor. The boards let out a creak as she tried to pull herself up.

Then she heard it. Above her, the screen door whooshed open.

Alison hung on to the balcony floor and tried not to

move a muscle. She still had her foot on one of the stones—so at least her arms weren't holding all her weight. She glanced down at Ryan. He was still looking up. But he must have heard the noise, too, because he had his back plastered against the stone wall.

The floorboards squeaked again as "Jenny" stepped out onto the balcony. "I thought I heard something," she said—obviously to someone on her cell phone. "Just a sec . . ."

Alison could see her shadow through the narrow gaps between the balcony planks. A few specks of dirt got in her eyes as she looked up, and she tried to blink them away.

"It couldn't have been anything," the woman announced, at last. "No, the little shit's still upstairs in his room getting ready for a birthday party. I'm driving him there. So—like I was saying, I want to wrap it up here by tomorrow night or the next morning. It depends on how soon you can get her here. You'll have the time difference working for you, a couple of extra hours. I can't do a damn thing until you deliver the real Jenny. Do I need to remind you? They all have to go at the same time . . ."

The floorboards squeaked again, and Alison turned her face away to keep from getting dust in her eyes.

"Two or three in the morning on Saturday?" the woman was saying. "Okay, that I can live with . . . What about the cat?" She paused. "Oh, for Christ's sake, bring it with you. I'll decide when you get here. Just don't get too attached to it . . ."

Alison listened to the sliding glass door squeak as

the woman shut it. She waited another few moments, and then hoisted herself up to the balcony. The railing creaked, but she kept pulling herself up. She ducked behind one of her mother's potted trees and watched "Jenny" approach the sliding door again.

She must have heard the creaking, because she glanced outside once more.

Trying to catch her breath, Alison stayed hidden behind the small tree. The open curtain inside covered the part of the window where she stood.

"Jenny" finally turned away from the sliding glass door and went to the breakfront in the dining room. Alison watched as she opened the cabinets and drawers. She inspected the crystal, china, and silverware. She opened the glass doors and checked out the various figurines on display, turning them over to look at the markings on the bottom. It was strange, but she seemed to know just where to look for everything that might have some monetary value. It was almost as if she'd been in the house before. And maybe she had been.

Maybe she was the one who had left the Diet Coke cartons on the kitchen counter the afternoon Alison had found her mother dead.

She couldn't believe her father had been duped by this bitch. Then again, she'd been fooled by her, too. She wondered who the real owner of the scarab bracelet was.

Danny stepped into the dining room—with his blond hair combed, and in a clean blue Izod shirt. He was carrying the birthday present their dad had bought with him last week. Alison had wrapped it for him. Her brother didn't seem to think it was strange that their houseguest had in her hand a Limoges teapot from the cabinet. "Jenny" casually returned it to the shelf and closed the breakfront's glass door.

Alison could hear murmuring, but couldn't make out what they were saying. It seemed like they were getting ready to leave. She leaned over the balcony railing and signaled to Ryan, pointing to the front of the house. He gave her the OK sign, and then crept along the stone wall toward the street.

After a minute, she heard the front door open and shut. A few moments later, the car engine started.

"Jenny" hadn't completely shut the sliding glass door. Alison let herself into the living room, and hurried to the front of the house.

Outside, tires screeched.

Alison froze. It sounded like a car had stopped suddenly.

Opening the door a crack, she peered outside. She didn't see the Hyundai rental in the driveway or on the road. Ryan emerged from some bushes between the garage and the front door.

"What was that noise?" Alison asked. "Did she see you?"

He shook his head. "It was weird. She and your brother took off. Then from around that curve," he said, pointing, "came this white Taurus headed in the same direction. They must have seen me, because they slammed on the brakes."

"And then what?"

He shrugged. "Then they kept going—after her. Maybe it was her accomplice or something. Anyway, I hope I didn't blow our cover."

Alison opened the door wider. "C'mon, we better hurry. If they spotted you, we don't have much time before she comes back."

Alison locked the door after him. Then she led him downstairs to the guest room.

The large brown box "Jenny" had brought with her was shoved into the corner of the room, beside Danny's relief map of the United States. Alison made a beeline toward the box.

"Damn," Ryan muttered.

"What?" she asked. Leaning over the box, she glanced back at him.

He stood by the nightstand. "I was hoping she'd have a sound machine. My brother, Keith, said Lacee had a sound machine with jungle noises."

"Check out her clothes in the closet," Alison said. "Look through the pockets. See if there are any clothes with labels from boutiques in a certain city. At least maybe we'll find out where she's from."

"God, you're good," Ryan remarked, opening the closet door.

Alison found Jenny Ballatore's work portfolio in the box. She looked over the design samples, and was impressed with her designs—if they were really hers.

" 'Caroline's Casuals, Oakland, California,' " Ryan said, reading one of the labels.

Alison examined a blue plastic box, which was a little smaller than a hockey puck. She opened it. "Huh, a night guard," she said. She found some notebooks, and opened one to a middle page. The penmanship was neat:

2/16/12

Mom was having one of her more lucid days today. We had a little walk down memory lane, while I was in the kitchen making dinner. She actually helped & made the salad. I couldn't shut her up, but it was sweet. It's amazing how with-it she can be at times. But then she started talking about Aunt Dot as if she were still alive. Of course, I let her think she was . . .

Alison closed the notebook. She opened another, and saw more writing, the same penmanship. She found a handful of other books, too, novels with Jenny's name written on the inside cover.

"Nothing in the pockets except some Kleenex and two peppermints, still in the wrapper," Ryan announced. "Is Ellen Tracy a store someplace?"

Alison shook her head. "No, she's a designer." She ducked out of the guest room and tried the bathroom next door. On one shelf in the medicine chest "Jenny" had stored some face cream, her lip balm, a toothbrush, and some other things. There were no prescription bottles, nothing with a name on it. Alison even went through the trash basket. Nothing.

Ryan hovered in the bathroom doorway. "Did you say she had a night guard in the box? You mean, one of those thingies people put in their mouth when they're sleeping?"

She nodded. "So they don't grind their teeth."

"Well, if she slept here last night, why isn't it in here

with her other stuff—or on the nightstand? Why is it stashed in a box of junk?"

Alison stared at him for a moment. "Because—oh, my God, because *it's not hers*," she said, grabbing his arm. "It's the *real* Jenny Ballatore's—so are those books and journals, the portfolio and the clothes, even the coffee mug she was drinking out of this morning, I'll bet. I heard her on the phone when she was on the balcony. She said she wanted to wrap things up by tomorrow night. It's going to happen around two or three in the morning on Saturday. And this guy she's working with has to bring the *real* Jenny, because 'they all have to go at the same time,' she said. It's just what you've been telling me about the whole family dying together. I think he must be bringing Jenny's cat with him, too."

"Tomorrow night?" Ryan asked. He shook his head. "I thought we'd have more time. Usually she marries the guy first . . ."

"That's how they've been doing it," Alison said, half-listening to him. "They've got the real Jenny Ballatore locked up somewhere while this woman assumes her identity. That's why she didn't want her picture taken. They must have the real Jenny holed up somewhere in the Midwest, because she said to the guy on the phone that he has two extra hours to get her here, because of the time difference."

Ryan shook his head. "You're going too fast for me . . ."

"The idea is they bring the real Jenny here tomorrow night, and kill her along with the rest of us. The police will find the genuine article here, dead—along with her journals, books, and her night guard, and even her cat. And no one's the wiser."

"Do you hear yourself?" Ryan said. "They want to kill you and your family *tomorrow night.*"

"That gives us twenty-four hours," Alison said, patting his shoulder. She brushed past him out of the bathroom. "Come on upstairs with me. I want to check something out . . ."

She led him to the dining room. She studied her mother's silver pieces and the china displayed in the breakfront. "Whatshername was checking this out earlier. Something tells me she plans on leaving here with some souvenirs. Some of this stuff is really expensive, too. How much was your father supposed to have embezzled?"

"Three hundred and fifty thousand bucks," Ryan replied. "But my friend Stephanie was pretty sure Lacee got his work password information and stole it."

"Not Lacee, the woman pretending to be Lacee," she corrected him.

"They never found the money."

Alison slowly shook her head. "But that's not why they're doing this. It's not about the money and the expensive souvenirs they can pawn. Those are just perks. No, they're doing this for some other reason. It's got to be something else—something that involves our fathers and the other two."

He shrugged. "All I could think of is the waitress disappearing that same summer they were all at the country club. But I talked to her sister, and she didn't think they had anything to do with it."

Alison nodded. Ryan had already told her about that

in front of the school. She didn't want to believe her sweet father could have been involved in something so sordid.

Ryan wandered over toward the cellaret. "Oh, my God . . ."

She turned toward him. He was pointing to the bottles on top of the wine cabinet. "Are those hers?"

"Yeah, the two in front are hers. She brought them with her last night. Or maybe they're the real Jenny's . . ."

"They're hers," Ryan said with certainty. He picked up the liquor with the uniquely shaped bottle. "Keith was right. It looks just like Mrs. Butterworth's . . ."

Alison noticed the bottle wasn't quite full and the band around the top had been ripped. She'd watched "Jenny" take the unopened bottle out of the grocery bag last night. "She must have drunk some after I went to bed," Alison said. "What is it?"

"Frangelico," Ryan murmured. "She has a couple of shots after dinner every night. My sister told me."

Alison heard a car pull up in front. "Oh, crap, she can't be home already . . ." She raced to the front window and looked outside. The red Hyundai was in the driveway. Her mouth open, she watched "Jenny" climb out of the car. "Damn it, you're right," she whispered. "Somebody she's working with must have spotted you . . ."

"The balcony . . ." Ryan said.

"No, it's too late," Alison said in a hushed voice. Grabbing his arm, she pulled Ryan into the living room and then pushed him down on the sofa. She kicked off her sandals and unbuttoned the top of her sleeveless blouse.

"Whoa, wait a minute," Ryan said.

The front door lock clicked just as she climbed on top of him.

It took him a moment, but then he seemed to know exactly what she was going for, because he began to kiss her neck. "I can't let her get a good look at me," he whispered, his hands caressing her back. "She's gonna spot the resemblance to my dad. I'll need to get out of here right away. I'm staying at the Grove Inn. Call me there tonight . . ."

"Okay," she whispered. She heard the front door close.

Alison kissed him. He had soft lips and nice breath. For a brief moment, she almost forgot why she was on top of him like this.

But then she heard "Jenny" clear her throat. "Well, now, don't let me interrupt . . ."

"Oh, shit," Ryan muttered.

Alison swiveled around and gaped at her. "Oh, my God . . ." She untangled herself from Ryan and climbed off the sofa. Past the hair in her eyes, she saw "Jenny" standing there with her hands on her hips, frowning at them.

Ryan's black T-shirt had ridden up to his chest—so most of his stomach was showing. He put a hand in front of his face. "Oh, man, busted," he muttered. He kept his hand up in front of his face as he hurried past her toward the door. He was a good actor. He looked like he was really embarrassed or ashamed. "See ya, Ali!" he called, running out the door. He shut it behind him.

"I didn't think you'd be home," Alison said, buttoning up her blouse. All the while, her heart raced.

"Jenny" was shaking her head at her. She let out a surprised little laugh. "Who was that?"

"The guy I told you about—Shane." She pushed the hair back from her face. "Are you going to say anything to my dad?"

The woman seemed to mull it over. Then she cracked a tiny smile. "No. Your secret's safe with me. We're friends, remember?"

Alison nodded. "Friends," she echoed.

She put on her sandals, and then went over to the mirror and checked her reflection. She started for the door.

"Where are you headed?" the woman asked. "Are you going to chase after him?"

She glanced over her shoulder. "No, Jenny. I have to get back to school. I have chem lab in an hour."

"Nice way to spend your break," she replied.

Alison didn't say anything. She just slipped out the front door.

CHAPTER TWENTY-SIX

Thursday—12:09 P.M.

Ryan wasn't sure how to get back to the hotel from here. Walking along the roadside, he glanced back at Alison Metcalf's house, a half a block away. He hoped Alison would be all right. He figured the sooner he got to the hotel, the sooner she could call him.

He was pretty sure the way back was the long, straight roadway up the steep hill in front of him. The climb looked like a lung-burner.

A thousand thoughts raced through his head. He couldn't believe just moments ago he had been in the same room with the woman who, in all likelihood, had been involved in the murder of his entire family. A part of him had wanted to grab her by the throat, force a confession out of her, and then choke her to death. But she had at least one accomplice out there. And the life of the real Jenny Ballatore, wherever she was, hung in the balance. If he called the police right now, what would happen to that woman?

He had a picture of the phony Jenny on his iPhone. He was pretty sure Alison was right about how these murderers had conducted their killing spree. But he still didn't know why.

He wished he could tell Stephanie everything they'd figured out so far. If only he could dial her number, hear her voice, and talk to her. But at this point, hoping she was still alive seemed pretty futile.

He had to think of Alison and her family. He liked her. In fact, he couldn't believe that just a couple of minutes ago, she'd been on top of him, kissing him. He hated leaving her with that woman. He kept reminding himself that nothing was going to happen until tomorrow night.

Ryan heard a door slam, and wondered if it had come from the Metcalfs'. He swiveled around. He couldn't see the house anymore. Was it Alison? Or was that woman coming after him?

He spotted a white Taurus cruising around a curve in the road.

"Shit," he muttered, ducking into the bushes. Branches scratched his arms and burrs clung to his T-shirt, but he forged deeper into the woods. He had a feeling he'd already been spotted—a second time.

Ryan heard the tires screech on the pavement again. Through the trees, he could make out the Taurus, stopped on the road. He turned to go farther into the brush and almost ran into an old, rusty barbed-wire fence. The fence still looked pretty sturdy, and came up to his neck. There was no way he could jump it without getting all cut up.

An incessant *ding, ding, ding* rang out. He realized it must have been the car, signaling a door was open, and the keys were left in the ignition.

Ryan started to move alongside the fence. He hoped to find an opening in it. But his foot caught on something, and he nearly tripped. He looked down and saw it was a section of a fallen branch about as long as a baseball bat—only twice as thick. It was covered with mud, moss, and worms, but he bent down and grabbed it anyway. He wasn't scared anymore.

He was enraged.

If this person chasing him was a cohort of that evil bitch who had killed his family, he refused to run.

Through the trees, Ryan saw the car's hazard lights blinking. Someone was moving toward the edge of the woods. He couldn't tell if it was a man or a woman. But whoever it was, they suddenly became very still. He wondered if they had a gun.

"Ryan? Ryan, is that you?"

He dropped the branch, and closed his eyes. "Oh, thank God," he whispered.

He recognized Stephanie's voice.

Stephanie hadn't expected him to get so emotional.

Ryan emerged from the woods, scratched up and dirty. Without saying a word, he threw his arms around her and started sobbing. As she patted his back, she couldn't help thinking that they'd only met that one time, and yet they'd developed this long-distance bond on the phone and through e-mails. It was strange to feel this important to someone once again.

She gently pulled away from him. "Come on, we can't afford to linger here."

"Where the hell were you?" he asked, wiping his eyes. "Why didn't you call me? I was worried sick about you. I thought you were dead. Hell, everyone thinks you're dead . . ."

"I figured it was safer for me that way," Stephanie said. She moved around the front of the Taurus to the driver's door. "Now, hurry, get in the car."

The Taurus's motor churned as Stephanie drove up the steep hill. She kept checking her rearview mirror to make sure no one was following them. Ryan was strapped in the passenger seat. A breeze came through his open window, but his short, spiked blond hair hardly moved. She almost didn't recognize him when she'd spotted him in front of the Metcalfs' house about a half hour ago, though she really shouldn't have been surprised to find him in Seattle. She'd warned him—practically begged him—not to come here. So naturally, he was here.

He seemed a lot more surprised to see her.

"At five in the morning yesterday, I decided to sneak back home in a taxi and grab some things for this trip," she explained, her eyes on the road ahead. "If I'd left the hotel about fifteen minutes earlier, they'd still be picking up pieces of me on Hilliard Street."

Neither she nor the taxi driver, Steve, heard the blast. But about five blocks from her house, fire trucks and squad cars—with their sirens wailing and lights flashing—passed them on the street. Stephanie had Steve keep going to the start of her block, where the police were already setting up orange cones. Emergency flares hissed and glowed in the dim light of dawn. Her neighbors, dressed in robes and pajamas, were coming out of their homes.

As for her own home, flames consumed what was left of it.

"That's your house, isn't it?" the taxi driver asked.

"Could you—could you take me to the airport, please?" she managed to say.

"That was your place, wasn't it?" he asked again, turning the cab around.

She felt sick to her stomach, and started trembling. "Could you just drive, please?" she whispered. "Get us out of here . . ."

As they approached the airport, she explained to him that she was better off letting certain people think she was dead. Would he mind not saying anything to the police or anyone else for the next twenty-four hours? She would call and explain everything to him.

His eyes kept shifting back to her in the rearview mirror. Then he finally sighed. "All right, but you better call me."

"Thank you," she said. "Are—are you sure I can't pay you?"

"Positive. I don't have a fare, because I never picked anyone up."

At the National Car Rental kiosk in the Portland Airport, she thanked God for that cabdriver. She ended up calling him a lot sooner than she thought she would.

With all of her crouching down and ducking in the back of the taxi, her cell phone must have slipped out of her pocket. She didn't notice it was missing until she stopped for gas in Olympia. From a pay phone, she called her number. The taxi driver, Steve McKinney, answered. He promised to FedEx the phone to her hotel in Seattle.

She figured it was there at the front desk at the DoubleTree, waiting for her now. Meanwhile, she hadn't been able to get her messages. And she couldn't for the life of her remember Ryan's cell phone number. She'd been able to look up his grandmother's number on Hill Street in Highland Park. She'd called it from the pay phone in the hotel lobby several times, hoping Ryan would answer. She kept getting his grandmother or the machine, and kept hanging up. She was probably driving his poor grandmother crazy.

This morning, after reading about the Beaverton couple who decided to toss a brick through her window, Stephanie figured out what must have happened. While she was at the hotel, the man who had been trying to kill her must have wired the house for detonation. Obviously, the place had been rigged to blow using some kind of motion sensor. The brick through her window had set it off.

Unfortunately, if she was able to figure out what had happened, so could these killers. If they saw the news item about the Beaverton couple, then they knew she was alive. The police probably now assumed she'd escaped the blast. Considering her reputation with them, they probably thought she'd caused it.

Except for four hours of sleep at the DoubleTree last night, Stephanie had spent nearly all of yesterday and this morning following Mark Metcalf. She'd caught him meeting up with his new girlfriend last night in front of the TV station, and she'd followed them here to the Metcalfs' house in West Seattle. It looked like the woman was already moving in.

"I even got some pictures of her with a disposable camera I bought at the hotel gift shop," she told Ryan. "I'm not positive, but I'm pretty sure she's the same woman who drugged my coffee at the Portland Airport."

He nodded. "I got a picture of her, too, Stephanie. I e-mailed it to my grandmother. It's the same woman who married my father. There's no doubt about it. Alison and I—well, mostly Alison—we figured out how they're doing it . . ."

Thursday—7:19 P.M.

"I snuck in the guest room while she was in the shower," Alison whispered to him over the phone. "I went through her purse. It's all Jenny Ballatore's stuff in there. The photo on the California driver's license might look like her at first glance, but if you actually stop and study it, you can see it's not the same woman. I took down the real Jenny's address . . ."

"Just a sec," Ryan said into the hotel phone. He signaled to Stephanie, who was sitting over at the desk. They'd been eating Thai food takeout when Alison had called. "Paper and pencil?" he asked.

From the desk, she handed him the pad and pen, both with "The Grove Inn" printed on them.

"Thanks," he said, and then into the phone, "Okay, go ahead."

"She lives at 722 Bayview, Apartment 835, Emeryville, California 94608. The same address is on her checks, so I think it's up to date. She had her phone in the purse, too. I was hoping to find some of the real Jenny's friends' contact numbers for you guys, but this woman has it set up so you need a password." Ryan heard her sigh on the other end of the line. "I tried looking for a second phone—you know, her own—or a wallet or something that might tell us who she really is. But she must have it hidden pretty damn well. I even tried under the mattress. Anyway, if I can sneak into her rental car tonight—"

"No, don't take any more chances," Ryan said. "Don't push your luck." He realized he was talking to her the way Stephanie talked to him. "Have you said anything to your dad yet?"

"Not yet. Ever since he got home, whatshername has been clinging to him like a lecch. Besides, I'm not sure what to say to him. I mean, does your friend, Stephanie, have a theory about why all this is happening?"

"We're pretty sure it has something to do with the disappearance of the girl from the country club."

"But I seriously don't think my dad could ever be involved in something so creepy and horrible. Besides, didn't the waitress's sister even say the guys couldn't have had anything to do with her disappearance?"

"Stephanie thinks she seems a little too sure about it," Ryan explained. "She might be hiding something. Plus that photo you took of the fake Jenny, Stephanie thinks there's a resemblance to the newspaper photo of the missing girl. I have to agree. That's why I'm getting my friend to set up the Skype session with Mr. Jayne tomorrow morning . . ."

He'd called St. Paul's rectory, and got the priest to give him Mr. Jayne's number. Then he called Mr. Jayne and asked if he could have a friend come by his apartment tomorrow morning. He wanted to show Mr. Jayne something online. The old man was as grouchy and curt as ever, but he'd agreed to meet Ryan's friend at 10:30 in the morning.

What Ryan wanted to show Mr. Jayne was the photo Alison had taken of their houseguest. If Mr. Jayne recognized his daughter, then they'd have their answer.

It had been almost tougher to get Billy to agree to set up the Skype session for them. "I'm curious," he'd said. "Remind me again why the hell you don't just go to the police?"

Ryan had to go over it with him once more: they'd have to persuade police from all these different jurisdictions to reopen the cases; except for photos of the woman now claiming to be Jenny Ballatore, they had no physical evidence that these deaths were connected; the only person who might explain a motive for the murders was Mark Metcalf, and he refused to even acknowledge that he knew the other three guys. "Plus we're pretty sure this woman has an accomplice. Maybe two," Ryan had pointed out. "If the cops arrest her, what's going to happen to the real Jenny Ballatore?"

"The police will probably arrest *me* before they arrest this woman," Stephanie had chimed in from across the hotel room. "They think I blew up my house. I have absolutely no credibility with them. They think I'm a nutcase."

"Did you hear that?" Ryan had asked his friend on the phone.

"Yes. I think you're *both* nutcases," Billy had replied. "And I must be nuts to go along with this. But I'll set up your Skype session for you . . ."

If Mr. Jayne didn't recognize the fake Jenny as his daughter or a friend of his daughter's, then they were back to square one. Ryan figured he and Stephanie would have to come up with a whole new theory to determine the motive for all these killings. And they'd have only a few hours to follow up on it.

"I want to be there when you're Skyping with this old guy," Alison said. "You can keep me off camera. I just want to see how he reacts to the picture, and what he says. Then I'll talk to my dad, I promise. He has to be at the station during the day tomorrow. I can talk to him there—without that awful woman around. We'll still have time. They're not going to try anything until tomorrow night at the earliest. Worst-case scenario is if we haven't gotten anywhere, we call the police at six-thirty."

"Just a sec," Ryan said. "Repeat that last part for Stephanie."

He held out the phone.

"I said that if we can't work this out ourselves by six thirty tomorrow night, we should dump this on the police and hope for the best."

"Does that sound like a plan?" Ryan asked.

Stephanie nodded. "I guess so. It ensures all of us will be safe." But then she frowned and her voice dropped to a whisper. "I just hate to think about the real Jenny Ballatore, and where that leaves her."

Ryan got back on the phone. He knew Alison hadn't heard the last part.

As they finished up on the phone, he noticed Stephanie at the desk, pushing her food away. He said good night to Alison, hung up the phone, and then turned to her. "What's wrong?" he asked. "Are you thinking about the real Jenny?"

Stephanie nodded. "I wish to God we could do something to help her."

Thursday—10:32 P.M.
Sheridan, Wyoming

"I was going to try to make it all the way to Billings, but the last Red Bull is wearing off," he said into his Bluetooth. He sat at the wheel of the Winnebago. The yellow tabby clawed at the back of his cushioned driver's seat. Churning along the dark Interstate, he could see the twinkling city lights ahead.

He'd packed some of his things. But more important, in the back he had a plastic bag full of *her* things: the hairbrush and comb she'd been using, her soap, her underwear, used Kleenexes—anything from the bunker with her DNA on it. They'd be planted in the house, where the bodies would be found.

And he was on his way there now.

"Driving through those Black Hills at night was a bitch," he continued. "I think I'll pull over someplace, give her a sedative, and then go look for a trailer park in Sheridan, get some sleep. I may even have a drink or two. The side of my face is killing me—her with that fucking lightbulb. I swear, there must be a few pieces of glass still in there." He touched the big, white bandage along his jaw. "So—what are you doing?"

"I'm down in the guest room," his cohort whispered. "He just left about five minutes ago for his eleven o'clock newscast. I told him I'd wait up. The brats are in their respective rooms. The little one's asleep. The prom queen's been giving me the cold shoulder all night long. I'm not sure what's going on with her. What's your ETA?"

"If I put the pedal to the metal and we have traffic on our side, I should be there at two or three in the morning on Saturday."

"Perfect," she said. "There's a small parking lot by the beach just down the hill from the house here. I'll leave the rental there for you. Park the Winnebago down there, and transfer our friend to the rental. It's a red Hyundai. The keys will be on a magnet under the left passenger door. I don't want the neighbors seeing the Winnebago in front of their house."

"Have I ever parked the Winnebago in front of the house? Ever? I know the drill by now. Just text me the approximate address of the parking lot, okay?" He rubbed his tired eyes and focused on the road again. "Speaking of our package, I'm afraid there's some bruising. She has quite the shiner from our little scuffle early this morning."

"That's all right," his partner said. "There won't be much left of her face anyway."

Jenny heard murmuring.

She'd been awake for a while now, maybe an hour or

so. She wasn't sure. She still wasn't used to opening her eyes and seeing just blackness. Tied up inside the compartment under the Winnebago's full-size bed, Jenny tried to wrestle her hands free. She was sweating so much that the piece of tape over her mouth was starting to loosen a bit.

Over the hum of the wheels on the road, she heard a police siren. It seemed to be behind them, getting closer and louder.

"Oh, fuck me!" she heard her captor yell.

She could feel the Winnebago start to slow down. Loose gravel started to hit the underside of the vehicle. They were pulling over to the side of the road.

Jenny tried to move her mouth and jaw to put some slack in the tape. Her arms struggled to wriggle out of the rope binding her wrists together. She'd never have another chance like this. The next time he took her out of this drawer, he'd probably kill her.

She listened to her captor swearing as the Winnebago finally ground to a stop. The siren's wail ceased. She knew the cop would be coming up to his window or knocking on the trailer's door within the next minute or two. She kept moving her jaw like she was chewing a big wad of gum. The tape was tearing at the skin around her mouth. Her eyes watered up.

Outside, she heard a car door slam, and then footsteps on the gravel along the roadside. If she could hear the cop out there, he could hear her.

"I'm writing you up for speeding," the Wyoming State Trooper explained. He looked like a rookie, one of those stocky, baby-faced guys. He had to reach up to the open window to take the driver's license from him.

He smiled down at the cop from his driver's seat. "Well, officer, guilty as charged, I'm sure."

"I don't catch too many Winnebagos speeding around here. Usually, you're the guys everyone's trying to pass. Anyway, the speed limit went down to fifty-five when you passed the sign for Sheridan back there. You were doing sixty-six."

"Well, I believe it. I must have missed the sign. I'm getting pretty sleepy. Tell me, are there any trailer parks around here you'd recommend?"

"You're not too far from Peter D's RV Park on Joe Street," the cop replied. "Keep your eyes open, and you'll see a sign for it coming up." With the driver's license and his ticket pad, the trooper ambled toward the front of the Winnebago. He started jotting something down.

With his hand slung over the steering wheel, he watched the cop at work. He heard a muffled cry from back in the sleeping area. The cat must have heard it, too. Suddenly, the tabby turned and arched its back.

The cat recognized his owner's voice.

"Help!" It was clearer this time, but still muted.

He straightened in the driver's seat and stared at the rookie, who was still in front of the Winnebago, writing the ticket.

The cat scurried back toward the bedroom and scratched at the closed door.

"Help me, please!" she yelled, her voice faint. She started kicking against the side of the little compartment.

The state trooper suddenly glanced up. Then he looked from side to side.

"Shit," the man muttered. He reached over and switched on the radio. They were playing Johnny Cash's "Ring of Fire." He cranked it up.

The cop walked back toward his window. "Could you turn down your radio, please?" He had to yell to be heard over the noise.

The man obliged him, turning it down a few decibels. He started drumming his fingers on the half open window. The radio and the drumming competed with the muffled sounds from the bedroom.

"What happened to your face, by the way?" the cop asked. He handed him his license and the ticket.

"Oh, I was mowing a friend's lawn and ran over a bottle. Lucky I didn't get any glass in my eye . . ." As he took the ticket and his license, he heard her faint screaming.

But at that very moment, a plane passed overhead.

Explaining the different payment options for the ticket, the cop had to talk loudly over the jet noise.

All the while, the man just smiled and nodded.

Jenny kept screaming for help and frantically kicking at the drawer. But she was barefoot, and it hurt like hell to keep banging at that pressed wood material. The only noise she could produce was a dull, muted thud. With her throat so dry, her screams were more like whimpering. She knew the cop couldn't hear her past the radio and the jet noise.

"Okay, so long!" her captor was saying. Then the radio started blaring again.

Jenny made a last-ditch effort to be heard, banging

away at the side of the drawer, and screaming until her throat was raw.

But she heard a car door slam, and the engine start up. She knew it was useless.

Past the radio, she detected footsteps. The bedroom door opened. He let out a grunt, and then all at once, the compartment she was in started moving. The big drawer squeaked.

Jenny blinked at the sudden light. She hardly had any time to focus on him. She saw the white bandage on his jaw. She saw him haul back his fist.

"I don't have to worry about the way you look," he said.

Then he slugged her in the face.

The pain was staggering, but it didn't knock her out. She was still conscious enough to feel the throbbing ache along one side of her head. Her ears were ringing.

As she lay there dazed, he must have cut off another piece of tape. He slapped it over her mouth. He tightened the rope around her wrists.

Letting out another grunt, he shoved the drawer shut with his foot.

Then everything was black again.

Jenny felt herself passing out from the pain and exhaustion.

The last thing she heard was her cat yowling.

Friday, June 21—1:55 A.M.
West Seattle

Mark heard a glass clinking downstairs. It was the second time tonight he'd heard the sound. He figured

Jenny was going for another nightcap. Maybe she couldn't sleep, either.

He thought about going down there and joining her in a drink, but not that godawful Frangelico stuff. He'd have a shot of bourbon—in the living room, not in Jenny's bedroom. Maybe then, he'd relax a little and be able to get some sleep. Last night had been a toss-and-turn marathon.

At the studio, the makeup woman hardly ever touched his face. But when they'd taped their promos yesterday, she had kept working on his eyes. "Honey, these aren't bags, they're steamer trunks. Were you partying last night or what?"

When they weren't taping, he was online, reading about the deaths of his former friends. If the pattern was continuing, Dina's "suicide" meant his family had already been targeted. The other widowers had remarried. But he had no intention of remarrying. He thought about Jenny downstairs, and wondered if their accidental meeting had been prearranged by someone else. Had someone set her up? Or was she a willing participant? It made no sense that she'd get involved in some scheme, knowing she'd end up dead.

He thought of his kids, asleep in their beds right now. Dick Ingalls's kids and Brent Farrell's had died in their beds.

The Portland police had called him back at the station yesterday. They'd merely asked if he'd heard from Stephanie Coburn again. Apparently, they were pretty certain she hadn't been home at the time of the explosion. At least he could answer them honestly this time and say no, she hadn't gotten in touch with him again, not since her call on Wednesday night.

He could have told the police the truth about Stephanie's call. He could have told them that he had every reason to believe her warnings were valid. He could have told them what had happened on that private beach on a Wednesday night twenty-seven summers ago.

But he didn't say a damn thing.

He didn't have to wonder why this was happening. But why was it happening now, after all these years?

He remembered Selena's discarded blue dress on the pier, fluttering slightly in the breeze. An hour later, it was gone—and so were her sandals, her bra, and her panties.

Mark heard glass clinking downstairs once more. He climbed out of bed and threw on some sweatpants. This time, he put on a T-shirt, too. He crept down the stairs and headed into the dining room. The chandelier above the table was on, but at its dimmest setting. He found Alison, in her mother's oversized REM T-shirt. She used it as a nightshirt. She was standing by the cellaret.

"Are you sneaking some booze?" he whispered.

"No, Dad," she said, rolling her eyes. "Don't worry. This isn't going to be an 'After School Special' moment. I don't have a drinking problem. I was just curious. In two nights, she's put away almost half a bottle of this Frangelico junk. Or are you drinking it, too?"

He shook his head. "No, that stuff's too sweet for me. So she has a nightcap or two. Cut her some slack, honey. She's had a rough time—moving up here, and this stalker situation. And you know, she's been a lot of help to us around here."

"I don't trust her, Dad," Alison whispered. "And I don't think you should, either."

His hands clutched the back of a dining room chair. "Why do you say that?"

Alison shrugged. "It's just a feeling I get. Is she going to stay here much longer?"

Mark thought about it for a moment. "I'll find her a hotel for tomorrow night," he said.

"Good." Alison wandered over and kissed him on the cheek. "Anyway, g'night."

"Sleep tight, sweetie," he said.

At the dining room entrance, she turned to look at him. "Dad, when you were around my age, did you ever do something that you—you really regretted?"

His eyes narrowed at her. "Alison, what are you talking about? Are you in some kind of trouble?"

She shook her head. "No, Dad. I'm asking if you ever were."

Mark felt his stomach clench. He shrugged and let out a puzzled little laugh. "No more than any normal kid. Why do you ask?"

"No reason," she murmured. "Good night."

She turned and headed toward the front hallway. Mark trailed after her. He watched her retreat up the stairs. He wondered if someone had been talking to her—and what exactly she knew. He wanted to call to her, but he didn't.

Mark stood at the bottom of the stairs. Alison disap-

peared down the hallway, and then he heard her bedroom door quietly closing.

He sighed, and turned away. Then something caught
his eye.

He glanced down the steps to the lower level. He
saw a shaft of light in the darkness. It was there for just
a moment before a shadow swept over it. Then everything was dark again.

Downstairs, someone had just closed another door.

CHAPTER TWENTY-SEVEN

Friday, June 21—8:32 A.M.
West Seattle

On the laptop screen, Mr. Jayne was staring back at him. His dark eyes kept shifting from side to side under his heavy, wild-haired brows. He wore his denim work shirt, and Ryan had to wonder if it was the same one from the other night—and if it had been washed. It looked like Billy had set up the computer notebook on Mr. Jayne's kitchen table. Ryan could see the avocado-colored refrigerator behind Mr. Jayne, with cards and snapshots on it.

Ryan was sitting at the desk in his hotel room. Alison stood over to the side near the bed so she could see the computer screen without being seen. She had her hair in a ponytail today, and was wearing a black T-shirt, jeans, and sandals.

They were recording the Skype session so they could show it to Stephanie later.

"You didn't tell me this friend of yours was an Oriental," Mr. Jayne grumbled.

Ryan was dumbfounded.

"Yes, I'm Oriental, just like the rugs," Billy said. His face wasn't in the shot, but Ryan could only imagine his peeved expression. His hand came into the picture. "The microphone's right there, Mr. Jayne," he said, pointing to the bottom of the screen. "Just talk normally."

"Thank you for doing this, sir," Ryan said.

"Well, it better not take long. I've got chores."

He and Alison had gone to FedEx Kinko's this morning, and blown up the photo she'd taken of the fake Jenny. Ryan reached for it now. "I just need you to take a look at this picture, and tell me if you know this person. Her hair and makeup might be different than how you've known her. But anyway . . ."

He held the photo in front of the screen. "Can you see this?"

"It's coming in clear on this end," he heard Billy say. "We can see it."

Squinting at the screen, the old man remained silent.

"Mr. Jayne?" Ryan said. "Sir?"

"Am I supposed to know who this is?"

"Well, possibly," Ryan said. "I was wondering if she's your daughter."

The old man shook his head. "That's not Nicole. Nicole's got blond hair."

"If you could just look past the hair for a minute," Ryan said. "If it's not Nicole, could it possibly be Selena—or a friend of Selena's?"

"Selena's dead, for God's sake," he snarled. "She was blond, too. Both my girls are blond. I don't know this woman at all."

"Mr. Jayne, do you have any pictures of Nicole that you can show us?" Ryan asked. "Just to confirm . . ."

With an impatient sigh, he got to his feet and turned to the refrigerator in the background. He removed a photo, and Ryan heard one of the magnets fall to the floor. Mr. Jayne plopped back in the chair and held the photo in front of the screen. His hand was shaking. "That's her, that's Nicole—with her sister," he said. "Are you satisfied?"

Ryan was staring at a blurry, washed-out color photo of a little girl—no more than five—with her adolescent sister. They were bundled in winter clothes, standing in front of a snowman. It wasn't any help at all.

"Mr. Jayne, I was talking about a more current picture . . ."

The old man shook his head. "I've had enough of this," he growled. He turned to Billy, who stood at his side. "How do you shut this thing off?"

Mr. Jayne got up from the chair.

"Shut it off!" Ryan heard him yell.

"Sorry," he heard Billy mutter. Then the screen went blank.

Ryan numbly stared at the monitor. A message was asking if he wanted to save or delete the file.

"Well, that was kind of a bust," Alison sighed.

"He's lying," Ryan said.

"What do you mean?"

He got up from the chair. "Can you retrieve it and play it back? I don't know how this works . . ."

Scooting in front of him, Alison worked the mouse and typed on the keyboard. "You haven't Skyped or recorded before?" she asked.

"No," Ryan replied. "When you bring it up, fast-forward until near the very end . . ."

"Well, you're mighty big with the pleases and thank-yous, aren't you?"

"Please," he said, hovering behind her. He watched the video in fast-forward. "Thanks. Now, could you freeze-frame it just when he gets up from the table at the end . . . please?"

Alison paused the video at the moment after Mr. Jayne left his chair. "Is that what you want?" she asked. "A shot of the refrigerator?"

Ryan was staring at the photos, postcards, holy cards, and a church bulletin on Mr. Jayne's refrigerator door. There were three greeting cards that had caught his eye. One had a photo of a baby's hand around a man's index finger; another showed a father and child on the beach at sunset; and another was a cartoon of a man's shirt and tie.

The image was slightly blurry, but he remembered those cards. He'd kept ones exactly like them in his desk drawer—after the first one, sent anonymously to his father, had caused an argument between his parents.

Ryan still remembered the line inside one of those unsigned cards:

But our family ties last forever!

Glenview, Illinois

Barton Jayne watched the tall Asian kid leaning over the kitchen table, closing up the thin little computer.

Barton glanced over at the knives in the butcher-block holder on the counter. He inched over toward the counter. "This friend of yours, the one I was talking to, where is he right now?" he asked.

The boy shook his head. "I'm not really sure. I think he's supposed to be in Madison, Wisconsin—at the university. He called me yesterday and asked me to set this up. Sorry it didn't work out for you guys."

"Did you fellas talk to anyone else about this?" he asked, reaching for one of the knives. He kept them sharp with the same file he used on the garden shears. "Does anyone else know you're here?"

The young man wasn't looking at him. He picked up a magnet from the floor and put it back on the refrigerator door. He frowned at him. "I'm not sure what you mean."

"I'm just wondering if he's going to be sending someone else here tomorrow."

"Beats me," he replied. "I'm sure not volunteering."

"Would you like a soft drink for the road?" he asked. He kept a hand behind him as he nodded to the refrigerator. "I've got some cold cans in there, on the bottom shelf. Help yourself."

"No, thanks," the kid said. "It's been a lot of fun, a regular laugh riot, but I think I'll just scram now."

As the boy turned and started for the stairs down to the garage apartment's entrance, Mr. Jayne stepped up behind him.

Suddenly, he heard the door open down there.

"Barton?"

He recognized Father Stutesman's voice. "Barton,

can you help us out over in the rectory? It's just going to take a minute . . ."

Mr. Jayne furtively set the knife down on the kitchen table, and moved to the top of the stairs. He watched the boy nod at Father Stutesman in the doorway, and then duck outside.

The snotty little son of a bitch had no idea how close he'd come to getting his throat slit.

Friday—10:25 A.M.
Emeryville, California

"I just don't understand it," said the manager of the Bay Vista Apartments. "She was an ideal tenant, never late with her rent, no complaints from the neighbors. In fact, they adored her. Bob Gold, next door in 837, he was just telling me that when his daughter, Dana, was visiting from Ohio, Jenny went out of her way to—"

"Do you know if Mr. Gold has heard from Jenny lately?" Stephanie interrupted.

He shook his head. "I don't think so," he said. "No one here has heard from her since she took off and left this mess . . ."

He glanced around Jenny Ballatore's spacious eighth-floor apartment. It had a beautiful view of the Oakland Bridge. With pictures knocked askew on the walls, drawers left open, and trash scattered on the carpeted floor, the place looked ransacked.

Stephanie had risked getting nabbed by the police at Sea-Tac by booking a last-minute trip to Oakland this morning. She'd thought her "presumed dead" status might get her flagged in the ticketing agent's computer. To her relief, she made it past ticketing and the boarding gate without anyone stopping her.

Thanks in part to the detective she'd hired, she knew enough about these women whose identities had been stolen. She also knew something about the woman responsible for their murders. The impersonator couldn't resist taking as much as she could from her victims: stealing valuables, maxing out their credit cards, and draining their bank accounts. And she kept the victims' close friends and family members on tenterhooks with e-mails and texts—composed on her victims' computers and phones.

Stephanie wanted to talk with one of Jenny's friends, someone who had heard from the fake Jenny.

She imagined Halle's, Lacee's, and Vanessa's apartments all looking trashed and plundered like this one. She noticed cat food on the kitchen counter, but no bowl, litter box, or cat toys.

Alison Metcalf had said something about them bringing a cat along with Jenny. Dead or alive, they wanted Jenny's cat found with her when the police walked into the massacre scene at the Metcalf house.

The food in the refrigerator was rotting. The landlord said Jenny's mailbox had gotten too full, and the post office was holding her mail now. "I just called her emergency contact yesterday, and asked if Jenny had a forwarding address yet," the landlord explained.

"Were they able to tell you anything?" Stephanie asked.

"Yeah, her friend said she didn't have an address, but Jenny was supposed to be somewhere in Seattle, staying with a new boyfriend—a widower with a couple of kids."

"This emergency contact person," Stephanie said. "Could you give me their phone number and address?"

"Her friend's name is Carroll Jordan, and she lives on Cole Street in San Francisco," Stephanie said into her cell phone. She'd be eternally grateful to the taxi driver, Steve McKinney, for shipping the phone to her hotel overnight.

She stood in the parking lot of the Bay Vista Apartments. It was sunny, with a cool breeze coming off the water. She looked out at the Oakland Bridge. "I'm headed over there now," she continued. "She and the real Jenny were—*are* good friends."

She used the same cover story with Carroll that she'd used with the landlord. She'd lied and said Jenny had designed her Web site. Now she was in town for a meeting. She was trying to track down Jenny so she could take her out to lunch and give her a bonus check.

"So what are you seeing this Carroll lady about?" Ryan asked. "I mean, what do you think she'll be able to tell you?"

"It's complicated. I'm just here on a hunch and a lot of hope. I'll call you in a couple of hours and let you know more. How did the Skype session go?"

"The old man pretended he didn't know her, but he does," Ryan replied. "He lied. In fact, I'm pretty certain he's in on this whole thing. I just checked with my friend, Billy, to make sure he got out of there okay."

"Why do you think Mr. Jayne's involved?"

"He had Father's Day cards on his refrigerator door. I noticed them while we were talking."

"I don't understand," Stephanie said.

"These weren't just any Father's Day cards. My dad got the exact same ones for the last few years—all unsigned . . ."

"Father's Day," Stephanie repeated. She remembered Scott talking to her on the phone about Rebecca's suicide. "Did she ever say anything to you about a Father's Day card?" he'd asked.

"Stephanie?"

"Listen," she said. "I think it's possible the others got Father's Day cards, too."

"Alison isn't sure if her dad got any. But here's what I was thinking. Maybe my dad, Alison's father, your brother-in-law, and Dick Ingalls all had sex with Selena that summer. Getting pregnant is a pretty good reason to run away, isn't it? I mean, especially when you have an old man like hers. Maybe Selena never knew who the baby's father was. I think that's why this fake Jenny woman looks like Selena Jayne, because that's her *mother* . . ."

"Ryan, honey, I—I think it's a good theory, but I studied the photo Alison took and watched that woman from my car, and I can tell you, she's not twenty-seven years old. She's closer to thirty-seven."

"Damn, Alison said the same thing," he admitted. "I just couldn't help thinking she was sending everyone—including her own father or *grand*father—the same cards every year."

"Well, you might be on to something there," Stephanie

said, starting toward her rental car. "Listen, I've got to go. What are you and Alison doing? Is everyone okay?"

"We're just hanging out here at the hotel," he answered. "She's going to the TV station to talk to her dad during his lunch break. Her brother Danny's all right. He's at a friend's house for most of the day."

The rental car's lights flashed as Stephanie hit the unlock button on her key fob. "Stay put and don't take any chances," she said, climbing into the car. "I'll talk to you in an hour or two."

"Okay, so long—and good luck with whatever you're doing down there."

"Thanks, I need it," she said, clicking off.

Stephanie started up the car, but then sat there at the wheel for a moment. She thought about Ryan's theory, and figured he was right about something.

Whatever happened back in the summer of 1986, however horrible, a child must have been involved.

Friday—10:48 A.M.
West Seattle

"I hope to get out a little early this afternoon—in case you need any help finding a hotel. And I'll be happy to loan you some money if you need it. I don't want you settling for some fleabag place. You should stay somewhere comfortable—and safe."

With big, sad eyes, she stared up at him.

She and Mark stood by his front door. He wore a tan suit with a white shirt and no tie. He was headed to the TV station for some meetings.

"Am I in the way here?" she asked meekly.

"Not at all, just the opposite," he said. "But until I figure out whether or not this threat is real, I need to keep you out of harm's way."

"What about your kids? Aren't you worried about them?"

"Terrified," he said. "That's why I'm sending them to stay with my in-laws for a couple of weeks—until this blows over. I just need to figure out what to do about Alison's summer school."

Her cell phone rang, and she dug it out of the pocket of her slacks. But then it stopped after one ring. She pushed the phone back in her pocket, and then moved in closer to him. Her arms slid up to his shoulders. "Well, I guess this is my last chance to see you off to work, and kiss you good-bye like a real wife."

Getting up on her tiptoes, she kissed him on the mouth. Her lips opened.

Mark took a step back, and gingerly pried her arms off his shoulders. "Thanks. That was—sweet. I'll see you in a couple of hours."

He opened the front door and retreated outside.

She lingered in the open doorway, and watched him climb into his vintage Mustang, parked in the bay beside the garage. She waved at him as he pulled away from the house. He didn't wave back.

She wondered how much that car was worth.

Ducking inside, she closed the door and hurried down the stairs to the guest room. She tugged at the nightstand, moving it away from the wall. Then she reached in back of it. She peeled off the tape that held her cell phone to the back of the stand. She clicked on the phone and speed-dialed a number.

She counted two ringtones. Then he answered: "Nikki?"

"I got the signal on Jenny's line," she said. "What is it, Daddy?"

"The Farrell kid, he just had me on some computer conference call. He showed me a picture of you—"

"What picture?" she asked.

"Well, you look like that Jenny girl, and you're in somebody's kitchen."

She remembered Alison taking the photos yesterday morning—and then *pretending* she'd deleted them. "That little bitch," she growled. "The Metcalf girl took that shot. If Ryan Farrell has that picture, it means he's working with her. Damn it, he must be in Seattle—"

"I tried to find out where he was," her father interrupted. "Maybe he and the girl are carrying on long distance. Farrell's friend, who set up the computer for the conference, he said Farrell was in Wisconsin."

"Wait a minute. Who's this friend?"

"Oh, some smart-mouthed Oriental kid," he answered. "I don't think he knows anything. I took down the license plate number on his car in case we need to take care of him later."

"So about the picture," she said, sitting down on the guest bed. "What did you tell them?"

"I acted like I didn't recognize you, of course. Still, we don't have much time. You need to finish this tonight."

"Laird's on the road right now," she said. "He should have my replacement here by two or three in the morning."

"Contain this as soon as possible. Get them all together, tie them up. Do whatever you have to, but find out from the girl where the Farrell kid is. You never should have let him slip away in April when you got rid of the rest of the family."

"Daddy, I explained that to you," she sighed. "Once I'd taken the money, I couldn't afford to wait—"

"Never mind that, just—just—just get them all together in the house there as soon as you can. Finish this tonight. I'm counting on you, Nikki. After this, it'll all be over. We can get on with our lives."

"What life?" she wanted to ask. She didn't have a life of her own. She'd spent most of the last two years pretending to be other women. But she didn't say anything to her father about that now. Instead, she said she'd call him back later. Then she hung up.

She set her cell phone down on the nightstand. She didn't bother hiding it. There was no need to anymore. The next person to come into this house wouldn't leave it again—until they were carried out in a body bag.

Nicole Jayne got to her feet and started up the stairs. She thought of that conniving little prom queen, Alison, and remembered back to when she was her age. Her sister had been dead—officially "missing"—for five years. Nikki was struggling at school. She spent her weekends and the previous two summers working as a ladies' room attendant at the country club. It was a disgusting, thankless job. All day long, she smelled shit, perfume, and Aqua Net. She loathed everyone there. Even the nice women seemed condescending and superior. And all of them were tightwads. Meanwhile, at home, she lived under her father's strict rules—even more inhibiting after her older sister had strayed. She was terrified of him—and for good reason.

As soon as she had enough money, Nikki got the hell out of there. She ended up in Las Vegas, working in the casinos. She got to know the ropes, and pretty soon, she was working some of the high rollers. Nikki became a first-class hooker and grifter. She teamed up with a small-timer named Laird Bikel. Together, they made a small jackpot on con jobs, some very clever scams, too. A few of their marks died in fatal "accidents" that she and Laird arranged. The first one had been tough going for her, but it got easier with each new mark. It never seemed to bother Laird.

Nikki might have gone on like that and saved up a nice little early retirement bundle for herself. But five years ago, she read about a young woman who was raped by three teenagers in Los Angeles's Griffith Park. It was a big story, because each of the teens responsible was from a "good family." Their victim, who took a beating for resisting them, was just some nobody. Apparently, a deal was worked out. The charges were reduced and the privileged preppies got off with light sentences that amounted to a slap on the wrist.

Nikki couldn't help thinking about that poor girl. They didn't show her photo in the newspaper, but Nikki pictured her sister. Everything she'd been suppressing for years about Selena and those four boys from Lake Ridge Country Club suddenly surfaced. She became more and more obsessed about it. Nikki did extensive research and learned that each of her sister's seducers was now a successful, happy family man.

Meanwhile, her sister was dead, and her own life was a mess.

Among the four young men, the one who fascinated and repelled her most was Dick Ingalls. He seemed to be their leader. Selena had had a terrible crush on him. Nikki's father would have called it "divine intervention" that Dick Ingalls's pretty wife died of a stroke.

Suddenly, Dick was a widower.

Nikki was still reading his wife's obituary when she started to formulate her plan to seduce Dick Ingalls, marry him, and then destroy his entire life. She found a willing accomplice in Laird. It was just the kind of elaborate con he enjoyed.

After the Ingallses' Lake Geneva summer home had gone up in flames, she and her partner walked away with about eighty thousand dollars in cash, silver, and jewelry. Dick hadn't any idea his new wife was dipping into his accounts and bleeding him dry. She and Laird had also collected over twenty thousand dollars from that Karla woman they'd abducted in Des Moines, Iowa. Nikki had been all set to assume Karla's identity and start working on Dick Ingalls. But that whole plan had to be scrapped, because the girl killed herself in the bunker. Ultimately it was Vanessa Black whose name went on the marriage license—and the death certificate. They'd made only about ten grand off her.

In the year after Ingalls's death, Nikki wavered between feeling triumphant about what she'd done and feeling vaguely dissatisfied. She started sending the three others unsigned Father's Day cards every year. She wanted them to think about all the women they'd been with, all the children they might have spawned. She wanted them to think about Selena, and her unborn baby.

She signed the cards she sent to her father—every year. That was her only communication with him in the last decade.

Then Nikki started to realize why she still didn't feel completely satisfied. Her father had no idea what she'd done. She didn't want to keep it a secret from him anymore.

So on Easter Sunday, 2012, she paid him a visit in his little garage apartment behind the rectory of that church in Glenview. She sat down with him at his kitchen table, and told him how she'd murdered Dick Ingalls and his family.

Her father broke down in tears. Then he hugged her, and whispered in her ear: "Good job, baby. Now, let's get those other three bastards."

Maybe she knew it was her mission all along. Maybe that was why she kept renewing the lease every year on that old house with the underground bunker in Cedar Rapids. The house was roughly halfway between Karla's home in Des Moines and Dick Ingalls's house in Glencoe, Illinois. Now the place was centrally located for their work in Chicago and on both coasts.

One problem: she couldn't wait around for the other three to become widowers. So they sped things up. Making it appear as if the wives had killed themselves had been her father's idea. "Let these rich, snot-nose sons of bitches know how it feels to walk in and find someone they love has died by their own hand," he said.

To Nikki, it seemed very karmic, like things coming full circle.

She made her contact with the new widowers while they were still vulnerable and confused. She built them up again and gave them confidence. They trusted her—the same way her sister had trusted each of them that summer night in 1986.

It was too bad she wouldn't have time to drain Mark Metcalf's bank account and run up his credit cards. A part of her really wanted to stretch this one out.

On the upper level of the Metcalf house, she stepped into the master bedroom and headed for the closet. From the shoebox on the shelf, she took out the Glock 19 and the bullets. She'd found them there yesterday afternoon, when she was alone in the house. It wasn't very original of Mark to leave the gun there. Scott Hamner had kept his gun in the bedroom closet, too—under a pile of sweaters.

Nikki sat down on the bed she would never share with her sister's seducer. In a way, it made her feel like a bit of a failure this time.

Humming a sad little tune to herself, she started to load the gun.

Friday—11:44 A.M.
San Francisco

"The last time I actually talked with Jenny, she was 'cautiously optimistic' about a blind date through this online service she'd signed on with," Carroll Jordan said. "She was supposed to meet the guy at the Public

Market in Emeryville. That was the first week in June, a Tuesday night."

Stephanie sat in the kitchen of Carroll's townhouse apartment in the Upper Haight neighborhood. Carroll's towhead baby daughter was in a high chair, with Gerber's mashed carrots all over her cute face. Spooning it out to her, Carroll had a little dollop of the stuff in her close-cropped red hair. But Stephanie didn't say anything. Her host was barefoot, and wore a black sleeveless blouse and white shorts. A box fan on the kitchen floor provided a cool breeze.

"And after that, it was just e-mails?" Stephanie asked.

"That's right," Carroll said. "It was like she was mad at me or something. Suddenly, she got distant and impersonal. I've left several voice mails. But not once has she called back." She waved the spoon in front of her daughter's face. "C'mon, Suzy, a few more bites for Mommy." She sighed. "It's so unlike Jenny. You know what else is unlike her? In the e-mails she's sent, she hasn't once mentioned how her cat is doing."

"That's right," Stephanie asked. "She has a cat, doesn't she?"

"Oh, she's obsessed with him," Carroll said, nodding. "Simon—that's her cat—he got lost for a day last year, and Jenny went crazy. When she finally got him back, she spent a small fortune on this state-of-the-art tracking collar. She even gave me a tracker device—for emergency backup. Ha, you know what you should do? You should take the tracking device to Seattle, and hunt Jenny down along with her new boyfriend—because where Jenny goes, the cat goes. And when you find her, give her a swift kick in the pants for me for acting like such a flake lately."

Stephanie bit her lip. "Do you still have the tracking device? Do you think I could borrow it?"

Carroll squinted at her and then laughed. "Are you serious? It's only good for detecting things a mile or two away."

"That may be all I need," Stephanie said.

Lowering the baby spoon in her hand, Carroll warily stared at her. "What is all this?"

Stephanie sighed. "Jenny didn't design my Web site. And I'm not looking to take her to lunch and give her a bonus check. But I want very much to help her. It's a long story, Carroll, but what it boils down to is that I think your friend is in terrible danger right now. Those e-mails you got, they weren't from her."

The baby started crying. Carroll shifted the tray, undid a strap, and lifted her out of the high chair. Rocking her daughter, she gazed at Stephanie with tears in her eyes. "I had a feeling it wasn't her, but I didn't want to believe it. If Jenny's really in trouble and you're serious about helping her, why haven't you called the police?"

"Because I'm worried she'd be in even more trouble if I did."

"I want an explanation about all of this," Carroll said.

"I won't leave here without giving you one, I swear. But right now, I need your help."

"Help you help Jenny, is that it?"

"Yes."

Carroll nodded toward the kitchen counter. "The cat tracking device is there in the middle drawer. It's our junk drawer, so it's kind of a mess. I think the instructions are in there, too."

Amid the candles, cereal box toys, extension cords, and other items, Stephanie found the pet tracking device, along with the instructions. She knew her plan was half-baked: hoping to track Jenny's abductor a couple of miles before he arrived at the Metcalfs' house—on the off chance Jenny's cat was still wearing the tracking collar. It was too much of a long shot.

Stephanie was thinking once again about how these killers stole their victims' money and walked away with all their valuables. She wanted to set a trap for them, something that seemed too good to resist.

She shut the drawer and turned to Jenny's friend. "If I wrote down what to say, could I ask you to send 'Jenny' a couple of e-mails—from you?"

"But will Jenny even see these e-mails?" Carroll asked.

"No, but the woman pretending to be Jenny will see them."

Carroll gazed at her and shrugged. "Sure, I guess. Just tell me what to write . . ."

CHAPTER TWENTY-EIGHT

Friday, June 21—12:32 P.M.
Seattle

"Mark?" She sounded upset.

"Jenny, is that you?" he said into his cell phone. He stood in his office doorway. They were about to break from their meeting for lunch. "What is it?"

"Oh, God, Mark I have something—something to tell you. I'm outside your building right now. Could you come down?"

"What's going on?" Mark thought it must be her stalker again.

"Could you just come down, please?" she asked, her voice shaking. "I'm parked right outside."

Grabbing his jacket out of his office, he headed through the newsroom toward the stairs. "I don't understand," he said into his phone. "Why can't you just tell me what this is about?"

She started crying. "It's Danny. His friend's mother took them to the park, and there was some sort of—

shooting incident. Mark, he's in the hospital. They called the house. They won't tell me his condition . . ."

Horrified, Mark rushed down the stairs, almost tripping. "God, no, is he alive? Tell me if he's still alive . . ." His voice echoed in the stairwell.

"I don't know, I swear. I'll take you to the hospital. He's at Harborview. That's all I know . . ."

Mark bolted out the lobby door. He spotted Jenny, across the street, pacing in front of her red Hyundai rental. Her arms were folded in front of her, and she held a sweater in one hand.

He ran toward her. A car horn blared, and tires screeched. But Mark didn't stop. He barely heard the irate driver screaming at him.

As he got closer to the Hyundai, Jenny opened up the driver's door and moved around to the passenger side. The motor was running. "You better drive," she said.

He climbed behind the wheel and shut the door. He was shaking, and his stomach was in knots. "Did you say they have him at Harborview?" he asked, out of breath.

She closed her door. "Yes, but we need to go home first."

"Home?" He turned toward her. "What are you talking about?"

Just moments ago, on the phone, she'd sounded like she was crying. But her eyes were dry now, and she gave him an icy stare. The sweater she was holding fell into her lap. In her hand was the Glock 19 he'd bought two days ago.

"Danny isn't in the hospital," she said. Suddenly her voice sounded different, too. "He's at the house with a friend of mine. Poor Danny, he keeps asking for you. I'm afraid he won't stop crying. You see, right now my friend has a gun just like this one, and he's holding it against your little boy's head."

Mark stared at her. He couldn't believe this was happening.

"So—let's go home and see Danny," she said. "And mind the speed limit."

Friday—12:40 P.M.
San Francisco

"Are you sure no one's going to be using the cabin tonight, Erica?" she asked.

With the cell phone to her ear, Stephanie stood by the window in Carroll Jordan's kitchen. Carroll sat at her breakfast table, hunched over her notebook computer. She'd put the baby down for a nap twenty minutes ago, but the monitor intercom still picked up some static-laced cranky crying.

"Steffi, the place is all yours," her friend said on the other end of the line. "Enjoy. Sleep in our bedroom. The sheets are clean, and the air conditioner is in there. I have no idea what's in the fridge, but so long as it's not moldy, you're welcome to help yourself. You remember where the key is—under the old butter churn on the front porch."

"Yes, I remember," she said. "Thanks so much, Erica."

After hanging up with her friend, Stephanie moved

over to the kitchen table. She'd written everything down for Carroll, who was composing it as an e-mail. Stephanie looked over her shoulder. She hoped they'd get a quick response from "Jenny."

Hi, Jen,

I know you want some space, but I'm hoping you can do a favor for Jim & Barb.

Does your boyfriend there in Seattle know someone in Spokane, someone he trusts? Here's the thing. Jim & Barb have taken off for Paris, and once again, they've left the cabin unlocked. You'd think with all the valuables they have in there (Jim's rare coin collection, for starters!), they'd be more careful. The nearest neighbor is at least ten miles away. They're hoping you or your friend has a Good Samaritan pal in Spokane who can make sure the cabin is locked up. If so, I'll give you directions to the cabin (right off I-90) and I'll let you know where they hide the extra key. They'll bring you back a bottle or two of wine for your troubles. Let me know! No pressure if you can't. They have a friend in Sandpoint who might be able to get there tomorrow morning.

Thanks, Jen. I miss you! Call me!

XXXXX—Carroll

The Spokane cabin, belonging to Stephanie's friends, Erica and Ben, was nothing luxurious—certainly not full of valuables. But it was isolated, and an easy mark for anyone wanting to break into a house undetected.

Stephanie figured if the real Jenny was being transported from somewhere in the Midwest tonight, they were most likely taking her in a truck or a camper via Interstate 90. If they planned on arriving in Seattle by two or three in the morning, they'd be passing through Spokane between ten and eleven. She just prayed that these killers grabbed the bait.

She and the Spokane police would be waiting for them there. They may even have a few minutes' warning when the camper would be starting down the private gravel road. According to the directions on the cat tracking device, it was good for up to 2.5 miles.

It was still a long shot. If every piece didn't fall exactly into place, the whole plan could fail. Still, it was all she could come up with for now. And Stephanie couldn't even count on that until they heard back from "Jenny."

"There you go," Carroll said, typing in her name at the bottom of the e-mail. "Should I send it?"

Stephanie patted her on the shoulder. "Yes, please. Send it."

Friday—12:49 P.M.
Seattle

White-knuckled, Mark clutched the steering wheel as they took a curve in the road at the end of the West Seattle Bridge. He could feel the sweat against the back of his shirt. He was terrified for his family—and confused. Yet a part of him knew why this was happening.

He'd known as soon as he saw the gun in her hand and heard her real voice. Suddenly, he'd detected a slight Midwestern twang. She was from the Chicago area. He would have thought after his terrible crush on her older sister that he might have recognized Nicole Jayne. Of course, she'd been eleven when he'd last seen her, hanging around the club—helping out at the snack shack and running errands for people. Still, he should have seen the resemblance to Selena past the dark hair and the makeup.

He took his eyes off the road for a moment and glanced at her. "Listen, I could stop by the bank," he said. "I have about twenty thousand in savings, and I can get more. It's yours—if you just promise not to hurt my kids. Do whatever you want to me. But leave my kids alone, okay?"

"Your wife pretty much said the same thing to us after we surprised her in the garage." Nicole brandished the gun in her hand. "So—I'm supposed to show you mercy? Back in the summer of 1986, you and your buddies from the country club didn't show my sister any mercy when you took turns raping her."

"I knew you were Nicole," he murmured. He shot a look at her. "Your sister wasn't raped. Did Selena tell you she was?"

Nicole glared at him and said nothing.

"So she survived that night . . ."

A car horn wailed, and Mark suddenly realized he was drifting into another lane. He shifted in the driver's seat and leaned closer to the wheel. "Dick was right," he said, almost to himself. "That night at the beach, he thought Selena might have been hiding in the bushes, just waiting for us to leave. I went back there an hour later, and all her stuff was gone . . ."

"She walked home that night—seven miles," Nicole

said. "I heard her come in at four in the morning. She was a wreck. She told me everything you rich, privileged pigs did to her . . ."

Mark shook his head. "You forget, I worked at the club, too. I wasn't rich, or privileged. And I don't know what your sister told you, but she wasn't raped. I think her judgment was impaired, because she'd had a lot to drink. But she was a willing participant that night. She went skinny-dipping with us. She made out with Dick Ingalls, and I'm pretty sure she enjoyed it. He started passing her around to the other guys . . ."

" 'The other guys?' " she echoed. "And you didn't touch her, right?"

Mark slowed down the car and came to a stop at a traffic light. "No, I participated. I was disappointed in myself. I was disappointed in your sister, too. I liked her a lot. But she liked Dick Ingalls, and I think she really wanted to impress him. The two of them swam off by themselves—and ended up on the pier. The other two, Brent and Scott, took turns with her. I'm sure Dick Ingalls must have talked her into it—"

Someone beeped their horn, and Mark saw the light had changed. He moved his foot to the accelerator and the car started moving again. "I was down the beach from where they were," he explained. "Your sister didn't scream or fight anyone. When it was my turn, I brought Selena her clothes, and she started kissing me. Then she pulled me on top of her . . ."

"You're a lying sack of shit," Nicole muttered.

"It's the truth," he said. "In the middle of it, she went kind of crazy. She hit me and lashed out at the other guys. There was a struggle. She slipped and fell into the water. I thought she might have banged her head against part of the pier. I dove into the water and looked for her, but for the life of me, I couldn't find her . . ."

"Funny," Nicole said. "Each one of your friends said he was the only one who dove in after her. Each one said he wanted to call the police or an ambulance."

Mark turned onto his block. "Well, then each one of them was lying. Dick Ingalls and I swam around and searched for her. The other two stayed up on the pier and didn't do a damn thing. I was furious with them. I was the only one who wanted to call the police, but I got outvoted. I can't believe they all switched it around like that. When did they tell you this?"

"I heard it from them individually. And each one of your buddies insisted it was true—right up until the moment I killed him."

Mark's cell phone rang.

"Let it go to voice mail," she said.

He kept driving, and didn't say another word until after he pulled into the driveway. Then he turned to her. "I'm going to ask you again. Please, leave my children alone. They have nothing to do with this."

Opening her door, she climbed out of the car and once again draped her sweater over the gun in her hand. "Just leave the keys on the car floor," she said.

He shifted into park, cut off the engine, and did what he was told.

"Come on, you lead the way. Danny's waiting for you . . ."

Mark got out of the car. Reaching into his pocket for his keys, he hurried toward the front door. He felt his heart pounding. He unlocked the door and stepped inside. "Danny?" he called anxiously. "Danny, it's Dad!"

He didn't hear anything except her footsteps behind him.

Mark turned around—in time to see Nicole Jayne raising the gun up in the air. She slammed it down onto his head.

Stunned, Mark collapsed to the hardwood floor. The blow didn't knock him out. He tried to call to Danny again, but it just came out as gibberish.

When he looked toward Nicole, she seemed slightly out of focus. She hovered over something on the table in the front hallway. He heard a rustling noise. He tried to get to his feet, but he couldn't.

All at once, she was on top of him. She had a rag in her hand. She slapped it over his nose and mouth. It was wet.

The last thing Mark remembered was an awful chemical taste in his mouth.

Friday—1:17 P.M.

"He's still not answering," Alison said, listening to her father's voice mail greeting. She clicked off, and wrote him a text:

Hi, Dad. Trying 2 get hold of U. I'm comin 2 the TV station 2 tlk 2 U bout something. Its important. W8 4 me there! C U round 2. Pls don't tell Jenny. Thx—XXX—A

Ryan stood by her at the bus stop three blocks from his hotel. "You sure I can't come with you?" he asked.

Alison sent the text, and put her phone back in her purse. "You better not," she sighed. "I need to be alone with my dad for this talk. Besides, you and I really shouldn't be seen together . . ."

That reminded her. Alison looked over toward the busy intersection near the bus stop. She'd been keeping her eyes peeled for the red Hyundai—as well as the bus. Ryan's friend, Stephanie, had been adamant about him laying low while he was here. They were taking a chance just standing on the sidewalk together.

"So what am I supposed to do?" he asked. "Just sit in the hotel and wait?"

She nodded. "I'll feel better if one of us sticks close to the house. If you're worried about me, I'll be fine. This bus lets me off right in front of my dad's work."

"Well, you're right, I am worried about you." He touched her arm. "I mean, you've probably figured it out by now. I think you're pretty cool."

Alison smiled at him. Then she saw something out of the corner of her eye. "Oh, there's the bus! Listen, after I talk to my dad, I'll give you a call. Meanwhile, please, just wait for me at the hotel. Okay?"

He nodded.

The bus pulled over to the stop. The door made a *whoosh* as it opened. A few people filed out.

Alison put her hand on Ryan's shoulder, then leaned in and kissed him on the lips.

When she pulled away, he looked startled. But he was smiling.

"I think you're pretty cool, too," she said. Then she stepped onto the bus.

Alison scanned her bus pass, and then took a seat

near the back. She waved at him as the bus pulled away. She kept staring out the window—until she was too far away to see him anymore.

As the bus started over the West Seattle Bridge toward the city, she heard her phone ring. It was a text from her father:

Got your msg. Unable 2 talk rght nw. I'm not @ TV station. I'm heding home & wil b ther s%n. Pls come & pls don't tel any1. I know U R communicating w SOME1. Don't trust them. It's urgent we talk. C U s%n. Love, Dad

The midday sunlight snuck through the closed curtains in the Metcalfs' house. Inside it wasn't dark, just dim and a little gloomy. Nikki sat on the stairs to the upper level. On the foyer floor, Mark Metcalf lay unconscious.

She was reading the text that had come up on Mark Metcalf's iPhone:

B ther s%n. XXX—A

Getting to her feet, Nikki ambled into the kitchen and set his phone down on the counter. She'd already cut off some sections of rope, and found a roll of duct tape. She had everything laid out on the breakfast table.

She'd made up her mind this was going to look like a robbery gone haywire. It had worked well for the Croton job—and allowed her and her partner to help themselves to any valuables. The police would find the

Metcalfs and their houseguest bound and gagged in the big utility room downstairs.

Grabbing the tape and some pieces of rope, she returned to the front hallway. Mark Metcalf didn't stir or groan as she stripped off his suit jacket. In his wallet, he had nearly eighty dollars in cash—along with his credit cards. Nikki tossed the wallet on the floor. She'd go through it more carefully later.

It was a struggle, but she managed to roll him over onto his stomach. But then she felt like a contortionist. She had to hold one of his hands behind his back with her knee while bringing the other hand around to tie them together.

She hated doing this alone.

"Get the knot good and tight," she could almost hear her father saying.

Nikki remembered that afternoon, twenty-seven years ago.

She remembered her father's gardening tools on their bathroom floor after he'd finished in there. He'd merely rinsed everything off. She could still see drops of water and blood on the various shears and the saws. Crimson smudges marred the bathroom tiles. Blood got trapped in the corners between the top of the tub and the walls. Even the white soap bar in the dish had pink swirls on it.

Four big, bulky green lawn bags sat on a tarp her father had laid out on the hallway floor. He didn't use twist ties to seal them up. He used rope—and he had her help him. She didn't see him load the bags, but she knew what was inside them.

"Remember, this isn't your sister anymore," he said. "She's already on her way to Judgment. These are just bones, tissue, and body parts."

Only hours before, those dissected body parts had been her living, breathing, beautiful, sweet older sister.

Their father had been asleep when Selena had snuck home just before dawn. Nikki and her older sister shared a bedroom—and a double bed. Selena sat on the bed and shook her awake. She looked terrible. She said she'd been at the beach with Dick Ingalls and his friends. Selena told her everything. At eleven years old, Nikki was both fascinated and repelled. The four boys from the country club had gotten Selena drunk and talked her into doing all sorts of sinful, perverted, sexual things. But Selena admitted that some of it had excited her. She'd enjoyed the attention—for a while.

"Then I heard one of them egging on his friend, who was on top of me," she explained. "And all at once, I felt so dirty—and used. They'd all been inside me. We didn't have any kind of protection, either. I panicked. I suddenly got so scared . . ."

Selena said the boys had surrounded her at the end of the pier. She was terrified they all would want to take turns with her again. She fought them off. But then one of them pushed her into the lake. She had a horrible bruise forming on her left hip from where she hit a little shelf off the jetty. For a few moments she'd had the wind knocked out of her. But she stayed underwater and frantically swam for the shore. She just needed to get away from them.

She was also dead certain one of them had already started something. "I'd rather be dead than be pregnant right now," she whispered. "And I can feel it in my body. It's already happening."

Curling up on the bed, Selena told her about the rest of the night.

While the boys argued on one end of the pier, she swam to the shore. She hid in the woods bordering the beach. Naked, shivering and scared, she waited it out. At a certain point, one of the boys said, "No one will miss her."

"When I heard that," Selena whispered, "I suddenly hated all of them."

She and Selena were still talking when they heard their father wake up. He always coughed and hacked for about ten minutes every morning.

They kept quiet—until after he'd had his coffee. They could smell it brewing in the kitchen. They heard him stomping around some more, and figured he was about to head off for the country club.

But then his footsteps seemed to change course, and it sounded like he was coming right to their door.

It creaked open. With the hallway light behind him, his face was swallowed up in shadows. "I could hear you talking in here," he said evenly. His voice was flat and cold. "I heard everything. By the time I get back from work, I want you out of this house, Selena. You're not my daughter anymore."

Then he closed the door.

Nikki listened to him lumbering down the hall. After a few moments, the front door slammed shut.

Dirty and sweaty, with her pretty blue dress full of sand, Selena fell asleep crying on the bed. Nikki held her and stroked her hair.

When her sister wasn't up by noon, Nikki tried to wake her. "C'mon, Selena, get up!" She shook her shoulder. "You've got to pack some things and find a place to stay—at least for a few nights. If you're not gone when Daddy gets home, he's going to kill you . . ."

Rolling over on her back, Selena reached out and took hold of her hand. She placed it on her flat belly. "Feel that, Nikki," she whispered. "It's a baby, growing inside me. I just know it."

Nikki pulled her hand away. She went to her dresser and retrieved her Miss Piggy bank. She emptied it out and counted thirty-one dollars and some change. Selena had said last night that she'd left her coin purse in Dick's car. She would need some money for wherever she was going. Nikki started to rummage through Selena's dresser for clothes to pack.

"Please, leave me alone and let me sleep," her sister groaned.

Selena finally crawled out of bed at three-thirty in the afternoon. Their father would be home in less than an hour. And here she was, still in her dirty, wrinkled blue dress. But she didn't change clothes or shower. Instead, she sat down in the rocking chair by their window.

Nikki was frantic. She was convinced their father would beat Selena within an inch of her life. She imagined how he might even hurt the baby.

"Listen, let me just sit here for a while longer," her sister said with a strange smile on her face. "Why don't you go wait for him outside? Come in and let me know when you see his truck coming down the block . . ."

"But that won't give you enough time!" Nikki argued.

Selena took her hand and squeezed it. "Don't worry. He'll forgive me. Just you wait and see. Now, scoot."

Nikki started for the bedroom doorway. She glanced back at Selena, who was gazing out the window. Nikki wondered how she could act so calm.

She did just what her sister told her to. She waited outside for forty minutes—until she spotted their father's old pickup rumbling down the street. Then she hurried back into the house and ran to the bedroom. Selena wasn't in there. Nikki noticed the bathroom door was closed. She pounded on it. "Selena, he's coming! Hurry up!"

There was no response.

She turned the handle. It was locked.

Ten minutes later, when her father kicked open the door, they found Selena's blue dress in a heap on the tiled floor. A section along the hem touching the puddle of blood had turned purple. Her sister looked as if she were asleep in the tub. The water was scarlet. One arm was draped over the bathtub's edge. The blood on the floor came from the slash marks on her wrist.

Her father said he didn't want any medical examiner discovering Selena had been promiscuous. No one had seen her come back from the beach. No one knew she'd come home last night. No one would ever know what she'd done.

He went down to his truck and fetched his gardening tools.

Nikki still remembered him carrying the shears and saws into the bathroom. "You're not to come in here," he said. Then he shut the door.

That night, after he came back from burying her sister's remains in the woods by the golf course, her father poured himself a glass of whiskey. He sat down at the kitchen table and drank half of it in one gulp. "I'll bet right now those bastards are getting drunk somewhere, bragging and slapping each other on the backs." He broke down and sobbed. "And meanwhile, my poor little girl . . ."

Nikki realized he didn't blame Selena anymore for what had happened. He blamed those boys from the country club.

Her sister had been right. He'd forgiven her after all.

And as long as those boys were guilty, her dead sister remained innocent.

"Get the knot good and tight." She imagined her father's voice again as she tied the rope around Mark Metcalf's ankles. She tore off a piece of duct tape, and firmly pressed it against his mouth.

Jenny's cell phone beeped.

With a sigh, Nikki straightened up and pulled it out of her pocket. It was just a tonal reminder that she had an unread e-mail—from Jenny's friend in San Francisco. Her calls and e-mails were becoming a major nuisance.

"Oh, give up already, will you?" Nikki muttered. She was about to delete the e-mail, but then decided to take a quick look at it:

Hi, Jen,

I know you want some space, but I'm hoping you can do a favor for Jim & Barb.

Does your boyfriend there in Seattle know someone in Spokane, someone he trusts? Here's the thing . . .

Friday—2:46 P.M.
Oakland

"Oh, no, no, no," Stephanie whispered, staring ahead at the standstill traffic on 880. The highway looked like four endless trails of parked cars, their brake lights glowing steadily. She didn't see an exit sign anywhere up ahead, either—not that she knew any other way to the Oakland Airport.

She'd been hoping to make a 3:50 flight to Seattle, with a connection that got her into Spokane at 8:05. That would have left her plenty of time to rent a car, drive to Ben and Erica's cabin, and then talk to the local police.

Slowing down to a stop, she impatiently drummed her fingers on the steering wheel. At least no one had gotten out of their cars yet. But there were the usual jerks who drove on the shoulder, trying to get a little farther ahead of everybody.

She'd hoped to call the Spokane police from the cabin, or at least near there, while on the way. She'd planned to report that a friend had been abducted in the vicinity by someone in a camper, trailer, or truck. She couldn't imagine a call from the Oakland Airport or Sea-Tac getting the same emergency response over in Eastern Washington. And once the police found out who she was, she seriously doubted they'd set up any kind of stakeout at the cabin site based on a hunch from the "presumed dead" crazy woman. Everything hinged on her being there and timing the 9-1-1 call so the police took it seriously.

A few people were honking their horns. Traffic didn't budge.

Her cell phone rang. Snatching it off the passenger seat, she checked the caller ID and switched it on. "Hello, Carroll?"

"Hi, Stephanie," she said. "I got an answer. It's the quickest response time I've gotten from her in nearly three weeks. It's an e-mail, just like you predicted. She says her boyfriend knows someone in Spokane who can swing by the cabin tonight. No problem, she said. She wants me to send the directions as soon as I can— along with where to find the key."

Stephanie bit her lip. She would have been thrilled they'd taken the bait—if only she weren't stuck in traffic right now. She hadn't budged an inch since stopping a few minutes ago. The next flight with a connection to Spokane would probably get her in there around ten o'clock. That was cutting it close.

"Did she give any indication when exactly her friend might be 'swinging by'?" Stephanie asked.

"No," Carroll replied. "By the way, are you flying out of San Francisco or Oakland? They just announced on the radio there's a backup on the 880."

"I'm in it right now," Stephanie said.

"Oh, no," Jenny's friend murmured. "Do you think you'll make your flight?"

"At this point, it's doubtful. And if I don't get there in time, this is all for nothing. We're screwed."

"So do you want me to send the response?"

"Yes, please, send it," Stephanie said. She prayed it wouldn't all be for nothing.

"All—" Carroll's reply was choppy. "—call you back if—" there was another break.

"Carroll?" She looked at the phone screen: "Low Battery." "Carroll?"

They'd been cut off.

Friday—3:37 P.M.
West Seattle

"See where the road takes a turn in a couple of blocks?" Ryan asked the taxi driver. He pointed to the spot where Stephanie had noticed him ducking into the woods near the Metcalfs' house yesterday. He dug a ten-dollar bill out of his wallet. "You can let me out there. I'd rather they not see me coming. I—I want to surprise them."

As the cab continued down the road, Ryan took out his phone and stole another look at the text he'd received twenty minutes ago:

Ryan, I can't tlk cuz I'm @ home & that woman is here. I need ur help. I left the basement window unlocked on north side of the house. Rng my fone 1ce & hang up. That wil b my signal that U R here. I'll meet U in basement. Don't let any1 C U. Pls hurry! –A.

After getting that text, he'd immediately phoned for a taxi. Then he'd tried to call Stephanie. But he'd gotten the automated voice mail from the service provider. That wasn't a good sign. She would have picked up for him.

Ryan left a message for her to call him back as soon as possible. Then it occurred to him, he'd better shut off the ringer if he planned to go sneaking around outside Alison's house. Now the phone was set to vibrate.

The taxi driver pulled over at the curve in the road, and Ryan gave him the ten for a $6.50 fare. "Keep the change," he said. "And can I ask you a really stupid question? Which way is north?"

Ryan retraced his footsteps from the walk yesterday with Alison. He kept to the edge of the woodsy road and stopped to check out the front of the Metcalfs' house. The red Hyundai was parked in the driveway. The curtains in all the front windows were closed.

Cutting through the neighbor's yard, he crept around to the back of Alison's house. Inching along the stone wall, he passed below the balcony Alison had scaled yesterday. He snuck up to a window and peeked inside. All he could see was darkness—and his own murky reflection. Ryan darted past the window. Then he paused for a moment and looked down at his sneakers. They were covered with mud.

He had no idea what Alison expected him to do once he got inside the house. Her text had been pretty vague. She'd merely said she needed him. Whatever for, he wanted to help her.

He turned the corner to the north side of the house. On his tiptoes, he reached for the first window and gave the lower sash a shove. He put his back into it. But it didn't budge at all. He slinked around some bushes and tried the next window down. At least it was easier to reach. As he gave it a push, the sash moved up with a squeak. Ryan hesitated. He tugged at it again, and the window creaked even louder.

He'd only gotten the damn thing open a couple of inches. Frustrated, he gave it one quick, forceful push. It let out a loud groan, but he'd pried the window open all the way. He kept wondering if anyone had heard it.

Ryan waited for a moment—for the sound of footsteps. He peeked into what looked like the furnace room. It was too dark to really see anything. The only thing he heard was a radio in some far-off room. It was playing an old tune: "I Only Have Eyes for You."

With a shaky hand, Ryan pulled out his cell phone. He dialed Alison's number, let it ring once, and then hung up.

Sticking his head inside the window opening again, he looked down at the eight-foot drop to the floor. He climbed up to the ledge, and carefully lowered himself down from the sill. He jumped the rest of the way. Because of the mud on his shoes, his feet almost slid out from under him as he hit the cement floor. He braced himself against the wall to keep from falling, and tried to catch his breath.

He was in the utility room—with the furnace and water heater in one corner, and the laundry sink, washer, and dryer in the other. Pipes ran along the ceiling. Three support beams were spaced down the center of the cavernous area. Boxes, old furniture, and toys were pushed against one wall.

Suddenly there was a muffled boom, and then a steady hum. It took Ryan a moment to realize it was the air-conditioning system starting up. He let out a grateful sigh.

But then a light went on.

He saw the brunette woman near the door to the basement hall. She clutched a skinny blond boy by his hair and held a gun to his ear. The poor little kid looked terrified. Tears streamed down his face and he was trembling. He'd wet his pants, too.

"Ryan, I don't believe you've met Alison's little brother, Danny," the woman announced. "He just got back from a friend's house a few minutes ago. Isn't that right, Danny?"

She gave his hair a tug.

The boy seemed too scared to talk. His lips moved, but no words came out.

With an icy smile, she gazed at Ryan. "Danny, this is Ryan Farrell. He's going to tie you up for me—just like I tied up your daddy and your sister upstairs."

Ryan stared at her. "You're Nicole, aren't you? Or are you her sister?"

"We just talked on the phone the day before yesterday," she said. "I should be insulted you don't recognize my voice."

"Listen, Nicole, you don't have to do this," Ryan said.

She pulled at the boy's hair again, jerking his head back. "Danny, did you know I was married to Ryan's dad? We're family."

"Damn it, you're hurting him," Ryan whispered.

She slowly shook her head at him. "I should have recognized you yesterday. You look just like that no-good prick father of yours."

CHAPTER TWENTY-NINE

Friday—4:15
Oakland International Airport

The screen on the self-serve ticket kiosk read:

WE ARE UNABLE TO PROCESS YOUR ORDER
PLEASE SEE THE TICKET AGENT

Stephanie was afraid of something like this happening. She had to remind herself that it might not be because the police were looking for her. People booking one-way tickets often got flagged for screening.

She hurried to the line for the ticket agent. The couple in front of her had a lot of baggage—in more ways than one. They bickered with each other and bickered with the agent. She was a stocky Asian American woman with a pretty face and a patient smile.

It had taken Stephanie over an hour to drive the last eight miles to the airport. Her flight had already taken off. The next available plane was at 5:40—with a connection in Portland. It got her into Spokane at 9:35.

That was cutting it close if she expected to intercept the real Jenny's abductor. Hell, it took twenty minutes to drive to Erica and Ben's cabin from the airport. She was really pushing it.

She wished the people in front of her would just shut the hell up, accept their seat assignments, and get out of the way. After this, she'd have to put up with the TSA screeners. They were bound to question her about the cat tracking device in her purse.

If she got past the ticket agent—and the police didn't come for her—she wanted to sit down someplace and find a plug to recharge her phone. She wondered what Ryan was doing.

"Next?" the agent said, patiently smiling at her.

Stephanie approached the counter. "Hi, I need to go to Spokane. I was hoping to catch the five-forty to Portland and connect there." She handed the woman her driver's license and credit card. "I tried to get the ticket at self-service, but it directed me here."

The woman set down the driver's license and typed something into her computer. She frowned.

"I'm going one way," Stephanie said. "And I'm not checking in any bags. I'm sure after your last customers, you're probably happy to hear that."

The woman didn't even crack a smile. "Excuse me for just a minute, Ms. Coburn," she said. Then she took the driver's license with her to the agent at the next station over. They talked for a moment. The other woman looked directly at Stephanie, and again, at the license. She typed something into her computer, studied it, and then reached for the telephone.

Stephanie stood there with her stomach in knots.

She couldn't exactly make a run for it. They had her driver's license. Any minute, she expected security guards to close in on her.

It seemed to take forever for the other woman to get off the phone. She eyed Stephanie again, and shook her head at her coworker. Finally, the ticket agent returned to the counter. She handed her the license, and got busy typing on the keyboard again. "Do you have a seating preference to Spokane today, Ms. Coburn?"

Stephanie wanted so much to ask her what the problem had been. But then she thought, why push her luck?

"Aisle, please," she replied.

The agent typed, and eventually a ticket was spit out from the machine.

All the while, Stephanie thought about Jenny Ballatore, tied up in the back of a minivan or a camper right now. Her captor was probably driving through western Montana—hauling his prisoner to Seattle for her execution.

Stephanie remembered Jenny's ransacked apartment.

They'd already taken away so much that belonged to her. And unless someone stopped them, they would take away her face, too.

For the last two or three hours, he'd had the radio cranked up. Maybe it was his way of keeping awake or fighting the monotony of highway driving. The bass was especially heavy. Jenny found she could keep up with the rhythmic *boom, boom, boom*. She'd managed to turn herself around in the tiny coffin-like compartment. In time with the music, she kicked at the drawer panel. She'd been at it long enough that her feet were bleeding. She could feel the wet, warm blood splashing with every kick. Each bang against that hard wood sent a jolt of pain that shot all the way up to her knees. Yet, she felt the panel loosening, splintering at the corners—and it only made her kick harder.

She tried to keep from crying, because as her nose filled up with mucus, it became more and more difficult to breathe. She hoped her tears and sweat would loosen the duct tape a little. She kept trying to move her jaw. She wasn't sure if it was wishful thinking, but the rope around her wrists seemed to be slackening, too.

Jenny kept telling herself she wasn't going to give up.

Past all her kicking and the booming bass from the car radio, she could hear scratching. She knew it was Simon. He was outside the Winnebago's bedroom door.

Right now, he seemed like the only friend who actually knew where she was.

Ryan did what he was told.

With the gun in her hand, Nicole Jayne barked instructions at him as he tied up Alison's younger brother. "Don't worry, we're going to get out of this," Ryan whispered into the boy's ear. He noticed the ear was bleeding a bit from her repeatedly jabbing the gun barrel at it.

When he was finished tying up Danny, she gave a tug to the rope around the boy's wrists and ankles. She tossed Ryan the roll of tape. "Tear some of that off and cover up his mouth, good and tight."

Ryan stared at her. "Why, for God's sake? The poor kid's terrified. He hasn't uttered a word in the last fifteen minutes. What's the point? Don't you have a heart?"

"Tape it up," Nicole said.

As Ryan obeyed her command, he thought about Stephanie's niece and nephew. This woman and her partner had done the same to them in a basement bedroom. They'd tied them up and shot them.

Ryan figured at least his brother and sister had been drugged—and died in their sleep. He hoped to God they'd been spared this kind of terror in the last minutes of their lives.

He gently fixed the tape in place over Danny Metcalf's mouth.

"All right, let's go upstairs," she said.

Ryan treaded out to the hallway, past the guest room to the stairs. With the utility room doorway open, he could hear Danny whimpering anxiously as they left him alone in there. He climbed the stairs—with Nicole a few steps behind him. She poked him in the back with the gun.

Upstairs, he found Alison facedown on the hallway floor. Her hands were tied behind her, and her ankles were bound. Alison's father was a few feet away from her, tied up in the same manner. They both appeared to be unconscious. Ryan caught a glimpse of the blood on Mark Metcalf's forehead. He figured Nicole Jayne must have clubbed him on the head with something.

"Take your girlfriend downstairs," Nicole said.

With the way Alison's hands were tied behind her, Ryan wasn't sure how to carry her. He finally lifted her over his shoulder like some stupid caveman. Then he took her down the stairs. One of her sandals fell off on the steps. He was careful not to bang her head or feet on the banister.

"Alison, can you hear me?" he whispered as he carried her into the utility room. "Alison?"

"She can't hear you," Nicole interjected. "With the stuff I gave her, she'll be out for at least another hour."

Gently Ryan set her down on her side next to her brother. But Nicole would have none of that. "I want her on the other side of the room," she insisted.

He did what he was told.

They went back upstairs for Alison's father. He struggled to hoist Mr. Metcalf over his shoulder. On the stairs, Ryan clung tightly to the railing, because he felt himself teetering on the steps under the extra weight. He almost tripped over Alison's sandal halfway down.

Just when he thought he'd regained his footing, he felt her kick him on the back of his knee.

Both his legs gave out from under him. Ryan lurched forward. Mr. Metcalf fell off his shoulder and toppled down the stairs like so much deadweight. Helpless, Ryan tried to grab at the banister again, but it was too late. He went tumbling down the stairs—just seconds after Alison's father. As he hit the floor, Ryan heard a loud snap and felt something crack in his lower left leg. The pain was excruciating.

Ryan couldn't move. The basement corridor seemed to be spinning.

He heard her footsteps as she slowly came down the stairs.

His leg was broken. He knew there was nothing he could do now to save Alison or her family—or himself.

That was his last thought before he passed out.

"Hi, Ryan, I really wish I was talking to you instead of your voice mail," Stephanie said into her newly recharged phone. She stood by herself, off in a corner of the boarding gate area. They'd just made the final boarding call—all rows—for her flight, but people were still lined up at the Jetway.

"Listen, I'm on my way to Spokane," she continued. "I'm hoping to stop this guy who has the real Jenny. If it all goes according to plan—fingers crossed—he'll be in police custody by ten or eleven tonight. I'll call you with an all clear when that happens. At that point, don't hesitate to call the police and have them nab his partner. Meanwhile, take care and just wait for my call, okay?"

She clicked off the line. It wasn't until five minutes later, when she was standing in line in the Jetway that Stephanie realized she shouldn't have left that message. What if Ryan's phone fell into the wrong hands?

But it was too late now.

"Would you turn that damn music down?"

"I like it loud," he said into his Bluetooth. "It keeps me awake." With his eyes on the road, he reached over and turned down the volume on the radio. "So—what's going on?"

"Well, they're all here, one big happy family, just waiting for you," she said. "I've had them tied up in the basement for the last three hours. I'm afraid Joe Quarterback's football career is a thing of the past. I'm pretty sure he broke his leg falling down the basement stairs."

"That's a shame," he said, drumming his fingers across the steering wheel. "I guess we'll just have to shoot him—like a horse, huh?"

"Must have smarted some, because he passed out," she said. "But he woke up a while ago. The others are awake now, too. I was just down there, checking on them."

"What are you doing now?"

"Inventory, chum," she replied. "I'm going over the living room and dining room, gathering things and trying to figure out what's worth stealing in this dump. I think we'll make out okay. So—how's our little package?"

"She was dead asleep about three hours ago when I last checked. I'll peek in on her again after I swing by this cabin in Spokane."

"Are you that close to Spokane?"

"I just gassed up in Kellogg, Idaho," he said. "So I should be at this place in about ninety minutes, tops. Then I'll be rolling into Seattle around two-thirty."

"Call me after you've checked out this cabin. I want to know what kind of haul you get."

"Will do," he said.

She hung up.

He turned the volume back up on the radio. He started slapping the steering wheel in synch with the *boom, boom, boom* of the bass.

Suddenly a deer ran out in front of the Winnebago. It happened so fast.

He slammed on the brakes. The tires screeched.

He watched the stupid animal scurry out of the headlight beams—and into the woods on the other side of the Interstate. He looked over his shoulder to make sure nothing had broken in the Winnebago. The cat was freaking out a little, but that was nothing new.

Turning down the radio, he listened for a moment, but didn't hear anything from the bedroom. He imagined that his friend in cargo storage had gotten quite a jolt. He imagined her banging her head against the side of that drawer. And the thought made him smile.

He moved his foot to the accelerator, and then cranked up the radio again.

The sudden stop sent Jenny's whole body crashing into the side of the drawer. Her shoulder got the worst of it. For a moment, when she heard the loud crack, she thought she'd broken something. And she had.

She'd broken the drawer panel.

"Sorry to be calling again," Stephanie said into her phone.

Hurrying to her boarding gate in the Portland Airport, she was wary of every security guard or cop she passed. This was her home turf, where the police had her listed as presumed dead or missing. Service people at the different stands, TSA employees, and other airport personnel knew her here. She couldn't afford to be recognized by anyone.

As worried as she was about getting stopped, she was more concerned about Ryan. She still hadn't heard back from him. In his last phone message at three-thirty—over five hours ago—he'd been on his way to see Alison at the Metcalfs'. He didn't say whether or not their houseguest was home.

"I'm starting to panic here," she said into the phone. "I hope you're all right. Give me a call just as soon as you get this. And to be on the safe side, please do me a favor, and erase my last message, okay?"

She clicked off the line and stashed her phone in her purse.

"Stephanie?"

It was a man's voice, and it seemed to come from someone over by the Hudson News stand. But Stephanie didn't dare stop or even look in that direction.

She just kept walking.

She counted the seconds—wondering how long it would be before he called her name again. After ten seconds, she figured she was safe. A part of her wanted to glance back and see if she recognized anyone in the crowd.

But she just kept walking.

Ryan's cell phone vibrated again.

It was tucked inside the pocket of his jeans, and he

was amazed the phone hadn't been damaged when he'd fallen down the stairs.

At least something had survived that tumble. His leg was killing him. If he didn't move, the pain was constant, but tolerable. However, one little flinch, and he almost went through the roof from the utter agony.

With his hands tied behind him, he was propped up against a support beam in the Metcalfs' utility room. She must have dragged him in here while he'd been out. He wondered just how bad the leg was. He couldn't roll up the cuff of his jeans to assess the damage. Then again, he probably couldn't have done that even if his hands were free. His leg had swollen up, and he would have had to cut open his pants to get a look at it.

He was pretty sure he had a fever, his body's reaction to the pain. Sweat poured off him, and his T-shirt was drenched. All the perspiration had loosened the duct tape around his mouth. He found he could whisper out of the corner of his mouth to the others. While Nicole was upstairs, he'd found out how Alison, her father, and her brother were doing. He'd ask them questions, and they communicated through a series of grunts and groans. He was the only one seriously hurt and immobile. Alison thought she had some slack on the rope around her wrists. At one point, she'd managed to roll over on the floor toward her father. With their backs against each other, she'd tried to untie the rope around his wrists. But Nicole had come into the utility room at just that moment. She'd kicked Mr. Metcalf in the stomach. Grabbing Alison by her hair, she'd dragged her to the other side of the room. Then she'd gone back upstairs.

Despite the intense pain every time he moved, Ryan had squirmed enough to almost dislodge the cell phone from the pocket of his jeans. If he could somehow move it toward his hands, there was a chance he could put in a 9-1-1 call. The vibration from that last missed call helped shake it just enough that the phone was about to fall out of his pocket.

He wiggled a bit, and winced at the jolt that went through his broken leg. The phone slid all the way out of his pocket and clattered onto the cement floor.

He looked over toward the doorway, and saw her standing there.

She must have crept down the basement stairs, because Ryan hadn't heard a thing.

Nicole folded her arms in front of her. She was holding a notebook, with a pen sticking out of the spiral binder. "I can't believe I forgot to go through your pockets! Is that a phone, Ryan?" She walked across the room toward him. "Your family's all dead. Who were you going to call?"

She nudged his broken leg with her foot. "Who?"

He grimaced at the pain.

She bent over him and snatched his cell phone off the floor.

As Ryan caught his breath, it dawned on him that Stephanie had probably been the one leaving him the message. Did Nicole know she was alive?

Nicole frowned at the cell phone in her hand. Then she hurled it against the wall. The phone smashed into bits.

As she turned away, Ryan noticed she had the gun

tucked in the back of her slacks. She took a folding chair that was leaning against the wall, and set it up between Alison and her father. She set her notebook on the seat. She looked like a secretary setting up a spot to take dictation.

Marching over to Mr. Metcalf, she grabbed him under the arm, turned him around, and sat him up. She tore the tape off his mouth. Just hearing that noise made Ryan wince. Mr. Metcalf seemed to stifle a scream.

Backing away from him, she grabbed her notebook and sat down in the folding chair. She stared at Mr. Metcalf. "All right, I need your bank PIN number," she said.

"Not until you take the tape off my kids' mouths," he said, still gasping for air. "And do it carefully. Slowly."

"You're not calling the shots here," she said.

"Danny's been crying. His nose is all stuffed up. He can hardly breathe with that tape over his mouth."

She didn't move from the chair.

"Boeing Employees Credit Union," Mr. Metcalf said. "The first two digits are nine, seven. You'll get the other two when you take the damn tape off my children's mouths."

Ryan was surprised to see her stand up, and walk over to Alison, who was lying on her side. She ripped the tape off her mouth—and wasn't gentle about it at all. Alison screamed from the initial pain. Nicole left a piece of tape dangling from her cheek. Then she went over to Danny. He tried not to cry when she quickly pulled the tape off his mouth. It was heartbreaking to hear him stifle the sobs.

Nicole went back to her chair and sat down again. "Nine-seven what?" she asked.

"Nine-seven-two-two."

"Your Chase card PIN number?"

"Four-five . . ." He trailed off. "I'll tell you the next two digits if you tell me what happened to Selena."

"She killed herself the next afternoon. She slashed her wrists in our bathtub at home."

"You blame me and the others for that?"

"Yes. You raped her . . ."

"What?" Alison murmured.

"She wasn't raped," Mr. Metcalf told his daughter. He turned to Nicole. "It was a bunch of stupid, drunk teenagers on the beach that night, and she went along with it. Did Selena say she was raped?"

Nicole straightened up in the chair. "Give me your goddamn PIN number for the Chase card."

"When she fell into the lake, I thought she'd drowned," Mr. Metcalf said. "You know, not a week has gone by in the twenty-seven years since that I haven't thought about that night, and wished I could take it back. I didn't rape anybody. But I walked away from that beach thinking she'd drowned there—and I didn't call the police. I didn't tell anyone. That's what I'm guilty of." He shook his head. "And isn't it ironic, Nicole? All that guilt and regret, and then it turned out she walked home that night. Tell me something, why did she go home to kill herself? If she was that traumatized by what happened on the beach, why not just drown herself there? She had that big, beautiful lake—just waiting. What happened when she got home? Did something happen with your father?"

"Shut up!" She jumped to her feet and threw the notebook at him. It hit Mr. Metcalf in the forehead.

Grimacing, he recoiled for a moment. "What happened to Selena's body?"

Enraged, she kicked him in the ribs and hit his face with her fist. Danny and Alison were screaming at her to stop. Mr. Metcalf curled up into a little ball.

Suddenly, she did stop. She reached back and pulled out the gun. She aimed it at him.

"No, please, wait!" Alison screamed.

Danny was shrieking.

"Shut the fuck up!" she growled, suddenly turning toward the boy.

He fell silent.

She seemed to take a deep breath. Then without looking at anyone, she turned and walked out the door.

Ryan heard her footsteps on the stairs a moment later.

He couldn't help thinking she'd gone to fetch a pillow to muffle the sound of the gunshots. Or maybe she'd gone to get a knife from the kitchen.

He couldn't help thinking the killing was about to begin.

CHAPTER THIRTY

Friday—10:11 P.M.
Spokane

Stephanie's hands shook as she clutched the steering wheel. She was seven miles west of the airport. At this time of night, there was hardly any traffic along this stretch of I-90. She could see someone's taillights in the distance up ahead, and in the last ten minutes, only a few cars had passed her heading east.

She checked the speedometer: 70 MPH. She pushed it up to seventy-five.

There was a chance he'd already arrived at the cabin. In the e-mail she'd had Carroll send, she'd lied about where to find the key. But that didn't mean he couldn't break down the door or bash in a window. Then he'd see there wasn't a coin collection or too many valuables. She couldn't help wondering if he'd come and gone already.

At least once she got there, she'd know whether or not she'd missed him.

Stephanie had her cell phone and the pet tracking

device on the rental car's passenger seat. Ideally, she should have arrived at Ben and Erica's place an hour ago. She'd have waited until she got a signal on the cat tracker, and then called 9-1-1. She wouldn't have to give the police a lot of details or any long, drawn-out explanations. Someone broke into the cabin and abducted her friend. He took off in a camper or RV. She didn't quite see what it was. He had a gun. Please come at once.

Stephanie had figured that would get a quick response from the police. In all likelihood, Jenny's captor would still be trying to break into the cabin when the first responders arrived. There was only one road going to the cabin. They'd have him trapped there.

The rental car's headlights swept across the milepost sign before the turnoff to Erica and Ben's. Stephanie reached for the pet tracking device to make sure it was on and working. Once off the Interstate, the road to the cabin wound through the woods for nearly a mile.

If he was there now, the device would have started blinking and beeping. Then again, he might have taken off the cat's collar and thrown it away days ago. Or maybe the trees were blocking the reception.

She set the device back on the passenger seat, and grabbed her phone.

If he was there now, what could she do to stop him? How was she going to save Jenny Ballatore? She didn't even have a backup plan—or a gun.

She dialed 9-1-1.

After two rings, the operator answered: "9-1-1 Emergency."

"Yes, my friend was just abducted," Stephanie said,

keeping her eyes peeled for the turnoff. "We're staying at a cabin, Number One Bonny Trail, Rural Route 37, milepost—"

"9-1-1 Emergency," the woman repeated.

Stephanie felt a pang in her gut. "Can't you hear me?"

"9—" That was all Stephanie heard on her end. It sounded like they'd been cut off.

"Oh, no, please," she murmured. She redialed, and listened. There was no ringtone or anything now. She looked at the phone screen: No Service Available.

Up ahead, she spotted the turnoff for Rural Route 37.

Stephanie put the phone back on the passenger seat. She took a few deep breaths, and then turned onto the access road. She reminded herself that nine out of ten times her cell phone had worked fine whenever she'd stayed at Ben and Erica's place. Maybe it was just that one spot that didn't have service. The mountains and trees around here made phone service a little quirky.

Her headlights pierced the darkness as she veered onto the unlit gravel road that wove through the woods. With the trees looming overhead, it was like driving through a dark tunnel. Stephanie slowed down to fifteen miles an hour. She reached over for the pet tracking device again. No blinking light, no beeping. It wasn't picking up anything yet.

Hunched close to the steering wheel, she listened to the gravel crunching under the tires. The drive along the crude one-lane trail was beginning to seem endless. Then she finally spotted a landmark—an old hitching post on the roadside. Bonny Trail and the cabin were just around the bend from here. Stephanie knew where she was now. She went to turn off the headlights, and for a moment, couldn't find where the light controls were on the rental car. At last, she located them and turned off the headlights. Through the darkness, she crawled off the gravel road onto a dirt path that wound around to a clearing behind some bushes. She knew this spot. If she parked the car here, it wouldn't be seen from the road—or the cabin.

Stephanie shut off the engine. All at once, everything seemed so deathly quiet. She tried 9-1-1 again on her cell. Still no service. She stashed the cell in her purse—along with the tracking device. It would have picked up something by now if he was there—and the cat still had its collar on. What had she been thinking with this stupid plan? So far, nothing had gone right. She nervously searched around the car floor for the lever to pop the trunk. She finally found it alongside her seat, and pushed it. Stephanie listened to the trunk hood click open.

Grabbing her purse, she climbed out of the car. She quietly closed the door, and went to the trunk. Peeling back the matting, she found the spare tire—and the tire iron. She wiggled it out of its clip-holder, and stashed it in her purse. Half of it stuck out, but that didn't matter. She pushed down the trunk hood until she heard the lock click.

She crept through the brush, toward the cabin. She heard something rustling in the bushes. Stephanie stopped in her tracks. A twig snapped, and the rustling sound got louder. Then whatever it was seemed to scamper off. Stephanie figured it must have been a raccoon or a possum. She forged on until the cabin came into view. It was a two-story log cottage with a front porch and a stone chimney. A light was on in the front window. Erica and Ben kept it on a timer. The other windows in the cabin were dark. They had some solar-activated lawn lights near the porch and around the clearing, where there was room for several cars to park. Stephanie didn't see a sign of anyone. The front door looked secure, and none of the windows had been smashed in.

She stepped up to the front porch, slightly cluttered with various potted plants and bric-a-brac. She checked under the old butter churn, and found the key.

At that moment, she heard a strange beep.

She realized it was coming from the cat tracker in her purse.

Stephanie looked toward the old gravel road. She spotted a light sweeping over the treetops. She had company.

There was another loud crash from above.

Ryan flinched at the noise, and the movement sent another jolt of pain through his broken leg.

It sounded like she was going through their cabinets and drawers upstairs. Every once in a while, she broke something—on purpose, it seemed. Maybe those were the items she didn't think worth ripping off. Or maybe she was just doing it to mess with them down here.

Ryan kept rubbing the restraints on his wrists against the support beam behind him. He hoped to wear away at the rope or at least loosen the knot. But even if he got free, he was helpless. He wasn't sure what he could do. Sweat continued to pour off him, and he couldn't stop trembling.

Alison still had a piece of duct tape dangling from her cheek. She'd managed to scoot over to her father once again. For the last fifteen minutes or so, she'd been trying to untie his wrists. They sat with their backs to each other while she blindly tugged and clawed at his ropes. She had tears in her eyes.

She kept glancing over at her kid brother, curled up on the floor.

Danny seemed to be in shock. About a half hour ago, shortly after Nicole had almost shot him, Danny lay down on his side and shrank into a little ball. He hadn't uttered a word or made a sound since. Ryan noticed that most of the time, Danny's eyes were closed, but when he opened them, he had sort of a dead stare. He was the only one who didn't jump a bit with each loud crash upstairs. In fact, he didn't move a muscle.

Considering their chances, Ryan wondered if the boy was better off in this state.

Mr. Metcalf had stopped struggling and squirming. He seemed beaten down. He whispered over his shoulder to Alison: "You were trying to ask me about it last night, weren't you?"

Ryan only caught snippets of the conversation. It sounded like Alison's father was telling her about that night with Selena Jayne and the others twenty-seven years ago. All the while, Alison had tears in her eyes. It looked like she didn't want to hear any of it. She kept picking and pulling at the rope around her father's wrists. But it didn't seem to be doing any good.

Ryan frantically looked around the room—for anything they might use to cut themselves free. Mr. Metcalf had already said all his tools were in the garage. The boxes along the wall contained old clothes and toys. A shard of glass might do the trick, but the windows were too high to reach. Ryan wondered if they could hurl something at the window, break it, and get a piece of glass. But how? Everyone's hands were tied behind them.

He looked over at Mr. Metcalf, still whispering to his daughter. Now both of them were crying. Ryan wanted to scream at them to stop talking and start thinking of some way to get out of there. It seemed odd that Mr. Metcalf had decided now to confess to Alison about his tired old sin.

Then it dawned on Ryan. Mr. Metcalf probably thought none of them were going to live through this. And maybe he just didn't want Alison to die thinking all this was his fault.

Stephanie watched the eerie light looming over the treetops.

With a shaky hand, she dialed 9-1-1 again, and prayed. She dreaded seeing that damn "No Service Available" message on the phone screen again. She waited. The pet tracking device in her purse let out a steady *beep, beep, beep*.

"9-1-1 Emergency."

"Oh, thank God," Stephanie murmured. "My friend was abducted by someone in a camper or trailer— maybe a truck. I didn't get a good look at the vehicle

I'm at number one Bonny Trail, off Rural Route 37. It—it's a cabin . . ."

"May I have your name please?"

Stephanie hesitated. Would they take her seriously if they knew who she was? She took a deep breath. "Stephanie Coburn. I'm staying at my friend's cabin. Did you get the address? I'm worried we might get cut off. I'm not sure about the phone service out here—"

"Stephanie, did you say your friend was abducted?"

The light over the trees seemed to get brighter. The beeping from the tracking device became more rapid—like her heartbeat. Stephanie was afraid if she took a step in either direction, she'd lose phone service. But she took a chance, and ducked around to the side of the cabin.

"Yes," she said, hiding behind some shrubs. "I didn't get a good look at the man, but he has a gun. He dragged her into a trailer of some kind. I can still see the lights on Rural Route 37—off the Interstate. Please come."

"Stephanie, could you—" There was a break.

"Hello?" she asked, panicked. "Can you hear me?"

Beep, beep, beep, beep . . . The tracking device was going crazy. Stephanie figured he'd hear it as soon as he stepped outside. Reaching into her purse to shut it off, she almost dropped her phone. "Are you still there?" she asked the 9-1-1 operator.

"—address again?" was all Stephanie got.

She tried to talk slowly and calmly. "Number One Bonny Trail off Rural Route 37, Milepost 14 off the Interstate," she said. "Did you get that?"

There was no response on the other end of the line.

Stephanie heard gravel crunching under tires. She saw the headlights through the trees. "9-1-1, are you there?" she said.

No answer.

"If you can hear me, please hurry. I think he's coming back here . . ."

She wondered if he'd seen her car parked in the spot after the hitching post. He must have passed it by now.

The big vehicle was like a monster tank rolling up the narrow little path. Tree branches scraped against its roof. For a second, Stephanie was blinded by the bright headlights as the Winnebago pulled into the clearing. She took a step back and pressed herself against the side of the house. The headlights went off before the Winnebago came to a stop.

"9-1-1, are you there?" she whispered. Again, no response. She clicked off. She put the phone on vibrate—in case they called back. She'd prayed they'd gotten the address.

The RV remained idling for a few moments. Stephanie couldn't get a good look at the driver. The windshield was up high and the lights were off inside the vehicle. He finally switched off the engine.

The driver stepped out of the Winnebago, and left the door open behind him. He tucked a gun in the back of his pants. Then he stood there and stared at the house. From his height and stature, Stephanie was pretty certain the wiry little man was the same one who had tried to break into her hotel room in Lake Forest, and the same one who had been hiding in her basement, ready to set up her "suicide." He had a bandage on the side of his face, and his receding dark hair was unkempt.

Clutching the phone in her hand, Stephanie remained perfectly still.

He strolled up to the cabin's front porch and peeked into the window. Once he moved toward the door, Stephanie could no longer see him from her vantage point. She heard the doorknob rattle. Then she listened to his footsteps on the porch. There was a shuffling sound—of him shifting around the potted plants. In the e-mail Carroll had sent, she'd said the key was under the third pot to the right of the door.

"Shit!" he muttered.

Stephanie listened to the clanking of pots as he moved them or kicked them aside. The man got noisier and more aggressive with each failed attempt to find a house key.

Glancing over at the Winnebago, Stephanie thought she saw it swaying slightly. Someone was in there. Was it Jenny?

The phone vibrated in her hand. Stephanie clicked it on.

"This is the 9-1-1 operator calling back for Stephanie Coburn . . ."

The operator's voice was too loud, too clear.

She heard his footsteps on the porch again. He seemed to be coming toward the side of the cabin. His shadow swept across the ground.

"Bonny Trail, off Rural Route 37," Stephanie whispered. "Hurry!"

Plastered against the side of the house, she clutched

the tire iron. She let the phone and her bag fall out of her grasp.

The boards on the porch's side steps creaked. He poked his head around the corner. His face was in the shadows—except for that white bandage on his jaw. He had the gun in his hand. "Well, well, well," he said, coming toward her. "If it isn't the bitch who won't die . . ."

Stephanie held the tire iron to her side. She was pretty sure he hadn't spotted it yet. She stole a glance over toward the rural road, hoping to see headlight beams over the treetops. But there was nothing.

"So—this was a setup, huh?" he said, pointing the gun at her face. "Are the cops on their way? Is that it? You think—"

The Winnebago shifted and squeaked.

He glanced over his shoulder.

Stephanie hauled back the tire iron and slammed it down on his arm. He let out a yowl, and the gun fell to the ground. She lunged at him, attacking him again, this time with a blow to his shoulder. She was like a crazy woman unleashed. She kept swinging the tire iron. With every blow, she thought of Rebecca and the kids—and all the others. She struck him again and again. But he was still standing, fending her off and cursing.

All of a sudden, he grabbed hold of the tire iron. Yanking it out of her hand, he hurled it into the bushes. She started to hit him with her fists, but he reeled back and belted her across the face. The blow sent her through the air. Stephanie slammed into a tree and crumpled to the ground. The whole left side of her face was throbbing. Spots swam in front of her eyes and everything was out of focus. A constant ringing filled her ear. He was muttering something, but she couldn't make out what he said.

Clinging to the tree, she struggled to her feet. She blinked until he came into focus. He was staggering toward her with the gun. His face was bleeding. The white bandage on his jaw was now crimson.

In this moment, when Stephanie was so certain she was going to die, she was glad to see what she'd done to him.

"What the fuck are you smiling at?" he said, raising the gun.

He started to say something else. But the roar of the Winnebago's engine drowned him out. The headlights went on. With the screech of its tires, the huge vehicle lurched forward. Dirt and gravel sprayed through the air.

Stephanie stumbled back toward the woods.

She watched as the man raised his gun again—this time aiming at the person driving the RV. A shot rang out just as the Winnebago plowed into him. Over the grinding engine noise, Stephanie heard his screams. The vehicle careened forward, carrying him across its front grating—right into a tall pine tree.

After that, the screaming stopped.

Clouds of dirt plumed around the base of the pine. They cleared as the Winnebago backed up. Stephanie watched the broken, lifeless body slide down the tree trunk and flop over onto the ground.

The dust was still settling when she noticed in the distance a red and white swirling light over the treetops. Someone was coming down Rural Route 37. Stephanie still had some ringing in her ear, but she could hear a police siren—not too far away.

Teetering, she took a few steps toward the clearing and the Winnebago. She saw the blood on the front of the vehicle, and a bullet hole in the windshield on the passenger side. Catching her breath, she stared at the woman in the driver's seat. She was a pretty brunette with a scar on her cheek.

It was her first look at the real Jenny Ballatore.

They'd never met before. They didn't know each other. Yet they smiled at each other like old friends.

Stephanie gave her a frail wave, and then hobbled over to the side of the cabin, near the shrubs where she'd been hiding. She found her cell phone.

With a shaky hand, she punched in Ryan's phone number.

Ryan wondered if any of the pieces of his broken phone were sharp enough to cut at the ropes around their wrists.

"Dad, is it loosening at all?" Alison asked. Her voice was hoarse from crying. She blindly picked and tugged at the restraints around her father's wrists.

"A little bit," he said. "Keep trying, sweetie . . ."

Alison started sobbing again. She shook her head. "That woman's not going to leave here and kill anyone else," she whispered. "I mean it."

"You guys," Ryan whispered. "Over by the wall where she threw my phone . . ."

He fell quiet at the sound of footsteps on the stairs. He could hear another sound—glass clinking.

Mr. Metcalf bumped against Alison, and they both tried to scoot away from each other. She put two or three feet between them before she fell to her side. Her father was still sitting up.

"I just can't keep you two away from each other, can I?" she said, appearing in the doorway. She held the bottle of Frangelico and two crystal old-fashioned glasses. She set them down by her folding chair. Then she pulled out the Glock 19, and briskly moved toward Mr. Metcalf. She slapped him in the face with the back of her hand. As he recoiled, she grabbed his arm and yanked at it.

Ryan could tell she was testing to see if the rope was loose. She moved over to Alison and tugged at the restraints. She seemed satisfied. "My father taught me how to tie a knot good and tight," she said.

Tucking the gun in the back of her slacks, she wandered over to the folding chair. "Tell you what, if you guys really like being close together, I'll make sure to arrange your bodies so each one is right beside the next—you two and little Rip Van Winkle over there." She opened the liqueur that came in the bottle that looked so much like Mrs. Butterworth's syrup. Ryan's sister had told him that she drank the stuff every night.

Sitting down in the chair, she glanced at Ryan. "But you, Joe Quarterback, you'll have to go someplace else to die. The police might start digging into things if the dead son of Brent Farrell turned up at a murder-robbery scene in West Seattle." She seemed focused on pouring the liqueur into the two crystal glasses. "No, it's better if you just disappeared. My friend will be driving back through Nevada. There are plenty of unmarked graves out in that desert. You'll end up being just another one of them."

"Nicole, think about it," Mr. Metcalf said, his voice calm and compassionate. "Your sister was a very sweet girl. What happened to her was a tragedy, but I'm guessing that had a lot more to do with the way she was brought up and how your father treated you both. I never thought she was happy. I felt sorry for her. I don't think she was spiteful. So be honest with yourself. How do you imagine Selena would feel about what you're doing—and what you've done?"

Her eyes narrowed at him. "You felt sorry for my sister? Well, before the end of this night, you'll be the one who's sorry." Suddenly, she changed expressions. Putting on a phony smile, she set down the bottle and hoisted one of the glasses. "Meanwhile, let's drink to Selena, shall we?"

Leaving one glass on the floor by the Frangelico bottle, Nicole stood up and moved toward Alison's father. "Maybe a little libation will get you to cooperate, and you'll give me more of your access codes and PIN numbers. If not, I may just have to fall back on some other means of persuasion. And I guarantee you, *Daddy,* the kiddies aren't going to enjoy it . . ."

Leaning over Mark Metcalf, she was about to put the glass of liqueur to his lips. But suddenly, Alison kicked upward with her feet and knocked the glass out of Nicole's hand. The Frangelico spilled across her father's lap, and the glass shattered on the floor.

Alison glared at her father. "I won't let you drink with the woman who killed my mother."

Nicole laughed.

Mr. Metcalf shook his head at her. "My daughter's right. I don't want any."

Ryan thought he saw a smile flicker across Alison's face.

"Fine, more for me then," Nicole said, retreating to the chair. She sat down and reached for the other glass. She drank it in one, smooth gulp. "You talk about my father and the way I was brought up?" she said. "Well, want to know what your little whore of a daughter was doing yesterday afternoon—with this one here?" She nodded toward Ryan and poured another glass. "She was skipping school so they could fuck on your living room sofa. I caught them . . ."

"Go ahead and drink up, bitch," Alison whispered.

"I know my limit, Alison," Nicole said, clearing her throat. "Don't for one minute think I'm going to be too drunk to take care of you." She took a sip and smirked at Mr. Metcalf. "Skipping school to screw boys, that's the kind of daughter you've raised." Nicole cleared her throat again and winced slightly. She quickly finished the rest of the glass in one gulp.

Ryan noticed her face was turning red.

"I didn't skip school," Alison said, glaring at her. "I told you I was going back for a class, remember?"

"Oh yes, I'm sure you did," Nicole said. "You probably went chasing after Joe Quarterback here . . ."

She nodded at Ryan. But then the smug look on her face disappeared. She started coughing. She slapped er chest with her hand. But the coughing fit continued. Ryan wondered if Nicole's favorite dessert drink had gone down the wrong way. Her eyes watered up.

"No, it's like I told you," Alison said—over Nicole's hacking. "I went back for chemistry lab. In fact, I brought home a sample . . ."

Coughing uncontrollably, Nicole stood up. She staggered back and tipped over the liquor bottle. She suddenly seemed to realize what Alison was telling her.

She reached back and pulled out the gun. Her hand wavered as she tried to point it at Alison.

Ryan automatically lurched forward, but his restraints held him back. The sudden movement drove a thunderbolt of pain up his broken leg. The big, dark room started spinning.

He caught only a glimpse of Alison's father—his hands still tied behind him—bolting up and hurling himself toward Nicole.

He heard Alison scream as the gun went off.

Alison's father fell on top of Nicole, pinning her to the floor. The gun flew out of her hand.

Ryan felt himself slipping away. Everything started to go black. He caught another glimpse of Mr. Metcalf, facedown on the floor, very still.

Nicole tried to reach across him for the gun. Her whole body writhed and shook as she choked to death from the poison in her system. Now Ryan knew what Alison had been thinking when she'd said, "That woman's not going to leave here and kill anyone else."

The last thing he saw was Nicole Jayne in convulsions, still struggling to reach for the gun.

He knew she'd never get ahold of it.

She couldn't even get a breath.

EPILOGUE

Saturday, June 22—6:40 A.M.
Glenview, Illinois

"I need to make a confession," Barton Jayne told the priest.

He was standing outside the rectory door. The old man wore an old, ill-fitting blue suit and a slightly threadbare maroon tie.

Father Stutesman had been getting dressed for seven o'clock services when the doorbell rang. He knew he didn't look very dignified in his T-shirt, black slacks, and stocking feet. He was a spry seventy-six, with receding gray hair and a goatee.

He opened the door wider. "Okay, come in, Barton."

"Not here," he said. "In the church confessional."

Father Stutesman glanced at his watch and sighed. "All right, I'll meet you over there. Let me grab a sweater and put my shoes on . . ."

Nodding, the caretaker headed toward the church.

The pastor finished dressing. He was the one who had hired Barton Jayne years back. He thought the old man was an odd duck. But Barton worked cheaply and he was dependable. He described himself as a Christian, but as far as Father Stutesman knew, he didn't belong to any particular church. Barton Jayne certainly didn't attend St. Paul's. Otherwise he'd have known they'd stopped hearing formal confessions ages ago. In fact, for years now, Father Stutesman had been using one of the two confessional booths to store prayer books.

Father Stutesman was pretty mellow about different rules and regulations. That was why he let Mr. Jayne put up a tombstone—with no actual grave—in their little cemetery. And that was why he was now walking over to the church to hear Barton's confession when the old man wasn't even Episcopalian.

Barton had unlocked the church door for him, but the only light he'd switched on was the one over the confessional boxes. Father Stutesman knocked on the cubicle they weren't using for storage. "You in there, Barton?" he asked. His voice echoed a bit in the quiet, empty church.

Mr. Jayne grunted an affirmative.

Father Stutesman stepped inside the cubicle and sat down. He put a purple stole over his shoulders, made a sign of the cross, and then slid open the little door between him and Mr. Jayne. Through the intricate latticework in the screen he could just make out the old man sitting there in the dark.

"Barton?"

He'd expected him to start with the formal confession recital. The door sliding open was his cue to pray, "Bless me, Father, for I have sinned . . ."

Mr. Jayne didn't bother with that. "Someone called me fifteen minutes ago, asking if I was Barton Jayne," he explained. "They asked if I was home at 1947 Harms. I said yes, and they hung up. I know it was the police. They're coming for me. In fact, I'm sure they'll be here any minute. So I want to confess . . ."

Puzzled, Father Stutesman leaned closer to the screen. He took a deep breath and tried to sound calm. "Um, what sins do you want to confess?"

"I helped my daughter kill ten people," he said—without a hint of emotion in his voice. "Some of them were children. She killed a few others, too, before I became part of what she was doing."

"What?" the priest asked. He couldn't believe what he was hearing.

"I'm not sure if this confession will work," the old man said, "because I'm not a bit sorry."

"Wait a minute, Barton. What—"

Father Stutesman heard a click.

The shot echoed throughout the empty church.

Horror-struck, the priest felt blood spray through the screen's latticework and onto his face. He heard the gun drop, and the body in the next cubicle crumpling to the floor.

And then, in the distance, he heard police sirens.

Monday, June 24—2:48 P.M.
Seattle

"Every Father's Day for the last few years, my dad got an unsigned card in the mail," Ryan said. "Did you get them, too?"

Mr. Metcalf nodded. Sitting up in the hospital bed, he had a tube in his nose. He was also hooked up to an IV drip. He wore a pale green hospital gown that made his complexion look sallow. The TV on the wall had a Mariners game on mute. The table across the room was full of flowers and cards. A shimmery orange, purple, and yellow Get Well balloon was tied to one corner of his headboard.

The bullet from the Glock 19 had punctured Mr. Metcalf's right lung. But he'd come through five-hour surgery the day before with flying colors. They planned to take him out of intensive care tomorrow—if his condition remained stable.

In his wheel chair, Ryan sat at Mr. Metcalf's bedside. He wore cargo shorts and a white shirt with the sleeves rolled up. His leg was in a blue fiberglass cast. Alison—and Danny especially—were disappointed they couldn't sign it. Danny had spent last night here at Swedish Hospital, mostly in observation to make sure there were no aftereffects from the two hours he'd been in shock. His older sister had spent half the night with him. He'd been discharged this morning.

Alison's father suddenly looked like he was in pain. "What did you tell the police?"

"About the Father's Day cards?" Ryan shook his head. "I didn't tell them anything."

He shifted in the bed. "Because of those cards, for a while there, I thought Selena might have disappeared on her own accord and had a child. But if she killed herself the next day, I don't understand what those Father's Day cards were about . . ."

Ryan shrugged. "It made you think of Selena, didn't

it?" he asked. "Maybe that was the point. I know those cards really unnerved my father."

"I don't see what good it'll do to tell the police about them. But if you feel it's necessary, go ahead. I'll back you up. I kept this thing a secret for so many years, I'm tired of it. I'd just as soon have it all out in the open."

"I wouldn't mind burying it," Ryan admitted. "I told Stephanie, and she didn't see any point in having people wonder about her brother-in-law possibly fathering a kid when it really didn't happen. It just gives folks the wrong idea. Plus my grandmother doesn't need to know. Right now, I think a part of her is just grateful to know my dad didn't embezzle all that money and then kill his family." Ryan shrugged. "I mean, he was kind of a—jerk. But he really wasn't that bad."

"I wish I could say I liked your dad, but—" Mr. Metcalf seemed to work up a smile. "Well, I think his son's pretty terrific. I know Alison has already developed a little crush on you, and I approve."

Two of Mr. Metcalf's coworkers from the TV station were waiting to visit him. There were limits on the number of visitors for patients in the ICU. Ryan awkwardly shook hands with Alison's father before he wheeled himself out of the room.

Dressed in a pink sleeveless shirt and khakis, Alison was waiting in the hallway. She had her curly brown hair in a ponytail. Her wrists still had burn marks on them from the rope. "Danny wants to push you around the block in your wheelchair," she announced. "Are you up for it?"

Ryan smiled and nodded. "Sure."

"He's waiting down in the lobby," she said. "He's really

hyper today. I almost liked him better when he was catatonic. I'll take you down to him." She started pushing him in the wheelchair down the hospital corridor. "How was your talk with my dad?"

"Enlightening," Ryan said. "He said you have a crush on me."

"Oh, he's so pumped full of drugs and painkillers. He's close to delirious."

Ryan laughed. He reached back and put his hand over hers.

"You know, you're going back to Chicago, and I'm staying here in Seattle," she said.

"You don't think we could handle a long-distance thing?" he asked. "I mean, I started thinking maybe I should apply to the University of Washington for next year."

"I'll still be in high school," Alison reminded him. She stopped in front of the elevator and pushed the Down button. "So that means I'll be one of those cool seniors who's dating a guy in college."

"And I'll be one of those d-bags in college who's dating a high-school girl," Ryan said.

She laughed, then bent down and kissed the top of his head.

"I'm cool with that if you are," he said.

"Well, let's just see what happens."

Ryan squeezed her hand. "I didn't ask your dad what he thinks will happen with his job. I mean, all this stuff coming out about what went on when he was a teenager, it could get kind of weird for him, being in the public eye and all."

The elevator doors opened, and she wheeled him

aboard. "Well, so far, the station's pretty supportive, and they have most of the facts. I guess we'll just have to see how the public reacts. Who knows?"

"It'll get weird for you, too," Ryan said, over the quiet hum of the elevator. They were alone in there. "You'll probably have to put up with a lot of shit from people at school. Will you be okay?"

"I was just thinking about that," she said. "I mean, I killed someone. I poisoned her. Like people aren't going to talk? But I don't have any regrets. I still remember how grateful I was to see her walk into the room with that liqueur in the Mrs. Butterworth's bottle. I just kept thinking and praying, *'Drink it, drink it.'* I don't think anyone at school would understand that, not the way you and I do. You know, I remember the day my Mom was killed. She came by the school, because she was worried about me. And I was so friggin' embarrassed. All I could think about was what people thought of me. I was such a brat to her. Now, when I wonder what they'll say about me or my dad, it doesn't really matter. I mean, the hell with them, you know?"

The elevator doors opened. Ryan squeezed her hand again. "I think my new girlfriend is pretty cool," he whispered.

Monday, June 24—6:55 P.M.
Oakland

Several of Jenny Ballatore's neighbors threw her and Simon a welcome home party when she returned to the Bay Vista Apartments. She was their local celebrity. She'd been in the news and on TV. She was even getting offers from film people and publishers for the rights to her story. One agent kept hounding her, "I can see Reese Witherspoon playing you in the film version!" Jenny took it in her stride. She had a feeling the media frenzy would die down soon enough.

All the attention took her mind off the fact that she had a broken ankle—from kicking at that drawer panel in the Winnebago for so long. It had taken her another hour to tear away at her restraints with a sharp hinge on the broken drawer. Jenny had hoped to signal a passing car on the Interstate. But then she'd discovered the bedroom window had been sealed shut and painted gray.

When her captor had parked the vehicle and left, Jenny hobbled from the bedroom to the front of the Winnebago. She'd thought there would be little chance of escape—until she discovered he'd left his key in the ignition.

Somehow, it hadn't hurt her foot too much to push down on the accelerator.

She'd made a new friend that night—in Stephanie Coburn. Stephanie kept saying that Jenny had saved her life. But Jenny thought it was the other way around.

Her landlord, along with a few neighbors, had cleaned up the mess left behind by her abductors. For Jenny, it felt good to be back, and know the sheer delight in another boring night at home with her cat.

Best of all, everything she'd written down on her wish list came back to her.

Wednesday, August 21—11:44 A.M.
Portland

Stephanie had only a few minutes before she needed to leave for the airport. She wasn't looking forward to this six-day stint coming up. The long, lonely stretches away from home were becoming tougher to handle now that things had changed.

It had been over a month since the FAA had cleared her of any misconduct charges. Pacific Cascade Skyways paid her the back wages lost while she'd been on the enforced leave of absence. Good thing, too, because she'd had to start all over with a new place to live, new furniture, and new everything.

She found a spacious two-bedroom apartment in Portland's trendy Pearl District. It had a fireplace and a panoramic view of the city. She was now surrounded by several pieces of furniture that had been in storage in Croton since last January. They were pieces from Rebecca and Scott's house—and before that, they'd been in her parents' home. Having these things around her every day, it was easy to forget they'd once been police-tagged or dusted for fingerprints. She held onto the good memories. The figurine of the old lady selling balloons had a spot in the bookcase by the mantel. Stephanie had even figured out where she'd put her Christmas tree in December. This year, it would be real.

She could have left early for PDX, then had her coffee and checked her e-mails there. But—for obvious reasons—she'd given up her guilty-pleasure ritual of coffee and a croissant at the airport's Beaverton Bakery Café.

She savored these last few minutes at home. She sat in front of her desktop computer in the guest room. The dark cherry antique desk, which used to be her dad's, was beside a window with a view of the river. Stephanie checked her e-mails, a task she'd faced with some trepidation back in June. Funny thing, with all the hate e-mail she'd received, only a handful of those people had bothered to write back with an apology after the FAA had publicly exonerated her. Stephanie figured they must have been busy writing nasty e-mails to new people.

She never heard from Ronald Mady or Calvin Davis— or their mothers. And that was just fine. But thanks in part to her, the New York police were forced to reconsider murder charges against the two Bronx teenagers.

Stephanie continued to be a pain in the neck to certain people. But it seemed to be paying off, or so she read in an e-mail from Halle Driscoll's cousin, Deborah Neff:

Dear Stephanie,

Thank you so much for your tireless efforts to redirect money from Nicole Jayne's estate back to the families of her victims. As you know, my aunt and uncle went broke covering the debts that woman racked up on Halle's accounts. They've been struggling emotionally and financially ever since. They couldn't afford a lawyer to get them any compensation. I doubt they could have found one who was as strong an advocate for them as you have been. I know you've met with a lot of resistance and had to cut through a lot of red tape to help us recoup some of our losses. Well, Stephanie, I just thought you should know. My aunt and uncle received a check today for $13,655. I know you had

a lot to do with that. I can't tell you how happy they were—
and how much they needed that money . . .

"Good," Stephanie whispered to herself.

After ripping off so many people, Nicole Jayne had about $290,000 in assets. For the last few weeks, Stephanie and Scott's lawyer friend, Bradley Reece, had been battling an insurance company and some law firm out of Las Vegas, both of which seemed reluctant to part with that money—even though it wasn't theirs. It belonged to the families of Nicole's victims and the people she'd robbed.

Stephanie marked Deborah's e-mail KEEP AS NEW and made a mental note to call Brad sometime during her layover. She wanted to make sure the other families were receiving checks, too.

She didn't recognize the sender of the next e-mail on the list: adele@bcurtisagency.com.

Dear Ms. Coburn,

I believe the story of your amazing journey during the last year would make an excellent book. Despite the odds, tragedies, and the attempts on your life, you never gave up your search for the truth. Yours is the kind of story that in-spires . . .

Stephanie didn't read any more. She and Jenny Ballatore compared notes on all the book and movie offers coming their way. So far, the tone of each offer was "act now while you're still hot." So they weren't acting now. They'd decided to wait.

She marked the e-mail KEEP AS NEW and stared at the name on the next e-mail. It was his private e-mail address: jimdunning22@gbmail.com. With a sigh she clicked on READ:

> Hey You,
>
> Well, you don't know how many times I've wanted to pick up the phone and call you. I've missed you terribly. It's taken me these last couple of months to realize just how right you were to break up with me. You were getting a raw deal. But you were very wrong about one thing. You underestimated just how important you've been to me. Though it might not have seemed that way, I always put you first . . .

"Oh, yeah, right," Stephanie mumbled. "Please . . ."

> . . . I've done a lot of soul searching in these last two months, two very lonely months. I'm not the same inflexible workaholic you knew. My relationship with my in-laws has changed for the better, and I now feel . . .

She clicked on DELETE, and watched his e-mail vanish. She thought about when Rebecca had died, and how Jim had arranged for a limo to take her to the airport. He couldn't even spare the time to drive her himself.

Well, she couldn't spare the time for him now.

Stephanie clicked on the next e-mail, this one from Ryeguy66@comcast.com.

Hi, Stephanie,

Thought of you this morning. Billy & I drove to St. Paul's in Glenview, and I put some flowers on Selena Jayne's grave at the cemetery there. I figured out it's the anniversary of her death, and no one else was around to commemorate that. So I decided to do something. It's weird. I know Nicole and her father were both cremated. Selena's the only one in the family with a gravestone, and she isn't even in that grave. I guess we'll never know where her body got buried. It's kind of sad.

I hope you're doing okay. I still talk and text with Alison every day. I wish I were like you and worked for an airline. I'd fly to Seattle every chance I got.

The cast comes off next week, but the doctor says there's no way I can play football this year. My dad's dream of me getting a football scholarship to Notre Dame isn't going to happen. But that was his dream, not mine. I'm keeping my fingers crossed for U of Washington next year.

Well, I should scram. I just wanted to tell you that you were on my mind today. I hope wherever you are when you get this, you're doing great.

Take Care,
Your Friend, Ryan

Stephanie clicked on the KEEP AS NEW option. Answering the e-mails would give her something to do at the hotel in Salt Lake City tonight.

There was a knock on her door.

Switching off the computer, she picked up her coffee cup and carried it to the door. She opened the door and smiled at the handsome man across her threshold. He had wavy brown hair and a bit of beard stubble. "Taxi's ready, ma'am," he announced.

"Thanks," Stephanie said, kissing him. "Your timing's perfect."

Steve McKinney took the coffee cup from her and sipped some. "I'm giving you the bum's rush, hon. Traffic's kind of nuts right now. So we better hurry."

"Okay," she said, touching his cheek for a moment.

He'd come to her rescue that night her house had been destroyed. And then again, when he'd FedEx'd her phone to her.

Stephanie still had his card from when he'd given it to her in his cab. She'd called and asked to take him out to lunch. Stephanie had owed him at least that much. At the restaurant, she'd apologized for lying to him about having a husband who knocked her around.

"I'm glad to hear you're not in that kind of situation," Steve had told her. "And I'm glad you're not married."

She often wished she could pick up the phone, call Rebecca, and tell her sister that she was in love. Yes, the guy was a taxi driver. The way Stephanie looked at it, they were both in transportation. He had a sideline as a freelance editor—fine-tuning everything from medical journals to the romance novels a Portland writer churned out three times a year. But until he got a few more steady clients, Steve would be driving a taxi as well.

"I'll take your bag down to the cab and wait for you," he said, handing the coffee cup back to her. He grabbed the pull handle to her carry-on, which was by the front door. "By the way, could you check your calendar and see if you're free on the Sunday after you get back? My folks want you to come to dinner."

"Sure thing," she said. "See you down there, sweetie. I'll just be a minute."

She watched Steve roll her bag out to the hallway. He closed the door behind him. In the two months since they'd started dating, she'd gotten together with his family four times. She'd spent three years with Jim, and as far as his family was concerned, she hadn't even existed.

Taking her coffee cup into the kitchen, she made sure the Mr. Coffee machine was unplugged and that the stove was off. She checked her wall calendar to confirm she was free that Sunday. She was.

Stephanie glanced out the kitchen window and down at the street. His taxi was parked in front of her building. Smiling, she watched him load her bag in the back seat. "I'm doing okay, Rebecca," she whispered.

At last, she'd found someone who was there for her, someone who put her first.

And he always made time to drive her to the airport.

GREAT BOOKS, GREAT SAVINGS!

When You Visit Our Website:
www.kensingtonbooks.com

You Can Save Money Off The Retail Price
Of Any Book You Purchase!

- All Your Favorite Kensington Authors
- New Releases & Timeless Classics
- Overnight Shipping Available
- eBooks Available For Many Titles
- All Major Credit Cards Accepted

Visit Us Today To Start Saving!
www.kensingtonbooks.com

All Orders Are Subject To Availability.
Shipping and Handling Charges Apply.
Offers and Prices Subject To Change Without Notice.